WHAT IF IT'S US

Also by
BECKY ALBERTALLI
Simon vs. the Homo Sapiens Agenda
The Upside of Unrequited
Leah on the Offbeat

Also by
ADAM SILVERA
More Happy Than Not
History Is All You Left Me
They Both Die at the End

BECKY ALBERTALLI
& ADAM SILVERA

WHAT
IF
IT'S
US

BALZER + BRAY HARPER TEEN

Imprints of HarperCollins*Publishers*

Balzer + Bray and HarperTeen are imprints of HarperCollins Publishers.

What If It's Us

Library of Congress Cataloging-in-Publication Data
Names: Albertalli, Becky, author. | Silvera, Adam, author.
Title: What if it's us / Becky Albertalli & Adam Silvera.
Other titles: What if it is us
Description: First edition. | New York, NY : HarperTeen, an imprint of
    HarperCollinsPublishers, [2018] | Summary: Told in two voices, when
    Arthur, a summer intern from Georgia, and Ben, a native New Yorker,
    meet it seems like fate, but after three attempts at dating fail they wonder
    if the universe is pushing them together or apart.
Identifiers: LCCN 2018013361 | ISBN 9780062795250 (hardback) | ISBN
    9780062868671 (international edition) | ISBN 9780062870506 (special
    edition) | ISBN 9780062889300 (special edition)
Subjects: | CYAC: Dating (Social customs)—Fiction. | Fate and fatalism—
    Fiction. | Gays—Fiction. | New York (N.Y.)—Fiction.
Classification: LCC PZ7.A434 Wh 2018 | DDC [Fic]—dc23 LC record
    available at https://lccn.loc.gov/2018013361

Typography by Erin Fitzsimmons
18 19 20 21 22   PC/LSCH   10 9 8 7 6 5 4 3 2 1

First Edition

For Brooks Sherman,
an agent of the universe who brought us together.
And Andrew Eliopulos and Donna Bray,
who made our universe bigger.

PART ONE
WHAT IF

CHAPTER ONE
ARTHUR
Monday, July 9

I am not a New Yorker, and I want to go home.

There are so many unspoken rules when you live here, like the way you're never supposed to stop in the middle of the sidewalk or stare dreamily up at tall buildings or pause to read graffiti. No giant folding maps, no fanny packs, no eye contact. No humming songs from *Dear Evan Hansen* in public. And you're definitely not supposed to take selfies at street corners, even if there's a hot dog stand and a whole line of yellow taxis in the background, which is eerily how you always pictured New York. You're allowed to silently appreciate it, but you have to be cool. From what I can tell, that's the whole point of New York: being cool.

I'm not cool.

Take this morning. I made the mistake of glancing up at the sky, just for a moment, and now I can't unstick my eyes. Looking up from this angle, it's like the world's tipping inward: dizzyingly tall buildings and a bright fireball sun.

It's beautiful. I'll give New York credit for that. It's beautiful and surreal, and absolutely nothing like Georgia. I tilt my phone to snap a picture. Not an Instagram Story, no filters. Nothing drawn-out.

One tiny, quick picture.

Instantaneous pedestrian rage: *Jesus. Come on. MOVE. Fucking tourists.* Literally, I take a two-second photograph, and now I'm obstruction personified. I'm responsible for every subway delay, every road closure, the very phenomenon of wind resistance.

Fucking tourists.

I'm not even a tourist. I somewhat live here, at least for the summer. It's not like I'm taking a joyful sightseeing stroll at noon on a Monday. I'm at work. I mean, I'm on a Starbucks run, but it counts.

And maybe I'm taking the long way. Maybe I need a few extra minutes away from Mom's office. Normally, being an intern is more boring than terrible, but today's uniquely shitty. You know that kind of day where the printer runs out of paper, and there's none in the supply room, so you try to steal some from the copier, but you can't get the drawer open, and then you push some wrong button and the copier starts beeping? And you're standing there thinking that whoever invented copy machines is *this* close to getting their ass kicked? By you? By a five-foot-six Jewish kid with ADHD and the rage of a tornado? That kind of day? Yeah.

And all I want to do is vent to Ethan and Jessie, but I still haven't figured out how to text while walking.

I step off the sidewalk, near the entrance to a post office—and wow. They don't make post offices like this in Milton, Georgia. It's got a white stone exterior with pillars and brass accents, and it's so painfully classy, I almost feel underdressed. And I'm wearing a tie.

I text the sunny street picture to Ethan and Jessie. Rough day at the office!

Jessie writes back immediately. I hate you and I want to be you.

Here's the thing: Jessie and Ethan have been my best friends since the dawn of time, and I've always been Real Arthur with them. Lonely Messy Arthur, as opposed to Upbeat Instagram Arthur. But for some reason, I need them to think my New York life is awesome. I just do. So I've been sending them Upbeat Instagram Arthur texts for weeks. I don't know if I'm really selling it, though.

Also I miss you, Jessie writes, throwing down a whole line of kissy emojis. She's like my bubbe in a sixteen-year-old body. She'd text a lipstick smudge onto my cheek if she could. The weird thing is that we've never had one of those ooey-gooey friendships—at least not until prom night. Which happens to be the night I told Jessie and Ethan I'm gay.

I miss you guys, too, I admit.

COME HOME, ARTHUR.

Four more weeks. Not that I'm counting.

Ethan finally chimes in with the most ambiguous of all emojis: the grimace. Like, come on. The *grimace*? If post-prom Jessie texts like my bubbe, post-prom Ethan texts like a mime. He's actually not so bad in the group text most of the time, but one-on-one? I'll just say my phone stopped blowing up with his texts approximately five seconds after I came out. I'm not going to lie: it's the crappiest feeling ever. One of these days, I'm going to call him out, and it's going to be soon. Maybe even today. Maybe—

But then the post office door swings open, revealing—no joke—a pair of identical twin men in matching rompers. With handlebar mustaches. Ethan would *love* this. Which pisses me off. This happens constantly with Ethan. A minute ago, I was ready to friend-dump his emojily ambiguous ass. Now I just want to hear him laugh. A full emotional one-eighty in a span of sixty seconds.

The twins amble past me, and I see they both have man buns. Of course they have man buns. New York must be its own planet, I swear, because no one even blinks.

Except.

There's a boy walking toward the entrance, holding a cardboard box, and he literally stops in his tracks when the twins walk by. He looks so confused, I laugh out loud.

And then he catches my eye.

And then he smiles.

And holy shit.

I mean it. Holy mother of shit. Cutest boy ever. Maybe it's the hair or the freckles or the pinkness of his cheeks. And I say this as someone who's never noticed another person's cheeks in my life. But his cheeks are worth noticing. Everything about him is worth noticing. Perfectly rumpled light brown hair. Fitted jeans, scuffed shoes, gray shirt—with the words *Dream & Bean Coffee* barely visible above the box he's holding. He's taller than me—which, okay, most guys are.

He's still looking at me.

But twenty points to Gryffindor, because I manage to smile up at him. "Do you think they parked their tandem bicycle at the mustache-wax parlor?"

His startled laugh is so cute, it makes me light-headed. "Definitely the mustache-wax parlor slash art gallery slash microbrewery," he says.

For a minute, we grin at each other without speaking.

"Um, are you going in?" he asks finally.

I glance up at the door. "Yeah."

And I do it. I follow him into the post office. It's not even

7

a decision. Or if it is, my body's already decided. There's something about him. It's this tug in my chest. It's this feeling like I *have to* know him, like it's inevitable.

Okay, I'm about to admit something, and you're probably going to cringe. You're probably already cringing, but whatever. Hear me out.

I believe in love at first sight. Fate, the universe, all of it. But not how you're thinking. I don't mean it in the *our souls were split and you're my other half forever and ever* sort of way. I just think you're meant to meet some people. I think the universe nudges them into your path.

Even on random Monday afternoons in July. Even at the post office.

But let's be real—this is no normal post office. It's big enough to be a ballroom, with gleaming floors and rows of numbered PO boxes and actual sculptures, like a museum. Box Boy walks over to a short counter near the entrance, props the package beside him, and starts filling out a mailing label.

So I swipe a Priority Mail envelope from a nearby rack and drift toward his counter. Super casual. This doesn't have to be weird. I just need to find the perfect words to keep this conversation going. To be honest, I'm normally really good at talking to strangers. I don't know if it's a Georgia thing or only an Arthur thing, but if there's an elderly man in a grocery store, I'm there price-checking prune juices for him. If there's a pregnant lady on an airplane, she's named her unborn kid after me by the time the plane lands. It's the one thing I have going for me.

Or I did, until today. I don't even think I can form sounds. It's like my throat's caving in on itself. But I have to channel my inner New Yorker—cool and nonchalant. I shoot him a tentative grin. Deep breath. "That's a big package."

And . . . shit.

The words tumble out. "I don't mean *package*. Just. Your box. Is big." I hold my hands apart to demonstrate. Because apparently that's the way to prove it's not an innuendo. By spreading my hands out dick-measuringly.

Box Boy furrows his brow.

"Sorry. I don't . . . I swear I don't usually comment on the size of other guys' boxes."

He meets my eyes and smiles, just a little. "Nice tie," he says.

I look down at it, blushing. Of course I couldn't have worn a normal tie today. Nope. I'm wearing one from the Dad collection. Navy blue, printed with hundreds of tiny hot dogs.

"At least it's not a romper?" I say.

"Good point." He smiles again—so of course I notice his lips. Which are shaped exactly like Emma Watson's lips. *Emma Watson's lips.* Right there on his face.

"So you're not from here," Box Boy says.

I look up at him, startled. "How did you know?"

"Well, you keep talking to me." Then he blushes. "That came out wrong. I just mean it's usually only tourists who strike up conversations."

"Oh."

"I don't mind, though," he says.

"I'm not a tourist."

"You're not?"

"Okay, I'm not *technically* from here, but I live here now. Just for the summer. I'm from Milton, Georgia."

"Milton, Georgia." He smiles.

I feel inexplicably frantic. Like, my limbs are weird and loose, and my head's full of cotton. I'm probably electric bright red now. I don't even want to know. I just need to keep talking. "I know, right? *Milton*. It sounds like a Jewish great-uncle."

"I wasn't—"

"I actually do have a Jewish great-uncle Milton. That's whose apartment we're staying in."

"Who's we?"

"You mean who do I live with in my great-uncle Milton's apartment?"

He nods, and I just look at him. Like, who does he think I live with? My boyfriend? My twenty-eight-year-old smoldering-hot boyfriend who has big gaping holes in his earlobes and maybe a tongue piercing and a tattoo of my name on his pec? On *both* pecs?

"With my parents," I say quickly. "My mom's a lawyer, and her firm has an office here, so she came up at the end of April for this case she's working on, and I totally would have come up then, but my mom was like, *Nice try, Arthur, you have a month of school left.* But it ended up being for the best, because I guess I thought New York was going to be one thing, and it's really another thing, and now I'm kind of stuck here, and I miss my friends, and I miss my car, and I miss Waffle House."

"In that order?"

"Well, mostly the car." I grin. "We left it at my bubbe's house in New Haven. She lives right by Yale, which is hopefully, *hopefully* my future school. Fingers crossed." It's like I can't stop talking. "I guess you probably don't need my life story."

"I don't mind." Box Boy pauses, balancing the box on his hip. "Want to get on line?"

I nod, falling into step behind him. He shifts sideways to face me, but the box looms between us. He hasn't stuck the shipping label on yet. It's sitting on top of the package. I try to sneak a peek at the address, but his handwriting sucks, and I can't read upside down.

He catches me looking. "Are you really nosy or something?" He's watching me through narrowed eyes.

"Oh." I swallow. "Kind of. Yeah."

That makes him smile. "It's not that interesting. It's leftovers from a breakup."

"Leftovers?"

"Books, gifts, Harry Potter wand. Everything I don't want to look at anymore."

"You don't want to look at a Harry Potter wand?"

"I don't want to look at anything my ex-boyfriend gave me."

Ex-boyfriend.

Which means Box Boy dates guys.

And okay. Wow. This doesn't happen to me. It just doesn't. But maybe the universe works differently in New York.

Box Boy dates guys.

I'M A GUY.

"That's really cool," I say. Perfectly casual. But then he looks at me funny, and my hand flies to my mouth. "Not cool. God. No. Breakups aren't cool. I'm just—I'm so sorry for your loss."

"He's not dead."

"Oh, right. Yeah. I'm gonna . . ." I exhale, hand resting for a moment on the retractable line barrier.

Box Boy smiles tightly. "Right. So you're one of those guys who gets weird around gay dudes."

"What?" I yelp. "No. Not at all."

"Yeah." He rolls his eyes, glancing over my shoulder.

"I'm not," I say quickly. "Listen. I'm gay."

And the whole world stops. My tongue feels thick and heavy.

I guess I don't say those words out loud all that often. *I'm gay.* My parents know, Ethan and Jessie know, and I kind of randomly told the summer associates at Mom's firm. But I'm not a person who goes around announcing it at the post office.

Except apparently, I kind of am.

"Oh. For real?" Box Boy asks.

"For real." It comes out breathless. It's weird—now I want to prove it. I want some gay ID card to whip out like a cop badge. Or I could demonstrate in other ways. God. I would happily demonstrate.

Box Boy smiles, his shoulders relaxing. "Cool."

And holy shit. This is actually happening. I can hardly catch my breath. It's like the universe willed this moment into existence.

A voice booms from behind the counter. "You on line or not?" I look up to see a woman with a lip ring raining down the stink-eye. No fucks given by this postal employee. "Yo, Freckles. Let's go."

Box Boy shoots me a halting glance before stepping up to the counter. Already, there's a line stretching out behind me. And okay—I'm not *eavesdropping* on Box Boy. Not exactly. It's more like my ears are drawn to his voice. His arms are crossed, shoulders tense.

"Twenty-six fifty for Priority," says Lip Ring.

"Twenty-six fifty? Like twenty-six dollars?"

"No. Like twenty-six fifty."

Box Boy shakes his head. "That's a lot."

"That's what we got. Take it or leave it."

For a moment, Box Boy just stands there. Then he takes the box back, hugging it to his chest. "Sorry."

"Next," says Lip Ring. She beckons to me, but I swerve out of line.

Box Boy blinks. "How is it twenty-six fifty to send a package?"

"I don't know. That's messed up."

"Guess that's the universe saying I should hold on to it."

The *universe.*

Holy shit.

He's a believer. He believes in the universe. And I don't want to jump to conclusions or anything, but Box Boy believing in the universe is definitely a sign from the universe.

"Okay." My heartbeat quickens. "But what if the universe is actually telling you to throw his stuff away?"

"That's not how it works."

"Oh really?"

"Think about it. Getting rid of the box is plan A, right?

The universe isn't going to thwart plan A just so I'll go with another version of plan A. This is clearly the universe calling for plan B."

"And plan B is . . ."

"Accepting that the universe is an asshole—"

"The universe isn't an asshole!"

"It is. Trust me."

"How could you possibly know that?"

"I know the universe has some fucked-up plan for this box."

"But that's the thing!" I stare him down. "You don't actually know. You have no idea where the universe is going with this. Maybe the whole reason you're here is because the universe wanted you to meet me, so I could tell you to throw the box away."

He smiles. "You think the universe wanted us to meet?"

"What? No! I mean, I don't know. That's the point. We have no way of knowing."

"Well, I guess we'll see how it plays out." He peers at the shipping label for a moment and then rips it in half, wadding it and tossing it into the trash. At least he aims for the trash, but it lands on the floor. "Anyway," he says. "Um, are you—"

"Excuse me." A man's voice reverberates through an intercom. "Can I have your attention?"

I glance sidelong at Box Boy. "Is this—"

There's a sudden squeal of feedback and a rising piano intro.

And then a literal fucking marching band walks in.

A marching band.

People flood into the post office, carrying giant drums and flutes and tubas, blasting a somewhat off-key rendition of that Bruno Mars song "Marry You." And now dozens of people—old people, people I thought were in line to buy stamps—have launched into a choreographed dance number, with high kicks and hip thrusts and shimmying arms. Basically everyone who's not dancing is filming this, but I'm too stunned to even grab my phone. I mean, I don't want to read too much into things, but wow: I meet a cute boy, and five seconds later, I'm in the middle of a flash mob marriage proposal? Could this message from the universe be any clearer?

The crowd parts, and a tattooed guy rolls in on a skateboard, skidding to a stop in front of the service desk. He's holding a jewelry box, but instead of taking a knee, he plants his elbows on the counter and beams up at Lip Ring. "Kelsey. Babe. Will you marry me?"

Kelsey's black mascara tracks all the way down to her lip ring. "Yes!" She grabs his face for a tear-soaked kiss, and the crowd erupts into cheers.

It hits me deep in my chest. It's that New York feeling, like they talk about in musicals—that wide-open, top-volume, Technicolor joy. Here I've spent the whole summer moping around and missing Georgia, but it's like someone just flipped a light switch inside of me.

I wonder if Box Boy feels it, too. I turn toward him, already smiling, and my hand's pressed to my heart—

But he's gone.

My hand falls limply. The boy is nowhere. His box is nowhere. I peer around, scanning every single face in the post office. Maybe he got pushed aside by the flash mob. Maybe he was part of the flash mob. Maybe he had some kind of urgent appointment—so urgent he couldn't stop to get my number. He couldn't even say goodbye.

I can't believe he didn't say goodbye.

I thought—I don't know, it's stupid, but I thought we had some kind of moment. I mean, the universe basically scooped us up and delivered us to each other. That's what just happened, right? I don't even know how else you could interpret it.

Except he vanished. He's Cinderella at midnight. It's like he never even existed. And now I'll never know his name, or how my name sounds when he says it. I'll never get to show him that the universe isn't an asshole.

Gone. Totally gone. And the disappointment hits me so hard, I almost double over.

Until my eyes fall on the trash can.

Okay. I'm not saying I'm going to dig through the trash.

Obviously not. I'm a mess, but I'm not *that* messy.

But maybe Box Boy is right. Maybe the universe is calling for plan B.

Here's my question: If a piece of trash never makes it into a trash can, can you even call it trash? Because let's just imagine—and this is totally hypothetical—let's say there's a crumpled shipping label on the floor. Is that trash?

What if it's a glass slipper?

CHAPTER TWO
BEN

I'm back at the start.

I had one job. Mail the breakup box. Not run out of the post office with the breakup box. In my defense, there was a lot going on. There was that cool and cute Arthur guy, who clearly hasn't been burned by the universe before, because he actually thought we were supposed to meet. On the day I was trying to mail Hudson's things back to him. I'm sure Arthur is changing his tune about the universe after that marching band broke us apart.

I hop on the train and head back to Alphabet City to meet up with my best friend, Dylan. I live on Avenue B, Dylan lives on Avenue D. Our origin story comes down to our last names, Alejo and Boggs. He sat behind me in third grade and was nonstop tapping my shoulder to borrow everything, like pencils and loose-leaf. Same deal as we got older when he'd need my two-versions-behind-everyone-else iPhone to text his Crush of the Week after his own battery died. The only time I ever quote-unquote borrow something is when I need him to spot me some lunch money. And I say quote-unquote because it's super rare that I can pay him back, and he doesn't care. Dylan's a good dude. He doesn't care that I like guys and I don't care that he likes girls. Shout-out to my main man the alphabet for this bromance.

When I get off the train, I stop at several trash cans, holding the breakup box over them, but I never catch that courage to actually dump the damn thing.

I guess I didn't expect the breakup to suck if I did the breaking up. But since Hudson's the one who kissed somebody else, it still feels like he really ended things. Things hadn't been right between us since his parents got divorced, but I was patient with him. Like when I let him plan my birthday and he took me to a concert of his favorite band. But I let it go because it was my first-ever concert and the Killers are awesome. Then he didn't show up to my parents' big anniversary lunch. I let it go again because celebrating my parents' marriage after everything with his parents was maybe too much for him. And when we went to the movies to see a rom-com about two teen boys and he just went off about how love, even our own, could never be Hollywood-worthy, I stormed off and thought he would chase me and apologize or call my name or literally anything a boyfriend should do.

Nothing for three days. Not until I called to ask him if we were ever going to talk again. Then he surprised me at my apartment and told me he thought we were broken up, so he kissed some random guy at a party. He desperately wanted another chance, but nope. I broke up with him. For real. Even if he thought things were over between us, he couldn't even wait a week before moving on? Pretty hard not to feel worthless after that.

I reach Dylan's building and press his apartment number, and he buzzes me up immediately, which is great because I'm not about that waiting life today. I'm carrying around a box of my ex-boyfriend's things. I'm wearing a backpack with summer homework. Today sucks.

I yawn in the elevator. I had to get up at seven because of summer school. Yay life. The universe keeps on swinging—brass knuckles to the heart and ego.

I step out of the elevator and let myself into Dylan's apartment because we're that tight. But I'm smart enough to knock on his bedroom door ever since a few months ago when I walked in and he was really going at it with himself.

"Hand out of your pants?" I ask.

"Unfortunately," Dylan responds from the other side.

I open the door. Dylan is sitting on his bed, texting away. He's cut his hair since I saw him last night for dinner. He's the only dude my age I know who's rocking a beard. For the longest time I swore I was behind on the puberty game since I haven't even grown a mustache, but Dylan's actually the freak show here—handsome freak show.

"Big Ben," Dylan sings, putting down his phone. "Light of my life. He Who Is Stuck in School." Summer school double-sucks because Dylan has been cracking jokes ever since that day I came out of the guidance counselor's office with the bad news. He's just lucky that no one he ever dated persuaded him to skip studying and to trust that the right grades would fall into place.

"Hey," I say. Cute nicknames aren't really my thing.

Dylan points at my chest. "That shirt is a thing of beauty, isn't she?"

His wardrobe consists primarily of T-shirts from indie coffee shops around the city, and he gave me this Dream & Bean shirt last night when he came over for dinner. Dylan hooks me up when his dresser gets too crowded. He doesn't usually let go of his favorites, like Dream & Bean, but I'm not complaining.

"I didn't have anything clean to wear," I say. "It's not, like, a cool shirt."

"That's hurtful, but I'm guessing you're in a mood because you're carrying a breakup box you were going to hand over to Hudson. What happened?"

"He didn't come to school today." I put down the box.

"Skipping day one of summer school seems like a bad start," Dylan says.

"Yeah, I asked Harriett if she would take it to him and she said no," I say. "Then I was going to mail it, but Priority shipping cost too much."

"Why did it have to be Priority shipping?"

"Because I want the box out of my face sooner."

"Regular shipping would've done the trick too." Dylan raises his left eyebrow. "You couldn't do it, could you?"

I put down the box I should've mailed or thrown away or tied to an anchor and dropped into a river. "Stop seeing past my bullshit, it's my bullshit."

Dylan gets up and hugs me. "Shh-shh-shh-shh." He rubs circles into my back.

"Your soothing voice isn't soothing me."

Dylan kisses my cheek. "It's okay, Pudding Pop."

I sit down cross-legged on his bed. I'm tempted to reach for my phone to see if I've missed any texts from Hudson, or to check Instagram to see if he has uploaded a new selfie. But I know there won't be any texts, and I've unfollowed him on every platform.

"I don't want to see him fail out of summer school because he's avoiding me. He'll get left behind if he's absent three times."

"Maybe. But that's his problem. If he doesn't show up, you won't have to spend the summer with him. Problem solved."

It wasn't that long ago when spending my summer with Hudson was all I could think about. A summer as boyfriends in pools and parks and each other's bedrooms while our parents were working—not exes who are in summer school because we spent more time studying each other than doing our chemistry homework.

"Wish you were in the trenches with me," I say. "He has his best friend, and I should have mine too."

"Oh man, remind me to never commit a crime with you. You'll get caught and out me so fast." Dylan checks his phone, like we're not even talking, which is my least favorite thing about humans. "That class would be all drama anyway. I can't be there with my ex, that's not a healthy environment."

"I am literally in there with my ex, Dylan."

"No you're not. He didn't show up, and if he does, don't forget you got the edge here. You won the breakup by being the Breaker Upper. It would double-suck if he broke up with you. It only single-sucks for you."

I'd trade my poor kingdom for a universe where single-suck heartbreak isn't a victory. But here we are.

Recent breakups prove that we should've never screwed up our friend circle by trying to date. Not to point fingers, but Dylan and Harriett started this. The four of us had a good thing going until Dylan and Harriett kissed on New Year's Eve. I was kind of into Hudson and I was pretty sure he was into me too, but when we turned to each other that night we didn't kiss, we just shook our heads because I knew my best friend and he knew his. This was never going to last. Maybe Hudson and I wouldn't have been inspired to give it a shot ourselves if we hadn't been left with a lot of alone time while Dylan and Harriett spent their weekends together.

I miss the squad days.

I get up and turn on the Wii because I need some shit-talking and entertainment to cheer me up. The triumphant opening of *Super Smash Bros.* blasts from the TV. Dylan's top character is Luigi because he thinks Mario is overrated. I go for Zelda because she teleports and deflects projectiles and shoots fireballs from great distances, which are all optimal moves for any player looking to avoid hand-to-hand combat.

We get the game going.

"On the sad scale, how are you feeling today?" Dylan asks. "Opening-montage-of-*Up* sad? Or Nemo's-mom-dying sad?"

"Whoa, no. Definitely not opening-montage-of-*Up* sad. That shit was devastating. I'd guess I'm somewhere in between, like last-five-minutes-of-*Toy-Story-3* sad. I just need time to bounce back."

"No doubt. Okay, I need to tell you a thing."

"Are you breaking up with me?" I ask. "Because not cool."

"Sort of," Dylan says. He does this big dramatic pause while hammering down on one button so Luigi keeps shooting green fireballs at Zelda. "I met this girl at a coffee shop."

"That is the most Dylan sentence you've ever said."

"Right?" Dylan's chuckle is very charming. "Okay, so after my doctor's appointment yesterday I went uptown to try this coffee spot."

"Of course you leave an appointment for your heart condition by going straight to a coffee shop. You're a little too on brand sometimes."

"The yearly ritual," Dylan says. He has a heart condition called mitral valve prolapse, which isn't as shitty as it sounds—at least not in Dylan's case. I don't know what he'd do if his doctors actually banned him from coffee. "Anyway. I walked past Kool Koffee, which I have avoided forever because you know I don't find cutesy spellings cute, and she stepped outside to throw away some trash and I became trash for her."

"As you do."

"But I couldn't walk in there wearing a Dream & Bean shirt."

"Why not?"

"Uh. Do you walk into Burger King with a Happy Meal? No. That shit is disrespectful. Have some common sense."

"My common sense is telling me to make new friends."

"I just didn't want to be disrespectful."

"You just disrespected me."

"I'm talking about her."

"Of course you are. Wait. Is that why you gave me this shirt last night?"

"Yes. I panicked."

"You're so weird. Go on."

"I braved Kool Koffee today dressed appropriately . . ." Dylan gestures at his solid blue T-shirt. Nice and neutral. ". . . and she was humming an Elliott Smith song while making someone's espresso, and I was *done*. Overdone. Big Ben, in a single moment, I gained a future wife and an unlimited supply of coffee."

It's really hard to be happy for someone finding romance when I've clearly just taken a loss in the same department, but it's Dylan. "I can't wait to meet my future sister-in-law."

"You remember that BuzzFeed post with the Harry Potter wedding? Samantha and I will do something coffee-themed. Everyone will wear barista aprons. Toasting with mugs. My face drawn in everyone's espresso."

"You are too much."

"One downside though."

"She has a downside already?"

"She's a huge supporter of Kool Koffee because they donate some portions to charities, and she thinks serious coffee drinkers should be better about where they're buying coffee. I mean, I'm not ready to be monogamous with Kool Koffee."

"Did she actually ask you to do that?"

"No, but . . . she asked without asking. And when the One comes along, there are things we must sacrifice."

"There's no way you're quitting Dream & Bean coffee."

"Oh hell no. I'm quitting drinking it in front of Samantha. What she doesn't know won't hurt."

"Only you could make drinking coffee sound nefarious."

"Anyway. I added other coffee shop shirts into your drawer so I don't get tempted."

I check out the shirts because maybe there's actually a winner in here. And yeah, I have a drawer in his bedroom and he has one in mine. We've slept over at each other's places enough that it makes sense. When I was first getting cool with the coming-out thing in school, I always felt super self-conscious in gym, like everyone thought I would try and check them out. It's really dope having a bro like Dylan who is super cool changing in front of me and me changing in front of him. I hope I don't lose his awesomeness again like I have every time he meets the One.

"Wait. Why didn't you tell me about seeing Samantha last night when you came over?" I ask.

"I don't know," Dylan says. Like that's a satisfying answer. Like I'm about to just go "Okay, cool," and go back to kicking his ass in *Super Smash*.

"You never tell me when you first get a crush," I say.

"Name one time."

"Gabriella and Heather and Natalia and—"

"I said one time."

"—and Harriett. It's just weird. We tell each other everything."

Dylan nods. "Not trying to jinx myself, I guess. You know how my dad always goes on about how he knew he would marry my mom when they met in freshman year? I'm getting those same vibes from Samantha."

I act like I haven't heard Dylan say this before, most recently with Harriett, who he broke up with in March, but I let it go. Maybe it will work this time. We keep playing as Dylan goes on and on about which hot beverage he and Samantha should name their firstborn after, and I refuse to be Uncle Ben to any child named Cider.

I'm a little jealous Dylan is in this phase of his new romance, where it feels like anything is possible. Like how Samantha could actually be the love of his life. Like when I thought Hudson was going to be mine. How I couldn't wait to wake up to his face—his beautiful lazy eye, the little bump on his nose, his suggestive dark eyebrows that don't match his short auburn hair. The way he changed my worldviews, like whenever he had to push back at idiots in school who got at him because of his effeminate manner-isms; he really helped me forget my own idiocy on what I thought a man was supposed to look like. And those nerves before we had sex for the first time in March, not knowing if it was going to be good or not. Spoiler: it was awesome.

Maybe I can kick so much ass this week at school that the teachers will realize I don't actually need to be stuck taking classes for the next month and I'll be Hudson-free.

Though I got to be real, I would've probably ended up in summer school even if Hudson was never in the picture. I'm not super tight with school.

"You'll always be my number one, Big Ben," Dylan says. "Until Baby Cider is born."

"Bros before babies," I demand.

"Tie?"

I shrug. "Tie."

"You won't be single long," Dylan says, like he's a Magic 8 Ball in white flesh. "You're tall, your hair is Hollywood ready, your style is effortless. If I didn't have Mrs. Samantha Last-Name-to-Be-Discovered-Before-I-Can-Properly-Hyphenate-It-with-Boggs, I'm positive you would have me changing gears within a year."

"That's sweet. You know getting someone to go gay for

me would be the highlight of my life." I don't go chasing after straight guys, but if one wants to experiment to see what's what? Welcome to House Alejo. Leave your shoes at the door, or bring them into bed with you if that's your thing.

I win the first round because I'm me and we get another round going.

"Let's talk about why you really didn't mail the breakup box," Dylan says, like he's going to bill me for this conversation.

"Only if you drop the therapist voice," I say.

"Maybe we can begin with why my tone bothers you. Do I remind you of an authority figure?"

I KO his character and flip him off.

"I just . . . I really thought I'd have the chance to hand over the box personally for closure. But then he didn't show up to school, and all of a sudden I'm at the post office talking to some guy about Hudson when a flash mob rolled through and—"

"Wait. Run that back."

"Yeah, flash mob. They were performing that Bruno Mars song and—"

"No. The guy. What. Who." Dylan turns to me, once again abandoning the complex sorcery of the pause button. "You're an asshole. You have me feeling bad for you and you're already slutting it up with someone else."

"What, no. This isn't real. There's nothing to pursue or slut up."

"Why not? Who is he? Name. Address. Social security number. Twitter and Instagram handles."

"Arthur. I don't know his last name. I definitely don't know his address. Ditto on the handles, but while we're on the subject, why can't people just have one handle for everything they do?"

"Humans are complex." Dylan nods sagely. "What do you know about him?"

"He's new to the city. Visiting from Georgia. He was wearing the most ridiculous tie in all the land."

"Gay?"

"Yup." It's always cool to find out immediately when a cute guy is gay or not. Trying to solve that mystery yourself isn't fun and rarely pays off.

"I'm getting hot vibes." Dylan fans himself.

"He's cute, yeah. Shorter than I usually go for though. Like five seven, maybe five six without the boots. Photoshop-blue eyes, like an alien."

Dylan claps. "Okay. I'm sold. I am shipping you with the boy you met when you were supposed to be shipping relationship relics to your last boy."

I shake my head and put down my controller. "D, no. I'm just a bad idea right now. I need to ship myself with me for a bit."

"You're never a bad idea, Big Ben."

"That's sweet, man. Thanks."

"In the not-so-distant future we're going to have too many drinks, I'll invite myself over at two a.m., and we're going to . . . cuddle so hard. And I promise not to call it a bad idea the next morning."

"You ruined the moment."

"Sorry. Game face back on," Dylan says. "You're being hard on yourself. Just because Hudson is an idiot who took you for granted doesn't mean the next guy will. And damn, you met a cute guy with bad taste in ties the same day you were moving past your ex. This is a sign."

I think about how Arthur and I talked about the universe, and he comes back into focus. He's not like the many cute guys I see out and about in the city where I dream up some epic love only to forget what they look like an hour later. Arthur's teeth were super white with his canine tooth chipped. Messy brown hair. He was too dressed up for anyone our age; an alien would probably dress up like that if it arrived from another solar system and was trying to pose as an adult but didn't realize how baby-faced it was. I shouldn't have run out of the post office when I did. Maybe Dylan's right, I just ignored that sign.

"I should get going," I say. Pretty bummed now. "Homework time."

"On a Monday in the summer. Living your best life."

Dylan gets up from the bed and hugs me.

"I'll call you later."

"If I'm not talking to Samantha, I will answer."

Don't I know it. I really hope I don't lose my best friend and boyfriend in one summer.

I'm heading out when Dylan calls me back.

"Forgetting something?" Dylan looks at the breakup box. "On purpose? I can *handle* this if you want. I'll get a ski mask and some gloves and handle this sumbitch in the dead of night. No one has to know it was us."

"You need help," I say. I pick up the breakup box. "I'll handle it."

I don't know yet if I'm lying or not.

I sit at my desk and turn on the laptop. It takes a few minutes to power up because it's not exactly the newest model, or even the newly old model. Playing *The Sims* would be way easier if I had an upgraded laptop.

I really should do my homework, but focusing on chemistry was hard enough when I didn't also have a box beside me with mementos from a relationship that was supposed to be everything and stopped being anything. Sometimes I focus on what went right in the relationship so I don't get pissed. Like the way Hudson would rest his jaw on my shoulder during our end-of-the-day hugs, almost as if he didn't want to go home or even step a few feet away from me. And how seen I felt with him, even whenever the brown of his eye was looking elsewhere, because I know he was looking at me. And buddy-reading books with him. And charging my phone in the lightning bolt–shaped power strip so we could stay on FaceTime late into the night.

But that Hudson went away when his parents' divorce was finalized on April 1 after twenty years of marriage. Hudson swore it was some ridiculous April Fools' joke from his mother because he'd been counting on them to get back together. Even when his parents announced they were separating and his mother moved out of Brooklyn to Manhattan, Hudson still had hope they would get back together. He had that spirit of some kid in a movie who creates a master plan to get his parents to fall in love again.

Watching a love that he really believed in fall apart wasn't playing out well for us. We were mega out of sync. There were times he didn't want me around to comfort him and other times when we would hang out and he would just be a total asshole about love. But there were only so many hits to the heart I could take before I needed to step away. I gave him a lot of chances—I gave *us* a lot of chances. I just wasn't good enough to remind him love could be a good thing.

My laptop is good to go. I have to let off some steam before homework, so I open up my self-insert fantasy novel that I've been working on since January. It's the only time I've actually honored a New Year's resolution, and I'm really obsessed with my story. *The Wicked Wizard War—TWWW* for short—is for my eyes only, but maybe one day I can share it with the world. Or at least Dylan, who's dying to see the character I modeled after him.

I jump back in where I last left off.

It's a scene with Hudson's character and starts off pretty simple. Ben-Jamin and Hudsonien sneak out of Zen Castle late at night and wander into the Dark Woods for a romantic rendezvous. And Ben-Jamin clears the mist with his wind powers, and whoa, a gang of Life Swallowers have suddenly shown up to execute the holy fuck out of Hudsonien. Shame. I go into great detail about the massive guillotine they're going to use to behead him because I really like to paint a picture, you know. And right when the Life Swallowers drop the blade from its frame, I shut down.

I can't do it.

I'm not ready to kill off Hudson—Hudsonien.

Or throw away the box.

Maybe we'll be able to talk things out. Get some closure. Really be friends.

I want to know how he's doing.

My heart races as I check in on Hudson's Instagram profile, @HudsonLikeRiver. One hour ago he posted a selfie, and I don't know why Harriett said he was sick because he looks pretty damn healthy. He's holding up peace fingers with the caption #MovingOn. It's really clear which finger he should've thrown up instead.

Hudson has to know I unfollowed him. Just like he knows me well enough that I would check his Instagram anyway since his profile isn't private like mine. But if he's so ready to move on, he should have no problem showing his face in school.

I wonder if he's actually moving on though. He said that guy from the party doesn't live in New York, but maybe they have a long-distance thing going on. I sometimes thought Hudson may have been into Danny from math class, but Hudson swears Danny isn't his type—too muscular, too obsessed with cars. Maybe it's someone else completely.

I mean, I can hashtag move on too. The universe definitely wasn't trying to help me out today, otherwise I'd probably be texting Arthur instead of looking up my exboyfriend. But Dylan has really gotten into my head. Playing to the romantic in me. But that was a problem with Hudson. When we broke up, Hudson said my expectations are too huge and that I sometimes dream too far. I don't get why that's so bad. Why shouldn't I want to be with someone who makes me feel worthy? Someone who wants to be with me for the long run?

I don't know how to find cute strangers in New York. I normally see them once and that's that. But I spoke to Arthur. I got his name. I click out of Hudson's profile and type *Arthur* into the search bar, and what do you know, the universe doesn't just push the Arthur I met to the top just to make my life easier. I have no clue if Arthur has Instagram, but if he's like everyone else at school, he'll post about every detail of his life on Twitter. I type *Arthur hot dog tie* to see if he's said anything about his ridiculous tie. Nothing except for a tweet about a hot dog eating contest with some dude named Arthur and a demand for a tiebreaker. I type *Arthur Georgia* and there's nothing but randomness, like a girl named Georgia binge-watching every King Arthur movie, and nothing about Post Office Arthur relocating from Georgia for the summer.

Damn.

This is New York, so Post Office Arthur won't pop up into my life again. I guess that's fine. It's not like something could've really happened between us.

Thanks for nothing, universe.

CHAPTER THREE
ARTHUR
Tuesday, July 10

Hudson. Like the river.

Lol, replies Jessie. You know you're creepy as hell for swiping his address label, right?

Sobbing tears emoji. I know, I swear I'm not a stalker

And even if I were—which I'm *not,* I would *never—* I'd be the worst stalker ever. I didn't even take the whole address label. It's ripped and crumpled to the point where I don't know if I'm looking at the *to* or the *from.* The address is torn in half, and the last name's completely illegible. Still, I text a picture of it to the group chat as the 2 train pulls in. Jam-packed, as always. I squish between a man with a *Cats* shirt and a woman with tattoo sleeves.

Well it definitely says Hudson, writes Jessie.

I lean into the pole. Right? But is Hudson the boy or the boyfriend?

I'm still kicking myself for letting him go. I always thought that was just an expression. *Kicking myself.* But nope, I'm literally standing here on the subway, kicking the back of my heel with my foot. All I had to do was ask for his number. That's it. I had one job.

Why am I such a gameless dumbfuck??

What?? Jessie writes. What are you talking about? You have so much game. I would never have had the guts to talk to a cute boy I just met. You're a badass.

God he was so cute. I don't think you understand how cute he was.

I'm serious, Arthur, that makes your game even more impressive. Muscle-arm emoji.

Agreed, chimes Ethan, you talked to a cute boy, you get props.

Okay, you know what's unsettling? Boy talk with Ethan. And the fact that he says all the right things makes it weirder. Because now I don't even know which Ethan is real. Supportive Friend Ethan from the group chain? Or our one-on-one chain, featuring a wall of unanswered texts from me? And I know it's just texts, and it's a weird thing to fixate on. My mom says I should just talk to him. But I don't even know what I'd say. And I bet he'd deny anything's wrong in the first place.

I tap into my photos. There's just this part of me that has to wallow, the part that cues up *Les Misérables* when I'm sad. I can't help it. If I'm going to feel something, I want to *feel* it.

I scroll back through time. Junior year. Jessie reading a book during the Roswell-Milton game. Ethan ironically-but-not-really-ironically wearing a fedora. Jessie napping in the passenger seat of my car. Scrolling further. Sophomore year. Ethan in front of a King of Pops cart. Ice skating at Avalon. A close-up of waffles drenched in chocolate syrup, because I always sneak chocolate syrup into Waffle House.

Then I switch over to my videos, and it's a million clips of Ethan singing. Sometimes belting. I'll just say Ethan's the reason I spent years assuming all straight guys were into musicals.

I kind of hate him.

I really miss him.

I look up from my phone to find an old lady watching me, and when our eyes meet, she doesn't look away. She doesn't smile. She just stares at me and pets her giant purse like it's a cat. New York is the weirdest.

Though it's weird in a good way sometimes. Like yesterday. My brain keeps wandering back to Box Boy. Hudson. The main thing I remember is his smile—specifically, the way he smiled when I said I was gay. I swear, he was happy to hear it. And yes, it could be a solidarity thing, like some

kind of Kinsey scale Sorting Hat. "Better be . . . GAY!!!!!!"
*cue cheers and rainbow flag waving from Hudson of Gay
House*

But maybe it wasn't just a solidarity thing. It didn't feel
like a solidarity thing. It felt like fate and recognition and
standing straighter and *oh hello*. I'm not an expert or anything, but I could have sworn he was interested. I just can't
figure out why he left.

I step off the train and into the smothering heat. Here's
something I didn't expect about New York: the heat's worse
than Georgia. I mean, it's hotter in Georgia, yeah, but in
New York you actually feel it. If it's ninety degrees, you
walk. If it's gushing down rain, you walk. Back home, we
don't even walk across parking lots in the summer. You
park by Target and go to Target. Then you move your air-
conditioned car a hundred yards to Starbucks. But here, I'm
sweating through my button-down, and it's not even nine
in the morning. Guess how much I love being the sweaty
intern. Extra great, because I work in the fanciest office
ever.

I mean, this whole building gleams. Artsy minimalist
light fixtures? Check. Mirrored elevators? Check. Crisp
gray couches and metallic triangular coffee tables? Check
and check. There's even a doorman, Morrie, who calls me
doctor, which is a thing that happens to me, despite me
being sixteen with no medical training. Because my last

name is Seuss. And the answer to your next question is no. Not twice removed. Not cousins by marriage. No, I do not like green eggs and ham.

Anyway, my mom works on the eleventh floor. It's the same firm she works for in Atlanta, but their New York office is at least three times as big. There are lawyers and paralegals and secretaries and clerks, and everyone seems to know one another, and they definitely all know Mom. I guess she's somewhat of a VIP, because she went to law school with the women who own this firm. Which is how I ended up here instead of directing six-year-olds in *Fiddler on the Roof* at the JCC.

"Yo," says Namrata. "Arthur, you're late."

She's got a massive stack of accordion files, which means I'm in for a fun morning. Namrata likes to boss me around, but she's actually pretty great. There are only two summer associates this year—her and Juliet—so they're always slammed with work. But I guess that's how it goes when you're in law school. Apparently 563 people applied for Namrata's and Juliet's positions. Meanwhile, my application process was Mom saying, "This will look good on your college apps."

I follow Namrata into the conference room, where Juliet's already thumbing through a stack of papers. She glances up. "The Shumaker files?"

"You got it." Namrata stacks them on the table, sinking

into a conference chair. I should mention that the chairs in here are squishy rolling chairs. It's probably the main perk of the job.

I scoot back in my chair, kicking off from the table legs. "All these files are for one case?"

"Yup."

"Must be a big case."

"Not really," says Namrata.

She doesn't even look up. The girls get like that sometimes: hyper-focused and irritable. But, secretly, they're cool. I mean, they're not Ethan and Jessie, but they're pretty much my New York squad. Or they will be, once I win them over. And I will.

"Oh, Julieeeettt." I roll back to the table, pulling my phone out. "I've got something for you."

"Should I be nervous?" She's still lost in her document.

"Nope, be excited." I slide my phone toward her. "Because this happened."

"What is this?"

"A screenshot."

Specifically, a screenshot of a conversation that occurred on Twitter at 10:18 p.m. last night with Issa Rae, who happens to be Juliet's favorite actress, per Juliet's Instagram, which I secretly follow.

"You told Issa Rae it was my birthday?"

I beam. "Yup."

"Why?"

"So she'd tweet you a birthday message."

"My birthday's in March."

"*I know.* I'm just saying—"

"You lied to my queen."

"No. Well. Sort of?" I rub my forehead. "Anyway, y'all want to hear about my latest screwup?"

"I think we just did," Namrata says.

"No, this is different. It's boy-related."

They both look up. Finally. The squad can't resist hearing about my love life, not that I have a love life. But they like hearing about the random cute boys I see on the subway. It's pretty awesome to actually talk about this stuff out loud. Like it's no big deal. Like it's just a thing about me.

"I met a boy at the post office," I say, "and guess what."

"You made out behind a mailbox," says Namrata.

"Uh, no."

"Inside a mailbox," Juliet suggests.

"No. No making out. But he has an ex-boyfriend."

"Oh, so he's gay."

"Right, or bi or pan or something. And he's single, unless he rebounds really quickly. Do New York guys rebound quickly?"

Namrata cuts straight to the point. "How'd you fuck it up?"

"I didn't get his number."

"Welp," Namrata says.

"Can you find him online?" asks Juliet. "You seem . . . good at that."

"Well, I also didn't get his name."

"Oh, sweetie."

"Well, I did. Sort of. I'm like fifty percent sure his first name is Hudson."

"You're fifty percent sure." Juliet's mouth quirks.

I shake my head slowly. I mean, I could show them the address label. But I'm not sure they need to know about me scrounging for trash on the floor of the post office. Even Jessie thinks that's creepy. And this is the girl who once told our entire math class she was related to Beyoncé and showed up the next day with Photoshopped pictures to prove it.

"So all you have on this guy is his first name, which . . . might not even be his first name."

I nod. "It's hopeless."

"Probably," says Namrata. "But you could put a thing on Craigslist."

"A thing?"

"A missed connection. You know those posts where it's like, *I saw you on the F train reading* Fifty Shades of Grey *and eating candy corn*."

"Eww, candy corn?"

"Excuse me, candy corn is a fucking gift," says Namrata.

46

"Um—"

"Seriously, Arthur, you should do it," says Juliet. "Just write a post that describes the moment, like, *Hey, we met at the post office and made out inside a mailbox*, so on and so forth."

"Okay, do people make out inside mailboxes here? This is not a thing we do in Georgia."

"Jules, we should write the post for him."

"Who even fits inside a mailbox?" I add.

"Yo," Namrata says. "Fire up your laptop, kid."

Okay, tiny pet peeve: when the girls call me *kid*. Like they're so mature and all-knowing, and I'm some kind of half-formed fetus. Of course, I open my computer anyway.

"Pull up Craigslist."

"Don't people get murdered on Craigslist?"

"Nope," Namrata says. "They get murdered for not getting on Craigslist fast enough and wasting my time."

So now I've got Namrata hovering over me, and Juliet beside me, and a million blue links arranged in narrow columns on my screen. "Um. Okay."

Namrata taps the screen. "Right here, under community."

"You seem to know your way around Craigslist," I say, and she smacks me.

I have to admit I love this. The fact that they're interested. I'm always vaguely paranoid that Namrata and Juliet are exasperated by me. Like I'm some high school kid they're forced to babysit when they'd rather be doing important things like consolidating the Shumaker files.

The thing is, they're the only squad I have in New York. I don't know how people make friends in the summer. There are a million and a half people in Manhattan, but none of them make eye contact unless you already know them. And I don't know any of them, except the ones who work in this law office.

Sometimes I miss Ethan and Jessie so much my chest hurts.

Juliet's taken over my laptop. "Oh god, some of these are really sweet," she says. "Look."

She rotates the computer back toward me. The screen says this:

Bleecker Street Starbucks/Not named Ryan— m4m (Greenwich Village)
You: button-down shirt with no tie. Me: polo with popped collar. They wrote Ryan on your drink, and you muttered, "Who the hell is Ryan?" Then you caught my eye and gave a sheepish smile and it was very cute. Wish I'd had the guts to ask for your number.

Fuck. "Ouch. That sucks."
I click to the next listing.

Equinox 85th Street—m4m (Upper East Side)

Saw u on the treadmill, u look good. Hit me up.

Juliet grimaces. "And they say romance is dead."

"I love the total lack of specificity," says Namrata. "He's like, 'hey, you look good. Why don't I give you absolutely no frame of reference for who I am.'"

"Well," Juliet says, "at least he's giving it a shot. Arthur, you want to have sex with this guy in a mailbox again, right—"

"That is not a thing. Mailbox sex is not a thing."

"I'm just saying—"

"Look, he's blushing!"

"Okay, I'm closing this now." I slide my laptop into the center of the table, burying my face in my arms. "Let's do the Shumaker files."

"And that," Namrata declares, "is how we get Arthur to do some fucking work."

CHAPTER FOUR

BEN

"I think she died," Dylan says over FaceTime.

Maybe I shouldn't have answered Dylan's call on my way to school. I'm on a Lorde kick this week and could be listening to more of her music before class, but I got my best friend pants on because Dylan is thrown off by Samantha right now. Last night he texted her some YouTube videos of underappreciated Elliott Smith songs and still hasn't heard back. Dylan's love for Elliott Smith can go overboard sometimes, like when he gave me shit for a solid week because I once spelled Elliott's name without the second *t*.

"I don't think she's dead. She probably has a life," I say.

"Doing what?"

"I don't know. Slaying vampires?"

"Sun's up. No vampires out. Try again."

"I'm sure everything is fine. You talked for two hours yesterday."

"Two hours and twelve minutes," Dylan corrects. He refills his mug of coffee. He didn't get a lot of sleep. I woke up to two middle-of-the-night missed FaceTime calls and ten thousand Samantha-related texts.

I really don't get the coffee thing and I especially don't get the coffee thing during the summer and I 100 percent don't get the coffee thing when you're already having a hard time sleeping. This math doesn't add up, but girls have this effect on Dylan.

"She has a last name," Dylan says.

"Whoa."

"Samantha O'Malley," Dylan says. He fills me in on every detail he learned about her yesterday: being a barista makes her way happier than it does her coworkers; her favorite movies are *Titanic* and *The Sandlot*; she takes her little sister out for seafood every week; she's great at video games. "And I thought she liked me."

I've seen Dylan go through a dozen "relationships" since third grade, but he's never been this insufferable on day two of knowing a girl. Even his crush on Harriett took a month to really take hold, which is years in Dylan Time. Dylan's heart-eyes for Samantha remind me of how I was with Hudson back when he used to race to find me after school. We know what happens next.

"I'm sure she likes you, dude."

"Liked. She's dead. I'll see you at the next Heartbroken Anonymous meeting."

I turn the corner and walk to the school's entrance. Belleza High in Midtown is not where Dylan and I go, but this year they're hosting a shitload of New York's summer mourners from other public high schools. I'm about to reassure Dylan that Samantha will reach out when I see Hudson and Harriett sitting on the front steps of the school.

Just like his Instagram picture yesterday, Hudson looks perfectly healthy. He sees me right before he can take another bite from his bacon, egg, and cheese roll, and he just turns to Harriett and busts out laughing. No shade to Harriett, because she's awesome, but hilarious she is not. Even she's looking at him like he's lost his shit.

"Oh," I say. "D, I got to go."

"What's happening?" Dylan asks. I flip the phone around and Dylan is also suddenly staring down Hudson and Harriett. "OH. Hi, guys."

Harriett shakes her head. "No thanks."

"Alrighty then," Dylan says. "Hudson buddy, you have ketchup on your face."

I shake my head and hang up FaceTime while Hudson wipes his face with a napkin.

"Hey. Hi," I say to Hudson and Harriett.

"Hi," Harriett says. But unlike yesterday, she doesn't give me a hug, because Hudson's here and she can't go betraying him. Really sucks since we knew each other before Hudson transferred to our school at the beginning of junior year. I really wish we could all be friends again. That Harriett and I could still talk about our favorite superhero shows. That Dylan and Hudson could still play chess. That Hudson and I could get our friendship back on track. Same for Dylan and Harriett. Maybe one day we can try being a squad again.

"Hey," Hudson says, not looking at me. No brave Instagram face today. He goes for another bite of his roll but holds out, probably still mortified from having ketchup on his face. Hudson always has been a sloppy eater, but I never called him out on that. Walking to school and eating cheap sandwiches while talking about whatever was a highlight for me. I know it shouldn't sting to see him having breakfast with Harriett, but it does. Like it's really that simple for Hudson to write me out of his life.

"You feeling better?" I ask. I'm really trying to make this summer not suck.

"Healthy and happy." Hudson wraps the aluminum around his sandwich. "And heading up." He goes up the steps and through the door.

"This is going to be a fun day," Harriett says.

"I'll never ask him how he's doing again, I guess," I say.

"He's going to need some time. Bruised ego."

"He's the one who made out with another guy," I say.

"He thought you guys had broken up," Harriett says.

"He kissed him two days after our fight."

Harriett raises her hands. "It's more complicated for him, and I think you know that."

"That's not fair. He broke my heart first," I say. "I don't get how Hudson gets all the pity points just because I'm the one who broke up with him. I had my reasons. You know all of them."

"I don't want to be in the middle any more than I am," Harriett says. "I'm sorry, Ben." She heads into the building.

I take a deep breath. I don't know what twisted world Harriett is living in where she's in the middle of this—she's clearly Team Hudson. None of this would be happening if Hudson and I had just stayed friends.

I go up the steps, dreading this class. But I don't turn back. I'm not repeating junior year because my ex-boyfriend scared me out of summer school.

Our teacher, Mr. Hayes, is outside the classroom flirting with the algebra teacher. Mr. Hayes is pretty young, like maybe midtwenties. He usually does missionary work in other countries during the summer, but in May he twisted his ankle during a Spartan Race, so he's keeping busy teaching us chemistry. He's not exactly my type because he's a little too fit, the kind of guy you see on a package for underwear, but there's no denying how handsome he is.

I take my seat at the back of the room, as far away from Hudson and Harriett as possible. I just open my notebook and keep to myself.

I've always sucked at school. Hudson telling me I didn't have to study as hard for exams definitely didn't help, but I've always had trouble focusing in class. I spend way too much time daydreaming, for starters. Whenever there's a test I study at home for twenty minutes and get back to my *Sims* and stories. Ma was so frustrated with me in my first semester that she confiscated the laptop until my grades improved, which they sort of did because I really needed to get back to my made-up worlds.

But even when I do my best to pay attention in class, I feel so far behind. Like if you miss a lesson because you're out sick or gazing out thinking about what it would feel like to be really loved back, the teachers don't stop class to reteach you. They keep it moving. I forget who fought in World War II. I can't name more than ten presidents. I'm geographically lost. Trivial Pursuit is my nightmare.

I want to know the real world better. Not just the ones I make up or the ones I play with on *Sims*. But right now I just feel lonely and unwanted in the real world.

Mr. Hayes walks in with a crutch under one armpit and carrying a duffel bag in his other hand, like he's about to work out instead of talk about chemical properties for the next two hours. "Good morning, friends," he says. "Let's roll through attendance."

Hudson raises his hand. "Hi. I'm Hudson Robinson. I missed yesterday."

Mr. Hayes nods. "You sure did. Feeling better?"

"One hundred percent."

"Great. Let's chat after class. I can walk you through what you missed," Mr. Hayes says. "Okay, Pete's here. Scarlett—"

"Wait," Hudson interrupts. "I'm not staying late. Coming to school during the summer is already over the top, thank you very much."

Harriett gives Hudson her signature dude-shut-the-hell-up face.

"I'm not the one who failed you. It's my job to make sure you don't fail again. Just hang back for thirty minutes after class so you don't have to spend the next year watching your friends get ready for prom and graduation and college while you're making friends with juniors." Man, Mr. Hayes knows how to go for the throat without sounding like a total dick.

"I'm not stupid, I know the material," Hudson says. I've never seen him talk to a teacher like this. "That's not why I'm here. I was just . . ." He doesn't look at me. "I only missed the first day. I got the basics covered."

"Cool. Tell us how ionic bonds are formed and you can earn your freedom."

Hudson doesn't say anything.

"Alloys are a combination of what?"

Nothing. See? School pauses for no one. Not even confusing ex-boyfriends.

Hudson shrugs and pulls out his phone, and holy shit, I hope he's going to google these answers and not just text away. This stretch of awkward silence is made even more awkward by how hard Hudson is blushing. I haven't seen him this quiet since Kim Epstein tried to call him one of the girls as an insult because he's a little effeminate, and Harriett blasted Kim's business for trying to swing at her best friend.

I'm killing the awkward silence. "Alloys are a combination of metals." We relearned that yesterday.

Hudson snaps away from his phone and stares at me. "I don't need anything from you, okay? *Don't* ask me how I'm doing. *Don't* help me out." He's so red in the face it's a miracle he doesn't not-so-spontaneously combust.

I want to prop up my notebook and hide.

No one here knows our history except Harriett.

They must think Hudson is a loose cannon and I'm the summer school know-it-all. I do know one thing: this is going to be a long summer.

CHAPTER FIVE
ARTHUR

On the subway ride home, it hits me: I really, truly, irrevocably messed up. I met the most gorgeous boy with the most sun-kissed cheeks, and the weird part is, I honestly think he was into me. That smile. It wasn't a solidarity smile. It was a smile like a door opening. But that door is now slammed shut, locked, and dead-bolted. I'll never see Hudson again. I'll never kiss him on his Emma Watson mouth. And isn't that just the story of my life. Relationship status: Forever Alone.

Wish I'd had the guts to ask for your number.

Jessie's dead wrong about me being a badass. The truth is, I have zero guts and zero game. I've never had a boyfriend, never had sex, never kissed anyone, never come close. It hasn't bothered me until now. It just felt normal. After all, Ethan and Jessie are right there with me in that boat. But now it feels like I'm auditioning for Broadway with no training and an empty résumé. Unprepared and unqualified and totally, totally out of my depth.

And all the way home, I feel too big for my skin. I hop off at Seventy-Second Street and step out into a mess of people and taxis and strollers and noise. There are three blocks between the subway station and home. I spend the whole time reading missed connections on my phone.

As soon as I open the door: "Art, is that you?"

I set down my laptop bag on the dining room table, which is also both the living room table and the kitchen table. My great-uncle Milton's apartment has two bedrooms, and I guess it's considered big for New York. Even so, it makes me feel like a mummy in a sarcophagus. I definitely get why Uncle Milton's hanging out in Martha's Vineyard all summer.

I follow Dad's voice, and he's sitting at my desk with a mug of coffee and his laptop.

"Why are you in my room?"

He shakes his head like he's baffled to find himself here. "I don't know, change of scenery?"

"You're scared of the horses."

"I love horses. I just don't understand why your uncle Milton needs twenty-two paintings of them," Dad says.

"Their eyes follow you, right? I'm not imagining it?"

"You're not imagining it."

"I just want to, like . . . glue sunglasses on them, or something."

"Good call. Mom would be thrilled."

For a moment, we just grin at each other. Sometimes with my dad, it's like we're two kids in the back of a classroom. Which means there are times we must throw wads of paper at the back of my mother's head. Metaphorically speaking.

I peek at my dad's computer. "Is this a freelance thing?"

"Nah, just tinkering." My dad's a web developer. In Georgia, he was the kind of web developer who made money, until he got laid off the day before Christmas. So now he's the kind who tinkers.

And here's something you learn when you live in a sarcophagus: sound travels through walls. Which means, most nights, I get to hear my mom calling my dad out for half-assing his job search. Which usually gets my dad muttering about how hard it is to job hunt in Georgia while living in New York. Which *always* ends in my mom reminding him he's welcome to head back home anytime.

Guess how totally not awkward that is.

"Hey, what do you think about Craigslist missed connections?" I blurt.

I don't know why I do this. I definitely wasn't planning

on telling my parents the post office story. Just like I wasn't planning on telling them about my sad crush on Cody Feinman from Hebrew school. Or my even sadder crush on Jessie's very slightly younger brother. Or the fact that I'm gay in the first place. But sometimes things just slip out.

"You mean like a personal ad?"

"Well yeah, but not like *must love dogs and long walks on the beach*. It's like . . ." I nod. "Okay, it's kind of like a lost cat ad, except the cat's actually a cute boy you met at the post office. But a human cute boy. Not a literal cat."

"Got it," Dad says. "So you want to put up an ad to find the post office boy."

"No! I don't know." I shake my head. "Juliet and Namrata suggested it, yeah, but it's a total long shot. I don't even know if anyone reads those things."

Dad nods slowly. "It's definitely a long shot."

"Right. Stupid idea. Okay—"

"It's not a stupid idea. We should post one."

"He's not going to see it."

"He might. It's worth a try, right?" He opens a new search window.

"Okay, no. No no no. Craigslist is not a father-son bonding activity."

But he's already typing, and I can tell from the set of his jaw: he's all in.

"Dad."

The apartment door creaks open, and I hear the click of heels against hardwoods. A moment later, Mom's in my doorway.

Dad doesn't even glance up from the computer screen. "You're home early," he says.

"It's six thirty."

Suddenly, everyone's quiet. And it's not even the normal kind of silence. It's one of those charged, atomic silences.

I dive into it headfirst. "We're making a thing on Craigslist to find that guy from the post office."

"Craigslist?" Mom narrows her eyes. "Arthur, absolutely not."

"Why not? I mean, other than the fact that it's pointless and there's no way he'd ever see it . . ."

Dad rubs his beard. "Why do you think he won't see it?"

"Because boys like that aren't on Craigslist."

"Boys like you aren't on Craigslist," says Mom. "I'm not letting you get killed by a machete murderer."

I laugh shortly. "Okay, I'm pretty sure that's not going to happen. Dick pics? Probably. Machete murderer—"

"Ooh. Yeah, as your mom, I'm going to go ahead and veto the dick pics, too."

"It's not like I'm asking for dick pics!"

"If you put an ad up on Craigslist, you're asking for dick pics."

Dad glances sidelong at Mom. "Mara, don't you think

you're being a little bit—"

"What, Michael? What am I being?"

"You don't think you're overreacting? Just a bit?"

"Because I don't want our sixteen-year-old son prowling around the underbelly of the internet—"

"I'm almost seventeen!"

"Craigslist?" Dad smiles. "You think Craigslist is the underbelly of the internet—"

"Well, you would know," Mom snaps.

Dad looks confused. "What's that supposed to mean—"

"Okay, please stop," I cut in. "Obviously, I'm not doing this. I'm not wasting my time searching for some random guy I talked to for five seconds. Okay? Can we just chill?"

I look from Mom to Dad and back to Mom, but it's like they don't even see me. They're too busy pointedly not looking at each other.

So I leave. Grab my laptop. Exit stage left.

My heart's beating so fast, it's almost stuttering. I hate this. It's never been like this with them. Yeah, I've seen them get snippy with each other. We're not robots. But they could always joke their way out of it. It's just that these days, even the jokey moments feel like a temporary cease-fire.

I sink onto the living room couch and shut my eyes—but I swear I'm being watched. By horses. Specifically, by the giant oil painting hanging above the table, which I can only assume is an early portrait of BoJack Horseman painted by

Leonardo da Vinci himself.

Mom's voice drifts in from my bedroom. ". . . home early. Excuse me? I rescheduled two conference calls to be . . ."

"Yeah. Like I said . . ." Dad's voice drops off. ". . . early."

"Oh, come off it. Are you kidding me? That's not . . ."

"You're reading too much into . . ."

"Okay, you know what you're not going to do, Michael? You're not going to spend the day playing computer games in your boxers, and then come after me for—"

I open my laptop. Click into iTunes. *Spring Awakening*, original cast album. I jam my finger down on F12 until the volume's as high as it will go.

"Mara, can you please—"

And I let Jonathan Groff drown them out.

Because that's what cute boys are for.

CHAPTER SIX
BEN

I wish I felt Puerto Rican out in the world the way I do at home.

Some friends in middle school told me I wasn't really Puerto Rican because I'm so white-passing and only know a dozen basic Spanish phrases, stuff like te amo and cómo estás. I told Pa that day, begging him to put Post-it notes on different objects around the apartment to teach me Spanish so I wouldn't get bullied again. Pa was happy to do so, but he broke it down for me that being Puerto Rican didn't come down to my skin or knowing Spanish, but my blood and family. I really liked that. But that doesn't mean that I'm not constantly having to basically say, "Hi, I'm Ben. I'm Puerto Rican." Pa's complexion is the darkest in our family, though still really light, like a white person's tan, and how he looks is how everyone expects me to look. No one ever questions my dad being Puerto Rican.

If only everyone could see me at home, completely killing it while I'm on sofrito duty, mellowing out to Lana Del Rey while mixing the cilantro, peppers, onions, and garlic, along with the fresh oregano my mom's coworker gave us. My dad prepares our plates with salad first, piling his rice and pigeon peas on top. He hooks me up with extra pegao because I've always loved crispy rice since I was a kid, maybe because it's crunchy like some of my favorite candy. My mom sets her coconut pudding in the oven and we're pretty good to go.

Ma taps my shoulder and says something I can't hear over the music. She pulls out one earbud. "What's going on with you?" Her dark hair rests over her shoulder, smelling like cucumber shampoo from her post-work shower. She's a bookkeeper at Blink Fitness, and even though she's in an office all day the smell of sweat clings to her like a gym bro on a pull-up bar, so she's always quick to hit the showers when she gets home.

"It's been a day," I say.

"Hudson?" Pa asks.

"Ding-ding."

Pa shakes his head while cleaning the pots and pans before we eat so the dishes won't seem as mountainous when our stomachs are filled, a trick Abuelo taught him. The soap foams over his hands.

"Diego, hurry up, I'm starving." Ma hands me utensils. "Benito, set the table. Catch us up after prayer."

I set the forks and knives on our individual place mats, these impulse buys at the corner store when our money situation was a little better than it is now. Ma's is shaped like an owl, her favorite animal. Pa's is a black-and-white linen stitch that he always scratches while waiting for us to finish our dinner. And mine has a T. rex trying to drink from a water fountain, which hasn't won a smile out of me since I broke up with Hudson.

We sit really close to one another. There's never been a time where my parents are both sitting at the heads of the table. Ma says it feels too regal, like we're eating a feast in some castle's massive dining room instead of a super-cozy two-bedroom apartment. And Pa just doesn't like being that far away from Ma.

We take one another's hands and Ma says grace. My parents are big on faith and we like to say we have a healthy relationship with religion. We're not old-school Catholics who live by the Bible and conveniently ignore all the verses that contradict the hate coming out of their mouths. We're the kind of Catholics who think people shouldn't go to hell for being nonhetero, and that was before I even came out. My parents pray to God on the regular and I jump in

67

during dinner. This evening Ma is thanking God for the food on the table, for my abuelita who fell getting out of the car and my aunt who's taking care of her, for Pa's modest pay raise kicking in at Duane Reade, and for everyone's well-being.

"Okay." Ma claps her hands. "Hudson. What's going on with him?"

I like that my parents are so in my face but know to give me space too. "I was trying to help him out in class and he flipped on me."

Pa's eyes narrow. "I thought you said he wasn't the fighting type."

"He's definitely not," I say, and he cools down. Two years ago I got robbed outside a grocery store and my parents locked me down with tight curfews, which felt like punishment for being a victim, but I know it was all love with the way Pa trained me to throw up my fists and run. Still, that was a summer I lost, and it's not like they come around as quickly as weekends. "He just shouted at me in front of everyone. And I didn't argue back."

"Good," Ma says.

"Also good that you can take him if you need to."

"Definitely." There was that one time where I picked up Hudson and kissed him against a wall because we saw a guy-girl couple doing it in a movie and we wanted to see what it was like for a guy-guy couple. Then we flipped and even though we're the same weight, he had a harder time carrying me.

"Okay, barbarians." Ma shakes her head because she's not about any talk of violence. She doesn't even like action movies, which Pa and I are openly fine with since she will ask you ten thousand questions during a movie, even if everyone is seeing it for the first time. "I hope it smooths over soon."

"Not holding my breath."

I try to stretch dinner for as long as possible because being alone is really getting to me. Ma tells us about the new thriller podcast she's been listening to, and how each episode ramps up the tension so much that she almost wishes the series was over already so she could breathe and not be held in suspense anymore. Pa tells us about how this afternoon a father and son were buying condoms at the same time without realizing the other was there.

"How's your story going, Benito? Have I made a reappearance yet?" Ma asks.

The only people who know I'm writing this novel are Dylan, Hudson, Harriett, and my parents. This year I couldn't afford to buy Ma anything for Mother's Day, so I wrote her into the story as a sorceress who doesn't age and casts peace spells. I printed it out, but at the last second my insecurities kicked in and I just told her what her character does instead of letting her read for herself. I've gotten so far with this story that I'm nervous any negative feedback might make me quit.

"Nope. Isabel the Serene needs to stay in her tower. Can't have any more peace spells in a war with wizards."

"Maybe they can reach a place of understanding by talking."

"Ma, no." I smile a little. "The laptop has been acting up lately. It gets overheated after twenty minutes."

"Maybe if you pass summer school, we can get you a new one," Ma says.

"No," Pa says. "His reward for passing summer school is not getting left behind."

"Better to have me home writing than outside getting robbed, right?"

"Cheap shot," Pa says. "But well played. Hector the Haggler taught you well." Hector the Haggler got even less page time than Ma's character.

"We can find another on Craigslist," Ma says.

I think getting a laptop on Craigslist was the problem to begin with, but I can't complain.

"Frankie connected with his new girlfriend on Craigslist," Pa says.

"Which Frankie? Employee Frankie or Mailman Frankie?" I ask.

"Employee Frankie. Rodriquez. He was telling me about this page on Craigslist where you can find people you met or almost met. Missed you connections, I think." Pa looks at me and Ma like we're supposed to know what he's talking about. He shrugs. "Well, Frankie first met Lola on the train and they didn't trade numbers before he got off. His friend told him to check out Craigslist, and he found a listing from Lola. Been dating two weeks now."

"That's so wonderful," Ma says.

"Impressive," I say.

It's like Craigslist is some agent of the universe. Handling business. And maybe the universe is speaking through my dad right now to encourage me to do the same. To see if Arthur, my Lola, tried finding me too. I get up from the table.

"I have to check something," I say.

"What about dessert?" Ma asks.

I halt and almost double back, but keep it moving. Dessert will still be there. I have this I-must-do-this-right-now-or-explode feeling in my chest. I close my bedroom door and sit on my bed with the busted laptop that started this whole Craigslist conversation. There's this exciting hope of possibility filling me up, like when Hudson and I started texting for the first time, like when Arthur said hi and we flirted and talked about the universe.

I go on Craigslist and find missed connections—not missed you connections, Pa, wow—and I look through their dude-for-dude listings in Manhattan. What starts out as hopeful scrolling quickly turns into defeat, and I sort of wish I could start a support group for all these people with their regrets and what-if fantasies.

I close the laptop.

I guess that's it on this Arthur business.

CHAPTER SEVEN
ARTHUR
Wednesday, July 11

"Arthur, shoes. Come on. We're going to be late." Mom checks her phone. "Oy. I'm getting a Lyft."

I peer up at her from the couch. "It's only eight."

"Well, since your dad finished off the coffee without telling me," she says loudly, in the general direction of their bedroom, "we need to stop at Starbucks before the Bray-Eliopulos call. You've taken your pill, right?"

"Yeah, but." I sit up slowly. "Why don't I just take the subway?"

"You'd need to leave now anyway for the subway."

"Not really. Not until eight twenty."

Mom scoffs. "Is that why you keep rolling into the office at nine fifteen?"

"That was one time!"

She ruffles my hair. "Come on. I already called the Lyft."

But then the door to my parents' bedroom nudges open and out shuffles my dad, wearing plaid flannel pants and yesterday's T-shirt. "Morning." He yawns, rubbing his beard. "Hey, Art. Want to grab bagels?"

"Yes!"

"Michael, can you just . . . not." Mom exhales. "Not right now."

They look at each other, and it's one of those lightning-fast wordless parental debates—if you can even call it a debate. It's more like watching a bulldozer run over a worm.

Dad pats my shoulder. "Let's do bagels tomorrow."

"But I don't want to be stuck in a Lyft with pre-coffee Mom," I whisper.

"You'll survive."

The Lyft pulls in front of our building, and I slide into the back seat after Mom. She smooths her skirt and sets her phone on her lap, screen down, hands clasped together. She's regained her chill now that we're moving, but she's watching me intently, and I think that's almost worse. No doubt she's gearing up for a Chat.

She clears her throat. "So, tell me about the boy."

"What boy?"

"Arthur!" She nudges me. "From the post office."

I look at her sidelong. "I already told you about him."

"Well, you just told me what happened at the post office, but I want the whole story."

"Okay. Um. You didn't want me to look for him, so . . . that is the whole story."

"Sweetie, I just don't want you on Craigslist. Did you read that article about—"

"I know. *I know.* Machetes and dick pics." I shrug. "I'm not doing Craigslist. I don't even care that much."

"I'm sorry, Arthur. I know you were hoping to find him."

"It's not a big deal. He's just a random guy."

"Well, I just think," Mom starts to say—but then her phone buzzes in her lap. She peeks at the screen and sighs. "I have to get this. Hold that thought." She twists her body toward the window. "What's up . . . yes. Okay, yes. On our way. Ten minutes, and we're swinging through Star-bucks . . . what? Oh. Oh no." She drums on her briefcase. Then she turns to me, eyes rolling slightly, and mouths, "Work."

Which means she's not hanging up the phone anytime soon. So I turn to stare out my own window, mentally cata-loging the restaurants and storefronts. It's not even nine, but the sidewalks are jammed with commuters. They all look exhausted and generally underwhelmed.

Underwhelmed. By New York!

I don't know. Sometimes I feel like New Yorkers do New

York wrong. Where are the people swinging from subway poles and dancing on fire escapes and kissing in Times Square? The post office flash mob proposal was a start, but when's the next big number? I pictured New York like *West Side Story* plus *In the Heights* plus *Avenue Q*—but really, it's just construction and traffic and iPhones and humidity. They might as well write musicals about Milton, Georgia. We'd open with a ballad: "Sunday at the Mall." And then "I Left My Heart at Target." If Ethan were here, he'd have the whole libretto written by the time we stepped out of the car.

"Oh, I don't think so," Mom's saying into the phone. "Unless Wingate filed a brief. Okay, we're a block away." She pauses. "No, that's fine, I'll send Arthur. Be right up."

Already, she's fishing a twenty from her purse. "Tall nonfat latte," she mouths.

Hashtag intern life.

I text Ethan while waiting in line at Starbucks. **Concept: a musical set in the Atlanta suburbs called . . . wait for it . . . Ha-Milton.** Mic emoji. Down-arrow emoji. Boom.

But Ethan doesn't text back.

Thursday, July 12

It's radio silence until the next morning, when Ethan texts a selfie to—surprise, surprise—the group chain. It's him and Jessie at Waffle House holding up a bottle of chocolate syrup. You're here in spirit, my dude! he writes.

It just sucks. Any other summer, I'd be next to Jessie in that booth, eating hash browns and ranting about politics or Twitter or stage-to-screen adaptations. I'd give Ethan and Jessie the full, unabridged post office story, and we'd probably make a football-style Operation Hudson game plan in my notes app.

As opposed to here, where the girls shut down every time I say the word *Hudson*. I swear, they're even worse than usual today. One of the paralegals drops off a package for Namrata, and she barely even looks at it. It's like she can't stop typing. For a moment, I just watch her.

"What's that?" I ask finally.

"I don't know."

"Maybe you should open it."

"I will."

Namrata's fingers still on the keyboard for a moment while she reads something on her screen. Then she glances at a stack of documents, back up at her screen, and starts typing again.

"When, though?"

"What?"

"When do you think you'll open it?"

"Let me guess." Namrata sighs so hard, it ruffles the Shumaker documents. "You're not going to let me work until I do."

"That's probably true."

"Then let's go." She rips the package open and peers inside of it for what feels like ten minutes—but when she finally turns back toward me, she's smiling. "Why the fuck did you buy me five pounds of candy corn?"

"It's actually four pounds and fourteen ounces—"

"Of candy corn."

"In July," adds Juliet.

"Arthur, you are something else," says Namrata. Translation: I nailed it.

Juliet ruffles my hair. "Want to grab lunch with us?" Translation: I *super* nailed it.

I'm so happy, I could sing. If the girls and I are lunch friends now, we're probably on track for tasteful matching BFF tattoos by next week. And then they'll introduce me to cute law school boys, cuter than Hudson, and I'll never go home. I'll just stay here in New York with my awesome new squad. My new best friends. I mean, who even needs Waffle House? I'll just be here grabbing business lunch in New York fucking City, the culinary center of the universe. Ethan and Jessie can spend the rest of their lives eating at chain restaurants. From now on, I'll only eat at farm-fresh artisan food trucks and iconic celebrity delis.

"I've always wanted to try Tavern on the Green," I say.

"Arthur, we have thirty minutes."

"Sardi's?"

"How about Panera?"

I gasp. "I love Panera."

"Yeah, I figured," says Namrata, throwing back a fistful of candy corn.

Five minutes later, we hit the streets, and I can't get over how different the girls are outside the office. They're so *open*. Up until today, most of my Namrata and Juliet intel came from one of three sources: eavesdropping, Instagram, and my mom. Now I know Juliet's a dancer and Namrata's a vegetarian, and they hated each other their whole first year of law school, but now they're best friends and they go on runs together and eat cupcakes, and neither of them has skipped a single reading for any class ever. All this before we're even in line at Panera.

"I'm beyond disgusted," Namrata's telling Juliet. "I was like, you know what? That's fine, don't call them out, but guess what. I'm done spending the night there. Sorry, David, but dinosaur porn crosses a line for me."

Juliet moans. "Ewwww."

"Wait, who's David? And why is he into dinosaur porn?"

Okay, real talk: I hate when people drop a random name like I'm supposed to magically know it.

"No, it's David's roommates," Juliet explains.

"And they're not only into dinosaur porn," adds Namrata, "but they're actually creating their own—I'm not even kidding—*dinosaur porn webcomic*. Which—okay, you do you. But then they leave their sketches in the fucking living room, and I'm like, David, can I please not have to look at this picture of a T. rex getting himself off?"

"But . . . T. rex arms." Juliet looks baffled. "How?"

"Seriously, who's David?" I ask.

Namrata looks amused. "My boyfriend."

"You have a boyfriend?"

"They've been dating for six years," Juliet says.

"What? No way." I turn to Juliet. "Do you have a boyfriend?"

"I have a girlfriend," Juliet says.

"You're a lesbian?"

"Next," says the guy behind the counter.

Juliet steps up and orders a soup. Then she turns back to me and says, "Well, I'm biromantic ace, which means—"

"I know, I know. But you never mentioned it. Why don't you guys ever tell me anything?"

"We tell you to get back to work," says Juliet. "We tell you that a lot."

"But you never tell me about your love lives. I've told you every single thing about Hudson, and I didn't even know you had a girlfriend! And I definitely didn't know Namrata had a boyfriend named David who draws dinosaur porn."

"No, David's *roommates* draw dinosaur porn," Namrata

interjects, drifting back from the counter. "That is a critical piece of information. Arthur, you're up. Go order your PB and J Happy Meal."

"Pssh. I'm getting grilled cheese. Grown-up grilled cheese."

Namrata pats my head. "Very sophisticated."

"Hudson," someone says over a microphone, and I freeze. Namrata and Juliet freeze. The whole world freezes. "Hudson, your order's ready."

"Arthur." Juliet presses a hand to her mouth.

"It's not him."

"How do you know?"

"It can't be him. That would be too weird. Like, what are the odds?" I shake my head. "It's some other Hudson."

"We're near the post office," says Juliet. "He probably works around here or lives here or something. It's not really that common of a name."

"Yeah, we're going up there," Namrata says.

"No way. That's shady!"

"No it's not." She gives me a not-so-gentle yank toward the pickup counter. Standing with his back to us is a boy in jeans and a fitted polo shirt—white, taller than me, hair totally covered by a backward baseball cap. "Is that him?"

"I don't know."

"YO, HUDSON," Namrata says loudly.

81

My heart stops.

And the boy turns around, looking slightly apprehensive. "Do I know you?" he asks Namrata.

It's not him.

It's not Hudson. Well, apparently it *is* Hudson, or at least he answers to Hudson, but he's not *my* Hudson, if my Hudson's even a Hudson in the first place. My head's kind of swirling. This Hudson isn't terrible-looking. He's got really nice cheekbones and incredible eyebrows. He's staring at us now, looking bewildered, and I'm absolutely pissing-my-pants mortified.

"Hudson. From band camp?" Namrata asks smoothly.

"I didn't go to band camp."

"Oh well. Must be someone else."

"Someone else named Hudson?" he asks.

Namrata doesn't even bat an eye. "Yup, Hudson Panini."

Hudson Panini. Did Namrata seriously just pull a fictional camp friend out of her ass and name him Hudson Panini?

"Oh wow. Way more epic than Hudson Robinson."

"I'm afraid so." Namrata grabs my hand. "But enjoy your bread bowl, Hudson Robinson."

"I ordered a panini," Hudson says faintly.

But by then, we're halfway back to the table.

Juliet's on us immediately. "How'd it go?"

"I'm going to murder Namrata," I inform her.

82

Namrata snorts. "Excuse me?"

"HUDSON PANINI?"

"I saw a panini."

"Genius," says Juliet.

I sink back into my chair. "That was so humiliating."

"Whatever. You were being a wimpy little butt," says Namrata. "You weren't even going to talk to him."

"That wasn't even him! It was the wrong guy."

"Well, obviously. He didn't recognize you at all."

Juliet leans back in her chair. "So it was a totally different Hudson?"

"Or it's the ex-boyfriend," Namrata says casually. "In which case, you're welcome. I just got you his last name."

"Wait," I murmur.

But the rest of my words evaporate.

Because maybe Namrata's wrong. But maybe she's not wrong.

Maybe Hudson Robinson—backward-cap-wearing, eyebrow-god Hudson Robinson—is Box Boy's ex. I bet he's been too depressed to wash his hair since the breakup, *which is why he's wearing the hat.* Holy shit.

Hudson Robinson. I'm not a stalker or anything. It's not like I'm going to show up on his doorstep. But everyone's on the internet somewhere, right?

I mean, maybe I was actually fated to meet the boy from

the post office. Maybe I'm fated to find him again. And maybe—just maybe—I'm supposed to find him by following the boy who brought him to the post office in the first place.

Hudson Robinson, I type. And then I click enter.

CHAPTER EIGHT
BEN

Class was rough and the last thing I really want to be doing is meeting Dylan's future temporary girlfriend, but I rush downtown anyway as if getting far enough away from school can help me forget about how much it hurts to be excluded from all the laughs Hudson and Harriett share at the beginning and end of class. I get off the train and Dylan is outside a pharmacy holding a Dream & Bean thermos and a bouquet of flowers.

"You have Murderer Face going on right now," Dylan says. "Guilty Murderer Face. Maybe we can turn that frown upside down before you meet Samantha. Happy Best Friend Face, if you need any suggestions." Dylan winks.

I will play along with Happy Best Friend Face because it's

Dylan. But it really is getting exhausting getting to know all of his girlfriends, bonding with them, and losing their friendship pretty quickly after Dylan cuts ties with them.

"You got it. What's going on with the roses?" I ask.

"Samantha mentioned roses are her favorite flower while we were watching *Titanic*," Dylan says, beaming, like it's a superhuman trait to remember something that was said less than twenty-four hours ago.

"You guys hung out?"

"Over FaceTime last night."

"You were on FaceTime the whole time? Isn't that movie over three hours long?"

Dylan nods. "It took us over four hours to get through it. We kept pausing to talk."

"That's impressive," I say. I mean it. Especially considering how much sleep he lost the night before because Samantha hadn't texted him back about Elliott Smith. It turns out she just hadn't had a chance to listen to the songs yet. And she loved them all. "Did you like it?"

"I thought the ship was going to sink a lot sooner, if you catch my drift."

"You were bored until the ship started sinking—"

"I was bored until the ship started sinking, yes."

Dylan has some serious pep in his step as we rush to the coffee shop. He's dodging people left and right, and I can barely hear him go on about how there was room for Jack and Rose on that floating door or how they could've at least taken turns. Dylan stops at the corner.

"Okay. How do I look?"

He's got bags under his eyes and he's wearing a Kool Koffee T-shirt, which feels super extra, but otherwise good. Except: "Might want to toss the Dream & Bean cup."

Dylan tosses the thermos at me like it's a grenade and we pass it back and forth before I finally throw it in my backpack.

"You're ridiculous," I say as we walk inside Kool Koffee. The coffee shop smells like pretentious writers who would hate the stuff I write.

Samantha is behind the counter in all her glory. She stops taking someone's order and waves. Her dark curls are flattened by a khaki cap, and her blue-green eyes are beaming at Dylan. And boom, bright white teeth when she smiles over a customer's shoulder. I'm certain that I'm 100 percent gay because if I was even 1 percent bisexual I would be crushing hard on Samantha for looks and high energy alone. Dylan watches Samantha as if she were glowing, and I wonder when I went dim for Hudson. If I ever really glowed for him at all.

Oh shit. One free table left. "I'm grabbing that table," I say.

Dylan wrenches me back. "You have to order. Also, I'm nervous I'll say something stupid."

"You'll be fine."

"I almost walked in here with coffee from the enemy."

I stay put.

I have my Happy Best Friend Face on, even when some hopeful novelist-looking type our age takes the last available table, opening his laptop to write the Next Harry Potter before I can. He's cool to look at, at least. Bright eyes, dark brown skin, Caesar cut, a shirt with the Human Torch on it. If I were ballsier, sort of like that Arthur dude or Dylan with Samantha, I would make the first move. I'd sit across from him, say what's up, chat about writing, find out if he's into guys, call him pretty, pray he calls me pretty back, get his phone number, fall in love. But I'm not ballsy, so I don't.

We reach the front of the line and Samantha reaches over the counter, almost knocking over a spinner of impulse-buy cookies. "I'm a hugger," she says. She's undersold herself because she's not simply a hugger, she's a damn good hugger. "So nice to meet you, Ben."

"You too, Samantha. Samantha, right? Not Sam? Not Sammy?"

"Only my mom calls me Sammy. Weirds me out whenever anyone else does. Thanks for asking," Samantha says. She turns to Dylan. "Hi."

"Hi," he says. "How you doing?"

"Good. Busy." She smiles at the roses. "You're sweet. Unless those aren't for me, then I'm spitting in your coffee."

"All yours," Dylan says.

Samantha picks up a cup, writes Dylan's name inside a heart, and gets his spit-free large coffee started. "What can I get you, Ben?"

"I don't know. A strawberry lemonade, I guess." Sugar FTW.

"Small, medium, large?"

I look at the prices on the menu. "Small. Definitely small." Holy shit, $3.50 for a small cup of half ice, half juice? I could go on an adventure with a $2.75 single ride MetroCard with change to spare. Buy a gallon of orange juice. Three packs of Skittles and five Swedish Fish at the corner store.

"You got it," Samantha says. She draws a smiley face under my name. "I'll be free in a couple minutes. Let me just close out this line."

We wait at the end of the bar. I take another peek at the dude in the Human Torch shirt. He's wearing headphones now and I wonder what he's listening to. Hudson liked a lot of classics. I'm more into whatever is trending that month. I don't seek out new songs, but if it's catchy, I'm set. It'd be cool to date someone who liked the same stuff I did. We wouldn't clash during road trips to see life outside the city. We could share earphones and vibe to the same song while relaxing somewhere quiet.

A girl gets up from her corner table, wiping it down with

napkins, and before I can charge to see if she's leaving, two vultures—excuse me, dudes in suits on their lunch break—swarm in and take the table.

"You should've let me get the table," I say.

"Isn't she awesome?" Dylan asks.

"Yup," I say automatically.

Samantha comes out from behind the counter, singing our names. "Here you go." She walks to the standing bar. "Thanks for stopping by."

"Dylan wouldn't miss it for the world," I say. "Me either, obviously."

"Beats going home and doing homework, right?" Dylan says.

I just nod.

I don't really want anyone knowing I'm in summer school. It was embarrassing enough sitting in homeroom toward the end of the school year when I wasn't handed my report card and had to go meet with the guidance counselor. Everyone in homeroom knew it meant I was getting the go-to-summer-school-or-repeat-eleventh-grade-in-a-different-school chat. I should've gone that second route. I would have my summer and be Hudson-free in September and beyond too.

Samantha takes a sip from her iced quad nonfat one-pump mocha with whip. I think she can tell talking about summer school is awkward and touchy for me. I wish my best friend was as quick on this front. "I love working here, but I sort of miss my freedom too. But I want to work in business one day, and my mom said it's best to work at every stage possible before climbing the ranks so I never turn into some monster expecting masterful work from employees making just enough to get by."

"What kind of business?" I ask.

"I would love to start my own app games. I have this one idea. It's like *Frogger*, but instead of heavy-traffic streets, it takes place on the sidewalks of New York. You die if you get hit with someone's shopping cart and you lose points if you cross a tourist's path while they're taking photos. Stuff like that."

"I would play the hell out of that and dominate the leaderboards," I say. "Dylan was practically playing a real-life version of it on our way over here."

"What? I didn't want to miss the start of her break," Dylan says. He's sheepish about it, which is not a word I would usually tag on Dylan. It's kind of adorable how every minute counts for him. The classic honeymoon stage where everyone feels like they're riding a unicorn on floating rainbows while drinking Skittle smoothies. But eventually you realize the unicorn was just a horse in costume and now you have cavities.

Samantha smiles at him, like she wants to call him sweet but is holding back. "So yeah, video game apps for me. If you ever have any ideas you want me to profit off of, let me know." She winks—it's not a perfect wink, but it's still charming.

"Can you make a one hundred percent foolproof app that helps people find their soul mate?"

"I was hoping for suggestions on something easier, like a dog-walking app with some sort of twist, but sure."

I really like her; it's going to suck to see her go. Maybe I can befriend her behind Dylan's back. A friendship affair.

"I know it was your call, but how are you doing post-breakup?" Samantha asks. It throws me that Samantha is caught up on Hudson. Probably too soon for Dylan to fill awkward silences by telling Samantha why he broke up with Harriett. He claims it was because Harriett liked being someone's girlfriend on Instagram more than she actually liked him. But I know it's because Dylan just woke up and wasn't feeling it one day. Yeah, definitely not something you tell your potential next girlfriend.

"First relationship. First breakup. First time someone really hates me. I just wish we could be friends," I say.

"I'm sorry," Samantha says.

"It is what it is." I down my sour strawberry lemonade in four sips, like some depressed adult throwing back shots, and I chew the ice because I paid for that too dammit.

"I hope he comes around," Samantha says.

"His loss," I say, trying to shake it off. I throw my Happy

Best Friend Face back on. "So, *Titanic*, huh?"

"I've loved it since I was a kid," Samantha says. "Though now I want to see a favorite of Dylan's."

"*Transformers*, hands-down," Dylan says.

Samantha cringes. "Maybe dinner tomorrow instead. I can take you to the seafood spot I was telling you about."

"Tomorrow is Friday the thirteenth," I say.

"Oh right! I'm not superstitious, don't worry," Samantha says.

"Me either," Dylan says. "I walk under ladders like it's no one's business."

"Yeah, like when you were eight and you broke your arm an hour later," I say. He was so freaked out by the pain that he had a panic attack. He swore he was dying, it was so bad. But I'm a good friend and I never bring that up. I'm so glad I wasn't around to see him fall off his bike.

"Bad coincidence," Dylan says.

"Or bad luck." I shrug. "Anyway. We have a tradition. Horror movies at House Boggs on Friday the thirteenth." This has been running strong since eighth grade. "I'm in a Chucky mood."

"Why Chucky?" Samantha asks.

"It's awesome. It's like *Toy Story* but fucked-up."

"I'm definitely not messing with tradition," Samantha says. "This sounds amazing."

Dylan side-eyes me.

I really don't want to be a cockblock, but I'm pretty sentimental. And Dylan can't blow me off for a girl he's known for less than week, no matter how awesome she is. Back in April Hudson and I were going to watch the new X-Men movie, and it was one of the few things he was excited about after the divorce, but it released on Friday the thirteenth, so I canceled our plans like a good friend and Hudson saw it with Harriett.

"You should hang with us," I say. I mean it. "I'm cool being the third wheel."

"I feel like *I'll* be the third wheel," Samantha says.

"Ben, find a dude and let's make it a double date."

"Okay, sure, yeah, I'll just spin around and choose someone here."

I turn as a joke and I make eye contact with the cute guy in the Human Torch shirt. I spin back to Dylan and Samantha with flushed cheeks. This is the universe popping up again. I want to make a move here. Because what if he's the one who's really supposed to fill the space that was carved out for Hudson?

"I'm going to say hi to that guy," I announce.

"Ooh, which guy?" Samantha asks.

"The dude with the laptop." I realize there are four dudes with laptops in my line of vision. "Human Torch shirt."

"Go for it," Dylan says. "Get yours. Do it! Do it!"

Get mine. Hudson isn't the only one who can move on.

I'm not going to psych myself out. I'm walking over and going to tell him he took my table as a joke and—

A gorgeous black girl approaches his table and she kisses him right on the lips.

I return to Dylan and Samantha.

"Of course he's straight," I say.

"Maybe he's bi," Dylan says. "And in an open relationship."

"Or my life sucks," I say. "And maybe Hudson will be the last person who wanted me."

"That alien wanted you," Dylan says.

"Alien?" Samantha asks.

"But I'm never going to see him again," I say.

"Come on, there's got to be something about him we can try to find."

"*What alien?*" Samantha asks again.

"I met a guy at the post office," I say. "His name is Arthur. But I didn't get his last name and I don't remember giving him my name at all."

"Oh my god." Samantha squeezes my arm while bouncing. "I love a mystery. My best friend, Patrick—"

"Your best friend is a guy?" Dylan asks.

"—calls me the Nancy Drew of social media—"

"Is Patrick gay?"

"—because I helped him find some girl online—"

"Bisexual?"

"—that he met at his brother's graduation."

I ignore Dylan's dizzying interruptions and focus on Samantha. "How did you find her?"

"He told me everything about the graduation that I could use as keywords for Twitter searches, like the ugly beige gowns and some quotable moments from the valedictorian's speech. But then we just went down a rabbit hole of the graduation's hashtag on Instagram and found her. Turns out she doesn't have Twitter."

"Whoa."

"Okay, but really, back to Patrick," Dylan says.

Samantha grabs Dylan by the shoulders. "Patrick is like a brother to me, creep. Good? Yay. Ben, tell me everything you know about Arthur."

"No point. I already did the Twitter hunt and I came up with nothing."

"Are you also the Nancy Drew of social media?" Samantha asks.

I smile. It's cool that she's so generous—or maybe she's really bored. Either way, I fill her in on everything I already searched for on Twitter.

"I need more than hot dog ties and Georgia," Samantha says. "I'm good, but come on. Why is he here for the summer?"

"Oh, because of his mom. She's a lawyer and she's working a case."

"Do you know the firm? Or anything about the case?" Samantha pulls out her phone and takes notes on her phone. Screw the app business, she needs to become a detective.

"No times two. But it's a firm that also has offices back in Georgia. Milton, Georgia! Milton like his uncle who's great," I say.

"Is his uncle a great guy or is he a great-uncle?"

"Oh." I don't remember. I shrug.

"There's that summer school brain kicking in," Dylan says.

Samantha slaps his shoulder. "It's okay. It won't matter too much. Anything else?"

I'm too hung up on thinking about Dylan's comment. I know I'm in summer school, I wake up with that FML tightness in my chest every morning. Summer school is where I have to face my ex-boyfriend and scary future. I'm not someone like Arthur who's dreaming about amazing colleges.

"Yale!" I say.

"Say what?" Dylan is super puzzled.

"Arthur said he stopped by Yale's campus. He's kind of baby-faced, but he can be starting there this fall, right?"

"This is all super helpful," Samantha says. "I should head back behind the counter in a sec, but anything else?"

I think about all the good stuff that probably won't be helpful. Like how awkward he was when talking about my "big package." How he lit up when he realized I was gay too, even though I was in the middle of telling him about my breakup. His enthusiasm for the universe like it's actually a friend of ours. Then I remember something useful.

"He's leaving at the end of summer," I say. There's no point.

"Incentive to work faster!" Samantha is beaming like she has all the hope in the world, and I wish she would share some because there's no way that the same universe that locks me away in summer school with my ex-boyfriend will also reunite me with a cute guy. "Okay, I have to run back." She hugs me. She smells like espresso and scones. "It was so great meeting you, Ben. I hope I can put this puzzle together for you and find your boy. But if not, I have no doubt someone awesome will cross your path and fall for you hard."

"Maybe that someone has been in your life for years," Dylan says, placing his hand on mine.

Samantha laughs. "I knew it. I'm totally going to be the third wheel tomorrow."

"Fear not, future wife of mine. If you get scared tomorrow night, I'll only tend to you." He smiles at her.

Samantha isn't smiling back. She stares at the floor and scratches her head.

I catch the moment Dylan realizes he's really overshot it with the flirting—that maybe Samantha isn't about marriage talk after two days.

"I'll catch you guys later." She goes behind the counter, puts on her hat, and gets back to work.

"Oh no," he says.

"It's okay."

"It was just a joke."

"Give her some space. She's working. You can talk later." Dylan leads the way out. "Is it that bad? Really?"

He turns around a few more times, like maybe he's trying to see if she's paying attention to him walking out. Maybe he's getting one last look at her.

CHAPTER NINE
ARTHUR

Okay. Fuck Google.

No, seriously, *fuck Google*. And fuck Kate Hudson and Chris Robinson. Fuck them for getting married and fuck them for getting divorced and fuck them in general. Because do you know what pops up when you google Hudson Robinson? Spoiler: it's not the boy from Panera.

I sink backward onto my bed, staring up at the ceiling. I feel wired and on edge, and my room feels even smaller than usual. Sometimes New York feels like a full-body corset.

Five seconds later, my phone starts vibrating. And it's Ethan.

I stare at the screen. Six weeks of ignoring my texts, and now he's FaceTiming me out of nowhere. Which isn't a big deal or anything. It's just unexpected.

I press accept.

"Arthur!" says Jessie. They're mushed up together on Ethan's basement couch. Otherwise known as the group text in video form. But it's fine. I mean, it's great. Ethan and Jessie are great, and I love them, and their timing is actually kind of perfect.

I smile. "Hey! Just who I needed to talk to."

They glance at each other so fast it barely registers. But then Jessie says, "Oh really? What's up?"

"I found Hudson."

"Excuse me. WHAT?"

"But it's not him," I say quickly. "It's not the post office guy. But I think maybe it's the boyfriend?"

"*Ex*-boyfriend." Ethan points his finger. "You're the boyfriend."

"Pshh. I wish."

"Soon-to-be-boyfriend," says Jessie. "Wow. How did you find him?"

I tell them about Panera and the panini and the last name and the eyebrows, but when I finish, Jessie looks perplexed. "Wait, how do you know it's not just some random guy named Hudson?"

"Because . . ." My stomach sinks. Suddenly, Juliet's logic seems specious at best. "I don't know. Is it that common of a name?"

"Devon Sawa named his baby Hudson."

"Of course you know that." Ethan nudges Jessie sideways.

"Anyway, nothing's coming up on Google or Facebook or Instagram or Tumblr or Snapchat or Twitter or literally anywhere, and I hate this."

Jessie's expression softens. "You really like this guy, huh?"

I groan. "I don't even know him. I met him for five minutes. Why am I still thinking about him?"

"Because he's hot," suggests Ethan.

"I just don't understand. Why would the universe introduce me to this boy and then take him away from me five seconds later?"

"Maybe the universe will send him back to you," Ethan says. "Slightly used, though. A little wear and tear. Mostly good condition."

Jessie's silent for a moment, chewing her lip.

"Maybe the universe wants to make you work for it," she says finally.

"I am working for it! I just spent an hour googling some random dude who likes paninis and didn't go to band camp."

"Hmm," says Jessie. She stands, suddenly out of frame.

"Wait, where are you going?"

"I have an idea."

I look at Ethan, and he shrugs. Jessie's footsteps thud across the floor.

So now it's just Ethan and me, and we're totally silent. He can barely meet my eyes.

"So this is . . ."

"Yup." He blinks.

"Everything good?"

"Totally good."

"Okay. Great."

"Yup." He presses his lips together and stares at his lap. "So how are M&M?"

Otherwise known as Michael and Mara Seuss. Who I'm pretty sure are on the express train to divorce town.

"Great!" I say. "Perfect!"

This is painful—and there's no sign of Jessie. I'm sorry, but she needs to pull the plug on this mess right now. Ethan's still gazing somewhere above the webcam. Would he notice if I texted her? Just a quick SOS. And maybe a tiny threat that if she doesn't come back this second, I will ruin her. I will track down the video love confession she recorded for Ansel Elgort in eighth grade, and, God help me, I'll find a way to break into the projection room at Regal Avalon. If she thinks this won't be the most memorable screening *ever* of *Mission: Impossible 6*, she's—

"Hey!" she says breathlessly, sliding back next to Ethan on the couch. "I think I found Hudson."

"Wait . . . what?"

"Mmhmm. Oh my god. I'm just—Arthur, I'm so proud

of myself right now, you don't even know. This is—like, this is actually happening. Are you ready?"

I nod slowly.

"Are you okay? You don't look okay." She laughs.

"Neither do you." I pause. "Are you sure it's him?"

"I mean, you'll have to look at his picture and tell me."

"There's a picture?" My stomach twists.

"Don't ever underestimate my internet creepiness."

"I never do," says Ethan.

"Shut up. So I had a stroke of inspiration. I was thinking about the whole story with Namrata, and I was like, you know what? I'm searching for Hudson Panini."

"Um—"

"No, hear me out. So I go to Twitter, and I literally type in *Hudson panini*—and the first thing that comes up is a guy named @HudsonLikeRiver. So right away, I've got chills, because that's exactly what you said, remember? Hudson, like the river." She points at me, smiling. "Anyway, this guy HudsonLikeRiver has a tweet from 11:44 in the morning today, and it says *craving a panini lol.*"

"Okay . . ."

"Arthur, he was craving a panini today, thirty minutes before you ran into him *ordering a panini*. And his name is Hudson!"

"But how do we know he's *the* Hudson? Is he from New York?"

Jessie leans forward, grinning. "I'm not done. Anyway, I check his bio, and it's super vague, and all of his tweets are vague, too—and they're bad, they're bad tweets. Not even funny-bad. And his picture is a bitmoji. So I'm like, *fuck*. But then I get the idea to check Instagram, because people usually just use the same handle, right? And sure enough. Boom. @HudsonLikeRiver. Public profile, fifty zillion pictures, amazing eyebrows. He's from New York. Art, I'm freaking out."

"Oh. My. God."

"You have to go check it right now," she says. "We'll talk to you later, okay?"

She ends the call, and I just sit there, shell-shocked. A boy named Hudson. From New York. With great eyebrows. Who was publicly craving a panini for lunch today. Box Boy would be following him on Instagram, right? At least they'd be tagged in pictures together. Which kind of makes my stomach churn, but whatever.

Deep cleansing breath. I pull up Instagram and type in the handle.

Hudson like river. @HudsonLikeRiver

And I'm there.

Text from Jessie: Is it him??

I can't even form a reply. God. It's him. Hudson. Clarendon-filtered, wearing that backward baseball hat. Selfie upon selfie.

But I have to stay calm. Just because he's Hudson Robinson, random panini boy, doesn't mean he's Hudson from the address label. It doesn't mean anything. For one thing, Box Boy is nowhere. Not a single picture of him in Hudson's entire feed.

I click through them anyway, starting with the most recent—which is—I'm not even kidding—a picture of his fucking panini. The next one's a selfie with some girl, adorably named @HarriettThePie, and then a peace sign selfie with the hashtag MovingOn.

Moving on.

It's from the day I met Box Boy—which doesn't necessarily mean anything. There are lots of ways a person can move on. Hudson could have changed jobs. He could have gotten a haircut. He could have moved on from bread bowls to paninis.

But the comments. One particular comment.

@HarriettThePie: You're going to be fine without him, my beautiful friend. <3

Him.

Hudson doesn't need *him.*

I take a screenshot of the picture and Harriett's comment, and I text it to Jessie and Ethan. It's him.

Holy. Shit, writes Jessie.

Whoa, nice work, Ethan chimes in. Followed by three detective emojis, two white boys and a brown girl. As if Ethan—world's most underachieving online creeper—had anything to do with this breakthrough.

But I'm too nervous to care. I'm cranked up to a thousand. I scoot back in my bed to settle in with the app. Time to take inventory.

@HudsonLikeRiver. 694 posts. 315 followers. 241 following. His bio's kind of bare. *Huds in the house. NYC baby.*

I scroll again through his pictures, all 694 of them. There's not a single one of Box Boy, not even in a group shot, and they definitely don't follow each other. I check the pictures other people have tagged Hudson in. No trace of Box Boy there either.

I mean, maybe this is all one giant coincidence. Just another Hudson. Another Hudson in New York who dates boys and just had a breakup.

It doesn't feel like a coincidence.

Maybe Hudson and Box Boy deleted every single picture of each other and untagged the ones their friends posted. And of course they unfollowed each other, because they probably can't stand the sight of each other. *Which is why Box Boy was mailing the box in the first place.*

Any luck? Jessie writes.

Not yet. Frowny face.

I switch over to Harriett's profile, since she and Hudson seem close—and even if she's all for Hudson moving on, she probably knew the ex he's moving on from.

And. Holy shit. Four thousand posts. Seventy-five thousand followers.

Okay, so Hudson's friend Harriett is some kind of an Instagram celebrity, and that is . . . pretty fucking cool, actually. She posts a lot of selfies with dramatically contoured cheekbones and intricate eyeliner patterns, and now I can't stop looking through them. I'm not even a makeup guy, but it's just so awesomely theatrical. If I didn't think it would be next-level creepy, I'd follow the hell out of Harriett.

Except—wow. Eye on the prize, Arthur.

I scroll down to some of Harriett's earlier posts, where there are fewer selfies and more pictures with friends. Lots with Hudson, lots with various girls, and a whole series of a guy with a beard and shimmery unicorn eye makeup. But there are group pictures, too—I pause longer on those, carefully scanning the faces. I keep scaring the crap out of myself by almost liking Harriett's pictures. Not on purpose. It's my self-sabotaging fingers and their unstoppable compulsion to pinch and zoom.

By now, I've worked my way back to March, and there's a whole series of group pictures in the snow outside Duane Reade. Mostly action shots—a snowball fight—but

I notice Hudson in the background, looking out of frame and laughing.

I swipe sideways. Same snowball fight, but the image is shifted slightly to the right. Now you can see Hudson's laughing with a guy—but he's blurry.

I swipe again.

And then I forget how to breathe.

Because it's the boy. It's actually him. Center frame, pink-cheeked and smiling self-consciously, while Hudson's doubled over, cracking up.

Holy. Shit.

I take a screenshot and text it straight to Jessie and Ethan. No caption. No emojis.

As always, Jessie's the first to reply. **Omg Arthur, that's him?** She doesn't wait for me to reply. **He's beautiful.**

That's a handsome dude, adds Ethan. Multiple winking emojis. Ethan Gerson: my Totally Accepting Straight Bro Friend Who Can't Be Alone with Me. I'd be totally accepting of him shutting the fuck up.

I turn back to Harriett's feed and scan the post for Instagram handles. A few people are tagged in the snowball series, but not Box Boy. Or Hudson. Maybe they untagged themselves. I keep scrolling.

For hours.

Every single group post. I click on every single one. I scroll through Harriett's followers—all seventy-five thousand of them. I scroll through her follow list. I click on everyone tagged in the snowball pictures and check their followers, too.

Nothing.

And not a single other picture of Box Boy.

Still no name. Maybe Box Boy was right. Maybe the universe really is an asshole.

What I need now is chocolate. And I'm not talking about a weak drizzle of Hershey's sauce on a waffle. I need the hard stuff, like Jacques Torres or one of those giant double-chocolate-chip Levain Bakery cookies. The classic Upper West Side dilemma: when your heart says Levain, but your lazy ass remembers there's a candy bowl next to the coffee-pot.

Emotional blue balls. That's what it feels like. It's being handed everything you've ever longed for, only for it to slip through your fingers. And there's no way to fix it. Nothing you can do but slink toward the kitchen counter in a full-body mope.

The kitchen's fully stocked with coffee again—I guess Dad stepped up and bought some. And it's the nice stuff—not Starbucks. It's French roast artisan blend from Dream & Bean—

A tiny thrum in my chest. My heart's the first to re-member.

Dream & Bean. His shirt. How could I forget about his

T-shirt? If I were a detective, the chief would fire my ass right now. This is the game-changing clue, and it was right under my nose. Who even wears shirts from coffee shops?

Coffee shop employees, that's who.

I google it so fast, I almost misspell the word "bean." But there it is, two blocks from Mom's office. In the direction of the post office.

All my chill vanishes.

What if what if what if—

I'm going to find him. It's going to happen. My heart slams in my chest as I picture it. He'll be behind the counter, bored and dreamy and adorably disheveled. I'll walk in, in slow motion, perfectly centered in a beam of flattering light. And obviously the handlebar twins from the post office will be there too, but we'll barely notice them this time. Our eyes will be glued to each other, his Emma Watson lips trembling. *Arthur?* he'll say, and I'll just nod. I'll be so verklempt. *I thought I'd never see you again*, he'll say. *I looked everywhere for you.* And I'll whisper: *You found me.* And then he'll—

But wow. Okay. I need to strategize.

Because maybe he's off duty tomorrow. I should bring the picture, just in case. Would that be unforgivably creepy? Showing his picture to the barista?

Maybe I could hang his picture on the bulletin board, like a real-life missed connection post. Like Craigslist, but old-school. I mean, coffee shops always have bulletin boards. I think.

All I know is this: I refuse to miss this chance.

I scramble back to my room, open my laptop, and type.

Are you the boy from the post office?
I feel super awkward right now, and I can't believe I'm doing this, but here we go.
We talked for a few minutes at the post office on Lexington. I was the guy in the hot dog tie. You were the guy mailing stuff back to your ex-boyfriend.
I loved your laugh. Wish I'd gotten your number.
Want to give me a second chance here, universe?
Arthur.Seuss@gmail.com

CHAPTER TEN
BEN

"Kool Koffee coffee is the worst," Dylan says as we step out of Dream & Bean with a fresh cup of coffee instead of refilling his thermos in my backpack. He's become really bitter since telling Samantha she's his future wife the way he'd normally tell no one but me. It's fine and cool with me, but telling the girl? When it's only been a couple days? That was never going to play out well. "Maybe it's for the best. Bad coffee is bad coffee, and that's what Samantha serves. If I had future-married her, I would've been leading this second life of lies. I might have told her on my deathbed so I could die an honest man."

I shake my head. "Why are you the way you are?"

"Too many shitty cups of coffee, Big Ben."

"It's not over. I'm sure she's already realized that you're just so Dylan that you Dylan'd too hard."

"Dylan-ing isn't a bad thing. To Dylan someone is to adore them. Even if they brew the worst coffee on God's green earth."

We walk through Washington Square Park. There's a cute Mexican guy with hipster glasses sitting on a bench, nodding along to whatever song is playing on his headphones while he eats ice cream. Ice cream is one of Hudson's favorite foods—not dessert, food. We once played this game where I would close my eyes, he'd take a spoonful of whatever flavors were available in his freezer, and I had to guess which ice cream it was. This was back in early March, when doing little stupid things like that felt extra special. Something that was just for us.

Dylan's phone rings. "It's Samantha, Big Ben. Ha! I knew Wifey couldn't get enough of Daddy D."

"I hate everything you just said. Play it cool."

Dylan winks, but I know he's got to be freaking. He answers the phone. "Hey. I—" His smile goes away. "Oh." My heart drops a little for him. He turns to me. "It's for you."

Okay, so maybe that wasn't the happy plot twist we thought it would be.

I take the phone. "Hello?"

"I may have found your boy," Samantha says.

"Say what."

"It wasn't easy, but I did some digging. I looked into law firms in Georgia with New York connections and came up empty. I jumped to Instagram and searched through the hashtag for hot dog ties, and the most recent photo was last year, so that was out. And I checked Facebook for Yale newbie groups and there's a meetup for incoming freshmen in New York . . . today at five."

"You're kidding," I say.

"I'm texting a link to the Facebook group now."

The phone vibrates against my face. I open the text, click the link: class of 2022. Meetup at Central Park.

"There's no promise he'll be there," Samantha says. "I searched through the list of people who RSVP'd yes, but people, like yours truly, often don't RSVP, so I have hope."

"Wow. You're amazing," I say.

"I'm also talking on company time, so I got to leave the stockroom, but best of luck with your search and tell Dylan I said bye!"

"Thanks," I say, right as she hangs up.

"What happened? Was she talking about me?" Dylan asks.

"D, I'm sorry. She's about to go run off into the sunset with Patrick," I say. He tries taking his phone back, but I don't let go. "I'm kidding. But look: she may have found Arthur. There's a Yale freshman meetup thing today. It's almost too convenient, right?"

"Yes, it's very convenient that my future wife did all the work for you."

"You know what I mean. There are so many things Arthur can be doing in this city he doesn't live in. He'll see all these people in school. There's no way he'll be there."

"We don't have to go." Dylan snatches his phone and looks at the group. "Wow. Samantha is wasting her time at that sad excuse of a coffee shop. She can be the Hermione in our trio. Dibs on Harry."

"But that means I'm Ron."

"Sucks for you."

"Ron ends up with Hermione."

"Okay, but . . . I don't want to be Ron. No one wants to be Ron. Rupert Grint probably didn't even want to be Ron. How about this? I'm Han Solo and she's Princess Leia. You can be Luke."

"I don't care," I say. "Let's focus."

"Right, right. We should go to the meetup anyway. Maybe Arthur won't be there. But maybe he will be," Dylan says.

Knowing he could be there is more than enough to get me going. "Let's do it."

"May the Force be with you, Ron Weasley."

"We should have aliases," Dylan says.

We're walking through Central Park and toward

Belvedere Castle, where the meetup is happening. There's something really enchanting about reuniting with Arthur at a castle like some bomb-ass fairy tale. Too bad I smell like my dad's cologne and I'm wearing a polo shirt from last spring that's now super tight on me because that's the Yale bro look apparently.

"Aliases will only make this more complicated," I say. I wish we hadn't gone back home to change first. I just want to be in clothes I like.

"More awesome, you mean. I think I'm going to be Digby Whitaker. You can be Brooks Teague."

"No."

"Orson Bronwyn?"

"No."

"Final offer: Ingram Yates."

"No." We're approaching the stairs that lead up to the meetup. "Okay, D, real talk. I'm kind of freaking. I really want Arthur to be up there, but I'm also feeling weird getting my hopes up about someone new. I need wingman advice, Digby Wilson."

"Whitaker," Dylan corrects. He claps his hands. "Let's say Arthur is here and you hit it off. He's leaving at the end of the summer anyway, right? You can treat this like a rebound."

"No. I don't want to do that to anyone. Or myself."

"You're right. Bad advice, Big Brooks."

"Ben."

"Not getting anything past you." Dylan takes me by the shoulders and stares into my eyes, like an intense coach and his trainee. "Maybe you do need a break before you're really ready to move on. I will respect you if you walk away from this. But I know you're a dreamer, Big Ben, and maybe the universe is giving you this second shot."

I hope he's right. I hope the universe proves me wrong and actually comes through—for both of us.

"Maybe," I say.

"If you won't do it for yourself, at least do it for all the people on the train who had to suffer through your cologne in such tight quarters."

"Asshole."

We reach the top of the open space, the sun and lake and rest of the park hanging out behind the crowd of Yale's noobs. A lot of the guys here are tall, so I walk around, dragging my feet, but out of the twenty or so guys, some smelling like cologne way nicer than my dad's, none of them are Arthur.

"He's not here," I say. "And we're the only ones in polos."

"It's early," Dylan says. "Arthur may show up in a polo?"

I glare.

"We're here, and we should try to have some fun," Dylan says. "If you send me home, I'm just going to listen to sad music and stare out the window and jump whenever my phone buzzes and then be sadder than I was before when I see it's just you texting me and not Samantha."

"You've made me feel like shit, but sure, let's stay."

"Yay." Dylan looks around. "Yale has some lookers here. Aren't you feeling motivated to study really damn hard in senior year to try and get that full scholarship life?"

"Not a hot dog tie in sight."

"Is that a new fetish?"

"No, it's just . . . it's cool to see someone not take himself so seriously."

"Well, someone who is actually here is checking you out," Dylan says. "Eleven o'clock a.m."

"A.m. or p.m. doesn't matter."

"Yeah it does. He's got those a.m. breakfast-date vibes. Not the p.m. take-me-into-the-bathroom-and-let's-bump-butts vibes."

I check out the guy instead of asking Dylan if he knows anyone who bumps butt as a sexual activity because I know he'll have answers and I have my limits. The guy is really cute and definitely breakfast-date wholesome—dark brown skin, peach blazer, white T-shirt, navy slacks that end above his ankles, and white low-top sneakers that probably cost more than what I spend on clothes in three months. It looks pretty effortless, and if I learned anything from Instagram rising star Harriett, everything that looks effortless requires too much effort. But it's always worth it if you want the likes and the looks.

"Nice style," I say. I'm extra self-conscious in my tight polo. "But I feel like I'd rather *be* him than be *with* him."

"Maybe we say hi before you completely write him off?"

"We don't know if he's even into guys."

"Then you make an ass of yourself. It's not like you're actually going to have to spend the next four years at Yale with him."

Don't I know it. There's nothing about any of my report cards since sixth grade that have my parents expecting to find me graduating from an Ivy League school. Ma really wants me in college so no one can write me off the way no one took her seriously for so many years, but sometimes it feels pointless anyway. Like if I'm pitted against anyone standing here in this circle, they're going to see me as Community College Ben and not Yale Ben, and I'll lose out.

And now there's this cute guy who I just automatically feel unworthy of. I once felt that way about Hudson too and that worked out before it stopped working. I'm not big on talking to strangers, like I wouldn't have ever approached Arthur, but there's an opening here, so I drag Dylan with me to go say hi to this guy while he's in the middle of a conversation with a girl in a radiant yellow hijab.

"Hi. I'm Ben."

"I'm Digby Whitaker."

"Whoa. Hell of a name," the cute guy says.

"Thanks. What's yours?" Dylan asks.

"Kent Michele," he says, shaking Dylan's hand and then mine.

I turn to the girl. "Ben."

"Alima," she says. "So, you guys excited?"

Dylan clears his throats. "Oh yeah. Really excited to advance my education in Greek, Ancient, and Modern studies, you know. I kind of want to name my son Achilles because I think there's a lesson here about downfalls."

I don't . . .

I just . . .

It's like Dylan tries to out-Dylan himself sometimes.

"Sounds way more fun than Ethics, Politics, and Economics," Kent says. "Fun times." Oh good, he's not so full of himself that he thinks his major is riveting stuff. He definitely gets some cool points. "What are you into?"

And damn, the way he asks that gets me blushing a little. I realize I have no idea what courses are available at Yale. Or colleges in general. I'm not even a senior yet and haven't really been thinking that far. So I just keep it honest. "I'm big on writing."

"Me too!" Kent says. "Well, used to be. Don't make fun, but I used to write a lot of fanfiction."

"Oh, Ben definitely won't be making fun of you," Dylan says.

"I'm not the Little Mermaid, I can speak," I say with a forced laugh, like ha-ha-ha-shut-the-hell-up. I turn back to Kent. "What fandom were you writing?"

"Pokémon," Kent says, and he cringes a little like I'm about to make fun of him. He has dimples too because damn. "I know it's silly, but that was my everything growing up."

"Not silly," Alima says.

"Definitely not. I used to beg my parents to take me outside so I could catch a Squirtle," I say.

"I was a Pikachu guy," Kent says.

"Pikachu was my man," Dylan says.

I can't tell if Dylan is my wingman or competition. I give him a hey-maybe-go-away look and he actually gets my signal.

Dylan turns to Alima. "So, what do you do for fun? What's your drug of choice? Not literal drug, unless literal drug is your speed. Not speed as in the drug—"

My deepest apologies to Alima, but I feel a flicker with Kent that I like. And maybe I came here looking for someone who won't show up, but I'll leave with someone who could be even better for me.

"So how do I find this Pikachu fanfiction?" I ask.

"It's long gone. Destroyed. I threw it in a volcano and

then I threw that volcano into another volcano." If Kent's chuckle is this charming, then I can't wait to hear his laugh. "So where'd you grow up?"

"Alphabet City," I say.

"No way, that's not far from me. I live a couple blocks from Union Square."

Okay, now this definitely feels like the universe is involved. We've lived fifteen minutes apart from each other and we're just now meeting.

"My dad is an assistant manager at Duane Reade right across the street from Union," I say. I'm proud of my dad, but some dicks at school thought lesser of my family because my parents don't have "cooler jobs," and Dylan was the muscle who shut them all down. It feels good to get this out right now in case Kent is a huge snob.

"I go there all the time. I'm in charge of dinner on Tuesdays and Thursdays, so that's where I get my supplies."

"But Whole Foods is like a block down," I say. His sneakers and clothes suggest his family can spring the extra few bucks.

"The lines are always a mile long and everything I need to whip up Spanish dishes is there," Kent says.

"Oh cool. Are you Puerto Rican by any chance? Or—"

"I am, yeah," Kent says. Another smile. I still don't have any clear confirmation he's into guys, but it's going well, at least.

"Me too! Everyone always thinks I'm white. It sucks," I say. "It's pretty annoying always having to make that clear."

Kent bites his lip as he nods. "At least no one follows you around grocery stores like you're trying to steal something. And I bet no one is asking you if you got into Yale to meet some sort of diversity quota. That *actually* sucks."

I look away because wow, Kent didn't swing, but it still felt like I got punched. "I'm sorry, I . . ." It's quiet between us. Having to tell people I'm Puerto Rican is not a problem compared to what Kent faces regularly. I'm the worst. "I should rescue Alima from Dylan."

"Yeah. I'll see you around, Ben."

Of course he won't, and that's got to be a good thing.

I go to Dylan and grab his arm. "Excuse us a sec," I say. I drag him away. "I want to go."

"Are you kidding? I was wrong about the a.m. vibes. Kent is pure p.m. He wants you to take him into that bathroom and catch his Pikachu."

"I have no idea what that is supposed to mean. We need to have a chat about what dude-on-dude sex looks like." I shake my head. "I don't belong here. I'm not actually about to build a future at Yale or with Kent or Arthur. I'm done."

"You're not being fair to yourself," Dylan says.

"Maybe not. But I'm being honest."

I rush for the steps and head back down into the park.

This was such a waste. I can't believe we did all this, like

Arthur was ever actually going to be here. I was stupid to think that the universe had some master plan. All I know now is that I cared enough to show up here, and I'm walking away completely clueless on what's next for my future. I just know I'm back at the start with no idea which way to go.

Friday, July 13

I can't focus on *Angry Birds* when I hear Hudson and Harriett laughing while taking a selfie together.

"The bags under my eyes are so . . ." Hudson can't find the word.

"WWE cage match?" Harriett says. She flips her hair over her shoulders and sticks her chest out. "You should make a silly face. It'll distract from the beat-up look you got going on."

"Thanks for the ego boost."

"I'm just being honest. You need more beauty sleep," Harriett says.

Beauty sleep hardly seems important for someone who filters the holy hell out of her photos, but what Harriett does for the 'gram is her business—literally. She does these ads for healthy juices that she doesn't even like because they give her stomachaches. Doesn't stop her from making two hundred dollars a picture. Harriett once did a #Boyfriend-Tag with Dylan where she did his makeup—contour on his cheekbones and eyeshadow. Dylan was a total champ about it and loved the attention. Harriett was so proud of the photos that she didn't even delete them after he broke up with her. Harriett tagging me in photos was always wild. I would get a couple dozen followers. Then they'd all gradually unfollow because they could give a shit about my pictures of cool graffiti I'd find in bathrooms around the city. Or my pictures with Hudson.

"That photo sucks even more," Hudson says, after another attempt. "My face is not good today. Forget it."

Hudson is always hard on himself.

"Let's try one more," Harriett says. "Silly faces."

"You got it, Boss."

Hudson leans in, puts his fist underneath his chin, and stares off into the sky like he's just had the most epic eureka moment and is now ready to remake the world. Harriett is blowing a kiss at absolutely no one in the opposite direction. They review the photo.

"Love it," Harriett says. "I need a caption."

"Wait," Hudson says.

"You look hot!"

"No." He zooms in and they both turn around.

Staring at me.

I must've photobombed their selfie. Their one good selfie. And of course I was staring at them instead of casually looking at my phone. Hudson shakes his head and looks away. My face goes red. I get back into *Angry Birds* and mind my business.

Or try to, at least. I still have ears.

"He looks good too, I got to admit," Harriett says.

"No, you don't have to admit that," Hudson harshly whispers.

One more month until I'm free from this hellhole.

I walk into Dream & Bean and Dylan is sitting by the window.

"Big Ben, step into my office," Dylan says, removing his backpack from one chair so I can sit.

"Your office needs a bigger table."

"Who needs tables when you have this wonderful view." Dylan gestures to the window.

"There's literally trash piling up." Three bags' worth. There's a better view from Hudson's bedroom and it's just brick wall.

"Do you want something to drink? My people can get right on that."

"You're a regular, not the owner."

"Why are you so hurtful, Ben?"

"Quick recap: I'm in summer school with my ex-boyfriend. I thought I was going to reunite with a cute guy yesterday. I didn't. Life sucks."

I lost some sleep last night thinking about both Hudson

and Arthur. Hudson because I wasn't looking forward to another school day with him. Arthur because I realized I screwed up by moving along. Up until yesterday when Samantha got involved, I never thought there was a real chance of finding him. It's New York City and I know next to nothing about him. But then she got her Nancy Drew on and hope became a thing. And the Yale lead was a smart one, but it led to nothing except how much I wanted it to work out. To find Arthur and see what could happen between us.

"You won't stay single long with that face." Dylan's eyebrows bounce.

I'm not in the flirty mood.

"I feel like I'm being punished for wanting to be happy," I say. Like maybe life would've been fine if I gave Hudson a second chance. Maybe everything would've gotten better.

"Maybe you're just Friday the thirteenth's bitch."

"At least we have our marathon."

Dylan is quiet for a second. "Samantha-less marathon."

"I'm sure she'll reach out." I'm not sure. She never texted him back last night.

Not to be that person, but I'd be lying if I said I wasn't a little relieved things aren't coming together with Samantha. Don't get me wrong—I want him to be happy, he's my absolute best friend. But sorry, he's not good at being a best friend when he's someone's boyfriend. It's like the only topic in the world becomes his girlfriend, and I don't ever feel like I can get a word in about what's happening with me. Maybe this is a bad attitude for me to have. But I just get, I don't know, threatened and feel pretty worthless every time he starts liking another girl. My dad asked me if I had secret feelings for Dylan, which is seriously not the case. Dylan is just the best and I would drop-kick someone for him. But I just miss him whenever he's dating. And I don't only want to feel relevant when he's single.

I'm thirsty, so I get up and go to the condiment bar. While I'm pouring some complimentary water into a plastic cup, I check out this bulletin board with tons of flyers for campus internships, a Resist poster, some phone numbers, dog walker job listing, random ads and—

My face.

My face is on the bulletin board.

The water spills over the cup and I don't even have the common sense or decency to immediately wipe it because that's my face on the bulletin board.

What did I do? What am I wanted for? Wait. No. This isn't some police sketch or shady security camera snapshot. My face is cropped out from that picture where I smashed a snowball in Hudson's face. Is this from him? I almost call for Dylan, but I'm still speechless because there's a memo too:

Are you the boy from the post office?

I feel super awkward right now, and I can't believe I'm
doing this, but here we go.

We talked for a few minutes at the post office on
Lexington. I was the guy in the hot dog tie. You were
the guy mailing stuff back to your ex-boyfriend.

I loved your laugh. Wish I'd gotten your number.

Want to give me a second chance here, universe?

Arthur.Seuss@gmail.com

Um.

My heart races because the universe has got to be fucking with me.

I tear down the flyer from the thumbtack. That's definitely my face. This is for me. I'm supposed to find this.

I just found this.

This . . . this doesn't happen. Yeah. This doesn't happen.

I storm back over to Dylan. "This some dumb joke of
yours?"

"What? None of my jokes are dumb."

"Don't play stupid."

Dylan reads the paper. "Wait. Holy shit."

"Is this seriously not you?"

"Dude. Ben. This isn't me." Dylan looks me in the eye,
and he's not laughing. "Where was this?"

"Condiment bar. Bulletin board. He must've known to

put it up here since I was wearing that Dream & Bean shirt."

"You're welcome! Man, Samantha is going to be pissed she didn't solve this herself. Happy for you too, I'm sure." He grabs my shoulder. "This is it. It's happening. You're going to reach out, right? This is amazing. Hollywood will make a movie about you two. And a Netflix spin-off about your gay children."

"But how? I'm so confused. How did he get this photo? That's kind of creepy. Am I being stalked? Lured into a trap?"

"Maybe make sure you meet in a public place. With a Taser."

"I just . . . This doesn't happen. I see cute guys all the time."

"Do you ever see them again?"

"Nope."

Dylan waves the paper around. "Big Ben, your life just got so easy. Don't get in your head about this. No one wants to binge a Netflix series about someone who does nothing, no matter how cute your smile and freckles are."

I stare at the email at the bottom of the flyer.

I guess I'm not Friday the thirteenth's bitch.

I'm the boy from the post office.

And Arthur is looking for me too.

★ ★ ★

We're not ready to press play on *Chucky*. Dylan and I are sitting on his bed. He's on his phone and torturing himself by looking through Samantha's Facebook profile. And I can't stop staring at the paper from Dream & Bean, which I pocketed from the bulletin board since no one else will need a photo of my face. I've typed the email address into my phone already, but my message is blank.

"You got to help me out here, D. What do I do?"

"Just speak from the dick, Big Ben."

"You're canceled if you don't help me write a useful message to Arthur."

"Right. Okay. If you're not going to speak from the dick, I think you should speak from the heart. That seems like the next logical step."

"Speaking from the dick was never a logical step."

"Says you."

If you let Dylan go on long enough, like I do, he eventually hits on the thing a normal person would know to say immediately. Like how I should just speak from the heart.

I keep it really simple and say the thing that I've been feeling ever since I first saw my face on that bulletin board: *Is this for real?*

CHAPTER ELEVEN
ARTHUR

"You need to chill," Dad says. "Put it aside and check in an hour."

"Yeah, but what if—"

"What if he emails you? Perfect. You don't want to write back right away anyway."

"I don't?"

"No no no. God no. You have to play it cool, Art. Not *too* cool. But a little cool," says the man wearing an apron with a picture of a flash drive and the words *Back that thing up*.

My phone buzzes with a new email notification.

Dad makes a grab for it, but I swipe it out of his reach and tap into my inbox.

Two more. This blows my mind. The poster's only been up for eleven hours, and I've already gotten sixteen emails.

Saw ur poster, I'm not your boy but good luck!

OMG this is so romantic & the boy in the pic is so hot wow

Nothing from Box Boy, of course, but my heartbeat doesn't know that. It goes haywire every time.

I skim their subject lines quickly. The first one says, how old are you. No punctuation or preamble. The second one says: Is this real?

"Come on, I need you. We're making grilled cheese." He holds up a giant knife. "Lose the phone. Now."

"Or else . . . you'll stab me?"

"What?" His brow furrows. Then he glances at his knife. "Oh. Ha. No. I'm cutting the crusts off the bread. Go put your phone away, Wart."

"Wart?"

"Like *The Sword in the Stone*. No?"

"No." I tap into the second email from someone named Ben Hugo. I bet it's nothing. It's probably some random fuckboy. But there's this knot in my stomach, and I can't seem to untie it.

Because what if it's him?

"I think I'm going to call you Wart until you put your phone away," Dad says.

Okay, there's text. There's a paragraph. And—

Holy shit.

> Hey, so I don't know if this is supposed to be a joke or a prank or what, but I saw your flyer about the post office. I'm not going to lie, I'm a little freaked out. In a good way, though. Because I think I'm the guy you're looking for? I hope that isn't creepy. Anyway, hi again. I'm Ben.

I just stare at it.

I'm speechless.

My hands are shaking. I need to—okay. I'm sitting down. On the edge of my bed. Phone's in both hands. All the words are hazy. I can't quite—Ben. He has a name, and it's perfect. Arthur and Ben. Arthur and Benjamin.

I have to write back. Holy shit. This is *real*.

Unless.

I stare at the message. Okay.

Okay.

So, it's *technically* possible that someone's trolling me. Which means I can't get excited. Not yet.

I have to test him.

Hey Ben.

Ben. So you claim.

Thanks for your email. It's very nice to meet you. Please answer the following question in detail: on the day of our meeting at the post office, what type of piercing did the postal employee have?

Send.
A minute later: Is this a joke?

Excuse me?

In detail? You sound like my teachers. Smiley face.

Okay, that's rude, right?
I type quickly. Yeah . . . this actually isn't a joke, so if you're just here to make fun of me, please don't.
Send.
But Ben doesn't reply, for what feels like an hour.
"Wart, are you alive in there?"
Dad. I almost jump.
"Coming! Just—"
My phone buzzes. You think I'm making fun of you?

Well. Yeah.

Okay, wow. I'm sorry. I'm not, I promise.

My stomach flips. Okay.

Look, do you want to just call me? I think maybe that would
work better.

He wants me to call him. Like an actual phone call. With
Benjamin. Ben. Who isn't making fun of me. Of course
he's isn't. He's *Ben*. He would never.

He sends me his number.

I click call. And it's ringing. This is happening. This is—

"Hey."

Oh my God.

"Is this Arthur?" His voice sounds muffled. "Hold on."

I hear shuffling and footsteps. Then a door closing.

"Okay, sorry. It's just—my friend. Anyway, listen. I'm
not making fun of your email. It just—I don't know. It
sounded like something a teacher would write. It was cute."

"Teachers aren't cute."

That makes him laugh. Which makes me smile. But I
can't tell if it's him. I can't tell if Ben's my guy. I was so sure
I'd recognize his voice. I thought I'd know him as soon as
I heard it.

"You never answered my question," I say.

"Right."

"I'm not trying to be a jerk. It's just that I've been getting lots of responses from random people, and—I guess I need to know it's really you."

He pauses. "Well, I don't remember the piercing."

"Oh."

"But I can send you a selfie if you want. And you were wearing that hot dog tie. And there was a flash mob and those twin guys wearing rompers and I think I called you a tourist? Oh, and you mentioned your Jewish uncle—"

"Milton." My heart is thudding.

"Right." Then he seems to stop short. "So it's you."

For a moment, I'm speechless.

"I'm kind of flipping out," I say finally.

"Yeah. This is weird."

It's beyond weird. It's astonishing. It's the New York moment of my dreams. The lovers are reunited. Cue the orchestra. Box Boy is real.

He's real. And he's Ben. And he found me.

"I can't believe this. I told you the universe isn't an asshole. I told you!"

"I guess the universe did do us a solid."

"No kidding." I grin into my phone. "So now what?"

He pauses. "What do you mean?"

Oh shit. Okay. Maybe he doesn't want to meet. Maybe

this is it. This call. It's the end of the line for us. Maybe he *was* interested until he heard me on the phone. Because I talk too fast. Ethan told me that once. He asked me, *When do you even breathe?*

"What do I mean?" I ask finally.

"I mean . . . Do *you* want to hang out again?" He says it just like that. Emphasis on "you." As if I haven't made that crystal clear. Like, come on, my dude. I put up a poster to find you. I think you know where I stand.

"Do you—" I start to ask, but now we're both speaking at once. I blush. "You go first."

"Oh, it's just." I almost *hear* him bite his lower lip. "I gotta ask. Are those your real eyes?"

"What?"

"Those are contacts, right?"

"I wear . . . clear contacts."

"So, your eyes are that blue."

"I guess so?"

"Huh," he says. "That's really cool."

"Um. Thank you?"

He laughs. And then falls silent.

"So . . . ," I say.

"Right." He pauses. "So how do we do this?"

"Arthur?" calls my dad.

I slide quickly out of bed, nudge my door shut, and lock it. "How do we do what?"

"The hanging-out thing. Should we—"

"Yeah," I say, too quickly. Deep breath. "I mean. If you want."

"Sure," Ben says. "Want to grab coffee?"

Coffee. Really? I mean, technically, yes. I'd grab coffee with Ben. I'd sit in traffic with Ben and hang out with him at the DMV. But this feels bigger than coffee. I'm pretty sure this is fate. Like we were meant to meet, meant to lose each other, and meant to find each other all over again. So this date has to be extraordinary. This date needs scavenger hunts and carriage rides and fireworks and Ferris wheels.

God, imagine us holding hands on a Ferris wheel.

"What about Coney Island?" I blurt.

"What about it?"

"Like as our first . . . destination. For hanging out."

For a moment, we're both silent.

"Coney Island?" he asks finally.

"It's an old-timey amusement park."

"Yeah, I know what Coney Island is," he says. "That's where you want to go?"

"No—I mean, not necessarily. Not unless you want to." I drum on my bed frame.

"I mean, we can . . ."

"No, it's fine!" I take a breath. "Why don't you pick?"

"You want me to plan our . . . date?"

Date! He said it. Holy shit. It's a date. This is legit. He's romantically interested, and I'm romantically interested, which means this is actually, finally happening. An actual date with an actual boy. This is possibly, definitely the number one best thing that's ever happened to me. And I have no chill about it. None whatsoever.

But okay.

I should breathe.

"That's fine," I say calmly. SUPER COOL. MEGA CHILL. I shrug. "If you want."

"Yeah, that works. So. Okay. Are you free tomorrow at, like, eight?"

"Eight p.m. Yup!"

I can't stop smiling. I'm just. *God.* I have a date.

"Okay, I think I have an idea," he says slowly. "But I'll surprise you. Want to meet outside the subway at Times Square? Main entrance."

"That sounds good."

And by good, I mean *great.* I mean exquisitely perfect. I mean I'm living in a Broadway musical. THIS IS AN ACTUAL BROADWAY MUSICAL.

"Okay. See you then."

We hang up. And for a full minute, I sit frozen, staring at the screen of my phone.

I have a date. A date. With Ben. I'm dating Ben. And dear God. Dear universe. Holy fucking shit.

I cannot mess this up.

PART TWO

IT'S US

CHAPTER TWELVE
BEN
Saturday, July 14

It's almost time for my first date. Well, first date with Arthur.

It's 7:27 and I should start getting out the door. I throw on the black T-shirt Ma insisted on ironing. My parents are standing by the door as Dylan follows me out of my bedroom, where he's been hitting me with decent pep talk the past half hour. He only told me to think with my dick once. Improvement.

Dylan circles me while scratching his chin. "I sign off on this look."

"Thanks," I say. "Let's go."

"Wait, I want a photo of you two," Ma says as she runs into the kitchen.

"Why both of them?" Pa asks. "Dylan isn't his date."

Ma returns with her phone. "His best friend came all the way from home."

"Five blocks," Pa says.

"It's Ben's first date. This is an Instagram moment." Ma's Instagram profile is classic Ma. She heavily filters photos of meals and selfies. She's a total abuser of hashtags. #It #Is #Really #Hard #To #Read #Entire #Captions #Like #This. She noticed when I stopped following her.

"It's not my first date," I say. If you scroll back six months, Ma still has the photo of my first date with Hudson. We had gone to a comedy show that was uncomfortably homophobic. Hudson pulling me into our first kiss was the perfect middle finger to that comedian. And just perfect.

Ma stares me down. "You can keep correcting me or you can take the photo and leave."

"Fine."

Dylan stands in front of me, wrapping my arms around him prom-style. I smile and roll with it.

"Perfect." Ma takes her photo. "Thank you!" She kisses both of us on the cheek, sits down on the kitchen stool, and gets to work on her magical caption.

"Have fun, weirdos." Pa sneaks me some extra cash the way a drug dealer hands off a dime bag. He kisses me on the forehead and hugs Dylan. "Ben, home by ten thirty. Dylan, home whenever the hell you want, you don't live here."

"*Yet.*" Dylan winks on his way out.

I close the door behind us.

I'm speed-strolling to the subway instead of speed-walking because sweating through my shirt will not be a good look. We get to the station, swipe our way through, and I stand at the yellow edge of the platform to see if the L train is approaching. It's not. I'll be ten minutes late, that's fine. Fifteen tops. Still not bad for me—there were times when I was thirty minutes late with Hudson. Puerto Rican time is a joke, but it's also a real thing with Team Alejo. I wouldn't have racked up as many detention slips for lateness if it wasn't. For Thanksgiving, Títi Magda always tells the family to show up at two knowing we won't get there until four, which is the actual time the kitchen will be ready. It'll be fine.

"Are you sure you don't want me to hang around and observe the date?" Dylan asks. "Good ol' Digby Whitaker has no problem skipping his movie."

"I will strangle Digby with arcade tickets if he shows his face."

"Hot."

We're going uptown to Times Square. Dylan is going to see some horror movie while I hit up Dave & Buster's with Arthur. The L train arrives and we ride it to Union Square. We switch to the N train, which is waiting on the platform for passengers transferring.

"So," Dylan says. "A lot of pressure tonight, huh?"

"Literally the last thing I want to hear before a date. Before anything."

"I'm just saying. You guys have this epic beginning."

"I know that, but . . . I'm trying to be somewhat realistic here."

It's weird how six days ago I met Arthur at a post office and the universe reached out with both arms to pull us together. Still, I never move at this speed. Hudson and I were friends for months before he charmed me into taking it to a different level with him.

But Arthur? I barely know him. I guess that's any relationship. You start with nothing and maybe end with everything.

CHAPTER THIRTEEN
ARTHUR

We're minutes away from showtime, and I'm kind of freaking out.

How do people even do this? It's not like I'm the first almost-seventeen-year-old to go on a date. People date in Georgia. But back home, that means someone paying for your Zaxby's, not Saturday night at Times fucking Square.

"You look great." Dad catches my eye in the mirror. "Untuck your shirt."

"It's supposed to be like this."

"Mmm. I don't think so."

I peer at my reflection. I don't know what to think. I'm wearing a blue plaid button-down shirt, half tucked in like a J.Crew model. Like a really short J.Crew model. I'm wearing a belt, too, and I ironed my jeans. It's highly possible that this is the best I've ever looked. Either that or the douchiest. It could go either way.

Dad sniffs. "Are you wearing perfume?"

"It's cologne."

"Wow. Art. So this is fancy."

"No! I mean. I don't know." I press my hair down, and it springs back up immediately. I have that messy brown Jew hair, just like my parents. I should dig up some gel. I could go full Draco Malfoy.

"You might want to tone it down a little, don't you think?"

"Dad. It's a first date."

"Yes. Which is why you should probably tone it down."

"No. Okay. I don't think you . . ." I trail off, suddenly realizing I forgot to buy breath mints. And I'm not talking Tic Tacs. I need the hard stuff. I need Altoids. I've already brushed my teeth six times, gargled mouthwash, and googled *How do you know if you have old-man breath.* Seriously, what if he kisses me, and it's like kissing Uncle Milton? What if my first kiss and last kiss are the SAME KISS? I need a guidebook for this. I need a fairy godmother.

"So where is he taking you?" Dad asks.

"I have no idea."

I mean, I have theories. Not that I've given this a lot of thought or anything. Not that I was up all night mapping it out in my head. But okay. We're meeting in Times Square, which is the most iconic New York spot ever, so he's clearly going for that big-city, big-date vibe. It's probably too early in the relationship for a Broadway show, even with a TKTS booth discount, but I could see us doing Madame Tussauds. I would love that. We'd take tons of pictures, in case we ever need to trick people into thinking we know famous people. First kiss would happen next to my birthday twin and forever president, Barack Obama. Or maybe Ben's going for more of a classic rom-com feel, like a trip to the top of the Empire State Building. I'd be cool with that. More than cool.

There's a twist of a key, and our front door creaks open. "Anyone home?"

"In Arthur's room," calls Dad.

"Oh wow," Mom says, appearing in my doorway. "All dressed up for your big date."

"Oh." I blush to my hairline. "It's not . . ."

"You look great, sweetie. Tuck in your shirt."

"Or untuck it," Dad says.

"He's going on a date, not bingeing *Simpsons* reruns."

"Yeah, but he's already wearing a collared shirt and cologne."

Mom looks pointedly at Dad's sweatpants. "Right, God forbid he make an effort—"

"Welp. Gotta go," I say loudly. I'm out the door so

quickly, it's like I'm breaking out of prison. I'm flushed and practically buzzing with nerves. I don't think I actually breathe until I step onto the sidewalk.

I peek at my phone. No texts from Ben. But that's good. It means he hasn't canceled.

It means I'm walking to the subway. It means I'm riding to Times Square.

It means it's seven thirty on a Saturday night, and I'm four stops away from the first act of my love story.

CHAPTER FOURTEEN
BEN

It's 8:11 when we reach the stop. Dylan wishes me good luck with my future husband as I race half a block down to the main entrance of the Times Square train station. It's a Saturday night in summer, so this block is a nexus of tourists plus New Yorkers who made poor life choices that landed them here. There are police officers and men dressed as the Avengers standing underneath the giant subway sign that's lit up like the billboards for Broadway shows, American Eagle Outfitters, and more. And there's Arthur, half the size of the dude dressed up as Captain America. His shirt is half tucked in and he's staring at his phone, sneaking looks around every two seconds. He's looking for me.

"Hey," I call.

Arthur almost drops his phone. "Hey," he says. Blushing. Startled, I guess.

I go in for a handshake and he's coming in for a hug. "Oh. Sorry." I go in for the hug this time and he extends his hand and almost grazes the Ben Juniors. I grab his forearm before he can pull away and shake his hand. Great start. He smells nice, at least. Cologne. I didn't even shampoo.

"Thought you were ghosting for a second," Arthur says.

"Yeah, sorry. I'm usually right on time or super late. I thought I had it under control tonight though," I say. Ten minutes is nothing compared to how late I've been in the past.

"I thought I was going to have to put up another poster to find you," Arthur says. He cringes and shrugs, which scores a smile out of me. "So where are we going?" He talks a lot, which I'm fine with, and he's not good at maintaining eye contact, which sucks because I want to stare at his electric blue eyes. Punch me in the face if I ever compare them to the sky or the ocean, because they're much cooler than that.

"Just right up here," I say. A vendor on the corner is selling water bottles, candy, and newspapers, and I stop real fast to get Skittles since they double as an appetizer and breath mint. "I'm still feeling burned after green apple was replaced by lime."

"She was still sexy though."

"What?"

"The green Skittle. I've got some really gay DNA, but even I get it. She was strutting around in all those commercials and getting the red and yellow Skittles all riled up."

"You're talking about M&M's."

"Oh." Arthur blushes.

"The green one riled you up?"

"Not really. But she was sexy in that cartoon way. Like how you know Bugs Bunny or Puss in Boots are probably respectable in bed."

"I've never given thought to Bugs Bunny or Puss in Boots having sex . . . And now I'm thinking about them having sex with each other . . ."

Arthur bites his lip and shrugs. "Sorry for bringing up sexy cartoons in the first five minutes of our date," he says. "It's obvious I've never done this before, right?"

"Had a conversation?"

"Been on a date." More blushing, like he's going for a world record.

I really had no clue until he outed himself. It's not weird, but the pressure keeps on building. "You shouldn't feel bad for bringing up sexy cartoons. My best friend, Dylan, once sent me a link to some Harry Potter porn. You can never read those books the same after you've seen Hermione, Harry, and Ron in a potions lab shouting *Erectus Penis*."

Arthur's laugh is way different from Hudson's. Hudson's was harsher and always sounded exaggerated, even when it was real. Arthur's laugh is higher and louder, and I don't know much about him, but I have no doubts his laugh is legit. And I really like the sound of it.

We walk past Ripley's Believe It or Not! and Madame Tussauds, a tourist trap with wax models of celebrities that people take selfies with and share on Facebook. No New Yorker is ever impressed.

Arthur looks excited until we walk past.

Next door is Dave & Buster's. "Here we are."

"The arcade?"

"Every dude's wet dream," I say. "You been?"

"I've gone a couple times back home."

"Awesome. I could use some competition."

I lead us up the two sets of escalators.

I buy my card with game credits and he gets his own. I would buy his too, but, you know. Probably better to establish money stuff from the beginning anyway. In a heterosexual relationship, it's pretty clear who's expected to be the gentleman. . . . It's the gentleman. Things are hazy when you've got two gentlemen. The only person I feel comfortable paying for me outside my family is Dylan, but that's because I know he'll be in my life forever and I'll pay him back if I ever hit it big. Hudson wasn't a guarantee. Neither is Arthur.

There are a lot of fluorescent lights when you enter. A photo booth where Hudson and I kissed behind the curtains and made stupid faces. The bar where we casually ordered cocktails with all the confidence in the world that we weren't going to get carded. Maybe I shouldn't have brought Arthur here, but all the places where I know how to have fun all have memories of Hudson days. If things work with Arthur, we can make this place our own this summer.

It's pretty packed, but there are some free games open. "What should we do first?"

Arthur scans the room. "Claw machine?"

"Amateur move, Arthur. If you win something early, then you have to carry it around all night. Let's go race motorcycles."

We head over. Arthur looks even more compact on a motorcycle. His feet hover above the platform when they're not resting on the pedals. We choose the same track and rev up. I'm really focused because I always play to win.

"I'm so mad because I'd just gotten my license back home when we came up here, and now it's pointless," Arthur says. "It's all trains and buses and Citi Bikes. Maybe I'll rent a motorcycle."

Arthur is in last place and going the opposite direction. He should not rent a motorcycle.

I want to ask him more about Georgia, but I'm in third place right now and have to get ahead.

The game ends.

"You got second place!" Arthur says. "Congrats."

"Second place sucks."

"Oh, you're one of those. Second place is the first loser, right?"

"Sort of. A couple years ago my mother almost won the lottery. She was off by two numbers." I get off the motorcycle. Not going to tell him how big that jackpot would've been for my family. "We were first losers."

"What would you have done if you won the money?"

Moved into a bigger apartment. Bought a car because yeah, the trains and buses are fine, but if we had our own car, we could take trips outside the city where the trains and buses don't go. Get one of those memory foam beds. "Buy every gaming console." Admitting practical needs isn't first-date talk. "And maybe brave my first flight ever so I can go to that Harry Potter park in Florida."

"I've never been either! Maybe we can go one day," Arthur says. He's beaming, like a first date automatically equals a couple's trip to Universal Studios. Definitely jumping ahead a bit. "You need a new wand anyway."

"What?"

"The wand in that box you were returning to your boyfriend."

The box still sitting in my bedroom. "Yeah. Exactly." I lead the way to a Pop-A-Shot. "Have you made any friends here yet?"

"These girls at my internship, Namrata and Juliet," Arthur says. "They were rooting for me to try and find you. They had suggested Craigslist, but my mom wasn't having it."

I stop. "You talking about missed connections?"

"Yeah! You know it?" Arthur reaches out and touches my shoulder. "Wait. Did *you* put up a listing for *me*?"

"Oh. Um. No," I say. I wish I had lied to spare us from all this blushing. "But my dad had mentioned it, and I checked to see if you were looking for me too."

Arthur is smiling. "I didn't know you were looking for me. At all."

"Well yeah." I run my hands through my hair as I move toward the hoops again. "So . . . motorcycles weren't your speed, but maybe basketball? You just got to get the basketball in the hoop as many times as possible in one minute."

He nods, but I'm not sure he's actually heard me. I probably only need one guess to know what he's thinking: we were looking for each other. He went to greater lengths, but hearing I wanted to find him too? Well, we all love having our feelings reciprocated.

We play against each other plus some random kid being shadowed by his dad. Making two notes to myself right now: 1) Don't talk shit when I beat Arthur and the kid. 2) Don't call "bullshit" if Arthur or the kid wins.

The timer starts and I'm doing okay, six shots in ten

seconds. The kid is keeping up though. Twenty seconds in and Arthur scores his first shot.

"YES!" He turns to me. "King of the world!"

"You're wasting time," I say. He has no chance of catching up, but he can try harder. Or at least stop distracting me. I. Play. To. Win.

Arthur keeps at it until his basketball bounces out of the booth, and he chases it like a bull wrangler.

Time's up.

23 to 1 to 25.

"That's bull—" I don't give props to the kid because he's laughing at me. Maybe an arcade wasn't such a great idea for a first date. My sore-loser side is more third-date material, maybe fourth.

Arthur returns with his basketball. Shoots it. Misses.

Hudson was a better opponent. He would've also schooled that kid.

I pop some Skittles.

"Want to play air hockey?" Arthur asks. "I promise you'll come in first."

Or I'll end up in the hospital when Arthur sends a rogue striker my way.

"Let's do the claw machine," I say. "But we'll make it interesting."

He follows me into the corner. We're not playing for any stuffed Pokémon, screw that.

"Interesting? Like strip poker interesting? I hope I'm wearing the right underwear for this," Arthur says.

"Do you have wrong underwear, in general?"

"We all have our laundry-day underwear," Arthur says.

"Truth. Well, your pants are staying on for this challenge." There's a claw machine for jewelry. Pretty necklaces, ugly bracelets, fake diamond rings, and so on. "Whatever we win, the other one has to wear. Game?"

"Game!"

"I'll go first," I say. Might help him to see someone else play. "That jeweled necklace in the corner will go nicely with your eyes." I get moving with the claw, holding my hand on the lever while peeking around the case—this is good. I press the button and the claw reaches down, expands, hits the case, and is thrown off completely. It returns with nothing. "This is not my day."

"I wouldn't say that. Good chance you'll have a wonderful accessory in the next minute or so."

"Good chance?"

Arthur points at a necklace with a bejeweled peace sign the size of my iPhone. He gets the claw going and surveys the case from all angles—crouches, tiptoes, shifts left, shifts right, adjusts the claw, rinse and repeat—and hits the button. The claw scoops up the necklace and deposits it.

Arthur retrieves the necklace and smiles. "You won a necklace!"

"Did you just hustle me?"

He's laughing—impish, alien hustler. "You chose the game."

"That's what makes it such a brilliant hustle. I mean, you can't even get a basketball in a big-ass hoop, but you can grab a tiny necklace with a claw?"

"I have a very particular set of skills," Arthur says, quoting *Taken*, which gets him a dozen cool points. "I'm sort of a god when it comes to claw machines." He closes the space between us, staring at the floor before looking at me and holding up the necklace. "Okay. Peace time."

He's close to my face and I think about how kissing him will be awkward. Not this second, though that would be awkward too. Way too early. Talking about the height difference. Hudson and I were on an even playing field, and Arthur is not at my level. That sounds bad. And I hate that I think about this, but I do. I can't help it if height is important for me. The way other people refuse to date someone who plays in a band or someone whose geekiness is so strong they can name all of the original one hundred and fifty Pokémon.

Arthur puts the necklace on me and his knuckles brush against my skin. He looks like he wants to kiss me. I can't see him making the first move. Not like at the post office.

"How do I look?" I ask.

"Like someone who wants gay peace on earth," Arthur

162

says. "And whose breath smells like the wrong green Skittles."

"Like sexy Skittles?"

"Like sexy Skittles," Arthur says. His shoulders straighten. His neck cranes.

"Let's grab a drink," I say.

We go to the bar. I get water and Arthur gets a Coke. I'm a little hungry, but I don't want to make this a dinner date because I get uncomfortable eating across from people. Not friends. I can watch Dylan talk with his mouth full for a disturbingly long amount of time. But with Hudson, we only ate at places where we didn't have to sit across from each other, like counters at pizzerias and in our bedrooms while watching movies. It's this strangling fear that we'll be sitting there and we'll run out of something to say and I'll be able to witness the exact moment someone falls out of love with me because I don't have enough substance to keep a conversation alive over a meal. Why would you want to talk to me for the rest of your life?

Our drinks arrive. "I got this," Arthur says. He pulls out his wallet and hands the bartender some cash. "I have that high-powered law firm intern money."

"Thanks."

We cross the arcade floor to the windows. Arthur is staring outside at Times Square like he wants to be out there getting an exaggerated portrait drawn for thirty dollars, finding his name on one of those license plate magnets, catching a musical, running into a celebrity, or standing around the sidewalk until he sees himself appear on one of those jumbotrons.

Arthur catches me staring at him. "Oh. I'm being an obvious New York noob."

"You are. It's cute. You still have that tourist glow. I can't remember what it's like to be wowed by Times Square. Or anything in New York."

"What! Let me mansplain your city to you." Arthur spills a little of his soda and rubs the rug dry with his sneaker. He recovers and keeps his cool. "You can order food at, like, any time. And if you can't order it, you can find it. These streets will still be busy at two in the morning. Movies are filmed in Georgia all the time, but they're not always about Georgia. Movies are *made* about New York. I could go on."

"I'm sure you can. You miss Georgia?"

He shrugs. "Yeah, I miss my best friends, Jessie and Ethan. And my house. The guest room we have at home is bigger than my uncle Milton's bedrooms."

"That's the New York way," I say. It's sad thinking about how if we picked up our lives and left behind extended family, ass-smacking Dylan, and late-night food-delivery services, I could live in a big house. "You excited to go back?"

"Not thinking about that right now. I'm just basking in

164

that New York magic." He points at me, himself, and me again. "The city made this happen."

I nod. "Good call." I look around at the other games. There's the roulette for tickets, where I once spent a lot of credits only for someone to come up right after me and immediately win five hundred tickets. There's Just Dance, which Dylan usually wins, and I wouldn't be surprised if Arthur has moves. *Mario Kart* racing is always fun. "Are you a scary movie fan?"

"I don't totally hate them."

"So yes."

"Sure."

"Great."

We go into this booth for Dark Escape 4D. It's a really immersive game that plays on people's fears. The seats vibrate, air blows at your face, the surround sound makes you feel like a madman with a knife is creeping up on you, and there's a panic sensor to track your heart rate so you can see who was the most scared.

"What do we have to do to win?" Arthur asks. "Is it who can outlive the other?"

"It's a team game. We have to survive together." I put on the 3D glasses as we look over the stages: Prison for those scared of the dead, Death Chamber for those scared of the dark, Cabin for those scared of pursuit in tight spaces, Laboratory for those scared of vermin.

"Is there an option for a large green field with butterflies chasing us?" Arthur asks.

"Maybe in the next edition. But the butterflies will probably be bats. And the green field will probably be a cave."

"So not what I said at all. Got it." Arthur puts on his 3D glasses and grabs the blaster with a tight grip. "Let's kill some escaped zombie convicts."

The game starts off fairly creepy. The prison is only lit with a swinging lightbulb as our characters drag their feet into the darkness. A cell door creaks open, but it's just the wind—no, no, fuck, no, it's not just the wind, it's an old man with half a face.

"Why is he in prison?!" Arthur yells.

"I don't know!" I yell back.

"Death sentence him! Death sentence him!"

We shoot up the grandpa zombie—and wake up the entire prison and walking dead. One lunges at us in 3D and tries to choke me and Arthur blasts him to death. I shift closer to Arthur, like I once did with Hudson. Our legs are now touching and he scoots closer too. The vibrations of every step as the zombie convicts charge toward us has my heart racing.

"How are you—ah! Shit, he's eating my arm—doing?" I ask.

"Scared. But could be worse."

"What would be the scariest thing that can pop up on that screen? That fucker in the corner?"

We see a zombie in the corner eating a guard's decapitated head like it's roasted chicken. "Him too. And I don't know. Maybe my parents getting divorced?"

"Oh. Is that . . . happening?"

"I think so. I don't know, they're just—zombie on your right!"

I let go of the blaster and push my 3D glasses to the top of my head. The zombies have their way with my character. "Want to talk about it?" It's weird to picture anything bad happening in Arthur's life. He's a "high-powered intern" at sixteen, just relocated to New York, seems really smart. I guess no one's life is perfect. Even those who seem to have it all.

Arthur pauses. "Okay, new scariest thing. Ethan hitting the high note in 'Music of the Night' from *Phantom*."

I'll take that as a no for talking about his parents. "Ethan's your best friend, right?"

"Yeah, I think?" Arthur turns to me with his glasses still on. I can't see his eyes. "Things have changed since I came out. I knew they would, but—I don't know. I didn't expect my best friends to exit stage left."

"Jessie too?"

"Oh no, she's cool. She's amazing. We've always been

pretty extra together, and now we're extra about boys." He finally removes the 3D glasses. "Can I ask how out you are?"

"Super out. In freshman year I was sleeping over at Dylan's and we were watching *The Avengers.* He went on about how many crimes he would commit if it meant Black Widow would track him down so he could meet her. I talked about hammering Thor and he respected that choice. That was that." Now that I hear about Ethan sucking in this department, I'm extra grateful for Dylan. "Same deal with my parents. I came out over dinner while Dylan was there, and my dad assumed we were dating. I just thought my parents would make a bigger deal about it. When they didn't, I was underwhelmed. I thought it was going to be some major event. Balloons, parade, I don't know."

"That's good though, right?"

"Yeah, now I'm glad it wasn't. I wanted it to be normal and it was."

"Because it is. You said you're super out. So everyone knows?"

"Yeah. I put up an Instagram post on Thanksgiving a couple years ago. Said that I was thankful for all the people in my life who are cool enough to love me as I am. And everyone else could unfriend me online and in real life. I had even checked my follower count before posting."

"Mass exodus? Modest exodus?"

"No exodus," I say. It's surprising. I thought people were going to care more than they did.

"Can I be honest about something?"

"You *are* a cartoon porn fanatic, aren't you?"

"Well yeah, but . . . I'm *not* an arcade fanatic. I have failed you."

"This explains a lot," I say.

"We make a great team though!"

"No we don't. We literally lost because we stopped playing midway."

"Logistics."

We put away the 3D glasses and get out.

"So no more playing is what you're telling me," I say. I still have credits, and they don't exactly let you get your money back because your date doesn't like arcades. He really is an alien. "Now what?"

"I have an idea," Arthur says. He leads me to the photo booth, puts in five dollars, and takes a seat. "Come on!"

I don't even get the chance to decide if this is what I want—the photo, this moment with Arthur—but I follow him inside the booth because not doing so is awkward and a waste of five bucks. I sit and all I can think about are the stupid faces Hudson and I made when we were here months ago. But Arthur is not Hudson. And I can't let Hudson spoil any chance at making new memories in old places. Not just here at Dave & Buster's, but everywhere in the city. School, parks, you name it. Arthur is his own person. Not a plaything. Not a distraction. I got to do this right.

"What's our motivation?" I ask. "We get three shots."

"I am not throwing away my shot," Arthur says. He looks at me expectantly. "*Hamilton*?"

"Oh. Right." People are obsessed with that show. I haven't heard a single song, but it's not something I should bring up now.

"I have so much to teach you, Ben."

A timer counts down from three. For the first photo, we wing it. Arthur leans against me and we both smile, super simple. For the second photo Arthur sticks out his tongue and says "Aaaaaah" like a doctor is inspecting his mouth. I do an exaggerated wink. For the third photo Arthur turns to me. My heart is racing because he looks like he wants to kiss, but I'm not there yet. I know this is all really cute, that I'm actually reunited with the boy I met at the post office, but no matter how charming he is, I can't force myself to kiss him before I'm ready. Before I mean it. We just stare and smile at each other when that last flash goes off.

We step out of the booth and we each get a reel to keep. We're actually really cute together.

"That last photo is something," Arthur says. "I . . . Never mind."

"Go ahead."

Arthur stares at his sneakers. "I look way happier than you. It's cool if you want to call this quits. If you're still caught up on your ex, I get it. Well, I don't get it. But I can imagine."

"No, I just . . . I had a lot of fun, but I know I wasn't fully here," I say. That's my fault. I brought my date somewhere I used to come with my ex-boyfriend. I also don't know how much I should really be investing in this since Arthur is just going to leave at the end of the summer anyway.

We're both quiet. I really want to see Arthur the way he sees me. It might take time though, and time isn't really on our side.

Arthur sighs and stares at the floor. "I screwed up my first date. Go me."

"No, you didn't screw it up . . . I'm the one who messed up. I'm always ready to flip off anything good the universe throws my way since I swear the universe hates me. But maybe the universe is just playing the long game. Like everything that's ever gone wrong was so it could be right later. I don't know."

"So the date was good? Or wrong?"

"The date wasn't wrong, I just think that if the universe is setting us up here that our story deserves a more epic first date," I say. "I really want to see you again. Maybe we should have a do-over date."

"Like a first date? Again?"

"Exactly. This time you can plan it. Whatever you want."

"Challenge accepted."

We smile as we shake on it.

CHAPTER FIFTEEN
ARTHUR
Sunday, July 15

A do-over date. And I'm the one who's supposed to plan it.

I didn't even know this was a thing. I thought they were just called second dates.

A do-over.

But at least I get to see him again. Which is convenient, since he's all I can think about. I can't even get out of bed. I'm too busy staring at the photo strip of us together. And yeah, we look a little like Pepé Le Pew and his bewildered cat girlfriend, but we really do seem like a couple. If you saw these pictures, you would not conclude that Ben and I are platonic bros. But the idea of myself as part of a couple is so intensely surreal, I can't even wrap my head around it.

I finally wander out into the living room around ten in

gym shorts and glasses. Dad's on the couch, drinking coffee with the news on mute. "Why are we watching the orange guy?" I ask, sinking into the cushion beside him.

Dad shuts the TV off. "Good morning, Romeo."

"Wow. Please don't."

Dad's brow furrows. "Don't what?"

"Don't be weird."

"Uh-uh. Nope," Dad says. "This is not *My So-Called Life*."

"I don't understand that reference, Dad."

"You're not *The Perks of Being a Wallflower*. I did not just rent *The Breakfast Club*."

"What does that—"

"It means chill with the fake teen angst. This is your first date, and I want to hear about it."

"Don't you think it's weird that we talk about this stuff?"

"Why? Because I'm your dad?"

"Yes. Obviously."

He just gapes at me, like he's trying to process that.

I sigh. "It was fine, Dad. It was an okay date. We have another one tomorrow."

"Whoa. Look at you. Second date."

"Well, it's not a second date. It's a second *first* date. We're having a do-over."

Dad strokes his beard. "That's interesting."

"I know."

"But he clearly likes you."

I sit up. "You think?"

"Well, he wants another date."

"Yeah. God. I don't know how to do this."

"How to plan a do-over date?"

"I don't even know how to plan a regular date."

Honestly, how am I supposed to know how to pick a destination and set the mood and charm Ben's pants off? Not literally. Kind of literally, though.

I glance sideways at Dad. "Okay, so if tomorrow's the first date, how do we talk about Dave & Busters? Do we pretend it didn't happen? Do we call it Date Zero?" I rub my forehead. "Do we try to reenact it?"

"Why would you reenact a bad first date?" Dad asks. "Just relax. This is going to be great. Just stick with the tried-and-true, like a diner. Something basic."

Basic.

I nod. "Okay."

Monday, July 16

Okay, no.

I'm not doing basic. I'm sorry, this isn't some random guy. This is *Ben.* Which is why I'm here on a Monday evening, crammed into a corner table at a restaurant in Union Square called Café Arvin. It's one of those places that looks like a nightclub shoved into a warehouse, with oddly geometric light fixtures and a menu that changes every day. But Yelp says it's a Best Date Restaurant, so hopefully Ben will be into it. Assuming he shows up. He was supposed to be here fifteen minutes ago, but he hasn't texted to say he's running late.

Just like last time.

I should check on him. *Are you coming—are you even alive—are you—*

Now I sound like my mom. Which is probably the wrong note to hit on a date.

I just never knew dates required so many little decisions. When to text, when to chill, what to do with my hands when I'm waiting. When he walks in, should I look up at him and smile? Should I be nonchalantly reading my phone? I need a script for this. Maybe I just need to stop overthinking.

But the moment I see him, I stop thinking altogether, because, wow: he's gotten even cuter. Or maybe I just keep noticing new cute things about him, like the curve of his jawline, or the slight hunch of his shoulders. He's wearing a gray V-neck and jeans, and his eyes scan the room as he talks to the hostess. When he finds me, his whole face lights up.

Suddenly he's settling in across from me.

"This place looks fancy," he says.

"Well, you know. Nothing but the best for our FIRST date."

"Yeah. First date. Never been on a date with you before." Ben smiles.

I smile back at him. "Never." And then my brain goes totally blank.

Unanticipated complication: apparently, I don't know how to talk in nice restaurants. Everything's so hip and elegant here, and no normal conversation feels worthy. It feels like we should be talking about deep things—classy, intellectual things, like NPR or death. But I don't even know if Ben likes NPR or death. To be honest, I barely know anything about him.

"So what do you do?"

"What do you mean?"

"Do you have an internship? What do you do all day?"

"Oh, it's . . ." He trails off, peering down at his menu, and I watch his face go pale.

"Is everything okay?"

"It's fine. I'm just . . ." He rubs his cheek. "I can't afford this."

"Oh," I say quickly, "don't even worry about it. This is my treat."

"I'm not letting you do that."

"I want to." I lean forward. "I'm still rolling in bar mitzvah money, so it's all good."

"But I can't. I'm sorry." He holds up the menu. "I can't eat a thirty-dollar burger. I literally don't think I'm capable of doing that."

"Oh." My stomach drops. "Okay."

He shakes his head. "My mom could buy dinner for us for three days with thirty dollars."

"Yeah, I get that. I guess—" I look up, and my gaze snags on a guy sitting one table over. "Holy shit."

Ben leans in. "What?"

"That's . . . is that Ansel Elgort?"

"Who?"

"He's an actor. Oh my God."

"Really?" Ben cranes his neck around.

"Don't stare at him! We have to play it cool." I grab my phone. "I have to text Jessie. She's going to *flip*. Should I talk to him?"

"I thought we were playing it cool."

I nod. "I should get a selfie, right? For Jessie?"

"Who is he again?" Ben asks.

"*Baby Driver. The Fault in Our Stars.*" I push my chair back and stand. Deep breath.

I walk over, and Ansel shoots me a polite half smile. "Hi."

"Hi! Hi."

"Can I help you?"

"Hi! Sorry. I'm just." I exhale. "Wow. Okay. I'm Arthur,

and my friend Jessie loves you. Like a *lot*."

"Oh!" Ansel looks surprised.

"Yeah, so."

"Well, that's . . ."

"Can I get a selfie?" I ask.

"Um. Sure."

"Awesome. Oh man. You're awesome. Okay." I lean in and snap a few quick ones. "Wow. Thank you so much."

I mean. That just happened. I just . . . walked right up to an actor. Like, a really famous actor. Jessie's not going to believe this.

"Wait," Ben says as soon as I sit down. "You think that's the guy from *Baby Driver*?"

I nod happily. "I'm freaking out."

"Mmm. I don't think that's him."

"What?"

"Oh, and I ordered us truffle fries. Is that okay? They're like twelve bucks, which is ridiculous, but I'll totally chip in—"

"No," I say, and it comes out sharp. I exhale. "I mean, yes. Fries are great. But wait. You don't think that's Ansel?"

"I mean, maybe?"

Suddenly, the waiter appears, setting a pale pink mixed drink in front of Ben. Ben looks up at him, confused. "Oh. Um, I didn't order this."

"The gentleman in the blue shirt sent this over for you."

I gasp. "What?"

"Awesome," says Ben. He takes a sip, and then turns to smile at Ansel.

I gape at Ben. "You're going to drink that?"

"Why wouldn't I?"

"Because." I shake my head. "Why is Ansel Elgort buying you drinks?"

"That's not—"

I cut him off. "Shit—okay. He's coming over."

"Hey," Ansel says, pressing his hands on the edge of our table. He turns to Ben. "Jesse, right?"

Oh.

Oh.

I laugh. "Oh wow, I'm sorry. Okay, Jessie's actually my—"

"Yup, I'm Jesse! Thanks for the drink."

I stare at Ben, dumbfounded, but he shoots me a tiny smile.

"Sure. Hey. I'd love to get your number."

Ansel Elgort. Asking for Ben's number. During our date. What the actual fuck?

"Did you just buy my underage date an alcoholic beverage and then ask for his number?" I ask Ansel loudly.

His eyebrows jump. "Underage?"

"Yes, Ansel, he's seventeen."

"Ansel? Dude, my name is Jake."

180

For a moment, we just stare at each other.

"You're not . . ." I trail off, cheeks burning. "I'm . . . gonna shut up now."

"Good call," says Jake, already retreating to his table.

I sink deeper into my chair, while Ben gulps down his drink. "I think that went well," he says, grinning. World's cutest asshole.

I cover my face with both hands. "That was so—"

"Sir, I'll need to see your ID."

I peek through my hands. It's an older guy, wearing a tie. And he's talking to Ben. My heart leaps into my throat.

"Oh. Um." Ben looks startled. "I think I left it—"

"He's seventeen," I interject.

Ben shoots me a look.

"Please don't call the police." My voice cracks. "Please. God. I can't go to jail. I can't—my mom's an attorney. Please." I fling down a twenty and grab Ben's hand. "We're leaving now. I'm so sorry, sir. I'm incredibly sorry."

"Bye, Ansel," calls Ben.

I drag him out the door.

"I can't believe how fast you just sold me out," Ben says. "Wow."

"I can't believe you let a random guy named Jake buy you a drink!"

"I did." Ben smiles proudly.

"You almost got us arrested."

"No way. I just rescued us from those thirty-dollar hamburgers," he says. "And now look at us. Two-dollar hot dogs. Amazing."

And even I have to admit it: street vendor hot dogs make a perfect dinner. It helps that Ben has a pretty cute hot dog technique. He pulls the bun up around it like a cardigan, takes a tiny bite, readjusts the bun, and starts all over again.

"How are you eating that without ketchup?"

Ben smiles. "Blame Dylan. He told me I'm forbidden, especially on dates."

"I don't get it."

"I don't either." He shrugs. "But he says, and I quote, 'Ketchup breath is both a dealbreaker and a relationship ruiner.'"

I open my mouth to say something, but all I get is air. No words whatsoever.

Because if Ben's thinking about ketchup breath, I'm pretty sure he's thinking about kissing.

Specifically: kissing *me*.

I watch him put this together. His neck and cheeks go pink.

"We'll keep it in mind for our next do-over," he says quickly. "Third do-over will be the charm. Nothing too pricey next time, okay?"

"Yeah. And we won't order garlic fries."

"I thought they were truffle fries."

"Right."

He smiles. Then he loops his arm around my shoulder, and I'm so happy, I can barely breathe. Even though it's just a shoulder thing. People on the street probably think we're just bros. Just two bros eating hot dogs with their arms around each other.

"Okay, so truffles," Ben says. "Since when do truffles not involve chocolate?" He slides his arm off my shoulders and takes out his phone. "I'm looking this up."

"Looking what up?"

"What . . . are . . . truffles?" he says, typing.

"They're some kind of seed, right?"

"Nope. Fungus." He holds up his phone. "See?"

"What? No way." I lean in closer. Our arms are brushing. "I really thought they were seeds."

"I think you're thinking Truffula Seeds from *The Lorax*, Arthur *Seuss*."

I burst out laughing, and Ben gets this look on his face. Like he's surprised and self-conscious and a little bit pleased with himself. I guess he doesn't know how funny he is. Probably his jerkface ex-boyfriend never laughed at his jokes.

"So how'd you figure out my last name?"

"From your email address?" He tugs me sideways to let a woman and her kid go by. It's pretty nice having a New

Yorker to help keep me in check on the sidewalks. "So, are you related to Dr. Seuss or something? No wait, it's a pen name, right?"

"His is. Mine's not." I smile. "And you're Ben Hugo?"

"Ben Alejo. Hugo is my middle name. It's harder to misspell than Alejo."

"Ben Hugo. I like that, it sounds like a poet's name."

"Nope. Not a poet. No picture book empire."

"Hey, you never told me what you do all day."

"Right." He presses his lips together. "I'm taking a class."

"You're auditing something? I thought about doing that at NYU. How is it?"

"Um. Pretty great."

"Very cool, Ben Alejo."

"I guess we're doing first and last names now."

"Well, I need to memorize it so I can google you."

He laughs. "I'm not that interesting."

"Yeah you are."

"So are you, Dr. Seuss."

CHAPTER SIXTEEN
BEN
Tuesday, July 17

@ArtSeussical started following you.

Screw homework.

I sit up in bed. Following each other feels like a step, one that I've been excited about because Arthur's profile has been on private. "Yo. Arthur just followed me."

"Finally," Dylan says, turning away from my desk, where he was playing *The Sims*. I've just rescued my Sim from doing homework too while Dylan's Sim lounges around playing games on the laptop. The whole thing is too meta for real me.

"Do I follow him back right now? Playing it cool seems pointless since he's leaving at the end of the summer. No time to waste."

"And there's no playing it cool with someone who put up a poster with your face to find you," Dylan says.

"Good point."

I follow Arthur back and suddenly we have access to each other's profiles. Like we've given each other keys to our lives. Harriett's Instagram is radiant, but I see how much energy she puts into each photo. Arthur's Instagram feels real.

There's a photo of him eating his first slice of New York pizza.

Playbills for *Aladdin* and *Wicked*.

A mirror selfie in some lobby, and I notice it's the day we met—hot dog tie and all.

A prom photo of Arthur and Jessie and Ethan.

A laptop decal that says *WWBOD: What Would Barack Obama Do?*

Arthur sitting on a stool somewhere fancy, and at first I think it's a restaurant, but then I see photos of him on the wall. His house in Georgia is definitely way nicer than I built it up to be in my head. The idea of him visiting my apartment before he goes home for good just became a thousand times more intimidating.

Arthur sitting cross-legged in front of what looks to be his bedroom mirror stops me. Even Dylan is zooming in on his face.

"Holy blue eyes, Batman," Dylan says.

"Holy blue eyes," I repeat. I've seen them in real life, but still.

And then there's another photo of Arthur in glasses, which is a thing, and wow. In the next ten photos I look at, I find myself staring at his lips instead of his eyes. "Is Thursday too soon to go in for the kiss?"

"Not one bit. Make your move," Dylan says. His phone buzzes on my desk and he gets up to check it. "You're on the timer here, Big Be—" He stares at the screen. "It's her."

"Samantha?!"

"Beyoncé," Dylan says. "Of course Samantha. What do I do?"

"Open the text. Read it. Then respond with words. But not words of the 'future wife' variety."

He reads the text and hands me the phone. "Okay. This is good. I think. Help me not mess this up."

I check out the text:

Hey Dylan. I'm sorry I haven't reached out sooner. Every time I start writing something I just assume you no longer care and then I feel stupid and say nothing. I had this anxiety with Patrick during a falling out and he was happy I wrote to him and I'm hoping you might be too. I panicked a bit over your future wife comment because my last relationship just felt very obsessive and I don't like who I became during it or how I felt after. I think you're good and funny and I'd like to see you again if we can keep it casual. If you've moved on, I'm sorry to bother you.

"Wow," I say. "You have to respond soon. Don't leave her hanging."

"What should I say?"

I go through everything I know about Samantha. "Maybe invite her out to grab some seafood with her sister? So it seems less romantic?"

"That'll land me in the friend zone."

"Dude, she wants to see you. Texting you was clearly hard for her, but she did it anyway. You just have to take your time," I say.

"Right. I was kidding about the future-wife thing. Half kidding." He takes the phone back and reads over the message again.

"Can I help you with the text, please?"

Dylan shakes his head. "I got this." He takes a deep breath and narrates: "Dear future wife . . ."

I snatch the phone.

Thursday, July 19

Our third first date is pretty low-key. No arcade games where Arthur can't keep up. No meals I can't pay for. Figuring it out wasn't easy. Arthur suggested one of those disco parties where you wear headphones and dance to songs of your choice. I suggested Nintendo World, which was apparently too close to arcade games for someone—cough,

cough. He suggested a painting class. I suggested rock climbing. We've settled on a stroll through Central Park, and I have plans for where I can kiss him.

It's after six as we walk the same path I walked with Dylan last week. I even knocked out my homework and studied for tomorrow's test this afternoon so I can stay out until nine. Arthur and I split a pretzel while talking about how his favorite GIF is the one of the bald eagle that tries biting Trump's hand off, and all I can think about are all the things I want to know about him. And what that means since he's not here for good.

"What are some of the things you have to do before you go back to Georgia?"

"Win the *Hamilton* lottery. And I kind of want to see another show on my birthday. Visit Lady Liberty, maybe? Going to the top of the Empire State Building could be interesting."

"It's hell to get up there, but definitely worth the Instagram photo op. I really liked that photo of you in the hot dog tie," I say. "A lot of photos, actually. But I didn't want to be That Guy who likes all your old photos. That Guy isn't cool. I hope where I'm taking you is worth the 'gram."

The only photo we have together is from our first first date. I don't know if I'm ready to upload a photo of a new guy to Instagram because that's a huge statement, but it'd be nice to start having something to remember this summer by.

As we head up the stone steps to Belvedere Castle, I'm kind of wishing we'd waited a couple more hours for the sun to set for some city glow action. I really love the way lit windows pop like stars when it gets dark out. But at least Arthur will be able to appreciate the daytime view.

"Here we are," I say. "What do you think?"

"Definitely Instagram-worthy."

As we look over the balcony, I say, "I came here looking for you."

"What?"

"This girl Dylan is interested in, Samantha, she tried helping me find you. And I told her everything I knew about you because she's pretty much a social media detective, and she found a Yale meetup here and I checked it out. For you. But you weren't here." I inch closer to him and our elbows are touching. "I think you're cool."

Arthur nods and smiles, but the smile doesn't hang out for very long. I'm not getting kiss vibes.

"You okay?" I ask.

"I'm fine. That's really sweet," he says. "I just . . . I saw a photo of you and Hudson at Dave & Buster's. Did you bring him here too?"

Fucking Hudson. We're not even friends and he's still managing to ruin my life. "Nope. Hudson and I never came here." I shift, our elbows no longer touching. "I brought you to Dave & Buster's because I was nervous and that was comfortable for me. Is that why you're upset?"

"I'm not upset," Arthur says. It's pretty clear he's bothered.

"If there's stuff you want to know, just ask me. It's fine. Cool?" I massage his shoulder, hoping we can get this back on track. "Arthur, don't forget that if I never dated Hudson, then I couldn't have broken up with him. Then I wouldn't have gone to that post office. Then I wouldn't have met you."

I swore that would've made me feel better. Except Arthur still doesn't look happy.

CHAPTER SEVENTEEN

ARTHUR

Stop. Talking. Arthur.

It's like my mouth and my brain don't even know each other. They're not even in the same plane of reality. My mouth is the guy in the horror movie with his hand on the door. My brain's the guy on the couch screaming, "DON'T OPEN IT."

The Hudson door. I can't stop opening it.

And tonight was supposed to be the night when everything clicked into place. I spent all week plotting every minute of it in my head. I was going to be funny and cool, and he'd be totally charmed. Not even charmed. He'd be straight-up enchanted. I imagined we'd end up on a bench in Central Park, sitting without an inch of space between us, and Ben would tap my arm to tell a joke or make a point, but he'd leave his hand there a moment longer than he needed to. I'd catch him staring at my profile. We'd watch all the tourists walk by, and he'd lean in close with whispered running commentary. I actually lost sleep this week imagining the heat of Ben's breath on my ear.

And of course there would be kissing. My first kiss. Followed by the loss of my virginity in some quiet, starlit field.

But no. Not even close. Instead, it's me bleeding out all my neuroses, looking for answers to questions I have no right to be asking. But I don't know how to make myself stop asking them. People like me should come with a mute button.

"I mean, I understand why you have pictures of him. But do you really need fifty-six of them?"

"Why are you counting my pictures?" he asks.

I turn toward him, stopping on the path, but he grabs my hand and tugs me out of pedestrian traffic. Next thing I know, we actually are on a bench in Central Park, just like I pictured it. And he's still holding my hand, which is more than a little bit wonderful.

"I wasn't really counting."

"You just guessed there were fifty-six."

"Okay, I counted them."

He smiles slightly.

"It's just—your social media is basically a shrine to another guy."

"Why don't you just not look at those pictures?" Ben asks.

I untangle our fingers. "You're missing the point."

"Hudson and I were friends, too," he says. "You've got tons of pictures of Ethan and Jessie."

"Yeah, but Ethan and Jessie are Ethan and Jessie!"

Ben sighs. "And Hudson is Hudson."

I watch him fidget with his shoelace.

"Okay, I'm just going to ask." My voice is quiet, almost hoarse. "Why'd you break up?"

He meets my eyes, but I can't read his expression. "Do you actually want to know?"

"Yes!"

"Are you going to hold this against me?"

"Did you do something awful?"

"No!" Ben shuts his eyes briefly. "It's just—it was messy. He broke my heart. I told you he cheated on me, right?"

I bolt upright. "He *cheated*?"

Ben's staring out into the park, jaw clenched. "Kind of? I mean, he kissed some guy, so—"

"Um, that's not kind of cheating. That's cheating."

"But I guess he thought we were already broken up."

"Were you?"

"Not that I was aware of." Ben's voice is tinged with exasperation. "We had a fight, and I told him to get out of my face, but I wasn't like, hey, why don't you go hook up with some dude at a party whose name you don't even know—"

I gasp. "He didn't even know the guy's name?"

"He knew his gamer handle." Ben shrugs. "Yung10DA."

"Young tenda?"

"Spelled y-u-n-g. And, like, the actual number ten."

"Oh my god." I shake my head slowly. "Hudson dumped you for a guy named Yung10DA?"

Ben pauses. "Can we maybe stop talking about this?" I open my mouth to reply, but Ben cuts me off quickly. "Just for the record, though, I dumped Hudson."

"Right."

"Also, he didn't pick Yung10DA over me. That dude was just there."

"No, I get it—"

"And—"

"I thought you didn't want to talk about it," I say finally.

He exhales. "I don't."

"Okay . . ."

"Okay then," he says. "Done deal. All good. We're good."

But when I sneak a glance at him, he's wringing his hands, mouth pressed into a tight line.

★ ★ ★

195

Friday, July 20

It was brutal, I write.

Oh, come on, writes Jessie.

I'm serious. I bombed it. I trace the perimeter of a tile with the toe of my boot. I haven't even been at work for an hour, and I'm already sending panicked texts to Jessie and Ethan from the bathroom.

How do you know you bombed it? asks Ethan, but he puts a bomb emoji in place of the word.

Well, for one thing, he didn't ask me on another date.

And as soon as I write that, it's real—so real, it makes my stomach lurch. I took this well past the point where a do-over could fix it. I can't even blame Ben for cutting me loose. Why would he possibly want to see me again? So he can spend another few hours being interrogated about Hudson?

So what? You should ask him out, says Jessie.

I can't do that.

Why? You have his number. Thinker emoji.

Because he's not going to want to hang out again. I bite my lip. I don't think you understand.

Were you a wet kisser? asks Ethan.

Shut up, Ethan. Arthur, ignore him.

I didn't kiss him. Too busy asking him about Hudson, I write.

ARTHUR!!!!

I know, I know.

I can picture Jessie so clearly—lips pursed, frantically typing. You can't grill him about his ex on the third date.

I frown. Actually, it was the third *first* date.

Suddenly, Jessie's FaceTiming me. "Jess, I'm at work," I hiss.

"You're clearly in the bathroom," she says. "Look, I'm not going to—okay. Here's the thing. I know I'm not quote-unquote 'experienced' or whatever, and I'm obviously talking out of my ass here—"

I can't help but smile.

"But Arthur, don't listen to Ethan, okay? He is . . . not one to talk, trust me." Jessie rolls her eyes. "But you actually like this guy."

I shrug.

"Arthur, come on. You made a poster to find him. You stalked him all through New York—"

"I did *not*."

"It was sweet! And yeah, you screwed up, but come on. Remember how hard it was for you to even find him? The fact that you did? Arthur, that's a miracle."

"I know, but—"

"Arthur, this is fate! Don't you dare give up this easily."

I spend the subway ride home drafting the text in my notes app—which of course makes the whole thing loom even larger. It's hard to feel casual about a text that's gone through three rounds of revisions. I might as well write the final version out in calligraphy. Or engrave it. Tattoo it on my butt cheek.

Hey. So I know last night was weird, and I hope it's okay that I'm texting you. Feel free to delete this if you want, but I hope you don't. I'm really sorry, Ben. I shouldn't have asked about Hudson. It's not my business, and you were right, I was jealous. It's just, I think I like you a lot, and I'm kind of new to this whole thing of actually dating guys I like a lot. Or dating guys at all, really. And I honestly get it if you'd rather just end things (I wouldn't want to date me either, lol). But if you want to give this another shot, I'm totally 100% super madly up for that. Maybe we could have another do-over?

I copy it into my texts and click send before I lose my nerve. And for a moment, I just stand there, in the middle of the subway station.

I just did that. I told him I liked him. I mean, he probably figured it out, what with the whole chasing-him-around-New-York thing. But that was different. That was almost like a game I was playing with the universe. This time it's Ben, and this time it's real.

I shove my phone into my pocket so I don't obsess the whole way home, but it starts buzzing with texts before I even reach the end of the block. Jessie, I'm sure. Or Dad. Don't check and don't hope. I won't look until I'm home.

Yeah, that lasts approximately two seconds. I whip it out and tap into my texts, heart skittering in my chest. There are two.

No, you're fine, I totally get it. It's a lot. Anyway, no worries, Arthur, and I'm super madly up for a do-over, too. Maybe we keep it casual this time and go from there?

And then the second: Actually, I don't know what you're up to tonight, but I was going to hang out with Dylan and his maybe-girlfriend. No big deal if you're busy, but let me know if you want to save me from the whole third wheel thing. Apparently we're doing karaoke, so I'm warning you, it's probably going to be a disaster.

I whip around in a full one-eighty, already speed-walking back to the Seventy-Second Street station. I'm smiling so hard my jaw hurts. But right outside the entrance of the subway, I pause to text Ben back. Three words.

I like disasters.

CHAPTER EIGHTEEN
BEN

This is going to be a disaster.

We're running a few minutes late when I get off the train with Dylan and Samantha. They are so drunk from flirting that I don't trust Dylan to not ruin this for me.

"Dylan, what are tonight's dos and don'ts?"

"I don't care for pop quizzes."

I stop in front of him. "D, I'm serious."

"I promise not to talk about how you have sexy time with Hudson during summer school—" I glare. "Okay." Dylan turns to Samantha, who's just laughing. "Ben, I'm not going to blow up your spot. I will only talk up the good things. I'll start with how you're an awesome friend and an even better lover."

Samantha shakes her head. "I'm going to be honest, I can't tell if you guys have actually had sex or if this is an ongoing joke I need to accept."

"What happens in Ben's room stays in Ben's room," Dylan says.

Deep breath. "Hudson is a word we all have to forget about. If Arthur got bothered by seeing old pictures of Hudson on my Instagram, he would freak out if he knew I was stuck in summer school with him."

"You're planning on telling him, I hope?" Samantha says.

"Yeah. Just got to figure out the right moment," I say.

I keep it moving. We get to the karaoke center and Arthur is waiting in the lobby. He's wearing a short-sleeved, sun-colored plaid shirt and he's just really damn cute. "Hey," I say. "Sorry we're a little late."

"It's okay," Arthur says. "Hi."

I go in for a hug because I think we're past handshakes and awkward fist bumps. I think he breathes me in, but I might be making that up. Hugging Arthur is different from hugging Hudson; Hudson's chin was able to reach my shoulder whereas Arthur's face is pressed against my chest, kind of like I'd imagine it would be if we were lying on the couch watching TV.

"This is Dylan and Samantha. Guys, this is—"

"Arnold!" Dylan shouts, and hugs Arthur. "So great to

finally meet you. Ben has spoken so highly of you."

"Hi, *Arthur*," Samantha says. "He's trying to be funny. He's not funny."

"I'm mostly funny."

"Nope," Samantha and I say at the same time.

Arthur looks between all of us. Like he's just now realizing how outnumbered he is in this circle. "So . . ." He puts his hand on my shoulder. "Fourth first date and first double date."

"Fourth first date?" Samantha asks.

"We want the first date to be epic and worthy of how we met," I say. "So we keep calling do-over when things detour a bit."

"Our beginning was very epic too," Dylan says. "I was just smart enough to get Samantha's phone number."

I want to remind him that he almost messed up his epic relationship, but that's bad form in front of our future people; I'll save it for when we're alone.

Samantha grabs his arm and looks into his eyes. "It was very romantic and epic the way you came to my job and waited in line and talked to me. Everyone should follow your lead!" She half hugs his waist and looks back at Arthur. "The poster you set up for Ben sounds wonderful, by the way. I feel like I'm in the presence of romantic greatness."

Arthur blushes. "Thanks. Luck was on our side."

The woman behind the counter calls out Arthur's name.

He apparently put his name down when he got here. We're led into this boxy room with one L-shaped couch, a TV, and two microphones. In the center of the table is my worst enemy—the binder of songs that we'll be choosing from tonight. In front of one another. For the first time. Even Dylan and I haven't done karaoke together. We've sung together, but we've never ever had a microphone and we were never sober.

"Dylan! Go use your beard to get us some alcohol."

"I can't drink," Dylan says. "Still too nauseous after that seafood."

"Don't blame the seafood," Samantha says.

"Fine. Get yourself whatever and the rest of us something not boring," I say.

"I don't drink," Samantha says.

"Me either," Arthur says. "Doesn't mix well with my Adderall."

"I'll drink for all three of you," I say, which makes me sound like an alcoholic, but there's no way I'm getting through this hour sober.

Dylan rushes out of the room.

Arthur and Samantha flip through the binder.

"Do they have *Hamilton* or *Dear Evan Hansen* here? This karaoke place back home didn't have updated songs yet," Arthur says.

She flips through the pages. "That would've been

amazing, but I'm not seeing any here either. The Broadway selection is okay. Tons of Disney."

"I can do anything from *Hercules* and *Little Mermaid* and *Aladdin* and *Beauty and the Beast* and *Tarzan* and *Toy Story* and *The Jungle Book*."

"Is that all?"

"I know a couple songs from *101 Dalmatians*," Arthur says with pride.

Dylan returns with four cups. Thank god. He hands everyone a cup and I take a sip, expecting it to be harsh. But it's kind of flat and gross.

"Is this Coke? Without alcohol?"

"She not only saw past the beard, but she mocked me." Dylan shakes his head and downs his Coke like a shot. "It was awful."

Samantha convinces Dylan to perform a duet with her, which just gives me all sorts of anxiety because Arthur is probably going to want to do the same, right? I agreed to karaoke night in the first place because Dylan assured me we would all just do group songs. But Arthur showing up has completely changed the game. We went from a party of three to a double date. The rules are out the window. Duets are allowed, and this is going to be a shit show.

The disaster begins with "Telephone" by Lady Gaga featuring Beyoncé. Samantha pulls out her phone, recording herself as she sings Lady Gaga's parts beside Dylan, and damn, I love Dylan because he doesn't even need to look at the monitor to sing Beyoncé's parts. He just takes the phone from Samantha and sings straight into the camera like it's some old-school, punk-rock music video and not a song about boyfriends being thirsty for their girlfriends when they're out having fun without them.

Arthur sits next to me the entire time, our knees touching as he bounces and sings along.

The song ends. "Let's do 'Bad Romance' next," Dylan says.

"Not the most romantic choice." Samantha taps the microphone against his forehead. "Try again, dodo." She turns to me, and I get the sinking feeling like when I'm in class and a teacher wants me to answer a question. "You want to go?"

"You can go again," I say. "I like watching."

"Better be me you're watching, buddy," Dylan says.

Arthur pulls the binder into our laps. "Want to sing something together? I can take lead. My dad isn't big on singing either, but when we were road-tripping to Yale, I was singing whatever came on the radio and he'd jump in at the chorus."

"I might need another few minutes to get hyped," I say.

"I'll sing a duet with you, Arthur," Samantha says.

"My hero."

"I tried coming to yours and Ben's rescue with that Yale

meetup, so this'll make me feel better," Samantha says.

"I really didn't even know that meetup was happening," Arthur says. "I know it's not my year, but I would've gone just to get some tips on the applications." He rests his hand on mine. "God, how awesome is life right now. I mean, everything is really coming together. So many possibilities for where we'll all end up next year. I'm cool with any of the Ivy Leagues, though Yale and Brown are really hit or miss, you know. I may end up putting a bunch of liberal arts schools on my list, just to be safe."

I stare into my lap and nod along like Arthur's possibilities for the future are no different from mine. But he's seen me fake my way through enough already that he catches himself.

"Of course, there's financial aid and scholarships," Arthur says.

I shake my head. "I'm not getting a scholarship."

My heart is racing because I feel like such a loser now. Like I'm always going to be fighting some uphill battle to make a place for myself in this world. Like why bother if I'm not some rich valedictorian. You would think the universe would be cooler about taking care of those with less. Let's say I get financial aid. I'm not liking my odds of maintaining the high GPA to keep it. And if I can't afford college, why would someone as brilliant as Arthur want to be with me, someone who's struggling with high school?

"I said something stupid," Arthur says.

"You're okay," I say. Though I can't look him in the eye. I really wish Dylan would come through and fill this awkward silence with some stupid joke. Call Arthur Arnold, talk about sex, anything. Except this has become the quietest karaoke room ever.

Arthur's hand slides off mine and he tucks his hands between his legs.

"Um. Follow me," I say, going out into the hallway.

Arthur stands and turns to Dylan and Samantha. He's probably not sure if he should say bye or not. I guess that's up to him.

The hallway is echoing with songs from other people's private rooms. A group is butchering Journey, which is what you should expect during karaoke—awkward singing. What I didn't expect was an awkward talk.

"I'm an idiot, Ben. I don't know why, but I know I am. I'm sorry."

"No, *I'm* sorry. I have to remember you don't know every little thing about me. Like you don't know that I kind of suck at school. So Ivy Leagues are really not a thing that's going to happen for me. And I don't know you well enough to know if that's important to you."

He shakes his head. "It's not! I'm sorry. I just get excited."

"You should be super excited. That's awesome. I hope you get into Yale or Harvard or Hogwarts. Wherever you want. But school is sort of a sore subject for me right now. I'm . . ." I wasn't planning on telling him tonight, but why the hell not. "I'm actually in summer school. That's the class I'm taking."

He looks up at me. "Okay. That's cool."

"You think I'm stupid."

"Are you serious?"

The thing is, I am. Hudson, Harriett, and I had the same teacher as everyone else, and yet we're the only ones from our class wasting away in summer school. Even Hudson and Harriett had perfectly fine grades before the three of us got closer. I'm the only one in that entire class who actually deserves to be there.

"How could I possibly think that?" Arthur says.

"Because you're applying to Yale and I'm in summer school."

"So what?" He steps closer, taking my hand. "That doesn't mean anything. I almost went one year, too."

"Yeah, right."

"Okay. But for real, I did. Fifth grade. It was before I was on meds." He squeezes my hand. "I had a really hard time focusing—like a really hard time. The only reason I didn't have to go was my mom got me six tutors. I'm not even kidding."

"That's a lot of tutors."

"Listen, Yale and everything . . . You know I don't care

about that stuff, right? I don't care if you're in summer school."

"I believe you," I say. "And I'm sorry for not being happy for you without being hard on myself."

"We're saying sorry a lot," Arthur says.

"That's what people do when they want something to work," I say. "Do you want to go back inside?"

"I really, really do."

I'm about to open the door when I stop and knock.

"WE'RE HAVING SEX!" Dylan shouts from inside.

I open the door and Dylan and Samantha are flipping through the binder.

"Straight sex is so weird," I say.

We all settle back in. Arthur gets another round of Cokes and when he returns, he grabs the remote. "I know you don't want to do a duet, but can I do a solo?"

"Knock yourself out."

Dylan cuddles up next to me and Samantha accepts it because if she's in this for the long run, this is her new life.

Arthur selects a song. He clears his throat as the song starts. "This song is called 'Ben,' and I dedicate it to . . . Samantha and Dylan. Kidding. Karaoke humor. Ben, this one is for you."

Arthur has hit peak awkward, and even he's cringing at himself.

He looks nervous, but not as nervous as I am when I

see the first line dragging across the monitor. The song is "Ben" by Michael Jackson. I'm already half praying for a blackout and half smiling because this will be one for the books.

"*Ben, the two of us need look no more . . .*" Arthur isn't going to be on Broadway anytime soon, but he has a really nice voice, and I'm mortified and I'm charmed and I never thought that was a combo that would make sense. He takes a deep breath when the song ends.

Samantha claps first and cheers. "Yay! Go Arthur!"

Dylan is fighting back a laugh.

"I know, I was flat on the key change," Arthur says in response to Dylan. "I haven't practiced my falsetto in a while. I'm sorry—"

"Your voice is awesome," I say. I smack Dylan in the arm. "What's so funny?"

Dylan's laugh is stuttering. "That song is . . . about a rat."

"What?" Arthur and I say at the same time.

"It's about a pet rat," Dylan says. "It's from a horror movie. Same title. Literally about a boy befriending a rat." Samantha is laughing with him now. "Because rats . . . are . . . so . . . misunderstood."

"I—I had no idea," Arthur says.

Dylan laughs and points. "Rat!"

I get up and take Arthur by the arms. "Thank you for the song." I laugh, and he finally laughs too. "I'm going to choose the next song though."

"You're going to sing?" Arthur asks.

"We *all* are," I say.

We throw out options. John Legend. Elton John. Aerosmith. Yeah Yeah Yeahs. The Proclaimers. Destiny's Child. Nicki Minaj. I really want to sing "You'll Be in My Heart" by Phil Collins, which is from *Tarzan*, which I was obsessed with as a kid, but maybe a song about being in each other's hearts forever during a double date isn't the wisest choice just yet.

We go for Rihanna's "Umbrella," which is definitely not about rats, and I work up the nerve halfway through to share a mic with Arthur, and our voices don't ever really become one, but I like how we sound together.

Like two people trying to make it work.

CHAPTER NINETEEN

ARTHUR

"It was *so* nice to meet you," Samantha says, gazing right into my eyes. She's got a hand on each of my shoulders, and I'm calling it now: this girl's going to be a motivational speaker one day or a life coach or like some kind of tiny white Oprah.

And then there's Dylan, sneaking in from the side to snake an arm around each of our waists. "Man, I love this guy," says Dylan, and he punctuates it with a squeeze. "Listen, I *love* this guy. Seussical, you're a keeper. Do you hear me?"

"I hear you."

"You're welcome." He beams. "Now you two kids have fun. Don't do anything Rose and Jack wouldn't do in a steamy vintage car." He glances slyly at Samantha. "That's from—"

"Yeah, we know," says Ben.

"Well, okay then. I guess we're off." Dylan releases himself from the Arthur-Sam-wich to wrap Ben in a bear hug. I watch him whisper something in Ben's ear; Ben mutters *shut up* and smacks Dylan on the arm. It's weird, watching Ben with Dylan. They're just so . . . handsy. Ethan and I aren't like that at all. I guess a part of me wants to ask Ben about it, but—

Nope. No. Not going down that road again. Jealousy over the Hudson thing got me exactly nowhere with Ben, and something tells me Dylan's even more off-limits.

Anyway, Dylan and Sam are gone, and it's just us now. We're on the corner of Thirty-Fifth Street, and Ben looks as awkward as I feel. It's funny—I always imagined dating someone would be pretty straightforward, once you established you liked each other, but it's not. There's this whole new world of bewildering situations. Like how many days should you go between dates? How do you find out if he wants to be your boyfriend? And, of course, there are those moments like right now—moments where you don't know if it's time to say goodnight and get on the subway, or . . .

"So, do you want to walk around or something?" I ask, trying to ignore the nervous flutter in my chest.

"Sure." He touches my arm—more knuckles than

fingertips. And it's just for a moment, but my organs go wild. We start walking.

"So you like to sing," Ben says.

"Sort of."

"I bet you're in all the school musicals."

"Not really. I was in choir, though." I smile. "Ethan and I wrote a musical once, and we roped Jessie into performing it with us. We were twelve."

"You wrote a musical when you were twelve?"

"I mean, it was the worst musical ever," I say, and he laughs under his breath. "It was summer. We were bored. I don't know. It's stupid."

"I think it's cool," he says. "What was it about?"

"You want to know?"

"Definitely."

The sidewalk ends, but Ben barely pauses. He steps confidently into the intersection, slipping between cars and taxis. But as soon as I follow, someone honks at me, and I flinch.

I speed-walk to catch up. "So, it was about these two knights named Beauregard and Belvedere."

He grins. "Were you Beauregard or Belvedere?"

"Beauregard. He was the smart one. Belvedere was the muscle. And Ethan was like two inches taller than me back then."

"Was Jessie the princess?" Ben asks.

"She was the dragon. Named Cheese. It's kind of a long story." I have that antsy, prickly feeling like I'm talking too much. "Want to sit somewhere?"

"Sure."

Somehow we're at Macy's, which is wild—because this isn't just Macy's. It's *the* Macy's, straight out of my TV screen. It's like meeting a celebrity. We snag a little round table outside. I watch Ben peek at his phone, smile, roll his eyes, and shove it back in his pocket without responding.

"Dylan?" I ask.

"Yup."

"I really liked him. And Samantha. Your friends are great."

"Yeah, they're cool. They liked you, too. Like . . . a lot."

I nod without speaking, because if I speak, I'll unleash the millions of questions I'm dying to ask. Like, what do they like about me and tell me in detail and was this a test and did I pass? And do you like me a lot, too?

"So tell me more about Ethan and Jessie." Ben leans forward, onto his elbows. "They sound cool."

"They're . . ." I trail off. "Well, we grew up on the same cul-de-sac. We were like a nerd gang." I pull out my phone. "Here, I'll show you some exclusive, not-really-new footage of them."

"Okay." He scoots his chair beside me, and I'm suddenly aware of *everything*. My heartbeat and the sound of my breathing and an itch on my elbow. I swipe quickly through my albums. "So, here's me and Jess, and that's my car."

Ben's quiet for a moment. "Jessie's cute."

And she is, though I never really think about that. She's just Jessie. Short and pudgy, with a Cupid's bow mouth. Jessie's mom is Jordanian, kind of pale, and her dad's black—whereas Jessie's skin is sort of in between. In the picture, she's smiling, just barely. I'm wearing sunglasses and my hair's a little overgrown and unruly. I went through a lazy hair period sophomore year. It wasn't pretty.

Of course, in the first picture I find of Ethan, he's shirtless. He's leaning back on his hands at the edge of a pool, feet underwater, and his hair's wet, which makes it look jet-black. His eyes are wide open and his mouth is an O. He used to make that face in pictures.

"Still not picturing how Ethan's a tiny, nerdy guy," Ben says.

"I swear, he used to be!" I laugh shortly. "Now I'm the last tiny nerd standing."

"I guess so." Ben smiles. Then he reaches for my hand under the table. "That's not a bad thing. I like tiny nerds."

"You do?"

He laces our fingers together and shrugs. And I'm dead. I am actually dead. There's no other way to explain it. I'm sitting in fucking Herald Square, holding hands with the cutest boy I've ever met, and I'm dead. I'm the deadest zombie ghost vampire who ever died. And now my mouth isn't working. It's like I'm stunned into silence. That never happens. I just need to—

I kick back into gear. "So that's Ethan. Still nerdy, no longer tiny. He was really good at puberty."

"Apparently." Ben laughs. "Did you guys ever . . ."

"No," I say quickly. "No no no no no. He's straight. And he has no game. None of us have any game. We're kind of like three celibate stepsiblings."

"As opposed to stepsiblings who have sex with each other?" Ben's smile sets my whole body into overdrive. Like, I'm pretty sure there's a little Olympic gymnastics team practicing their floor routines in my stomach.

"I can't figure out if you like me," I blurt.

He laughs. "What?"

"I don't know." I laugh too, but my heart's pounding. "It's just. The whole time at karaoke, you seemed sort of . . . withdrawn, I guess? Like you didn't want to be there—"

"Karaoke's not really my thing."

"Yeah, but I keep thinking about how if you really liked me, it *would* be your thing. Not karaoke in particular, I don't care about that. But I think I'd find anything fun if I was with you. Even weird, violent arcade games where I can't turn around to look at you or a zombie will eat part of my body."

"Well, that's what zombies do," Ben says.

217

"I know."

"But I get what you're saying." He furrows his brow. "I'm being a shitty date."

"No you're not!"

He tugs my hand. "Come on, let's walk. I can't sit here."

"Why not?"

"Because you being honest makes me want to be honest, but I can't do that if I'm looking at you."

"Oh." My stomach twists. "Should I be worried?"

"Worried?"

"I feel like I'm about to get dumped. Not that we're in a relationship. Oy. I'm sorry. I'm so . . ." I exhale. "Why am I so awful at this?"

"At what?"

"At this." I lift our threaded hands. "At being with you and being a normal human being with, like, minimally functional conversational skills. I don't know what's wrong with me."

"There's nothing wrong with you."

"I'm just so new to all of this, and here you've already kissed people and probably had sex, and you had this whole other relationship before me. I don't know if I can live up to that."

We turn onto a side street and then into an alley, and the fact that there are no people around makes Ben twenty times more relaxed. I can feel it in his grip.

"But I don't see it like that," he says finally.

"How do you see it?"

"Well, for one thing, I'm the one with something to live up to."

"That's ridiculous."

He smiles slightly. "No, really. I just—like, the fact that you've never dated anyone before or kissed anyone . . . I don't know. What if I mess it up for you? I don't want to be the guy who fucks up your first kiss."

"You wouldn't."

"It's just this pressure, you know. I want to make it perfect."

"Being with you already is perfect."

He snorts.

"I mean, except for the parts where you tragically underestimate my claw-machine skills and get hit on by Ansel Elgort's doppelgänger and have fifty-six pictures with your ex and—"

He kisses me.

Just like that.

His hands are on my cheeks, and he's kissing me.

Holy shit.

I mean, I never realized how close someone's face gets when they kiss you. His head is right there. It's tilted down to meet mine. His eyes are closed, and his lips move against mine, and WOW, I don't know what the rules are around the appropriateness of getting a boner in this sort of moment, but—oh.

I should kiss him back.

I try to move my lips around like he's doing, like I'm trying to eat his mouth without my teeth. But I think I'm doing it wrong, because he pulls back a few inches, grinning down at me.

I grin back. "What?"

He laughs. "I don't know."

"That was a kiss," I say slowly.

"No question."

"I guess the pressure's off now, right? No more worrying about making the first kiss perfect."

"It was perfect," I say.

"You sure you don't want a do-over?" he asks, smiling up to his eyes. "Second first kiss?"

"Oh, I could do that."

He laughs, hands falling to my waist. And then we're kissing again, and it's the same startling closeness.

I slide my eyes shut.

And the whole world narrows. I don't know how else to describe it. It's like I'm not on the street and I'm not in New York and it isn't July and none of it matters. Nothing exists but Ben's hands on my back and his lips on my lips and my fingertips and his cheekbones and my thundering heartbeat.

I never knew kissing had a rhythm. I never even thought

of it, beyond lips mashed together. But I can feel it like a bass line, somehow steady and urgent at once. Ben pulls me even closer, not an inch between us, and this time I don't worry about boners, because if there are rules about that happening, he's definitely, *definitely* breaking them, too.

I kiss him even harder.

"Oh," he says faintly. And I have this limitless feeling, suddenly, like I'm capable of anything. I could stop time or lift a car or press my tongue between his lips.

"You're not bad at this," he says.

"I'm not?"

"I mean, we should definitely keep practicing. Always room for improvement." I feel him smile against my lips.

I smile back. "Infinite do-overs."

"I like that," he says. "It sounds like us."

CHAPTER TWENTY

BEN

I've been home from my fourth first date with Arthur for a couple hours now, but I'm still coasting on my happy high. It's like the satisfaction I just got from a scene I wrote, where an old nemesis of Ben-Jamin unexpectedly popped back in and is making things extra tense. It's this exciting feeling of everything falling into place. Except this happiness is a real thing everyone can see. Like holding Arthur's hand as we left karaoke. Like the first kiss. Like the second first kiss.

I can't focus anymore, so I close my laptop. All I can think about is how much I want to still be out on the streets hanging with Arthur. Or even having him over to hang out. Wherever.

I have to talk to him. I don't even text, I just call.

"Hello?" Arthur asks.

"Hey."

"It's actually you. Not a butt-dial. I get everyone's butt-dials. Always have. Always will. Unless I change my name. Identity change seems like a good idea since I sang you a song about a rat."

I have only said one word on this call—a call *I* made—and I'm already ready to settle into another few hours of Arthur rambling. It's better than my favorite Lorde and Lana Del Rey songs.

"You can sing a different song next time," I say. I like that we'll have a next time. That even though things have gone wrong, we've tried to make it right. "So I was nervous to admit this at karaoke, but—"

"Please don't tell me you're actually a bunch of rats wearing a cute boy as a disguise."

"Worse." I take a deep, dramatic breath. "I haven't listened to *Hamilton*."

He doesn't say anything. Then the line goes dead.

Arthur texts: I'm sorry for hanging up, but I'm speechless. I really need to know something: HOW DOES THIS HAPPEN? HAMILTON HAS BEEN OUT FOR YEARS!!!

I laugh at his ridiculousness. Whoa three exclamation points, I text back.

!!!!!!!!!!!!!!!!!!!!!! he says.

I'm actually glad we're doing this over text.

BEN HUGO ALEJO!!!!

So we're breaking out the full poet name.

So you've heard nothing of this millennium's greatest phenomenon?

I've heard some stuff. but I haven't gone out of my way to sit thru it all. It's like Terminator movies. I know I should watch them but I haven't gotten around to it

You did not just compare the history of our great nation to the Terminator franchise.

Haha

BEN. The entire album is on YouTube for free. You need this 142 minutes and 13 seconds in your life.

Pls tell me you had to google how long the soundtrack is

You have no idea what you've gotten yourself into.

Ok. if I agree to try it, can I call you back?

PUT IT DOWN IN WRITING.

Do u have a middle name?

Arthur JAMES Seuss is not interested in your changing the subject.

I promise I'll try out Hamilton for mega fanboy Arthur James Seuss

I'm shaking my head and smiling when Arthur calls me back. "I'm sorry I had to hang up on you," he says. "But *Hamilton* is very serious business."

"I get that now." I'm staring at my ceiling and I really wish he was here.

"Good. Because I don't want to hang up on you again. Not my finest moment."

"If you do, I'm going to write you into my story and kill you off."

"You're writing a book?!"

"It's never going to be a real book, but it's a story I'm trying to finish for me."

"Is it *our* epic story?"

"No chill. You have no chill."

"Nope. So what's it about?"

I hesitate, like I'm about to not be cool enough for him. Cool is the thing I feel like I've had going for me. It's not brains, it's not money. But coolness has been my plus. "You're going to make fun of me."

"I sang you a song about a rat."

"Good point." If Arthur takes away all my cool points and can't embrace my nerd-ness, we're not going to be a good match anyway. Loving the same things I do is really important for me this time around. In my former squad I was the mega nerd, and I wish they were as into things as I get. Like how Hudson took a week to read *Harry Potter and the Cursed Child* and I was done within six hours. Or how they'd shrug off my suggestions for fun group costumes like *Super Smash* characters or Hogwarts students.

"It's a fantasy book. *The Wicked Wizard War.* My character, Ben-Jamin, is the chosen one in this war between wizards."

"I want to read it," Arthur says. "Right now."

"Really?"

"It's you in a world of magic. Of course."

"It's really nerdy."

"I like nerdy and I like you. Has anyone else read it?"

"Literally no one."

"I have to have this."

"What if you don't like it? What if you don't like it so much that you no longer like me?" I'm not trying to get canceled right as we really sync up.

"This is impossible. Trust me."

It's weird how it's easier to trust Arthur than it is to trust people I've known way longer. Like Dylan and Hudson and Harriett. My parents. It's not even that it's kind of low-risk because I'm not sure how long Arthur will even be in my life—it's more that I'm counting on knowing him for a long time and I want him to know the real me as soon as possible.

"Okay, I'll let you read it, but I got to warn you. You're right that this is me in a world of magic. Which means Hudson is a character too. I get it if you don't want to read that."

Arthur goes quiet, and here is where he's going to jump ship. To write about someone is so personal, even in a world with fire-breathing children and flying dragon services, and a lot of the good stuff between me and Hudson is there. I don't know if that's going to be hard for Arthur or not.

"If you've written about Hudson, maybe this means I'll pop up in the story one day?" Arthur asks.

"Let's see how nice you are about the book."

"I'm going to be the most generous critic."

"And the only."

"That's me. The one." Arthur pauses. "I have an idea."

"Yeah?"

"You listen to *Hamilton* while I read *The Wicked Wizard War*."

"Deal."

We get off the phone.

I can't believe I'm attaching *The Wicked Wizard War* to an email that I'm not just sending to myself. I really hope Arthur genuinely likes it. I'll know he hates it if he just tells me he thinks Ben-Jamin is hot or that my chapter titles are cool. I hit send and cross my fingers.

I go to YouTube and get *Hamilton* going.

I press play, and I'm going to be really real here: I don't know who Alexander Hamilton is. I mean, I googled him earlier this year because I thought he was a past president and Ma corrected me, which embarrassed me even though the only other person in the room was Pa. But I'm not sure I still have a handle on what he's done. If you're not a superhero or a sorcerer, my memory is bad at retaining any information about you. But as I lie on my side, reading the lyrics of the first song as it's playing, I'm immediately pulled into Hamilton's story.

And Arthur is into my story. He texts me after reading about Ben-Jamin getting his powers during a snowstorm and how he already wants *The Wicked Wizard War* to be a movie so he can buy Hot Topic shirts and Ben-Jamin Funko Pops. He's being overly generous, but I really love it when he keeps texting me favorite parts. It's all the scenes that were really cool to me and I wasn't sure if they would be cool to anyone else. I really like hearing which parts have him laughing and which ones get his heart racing. It's the greatest ego boost. Like maybe I have it in me to entertain strangers too.

And for the next couple hours, we keep texting each other our favorite parts. Hamilton not throwing away his shot as Ben-Jamin rejects his destiny. King George sending a fully armed battalion to remind the colonists of his love as Enchantress Eva predicts tragedy for a ragtag group of wizards. Hamilton rising up as Ben-Jamin rides into battle on a one-winged dragon. The Schuyler sisters getting me helpless as Arthur loses it over Ben-Jamin getting drunk with Duke Dill. History's eyes and coming of age in their young nation and making a million mistakes. Flirty touches and first kisses and hearts that turn out to be wrong.

Arthur reaches the end of everything I've written, where Ben-Jamin is fighting some monsters in a glass town, and he wants to talk, but I can't pull away from the tension between Hamilton and Angelica Schuyler, or Hamilton being a dumbass and cheating, or Eliza's haunting song and shit just getting super real that I can't believe I'm so caught up in something that happened centuries ago. Then "It's Quiet Uptown" comes on, and wow, I'm about to cry, and by the end of it I press pause and call Arthur.

"You're not done yet," Arthur says. Of course he knows where I'm at in the musical.

"I'm calling it quits. This shit is getting too sad."

"Oh yeah. 'It's Quiet Uptown' is brutal. But you have to finish."

"Okay. Will you stay on the phone with me? It'll be easier for me to yell at you if this gets sadder."

"My pleasure."

I wait for Arthur to sync up with me and we press play at the exact same second. I close my eyes, listening to the last twenty minutes, and it feels like Arthur is right beside me.

"Wait, is Hamilton going to die here—"

"So Burr—"

"No spoilers!"

"It's history!"

"History that I don't know."

And the gunshot goes off.

"Burr is a bastard," I say.

"Hamilton really wasn't all that great himself—"

"No commentary!"

The last song comes on and a tear finally breaks through. The longing in Eliza's voice as she sings about aching to see Hamilton again, and wow, I loved every second of this.

"Whatever *Hamilton* fans are called, Arthur, I am one of them."

"You're not just saying that? You're not obligated to like it, though you would be wrong not to."

"No, I'm a total Hamil-head."

"We're called Hamilfans, actually."

I tell him how I want to write *Hamilton* and Harry Potter crossover fanfiction and call it *The Great American Fantasy Novel* and stage all those duels in the dueling club and what houses I would sort everyone in. I take a deep breath. "All history should be taught through rap by Lin-Manuel Miranda."

"Maybe *The Wicked Wizard War* will become the next Broadway hit!"

Arthur tells me everything he loves about *TWWW*, and all I can think about is how I wish he was actually by my side right now, so I could feel him laughing against me and kiss him for making me feel smarter than I actually am.

". . . and when Ben-Jamin cracked the enchantress's wand, I yelled and my dad came into the room to ask me if everything was okay and then told me to shut up."

It's almost two a.m., and I could talk to him until my

body forces a shutdown on me like an overheated laptop.

"Arthur?"

"Ben?"

"Thanks for reading. And for *Hamilton*."

"Thanks for listening. And for *The Wicked Wizard War*."

"I want to see you again tomorrow."

"Date?"

"Why not."

"So is this a fifth first date?"

"Second date, Arthur."

"Wow. Second date. We finally got there."

"How lucky we are to be alive right now, right?"

"Oh my god, you're speaking Hamilton—I'm just so into you. I'm helpless."

I'm so into him too.

Saturday, July 21

Dylan calls me on FaceTime as I'm getting ready to meet up with Arthur.

"Hey," I say. I'm naked from the top up because I'm not sure which shirt I want to wear yet.

"Morning strip show," he says. "Dylan like."

I hold up a solid white T-shirt and a solid green T-shirt. "Which one?"

"Green. What are you doing? Let's hang out. I'm bored.

Samantha has to work until six."

I put on the green shirt. "I'm meeting up with Arthur."

"Cool. Let's all go chill."

"I think I need some one-on-one time with Arthur."

"Whoa. Knife to the heart, Big Ben."

"You're kidding." He's not playing this card on me.

"You were going to hang with just me and Samantha last night before Arthur was going to come around."

"Yeah, but you guys needed me too after your future-wife comment. It took away the pressure. Same with me and Arthur."

"I love you, man, but we didn't need you there. I said something stupid, but Samantha and I would've hung out with or without you."

"Okay. But you only want to see me right now because Samantha is busy and you're bored." It was the same deal with Harriett.

"I'm not seeing what's wrong with that. You're my best friend."

I don't know what a fight between me and Dylan would look like because arguing has never been our thing. But it's hard to just joke my way through this one. "Right, and Arthur is becoming more than a guy I just like. I got to give that some time and attention. I want to hang with you too, but this thing with Arthur is just so new and limited. I got to see how this plays out."

Dylan nods. "What's the winning scenario for you here, Bennison? Long-distance relationship? Friends on Instagram who like each other's pictures?"

I shrug. "I'm just going to live in the moment. That's the only way to see where we end up."

"I will let you live in the moment because it sounds serious and awesome," Dylan says. "But be careful, okay? I like Arthur and don't want to have to kick his ass if he breaks your heart."

"No ass kicking needed," I say, hoping pretty damn hard that Arthur won't turn out to be Hudson 2.0.

Arthur and I leave the High Line holding hands.

After that conversation with Dylan, I really needed Arthur telling me how Ms. Angelica "Looking for a mind at work" Schuyler is a Ravenclaw, or how screwed the wizarding world would've been if Hamilton was not only a Death Eater but Voldemort's right-hand man. But with every good thing, like kisses while we wait to cross the street or our hands finding each other again after crowds split us up, I'm still rocked by this idea of everything ending.

Maybe this won't work out and I won't care about it ending. But I can't get from A to B without us being A and B first. Live in the moment.

Except it's hard to think about living in the moment

when Arthur brings up time travel. "If you could time travel," he says, "would you go to the past or the future?"

"I can only choose one, right?"

Arthur nods as we cross through Union Square to make our way to the Strand Bookstore since he hasn't been there yet. The Union Square area is the place to be for the bookish crowds. There's a four-story Barnes & Noble, where I attended a midnight release party for *Harry Potter and the Cursed Child*, and a few blocks over is Books of Wonder, where I've met some authors and gotten graphic novels signed.

It would be really helpful to jump into the future to see how everything with Arthur plays out. But I wouldn't even want to do it hypothetically. I want to trust that everything runs its course for some reason. Maybe meeting Arthur is supposed to teach me to be open to another dude in the future, to be bold and get his name and number if we meet somewhere out in the world.

"If I go to the past, can I change things?"

"Sure."

Part of me wishes Hudson and I never dated. We were better friends than boyfriends. The good times were good, but I don't think it was worth losing a friend over. "I would go back to the past, like a couple years ago, with the winning lottery numbers for my mom. Change the game up for us."

"You're nobler than I am."

"What would you do?"

"I'm Team Future."

"Because of school?"

"Other reasons too," Arthur says. He squeezes my hand. "Probably better I go to the future. If I go anywhere near the past, I'm just going to write *Hamilton* before Lin-Manuel Miranda can."

"You would dick him over?"

"Fine. Cowrite *with* him."

I spot a churros food truck parked by the Best Buy and across the street from the park. "Have you ever had a churro before?"

"Not sure I know what that is."

"It's just fried dough. I like them best with cinnamon, but sugar is cool too. Come on, my treat."

We rush to the cart. The guy asks me what we would like in Spanish and I answer in English. One cinnamon, one sugar, one chocolate, one raspberry. We go to the park to eat the churros so we don't get powder and crumbs all over the books at the Strand.

"Do you speak Spanish?"

"Not really. I picked up some stuff from just listening to my parents speak to my aunts and uncles, but I understand more than I can speak." Fourth-Grade Ben got really tired of not knowing what the other Puerto Rican kids were saying about him behind his back. I take a bite out of the cinnamon churro, which has that freshly baked warmness to it. "Which one you trying first?"

Arthur grabs the chocolate churro. "This is crack," he says, taking another bite. "Where have these been? Is this a New York thing?"

"I don't think so? Some Mexican restaurants might have them as dessert."

"I'm a cookie guy, but I can be converted to a churro guy." He takes another bite. "I feel like a whole new world has opened up to me. Between you being so white and not speaking Spanish I keep forgetting you're even Puerto Rican. Your last name always reminds me though."

I freeze with the churro between my teeth. Arthur continues chomping away at his chocolate churro, completely unaware that he's just nudged me really hard in one of my sore spots. It's 2018. How are people—even good people—still saying shit like this? I mean, I'm an idiot too—I learned that with Kent at the Yale meetup. I swallow what I can and drop the rest of the churro in the cardboard tray.

It's really not my job to train people on catching themselves.

It's really not my job to reprogram people so they not only don't say something stupid, but that they don't think it.

But I want Arthur to be better. To be worthy and see that I'm worthy.

I look around at all the other people around us, couples or family or friends or strangers, and I wonder how many of their days are going south because of nonsense coming out of someone's mouth. I stare at the ground because I can't look Arthur in the eyes right now.

"I used to wish my last name was Allen," I say. "Alejo was too hard for people, and teachers would never mispronounce Allen. My second-grade teacher kept calling me 'Uh-ledge-oh' until my mother shut it down." I can't explain, but without even looking at Arthur, I feel this thickness around us like he's realized what he said. "Not looking the part of Puerto Rican messed me up. I know I get some privilege points from looking white, but Puerto Ricans don't come in one shade."

"I'm sorry—"

"And not every Puerto Rican is going to run down the block for churros or speak Spanish. I know you didn't mean anything bad, but I like you and I want to trust you like me too for being me. And that you'll get to know me and not just think you know me because of society's stupidity."

Arthur scoots closer to me and rests his head on my shoulder. "If I could time travel, I'd rewind five minutes and not be so stupid. I know that's an empty gesture because this is a make-believe scenario, but I really would. I would even give up the opportunity to cowrite *Hamilton* with Lin-Manuel, which, let's face it, I have no place being anywhere near that anyway. But I really don't like hurting you or making you feel bad, and I know I've done that a few times now."

"It's okay."

"It's not. It's really not. I'm really sorry, Ben."

"I know you didn't mean any harm. I just want to put it out there. I love being Puerto Rican and I want to feel as Puerto Rican around you as I do at home because that's who I am."

"So I'm not getting the boot?"

"Nope. I take your time-travel answer to heart. Sucks that you won't get to hang with Lin-Manuel though. Guess you'll have to settle for another Puerto Rican."

"Good. I still have a lot to learn about you anyway."

"And you probably know everything there is to know about Lin-Manuel already, right?"

"I know nothing of Pulitzer Prize–winning Lin-Manuel Miranda, who was born on January sixteenth and attended Wesleyan and named his son after the crab in *Little Mermaid*."

"I'm walking away from you." I take the basket of churros. "And you've lost your churro privileges."

Arthur gathers up his shopping bag from the Strand, where he bought magnets, postcards, and a Strand shirt, and now we're riding the train uptown to his place on the Upper West Side. I know the neighborhood well. I used to go up there all the time with Hudson because of the skating rink, and yeah, he had a thing for the Hudson River too. Acted like it was named for him. Arthur wants to share his view of the Hudson River and just sit there with me, and I'm not bringing up the times I sat there with Hudson because what am I going to do, not go anywhere I've been with Hudson? Not happening.

Besides, our options are kind of limited. I can't bring him home without feeling too exposed—and it may be too soon to meet the parents. I wouldn't mind, but I can't force it the way I tried with meeting Hudson's mom. That was a fail on my part.

Arthur and I are tired now though. I'm probably better off just going home and sleeping, but I don't want to leave him. By the time I wake up, I would only be able to text or call or FaceTime him and I'll miss hanging out in real life.

"Too bad we can't charge ourselves like phones," I say.

"We can. It's called sleep," Arthur says. "It's just that phones don't take eight hours to charge."

"I like sleep. A lot. Summer school is costing me enough sleep, and now you? Betrayal."

The train is going local since it's Saturday, which means we might be sitting tight for thirty minutes. Maybe forty or fifty minutes if someone has pissed off the MTA gods.

"I'm going to power nap," I say.

"Can I join you?"

I wrap my arm around him and he comes closer to me. The car isn't packed and I'm able to spread my legs a bit to get more comfortable. "I can't sleep without sound. Mind if I put one earbud in?"

"What do you listen to?"

"I just put my songs on shuffle."

Arthur whips out his phone and boom, the *Hamilton* soundtrack. He plays it from the beginning as we close our eyes, cuddled up against each other. It's like everything I imagined for myself last night while I was alone in bed and Arthur was on the phone listening with me, except we're really together this time. This kind of freedom is enough inspiration to go away to college and live in a dorm room where I can hang out with whoever I want whenever I want.

I'm half-asleep, but awake enough that when our stop comes up, I'll be able to jump up and drag Arthur out of the train before the doors close. Someone kicks my foot and I open my eyes to apologize for stretching out because I'm definitely on some inconsiderate shit, and this guy is hovering over us. He's holding a little boy's hand.

"Sorry," I say.

"No one wants to see that," the man says, gesturing at me and Arthur with his newspaper. He keeps standing there. Other passengers pay attention.

"See what?" I sit up and Arthur opens his eyes; I get this

240

feeling like he wasn't really asleep.

"Just keep it at home, okay? I got my kid here."

"Keep *what* at home?" I say.

"You know what you're doing," the man says. He's getting red in the face, and I don't know if he's pissed or embarrassed because I'm not taking his shit.

"Yeah. I'm hanging out with a guy I like." I stand up. My heart is pounding because I don't trust this guy to not do something stupid. But someone is filming him, so if this really goes south, I have hope this will go viral so I can share it with the police so this guy won't harass anyone else.

"I don't need my son seeing shit like this on the train when we're just trying to go home."

His problem is not a real problem. I'm losing the courage to tell him this. Even though my shoulders are high, my knees are shaking. This guy is going to lay me out any moment. Arthur stands up and I push him behind me.

"It's okay, it's okay," Arthur says to the man. "We're not going to do anything else."

"Screw this guy," I say. I really wish Dylan were here to back us up.

The man's son starts crying, like I'm the real aggressor here, like I provoked his asshole father because I was resting with another boy in public. I really feel for this kid and the tough road he may have ahead of him if he likes anyone who isn't a hetero girl.

The man picks up his son. "You're lucky I don't want to pop you in front of my kid."

Arthur tries dragging me away, and I only step back because he's begging me and my name is a choked breath and he's crying and he's probably more scared than that five-year-old kid. Some guy with a gym bag steps in front of the man and tells him to keep it moving, that it's done and over.

Except it's not over, because Arthur and I have to carry this around.

We get off at the next stop and Arthur loses it. I hold his shoulders, like Dylan wants me to do when he's panicking, but Arthur shakes me off and looks around the platform. "I thought New York was cool with . . ." He takes a deep breath and wipes the tears from his cheeks. "Gay bars and Pride parades and same-sex couples holding hands. What the hell. I thought New York had it together."

"For the most part, I think. But every city has its assholes." I want to hug him, but he doesn't want to be touched right now. Like any affection is going to become a target sign on our backs. Like we'll get punished because our hearts are different. "Are you okay?"

"No. I've never been threatened before. And I was *so* scared for you. Why didn't you just stay quiet?"

I should've. I shouldn't have endangered Arthur just because I wanted to speak up for us and everyone like us.

"I'm sorry. I was scared too."

We stand there for a few minutes and when the next train comes, Arthur doesn't want to get on. Same for the next train. He's collected himself as best as can be expected by the third train, and he's only willing to get on because it's packed so there will be more people to protect us if something happens again.

I don't like that the same world that brought us together is also scaring him.

"I'm not leaving your side until you're home," I say.

Arthur looks around the train, and his tired, hurt blue eyes look up at me.

And his hand links into mine and he doesn't break the hold the entire ride.

CHAPTER TWENTY-ONE
ARTHUR

"Did they respond to your text?" Ben asks as I press the button for the third floor. "I don't want to walk in on your parents having sex."

"Eww. They don't do that."

"They did at least once."

"Never. No." I gag.

"You're funny." He takes my hand and smiles. "This place is nice."

"On behalf of Uncle Milton, thank you." I pause for a moment in the alcove. When you step off the elevator, there's not really a hallway—just a little nook with three doors, leading to apartments A, B, and C.

"A for Arthur," Ben says, like this is the most satisfying coincidence of his life.

"We planned that."

"I figured," he says smoothly—but when I glance back at him, he's chewing his lip.

"Are you nervous?"

"Yes."

I squeeze his hand. "That's insanely cute."

And—wow. I'm actually about to do this. I'm bringing this boy home to meet my parents. I'm pretty sure that's not a typical second-date activity. But maybe Ben and I aren't typical.

My parents.

I don't know why I suggested it. Tonight just rattled me, I guess. I can't stop thinking about the guy on the subway and his crying kid and the look on Ben's face and the way it made me feel like the whole world was watching me. All I wanted, in that moment, was to be alone. I've never wanted to be alone so badly in my entire life.

But Ben stayed. He just *stayed*. And now I don't want him to leave. I'm not ready to say goodnight.

I glance back at Ben as I fumble with the keys.

I'm not going to panic. I'm not. This is going to be fine. Totally great. Quick visit. Super casual. So what if my parents know a little too much about Ben. So what if they can barely keep it together around regular friends, much less boyfriends. Not that Ben's my boyfriend. I can just picture what would happen if I introduced him like that.

Me: Meet my boyfriend, Ben!

Parents: *showering us with condoms* HELLO, BOY-FRIEND BEN!!!

Ben: *launches self into the sun*

But—okay. If he's not my boyfriend, what do I call him? My friend? My gentleman caller? The guy with whom I think about having sex 99 percent of my waking hours? And yes, I mean that both ways. I spend 99 percent of my waking hours thinking about how I'd like to spend 99 percent of my waking hours having sex with Ben.

My parents don't need to know that.

Okay, I'm just going to casually open this door and breathe and—

"You must be Ben. So nice to finally meet you!" My mom beams up at him from the couch. Where she's sitting. Right next to Dad.

I gape at them.

She pauses the TV and stands, coming straight over to shake Ben's hand. "We've heard so much about you." Dad nods pleasantly from the couch, and that's when I notice they're both wearing pajamas and glasses. I'm sorry, but what kind of alternate universe did I just step into? What mythical creature bit my parents and turned them into a lovey-dovey Saturday-night-on-the-sofa kind of couple?

"Come hang with us," Dad calls from the couch, while Mom offers Ben some water.

Ben peers around the apartment, gaze flitting from painting to painting.

"Uncle Milton likes horses."

"I cracked that code," says Ben.

We settle onto the love seat.

"So, Ben, tell us about yourself." Mom slides back onto the couch, leaning forward to really nail that uncomfortable eye contact with Ben. "How's your summer been?"

"Um. Great."

"I bet you're keeping busy," Mom says. "I'm glad Arthur's finally spending more time outside the apartment, too. I kept telling him, when are you ever going to get the opportunity to explore New York for the summer? Go enjoy it. Don't spend your time watching YouTube videos of—"

"So, Ben actually grew up here," I interrupt. "He's a New York native."

"Very cool," says Dad.

"Did you always live in Georgia?" Ben asks, looking back and forth between my parents.

Dad shakes his head. "I grew up in Westchester, and Mara's from New Haven."

"Yankees," I say. Ben glances at me and smiles.

Mom turns casually to Ben. "So are you working this summer?"

"Uh." Ben looks like he wants to melt into the couch. "I'm taking a class."

"Oh, wonderful. For college credit?" She smiles expectantly.

"Mom, don't interrogate him."

"Oh, come on. I'm just curious. Your dad and I were just talking about how much summer jobs have changed. When I was younger, we were all camp counselors, or we worked at Ben & Jerry's. But you guys have these fancy internships or college-prep courses. I mean, I guess that's what you've got to do, these days—"

"Mom, stop it."

"Stop what?"

I glance sideways at Ben, who's staring uncomfortably at his knees.

"Just. Stop . . . talking." I don't think I've cringed so hard in my entire life. I get it, Mom's used to a particular kind of badass. The Ethan and Jessie kind, who come with rock-solid PSAT scores and debate team trophies and National Merit Scholarships.

"I'm actually in summer school," Ben says.

Mom's eyes widen. "Oh!"

Ben looks mortified, which makes me mortified, too. My fucking parents and their fucking achievement spirals. I want to send a secret message straight into Ben's brain. *I'm not like them, okay? That stuff doesn't matter to me.*

Okay, maybe there's a tiny, minuscule part of me wondering what it would feel like to announce, *Ben's actually the world's youngest surgeon* or *Ben's working in the mayor's policy office.* As opposed to, *Ben's really weird and cagey when you ask about summer school.*

But no. None of that matters. I don't care that Ben's in summer school. I don't care if he has a fancy job, and I don't care if he ends up applying to Yale. I care about how he stood up to that asshole on the subway and how I feel seeing his name in my texts. I care about how much he cared about making my first kiss perfect.

"Ben's a writer," I say. "And he's amazing."

"No I'm not." Ben shakes his head, but he's smiling.

"He is. I've read his work."

"That's wonderful," Mom says. "What do you write?"

Ben pauses. "Fiction, I guess?"

"Ooh." Dad sits up straighter. "You know, I've always wanted to write a novel."

"Oh really?" says Mom.

"I've actually been—"

"Oh, I sincerely hope you're not about to say you've been writing the Great American Novel instead of applying for jobs. I really hope you're not about to say that."

"Mara, let's not—"

"Oh wow. It's late." I stand, face burning. "I better walk Ben to the elevator."

Ben looks uncertain. "You don't have to walk me out. I can just—"

"Oh, I'm definitely walking you out." I side-eye the hell out of my parents. Dad's stroking his beard, and Mom clasps her hands, looking slightly abashed.

"Well, Ben, I'm so glad you came," Mom says finally. "We'll have to have you here for dinner sometime."

"Mom," I say sharply, but then I catch the look on Ben's face. His eyes are wide, but he doesn't look horrified. Just bewildered and happy.

"I'm so sorry," I say as soon as the door shuts behind us.

"Why? They're really nice."

"Yeah, for like five seconds at a time, until they start tearing each other's heads off. I can't believe they did that in front of you."

"You mean the Great American Novel thing?"

"Yeah." I presss my temple. "They're such assholes to each other."

"Really? I think your mom was just busting his balls."

"No, she's for real. She always does that. She gets on him for not having a job, and then he gets defensive, and it's nonstop, and I literally wake up every morning thinking today's the day they're going to pull me aside for the whole *your father and I both love you very much, Arthur, this isn't your fault*, blah blah, et cetera. Like it's basically inevitable at this point. I don't even think the universe is rooting for Team Seuss anymore. It's just a matter of when."

"God." Ben looks at me. "Arthur."

"God Arthur, what?"

"I'm just really sorry. That sucks so much. I didn't know."

He pulls me closer and kisses me softly on the forehead, like a butterfly landing. I might actually melt. I look up at him and smile. "It's fine. I'll be fine."

"You don't have to be fine."

"I'm just sorry you had to see them being weird and awkward."

"Mine are weird and awkward, too. You'll see."

And just like that, the awfulness vanishes. Because WOW. Ben Alejo . . . wants me to meet his parents. I'm going on the hometown date. I grin up at him, trying to think of the perfect flirtatious-but-not-too-flirtatious response. But then Ben says, "Now I want to tell you something."

"Okay."

He's quiet for a moment, just breathing. He looks terrified.

"You don't have to tell me," I say quickly. "I mean. Unless you want to."

"I want to."

My stomach's doing cartwheels. Is he . . . about to say what I think he's going to say? It feels soon. But I guess New Yorkers don't really mess around. I should plan my response. Do I say it back? Is it weird if I don't? But why wouldn't I? Seriously, why the fuck not?

"It's about summer school," he says.

I stare at him. Wow. I think I could burn this whole city down with my cheeks right now. Am I just a thirsty dipshit, or am I the literal thirstiest dipshit to end all dipshits? God help me if Ben ever finds out that I thought—I *actually thought* he was going to—

Anyway. Summer school.

"What about it?" I ask.

"It's . . ." He pauses. "Okay, I just want to say first that Hudson and I are really, really over. We're not even friends anymore. You know that, right?"

"I know." I take both his hands. "Let me guess. Hudson was a jerk about summer school."

Ben looks at me strangely. "Wait."

"He's an asshole. I'm sorry, Ben, I know he was a part of your history and everything, but fuck him. There's nothing wrong with summer school, okay?"

"I know. Yeah. Okay—"

"No, it's not okay. How dare he make you feel like that. I don't care if he made straight As. I don't care if he's a Rhodes Scholar. He doesn't deserve you. He *never* deserved you."

Ben stares down at the carpet. "I should call the elevator."

"Okay, but just promise me you'll stop giving Hudson

real estate in your brain. He doesn't know anything. You're so fucking smart. I wish you could see it."

The elevator light blinks and the doors slide open.

"That's really sweet of you."

"I mean it."

"I know." The elevator starts to close, but he catches it with his foot.

I wrinkle my nose. "I don't want you to go."

"Me either." He tugs me closer.

So I kiss him and I kiss him as the doors press in around us.

I flop back onto my bed, and my whole body's buzzing. Heart, stomach, fingertips, all of it. My brain won't stop spinning. I feel like I'm living inside a love song.

Kissing Ben. Holding Ben's hand. Ben's crinkly brown eyes.

I should text him.

But when I look at my phone, I see two texts from Jessie.

The first one: **Hey!**

The second one: **Wondering if you me and E can talk.**

Sure what's up, I write back.

She responds immediately. **Too complicated for text. FaceTiming you, okay?**

I accept the call, still lying down. Still smiling dazedly.

"Whoa. Looks like someone had a good night," says

Ethan. They're on the floor of Jessie's bedroom, backs pressed against her bed. And something about the familiarity of it all makes me ache: their faces, their voices, Jessie's purple floral bedspread.

I grin. "Y'all are up late."

"So are you," says Jessie.

"So, what's up? What is this complicated thing?"

"Well." They exchange glances.

"That should be in caps, right? Complicated Thing." I laugh.

No one else laughs.

"Wait." I sit up. "Is this . . . an intervention?"

Jessie looks startled. "What?"

"It's about Ben, right? I'm too obsessed with him." I press a hand to my mouth.

They look at each other again.

"You do talk about him a lot," says Ethan.

"Guys, I'm so sorry."

I'm the worst friend on earth. Maybe I'm one of those guys who gets tunnel vision whenever he falls for someone. Maybe I'm just incurably self-centered.

"It's fine."

"No it's not. I haven't even asked you how you are."

Another furtive glance. Jessie bites her lip.

"Well," Ethan says. "I guess . . ."

But then a text from Ben pops up, obscuring half of my

screen. So . . . I told my parents that your parents invited me for dinner, and my mom turned the whole thing into wanting your whole family to come have dinner at our house tomorrow—I know that's crazy, don't be freaked out. They just really want to meet my awesome new boyfriend.

My heart leaps into my throat. Ethan's still talking—I think—but it barely even registers.

"Boyfriend," I whisper.

Ethan pauses. "What?"

"Ben just called me his boyfriend."

"When?"

"Just now. Over text."

Jessie's mouth falls open. "Oh, Arthur, really?"

I nod wordlessly.

"Damn," Ethan says. "That was fast."

Jessie nods. "Wow. Are you . . ."

But another text pops up and Jessie's voice fades to the background. Shit. Okay. I didn't mean to say boyfriend. Unless you want to say boyfriend. We don't have to label it. Wow. I'm sorry. Don't freak out.

". . . the talk?" she finishes.

"Sorry, what?" I blink. Then I shake my head quickly. "Ugh. I'm doing it again."

"No, you're good," Jessie says. "This is a big deal. Boyfriend. Wow."

"Yeah." I blink again. "Yeah."

"Go respond to him!"

"When I'm done talking to you guys."

"Arthur. Go put your boyfriend out of his misery."

My brain feels foggy, almost waterlogged. "*Boyfriend.* I'm just—"

"Arthur, go!" Jessie laughs. "We'll talk later, okay? I'm hanging up."

I hang up, too, and tap back into my Ben texts, reading and rereading until I think I might burst.

Not freaking out, I write. See you tomorrow, boyfriend.

Then I stare at the screen of my phone for five minutes straight, smiling harder than I ever have in my life.

CHAPTER TWENTY-TWO

BEN

Sunday, July 22

My boyfriend's family is coming over for dinner. I've been pretty *say what* about this all day. I dusted the bookshelves and the TV and the space underneath the couch. I dumped out all the garbage bins. I wiped down counters and the table. I did laundry so we'll have fresh hand towels in the bathroom. I lit four black-cherry candles that are mixing surprisingly well with the feast my parents are cooking up.

The doorbell rings as I'm setting the table.

I check the clock. If that's Arthur and the fam, they're early. Well, they're on time. I should've known better, because this is Arthur. But damn.

"I'll get the door," I say.

Please don't be them, please don't be them . . .

"Hey!" Arthur says, holding a box of cookies. His parents are behind him with bottles of wine.

It feels a little next-level to kiss Arthur in front of his parents, so I hug him and shake their hands.

"How are you doing?" Mr. Seuss asks.

"Starving," I say.

"It smells great," Mrs. Seuss says.

I don't know if she's talking about the candles or the dinner, but it's a win either way. "Come in," I say. The hallway feels too tight for four people, and I'm more self-conscious of that now than ever before. No matter how much cleaning I did, there's no pretending that the apartment isn't way tinier than they're used to, or that the two chairs we borrowed from my neighbor don't stand out at the dinner table, where we'll all be elbow to elbow shortly. "Ma, Pa. This is Mr. and Mrs. Seuss. And Arthur."

My parents know better than to make fun of their last name considering how much shit they've gotten for theirs, especially my mom, whose maiden name is Almodóvar, and people pretty much made a game out of butchering how to pronounce it.

"Thank you so much for coming," Ma says. "I'm Isabel, this is Diego."

"Mara," Mrs. Seuss says while shaking their hands. "Your home is lovely. Thank you for inviting us over."

"Of course. And you, Arthur," Ma says, her head tilting

with a smile. "The legend."

He smiles at me and back at her.

"Nice to meet you, Mrs. Alejo." Not going to lie, I love the way he says our last name. It's not a perfect pronunciation, but he'll get there with time.

Arthur gives Ma cookies from Levain Bakery, which is a tiny shop on the Upper West Side known for its huge cookies and long lines out the door. The fact that they waited in that line to bring us dessert means a lot.

Dinner is almost ready, and I feel like the world's most unnecessary tour guide as I show them around the living room. But when I see Arthur studying every picture hanging from the wall, I remember that home isn't about how big the space is but how we fill it. Above the TV is the framed Puerto Rican flag that Abuelita brought over when she and Ma moved from their home city of Rincón to New York. The side-by-side first-day-of-school photos of me and Pa, where we would look like identical clones if it weren't for Ma's freckles across my face. The oil paintings my parents made on their first date because Pa wanted to wow Ma with an experience more memorable than just dinner. The coffee table we found on the curb outside our building, which slides open to reveal decks of cards and board games. I still feel exposed, but I'm no longer worried about being judged.

"Where's your bedroom?" Arthur says.

"Don't worry about it," Mr. Seuss says.

Pa walks over with some coquito for everyone to try, which is basically just coconut eggnog. Arthur and I get the virgin coquitos, and normally I can have some of the regular one, but they want to make a good impression in front of Arthur's parents, which I respect. Team Seuss seems into the coquito. Mrs. Seuss already wants the recipe, and she and Mr. Seuss follow Pa over to the kitchen.

"So far, so good, right?" I say. Arthur doesn't seem to hear me. He's looking around like he's in Hogwarts. "Arthur?"

"Oh. Sorry. What?"

"Nothing. What are you thinking about?"

"I still can't believe I'm here. I'm in my boyfriend's living room. I have a boyfriend. You are that boyfriend. This is your living room."

"You really like it?"

"I really do."

"I'll show you my bedroom later. Let's wait until they're super buzzed."

We rejoin the group and Ma gets everyone seated. She doesn't want the families bunched together so she's sitting next to Mrs. Seuss and Pa is sitting next to Mr. Seuss and I'm across from Arthur. We're all still really close, like we're huddled around a fireplace in a cold forest instead of a dinner table that has no business seating six people. The table is set with pernil, ham with pineapple sauce, yellow rice, pink beans, and salad. Maybe Arthur's family should come over every weekend so we can eat like kings more often. I just hope they like the food now. I was almost tempted to ask my parents to fry some chicken and mash some potatoes and grill some corn on the cob, but that would've only stopped Arthur from discovering more about me. The little things that form the bigger picture.

"Mind if we pray?" Ma asks.

"Ma, no, they're Jewish."

"Oh, it's absolutely fine. Please do," Mrs. Seuss says.

Ma looks mortified as she turns to Arthur's parents. "Oh no—Benito neglected to mention you're Jewish. I made pork. I am so sorry. I can make some—"

Mrs. Seuss leans forward. "Oh, please don't worry! We don't keep kosher."

"We love pork," Mr. Seuss adds. "No objection to pork. Pigs die for us constantly. It looks delicious, by the way. What do you call this dish?"

"Pernil," Pa says.

Team Seuss just got their word of the day.

I'm holding Mrs. Seuss's and Pa's hands and resting my foot on Arthur's as Ma prays. She thanks God for the food and for bringing me and Arthur together so we can enjoy this food with new friends, and I peek at Arthur, whose eyes are still closed, but he's smiling so hard I can see his beautiful teeth. Like he wished on enough stars that his dreams are coming true. We all say amen.

Mrs. Seuss takes a bite of the ham. "This is delicious."

Ma taps her elbow and places the other hand on her heart. "Thank you. Mami taught me when I was seven. She was an afterschool teacher, so I would have to fend for myself when I got home. I'd make a snack and get dinner started while doing my homework. I love cooking."

"Do you cook professionally?" Mrs. Seuss asks.

"No. I do accounting for a gym. I'm scared I'll fall out of love with cooking if someone's paying me to do it. It'll become work and I won't be excited to come home and cook with my family."

Man, I love my mom. She's the kind of person who will make everyone feel at home even if she has a problem with you, sort of like she was with Hudson. But I can tell she's already so comfortable with Mrs. Seuss, like I can maybe even see them hanging out. Except Mrs. Seuss will be leaving at the end of the summer and taking my boyfriend back to Georgia with her.

"You're an attorney, right?" Ma asks.

"Yes. At Smilowitz & Bernbaum. It's a great firm. One that's been very relaxed about Arthur following your son into a post office instead of running his coffee errand."

We all laugh. I never realized that Arthur went into the post office just to follow me in.

"How about you, Diego?" Mr. Seuss asks.

"I'm an assistant manager at Duane Reade. It's not fancy, but we're comfortable. I have a great team—mostly great. Bills get paid. Food makes its way to the table. Ben gets his allowance. Anything else would be extra."

I think about extra a lot. Vacations to all these tropical islands I'm always seeing in movies. Owning expensive sneakers that I can take out into the world and not keep in a closet, scared that I'll mess them up. Family car to get us out of here on weekends. Updated iPhones and laptops. College since I won't score a scholarship. These are all things Arthur's family doesn't have to worry about as much.

"Yourself?" Pa asks Mr. Seuss.

"Computer programming. I'm in between gigs right now because of the relocating," Mr. Seuss says. He turns to Mrs. Seuss immediately. "Which is not anyone's fault. I thought it'd be easier to find a position of interest that can be managed with our time frame before we go back home."

"Do you miss working?" Ma asks.

"So much. The first week I got to watch a lot of Netflix, but that's satisfying, not fulfilling. I've done a dozen consultations and not been hired yet, and it's really taking a toll on me—on *us*." He gestures to Arthur and Mrs. Seuss. "But we're hanging tight."

"The coquito will make you feel better," Pa says. "Embarrassing the boys might help too, right?"

"Yes, please," Mr. Seuss says.

"No," Arthur and I say at the same time.

Our parents trade stories about what we were like as kids. I thought I was in the clear with secrets because Arthur knows I'm in summer school now, but I wasn't prepared for him to learn about ten-year-old Ben and Dylan acting like we were on a reality show called *Being Bad Boys* without realizing how sexual that sounded. And Arthur sinks into his chair while everyone, myself included, bursts into laughter because of how often he used to take selfies with mannequins on his dad's phone while they shopped for school clothes.

"I have another one," Mrs. Seuss says.

"No you don't," Arthur says. "You're fresh out of stories."

"A few months ago, when Arthur found out we'd be spending the summer in New York, Michael and I came home early from a friend's birthday party and Arthur was—"

"Mom!" Arthur shouts.

"—watching a YouTube video of a *Dear Evan Hansen* song and *belting* along while dancing."

"It was magnificent," Mr. Seuss says.

I don't laugh this time because Arthur seems a little upset.

I stand. "Arthur, let's go to my room. I can show you the cover I drew for my book."

Arthur practically knocks into his dad getting out of his seat. "Yes, please."

"But wait, we're still eating," Ma says.

"Food isn't going anywhere," I say, taking Arthur's hand. "We'll be back."

"Keep the door open!" Mr. Seuss shouts.

We go to my bedroom with flushed faces.

Like we're going to lock the door and get wild in here with them outside.

Except when we enter my room, I lead Arthur out of sight and I kiss him with this howling hunger that's demanding more time with him each passing day.

I take a breath. "You okay?"

"Better now. I just don't like being teased about Broadway. The videos keep me going. I saw two shows last month, but they weren't my top shows." His eyes widen. "Oh. That's shitty to say. That my Broadway shows weren't good enough. I was lucky to go to any. I just keep entering the lottery for *Hamilton* and *Dear Evan Hansen*, but no luck."

"There's still time," I say. "And it could've been worse out there."

"True."

Arthur looks around the room. He walks over to my desk. "So this is where the future bestselling and global phenomenon *The Wicked Wizard War* gets written. Where's the book cover?"

I reach into my drawer and pull out a purple folder where I drew some of the little monsters in the story. And I pull out the book cover. It looks like a Harry Potter cover except there's a Ben-looking wizard in the center and he's hiding behind a demolished wall as evil wizards search for him. It is not good at all, and even Arthur laughs.

He looks around at the rest of the room. I put Hudson's breakup box in my parents' closet a couple hours ago. I should just get rid of it. I don't like hiding anything from Arthur. But it's just like the old posts on Instagram that I can't get myself to just delete. Like Hudson never happened. Like he's someone to be ashamed of. And throwing away the good memories feels like a slap in the face to our history. It has nothing to do with the future.

I don't know.

"I really like your room," Arthur says. "This entire apartment. I hope this doesn't come off as wrong, but I really love it because it feels more like home than my own house does. Everything here feels like it matters. If something broke or got lost, you would notice. So many things in my house feel so replaceable."

"Maybe you just don't know why some of it matters?"

"Maybe. I need to get better at asking questions." Arthur sits on my bed.

I sit beside him and I think about sex because that's what happens when your beautiful boyfriend is in bed with you. If we make a move to have sex while he's still in New York, it's going to be his first time. That's wild pressure. I want to prove myself to him so that no matter what happens between us, he won't ever look back at me and regret our choice. Like how I don't regret Hudson and me losing our virginity together and I hope he doesn't either. People change and he did and I did too, but who we were when we had sex still feels right to me. I hope I always feel right to Arthur.

I lean in to kiss him when my mom calls for us.

"We're done talking about you! Come finish your dinner."

I squeeze his hand and we go back out there.

The rest of dinner is painless. We're all laughing together, not at one another. The only thing that could've made the night a little extra perfect is if Dylan, and yeah, Samantha too, were here. I hate that I'll have to recount the night to Dylan and that I won't be able to do it justice. That I'll forget some jokes that had us all laughing so hard. But I guess that's just the cycle that comes with dating—time spent with best friends is minimized and you get this whole new life they're not always a part of.

Arthur and I help clear the table as my dad brings out the cookies Team Seuss brought over. The cookies are huge—like, it looks like someone put four globs of cookie dough too close to one another on the tray and a mega cookie happened. Two are double chocolate chip, two are oatmeal raisin, two are chocolate-chip walnut.

"Thanks so much for bringing these over," Pa says. He offers the box to Arthur.

"You get first dibs for hosting us," Arthur says.

"Kiss-ass," Mr. Seuss says with a smile.

Pa grabs one double-chocolate-chip cookie and Arthur watches him take a bite with this wide-eyed look, like my dad just took Arthur's car for a joyride and crashed it. Ma grabs the other double chocolate chip because she's never been big on anything with nuts or raisins. Arthur stares at her like she just got the last available ticket in the world for *Hamilton*.

Smart money is on Arthur wanting one of those cookies.

"This is so good," Ma says.

Arthur grabs the chocolate-chip walnut cookie and picks out the walnuts before eating it.

Mr. Seuss takes a bite out of the oatmeal raisin cookie. "I probably won't wait twenty minutes for a cookie again, but I'm glad we did it."

We talk a little more before calling it a night. As Arthur hugs my parents, I can't believe this is all happening. Whenever Hudson came over for dinner, he would just shake their hands like they were my bosses and not my parents. But it's also really awesome seeing our dads hug and Pa telling Mr. Seuss that they have to come back over soon since they never got around to drinking the wine they brought over. Mrs. Seuss trades numbers with Ma, and wow, if I ever write my mom back into *TWWW*, I'll have to include her enchantress BFF Mara.

Arthur and I kiss very quickly while everyone is saying bye and Team Seuss thanks us one last time before leaving.

"That was so fun," Ma says. "Arthur is wonderful. Adorable. Great manners. I really like him. The whole family."

"Me too."

"What's going to happen when he goes home?" Pa asks.

I shrug. This question sucks. "I'm just getting to know him while he's here."

I think about the way Arthur smiled so hard during dinner when he thought no one was watching him and what I could do to win as many smiles out of him as possible.

CHAPTER TWENTY-THREE
ARTHUR
Monday, July 23

"I leave the room for five minutes," Namrata says, "and now you're standing on a fucking chair."

"I'm taking a sensory motor break." I press my fist to my chest. "*Oh Benny booooooooy . . . the pipes, the pipes are calling.*"

Juliet glances up from her laptop. "I'm just glad he stopped singing 'Ben's Body Is a Wonderland.'"

"Anyway, big announcement time," says Namrata. "Guess who's dropping out of school and moving in with their parents."

I gasp. "You?"

Namrata snorts. "No, dumbass. David's roommates."

"The dino porn guys?"

"Their Kickstarter got funded, so they're taking the year

to work on *Jurassion Passion*. And apparently 714 people are willing to pay for that quality content, so." She shrugs.

"Good for them!" I bump back down into my seat, sliding the chair back to the table. "Let's throw a party."

"You want to throw a party celebrating dinosaurotica?" Juliet asks.

"I'm in a good mood, okay?"

"We noticed," says Namrata.

"Want to know why?"

"We know why. Starts with *B*, rhymes with 'when,' as in when are you going to start working on the Shumaker files?"

"Ten points to Ravenclaw!" I announce, holding my fist like a microphone. "But which Ben? Is it Affleck? Stiller? Carson? Nope, it's BENJAMIN HUGO ALEJO. My . . . boyfriend." I do a quick drumroll. "Also Ben Platt."

"Great speech," says Namrata.

Juliet peers at me for a moment, her chin in her hands. "It's pretty wild, actually," she says. "I can't believe you pulled this off. You put up a poster for this guy, then you actually found him, and now you guys are boyfriends."

"We are! We've even got the label. We're doing some heavy labeling."

"Jesus. And you've already met his parents," Namrata says. "It's been, what—two weeks?"

"Yup." I beam.

"So what the fuck is next?"

I mean, the thing that's so crazy is *I don't even know.* I don't know what comes next. Because Broadway tells me one thing, but Reddit tells me something *very* different. And no one's advice seems to fit how I feel.

Nothing's quite what I expected. I think I knew I'd feel giddy, but I didn't know I'd feel so *certain.* I didn't know it would feel like the whole world clicking into place. It's weird, because even I know that two weeks are nothing. So why do two weeks with Ben feel so earth-shattering?

It's scary how easy it is to picture a future with him. It's scary how every minute, something new reminds me of him. New York in general reminds me of him.

As far as I'm concerned, Ben *is* New York.

And that's terrifying.

Tuesday, July 24

Hi hello yes we still need to discuss the Complicated Thing!! You guys free?

Helllloooooooo Jess, helllooooo Ethan

JESSICA NOUR FRANKLIN ETHAN JON GERSON WHERE ARE YOOOOOU

Im alone in the group chat frowny face frowny face frowny face.

Y'all are in Target aren't you, why does Target have the worst signal WTF

GET YOUR BUTTS OUT OF THE DOLLAR SECTION AND INTO MY TEXTS

Wednesday, July 25

By Wednesday, I'm a human fireball. The moment work ends, I launch out the door of the building, skidding to a stop next to Morrie, the doorman. Ben's surprising me tonight. I don't know where he's taking me, but he's been hyping it all week.

"Whoa there, Doctor," Morrie says, blue eyes twinkling. "In a hurry?"

"Someone's meeting me here."

My boyfriend. My boyfriend my boyfriend my boyfriend.

Morrie steps away to open the door for someone, and I sneak a glance at my phone. Five fifteen, and nothing from Ben. I peer up the street, taking inventory of all the faces. I don't even see him in the distance. I bite back a twinge of disappointment and shoot him a quick text.

A moment later: Sorry, running late! Be there in 5

He shows up at five thirty.

I just look at him. "I thought you might be dead."

"No—sorry. Lost track of time." He hugs me tightly. "Hey."

And it's the kind of contradiction that makes my brain hurt. On one hand, here's Ben, late, yet again, and obnoxiously unperturbed about it. On the other hand, I don't want him to stop hugging me, ever.

We set off for the subway. "So, where are you taking me?"

"Downtown."

"Interesting." I take in his outfit. He's definitely dressier than usual. This may be the first time I've seen him in pants that aren't denim.

He checks the clock on his phone.

"Are you worried about the time?" I ask. "Should we Lyft?"

"We'll be fine."

"I can pay for it," I start to say, but the look on his face stops me in my tracks. "Or not. Subway's probably faster anyway."

But the subway isn't faster. The subway is a shitshow. It's literally one stop from Grand Central to Times Square, but the train never starts moving. They don't even shut the doors. I turn to Ben after a moment. "Do trains sometimes just . . . forget to go?"

He taps his hand on the pole, mouth pressed tight. "I

don't know what's happening."

"Should we tell someone?"

"Tell who?"

"The Metropolitan Transportation Authority."

That makes him smile. "I don't think so."

"I heard someone threw up," says a lanky guy in glasses. Ben checks his phone again.

"What does that mean?" I ask, but Ben doesn't seem to hear me.

The lanky guy chimes in. "Well, they have to clean the whole car and sanitize everything. We might as well settle in." He seems almost pleased about it. "We're not going anywhere for a while."

"We better walk," says Ben. "Come on."

I follow him out of the station and out to the street. "It's not much farther. We'll be there in ten."

But ten minutes turns into fifteen, and that's with him walking so fast, I'm practically jogging to keep up. He turns onto Broadway and then Forty-Sixth Street, and I open my mouth to ask where we're going, but then I see it, all lit up in yellow-gold.

"Ben." For a moment, I'm speechless. "You did not."

He exhales, grinning. "Okay, so Lin-Manuel Miranda was running this lottery promo for—"

"For teens enrolled in New York Public Schools. I know. I know."

Holy shit. This is happening. This is actually happening. My voice cracks. "You won?"

"I mean, I entered." Ben shrugs. "I don't know. I figured, even if we lose, we could still hang out."

"I'm sorry, what?" My mouth falls open.

He smiles uncertainly. "You okay?"

"Yeah, I just . . . are you seriously implying that seeing *Hamilton* and quote-unquote 'just hanging out' are two equally good alternatives?"

"I feel like there's an insult buried in there." Ben laughs.

I don't laugh.

"Anyway, I think they should have announced the winners by now. Let's check with the box office."

I nod, but I feel like crying. God, I actually let myself picture this happening. Just for a moment, but already the loss of it stings. No one ever wins the *Hamilton* lottery. I enter every single day. And yeah, maybe the odds are better on this promo thing, but I'll never be that lucky. The universe doesn't love me that much.

But I follow Ben inside the theater, where there's an immaculately made-up blond woman at the will call window. "Hi. Excuse me," Ben says, his voice an octave higher than normal. I'm sort of in love with how weird he is around adults. "So. Um. I entered a competition today for New York Public School students, and I don't know if you've announced the winners yet, or if I need to check in somewhere else, or . . ." He trails off. "My name is Ben Alejo."

"Benjamin Alejo?" The lady looks at him, eyebrows knitted. "Oh, honey. We just gave away your tickets."

"W-what?" he stutters. "I won?"

My heart sinks into my stomach.

"Two front-row tickets, but they had to be claimed by six p.m. I wish you'd called in."

Ben shakes his head wordlessly.

"I'm so sorry. I can enter you in the lottery for tomorrow if you'd like."

"Um. Sure. Thank you." His voice is almost a whisper.

But by the time we're back outside, he's raging. "That's ridiculous." He stalks down the street, and I hustle to catch up. "When does the show start? Eight? There's over an hour. They could have called me."

"Are you joking?"

"They had my number on the form."

I want to scream. Or tear something down. I have that tornado feeling in my stomach. "Do you have any idea how many people would kill for the tickets you just lost? Front-row seats?" My voice breaks.

"Yeah, well, if they're going to set an arbitrary time to claim—"

"It's not an arbitrary time. That's how this works. We were late."

"Yeah, if the train hadn't stopped—"

"If you'd been on time, we wouldn't have been on that train."

"Arthur, come on."

"I'm just . . ." I exhale. "Like, do you even get that you just lost *front-row* Hamilton *tickets*?"

"I get it! God." His voice is thick. "You have no idea how much I wanted this to work out. No idea. I wanted this so badly."

"Yeah, well. Me too."

"I know. Arthur. It's *Hamilton*. I'm just—"

"It's not just *Hamilton*, okay?"

"It's not?" He looks at me helplessly.

"How do you not get this? God, Ben." My chest feels so tight it could burst. "You've been late for every single date. Every single one."

"I know. I'm—"

"And you know what? If you were excited about seeing me, that wouldn't happen. It wouldn't. It's like you don't even care."

He looks at me like I've hit him. "I do care!"

"But not enough. You don't care enough." I stare at him, heart pounding. "Maybe I should care less."

CHAPTER TWENTY-FOUR
BEN

I don't think I've ever been a bigger disappointment than right now.

Boyfriends are supposed to be the ultimate hype men. The ones responsible for smiles and building each other up even when they're down. They're not supposed to be the reason someone is heartbroken in the first place. But I betrayed Arthur's trust and I'm the cause behind his un-Arthur-like face. I held Arthur's big Broadway dreams in my hands and crushed them.

I had nothing but his heart in mind and the worst of me got in the way.

"Arthur?"

He's standing there. Shaking. He hasn't looked this

pained since the night that asshole came for us on the train. Now I'm the asshole. I reach for his shoulder and he shrugs me off. He just sinks to the curb.

I want to say I'm sorry, but I know he won't hear it.

He's crying. This is not just about tickets. I'm a screwup and he thinks I'm not into him as much as he's into me. I take out my phone and sit beside him.

"Arthur? Can you look up for one sec? Please."

I pull up YouTube. I have to make this right now more than ever.

I hand him one earbud and keep the other. I type *Hamilton karaoke*, and when "Alexander Hamilton" comes on, I sing along. I put myself out there the way Arthur did with "Ben." I feel him watching me as I try keeping up with the lyrics, as I try not to focus on the various people walking by us as I make a mockery of the performance that will soon be happening right behind us. One minute in, Arthur doesn't react. But then:

"*My name is Alexander Hamilton,*" Arthur says. Lead role. Of course.

We vibe along to the rest of the song, singing together— one of us significantly better and more carefree than the other. But he's the only audience I'm caring about.

When the song ends, I'm ready to apologize. But Arthur takes my phone and looks up a cover of "Only Us" from *Dear Evan Hansen*, and he comes closer to me as he sings the words "*So what if it's us, what if it's us, and only us.*" This song is so beautiful. What it feels like to be wanted by someone who sees you for who you are. How the world—the business of Times Square—can feel like it's falling away when you're with the right person. When it's my turn to choose the next cover, I go for "Suddenly Seymour" from *Little Shop of Horrors*, a movie I saw with my parents a few years ago. He chooses "The Wizard and I" from *Wicked*. I step it up—I choose "Can You Feel the Love Tonight" from *The Lion King*. I wish I could read Arthur's mind as he sways along. Arthur chooses "What I Did for Love" from *A Chorus Line*, and every song we choose feels like we're having a conversation without saying a single word.

"One more," Arthur says.

"We can stay here all night," I say. "Though my phone only has twenty percent battery left."

He plays a high school chorus banging out to "My Shot," and I wish I went to the kind of school that had talent shows so I could see something like this in person.

Which only reminds me we should be inside the theater.

"I'm so sorry, Arthur. I will never forgive myself. We should be seeing the real deal."

"I know this may sound like bullshit, but I loved this even more."

"Really?"

"Ben, millions of people can say they were inside the

Richard Rodgers Theatre and saw *Hamilton*. We're the only ones who can say we sat on the curb and got so much of Broadway in one night."

"And you're sure that's better because—"

Arthur shuts me up with a kiss.

"Well played," I say.

We get up.

"Seriously, I'm sorry—"

Another kiss.

"Okay. But I messed u—"

Another kiss.

"Let me say—"

Another kiss.

"You kissing me while I try to apologize is a good problem to have."

"Ben, I'm happy. That was amazing and romantic and perfect. You're the King of Rebounds."

We go on into the heart of Times Square. Tons of foot traffic keeps splitting us up, but we always make our way back to each other, not letting strollers or group selfies keep us apart. When I get his hand next, I keep him close and I don't want to let go.

Not tonight.

Not ever.

CHAPTER TWENTY-FIVE
ARTHUR
Friday, July 27

Jessie texts me on the group chain as the train leaves Thirty-Third Street. **You free now?**

Gah—on my way to Ben's apartment. I'm sorry!!

I frown at my phone, trying to ignore the guilty twinge in my chest. It's been almost a week since I cut short our FaceTime, and we still haven't found time for a do-over. Jessie still hasn't told me her Complicated Thing.

It's like we're spinning in opposite directions, like everything's off-kilter. And I can't explain why, but it feels like my fault. Even when it's Ethan and Jessie who are busy. Even when they're the ones not texting me back. I guess it's just weird, being the first one in a relationship.

No worries, Jessie writes. **Are you gonna** eggplant emoji, peach emoji, two dads with baby emoji?

Are you asking if I'm going to conceive a child tonight?

Pshh you know what I'm asking.

And I know. Of course I know. I'm getting three and a half hours of alone time with Ben tonight, because Mrs. Ortiz from up the block (agent of God, champion wingwoman, all-time MVP) wants to play cards with Diego and Isabel. And yes, I'm aware of what can happen when you're alone in an apartment with your very cute boyfriend. But I'm not letting myself build this up in my head. No expectations.

"Next stop, First Avenue," says the intercom.

Almost there!!!!!! I text Ben.

He writes back. **Outside the station! Told you I wouldn't be late.** Smiley face. **Also six exclamation points, is that a relationship milestone?**

It means we're letting our punctuation balls hang out!!!!!! OKAY I'M HERE, coming up

See you now!!!!!!, he writes back.

And there he is, in his headphones and Iceman T-shirt, leaning against a fence outside the station. His face brightens when he sees me, which makes my stomach feel fizzy. All I want to do is kiss him on the lips. Just a hello kiss, nothing tongue-y. But I hug him instead and he breathes in my hair, and that's pretty amazing, too.

"It's weird that you're here."

"I was here five days ago," I remind him.

"But not *here*." He gestures vaguely at the subway. "And our parents were there. It's different." His cheeks flush. And if I wasn't thinking parent-free thoughts before, I'm definitely thinking them now.

"I'll carry your bag," Ben says.

"It's pretty heavy."

"I'm pretty strong," he says, smiling, so I smile back and let him take it. "Oof. What's in here?"

"Mostly my laptop."

Also six boxes of condoms. Not that I plan to have thirty-six rounds of sex. But if sex happens, I need options, including glow-in-the-dark options.

We set off down the sidewalk. "So this is the East Village. I guess you probably came through here on Sunday."

"Well, our Lyft driver didn't really give us the grand tour."

"Well then. You are totally not in luck."

"I'm not?"

"Empty apartment. Cute boyfriend wearing cute work clothes." He bites back a smile. "I'm probably not going to be the world's most thorough tour guide."

"Understandable." I grin back.

But here's the funny thing: he kind of is the world's most thorough tour guide. He's not exactly taking the long route, but he has a story for everything we pass. Like his school,

285

which he calls his Real School, as opposed to summer school at Belleza High in Midtown. Or the beauty store where he and Dylan cut off chunks of their hair with nail scissors so they could hold them up against the boxes of dye and finally know the truth of their own hair colors (Dylan: Chocolate Lava, Ben: Honey Brown). Or the bagel shop that sells cups of ice cream that you eat with tiny wooden paddles. Or how scared he got the day eight-year-old Dylan broke his arm and had a panic attack. I just soak it all in. I've never seen Ben so animated. I really love this side of him. I love seeing his neighborhood through his eyes, the way his memories occupy every block.

"Now we're in Alphabet City," he says.

"I can't believe Alphabet City is a real thing. It sounds like it's from *Sesame Street*."

Our hands keep brushing as we walk. "That show was almost named after my street," he says, smiling. "They were going to call it *123 Avenue B*."

"You live on Avenue B?"

"And you're staying in Apartment A. I think the universe is mocking us."

"Or high-fiving us," I say, high-fiving him. Except even when the high five is over, we go on holding hands. Just for half a block, maybe.

By the time we reach his building, my heart's slamming all over my rib cage.

There's no doorman and no elevator, but there's a big empty stairwell leading to an empty apartment. And as soon as the door shuts, he cups my face in his hands, tracing his thumbs along my cheekbones. But he doesn't kiss me right away. He just looks at me, smiling faintly.

"I have something to show you," he says, sliding my bag off his shoulder.

"What kind of something?"

"Something awesome."

"Is it something I've seen before?"

"I don't know." He smiles so sweetly, it makes my heart flip. "It's in my room."

"Oh."

"So . . . should we . . ."

"Sure. Yup. Yeah."

I follow him into his bedroom, which feels totally, unrecognizably different from Sunday in a way that I can only assume is due to sex vibes. I'm so nervous I'm almost shaking. I can't wrap my head and my heart around this strange new possibility. This thing my brain's been circling around for years. How could I ever have predicted the circumstances of this moment—this particular night, this particular place, this particular boy. I always thought it would feel larger than life, and it doesn't, but I like that. It's not a starlit field, but it's better, because it's Ben.

"So." He sits on his bed, and I settle in beside him. Then

he strains sideways and slides his laptop off his nightstand. I watch as he cracks it open and scrolls through his applications. I have to admit, this is an unexpected part of the process. But maybe it's porn. I think I've heard of people who do that—have sex with porn in the background. I don't entirely see the point. It seems kind of like watching YouTube videos in a movie theater. But maybe this isn't porn-related. Maybe this is *The Wicked Wizard War*–related, and he's opening up a freshly written sex scene to inspire us. *That* I could get into.

"Oh, here we go." Ben scoots backward on the bed. We end up side by side, our backs pressed to the wall, and he tilts his laptop toward me.

It's . . . a computer game.

"I made you a Sim," he says shyly. "Look, that's you."

And there I am, center screen, tousled dark hair and button-down and a bow tie. It's actually somewhat creepy how much my avatar resembles me. I know a little bit about this game, mostly because Jessie loves it, but the level of detail catches me off guard. It's not even just the clothing or the coloring. Sim Arthur has my facial features. I blink. "Why do I have a green diamond floating over my head?"

"Have you never played this?" Ben asks. I shake my head. "Really?"

"Really."

"Then this is going to be a big night for you."

I force a grin, but my mind is whirling. So this is it. We're playing *The Sims*. This is Ben's big night. He introduces me to his avatar, who basically looks like Ben in Harry Potter robes, and under normal circumstances I'd be super charmed by this, but all I can think about are those thirty-six condoms burning a hole in my messenger bag. It's just hard to get excited about losing my Sim virginity when I was sure I was going to lose my actual virginity. But I guess that's my own fault for coming in with expectations.

But seriously, three and a half hours in his apartment with no parents, and this is how he wants to spend it? This is the only activity he could come up with to do in this bed?

"We have a really pimping house," he informs me. "Oh, and we live with Dylan."

"Of course we do."

I have to admit, our Sim house fucking rules. Ben's not shy about using cheat codes for money, so we've got a huge indoor pool and a sunroom for parties. There's a dragon sculpture in the foyer and a light-up dance floor in Dylan's room, and also the entire backyard is an amusement park, with a roller coaster and a carousel and a Tunnel of Love.

"For you and Dylan?" I ask.

"We don't let Dylan ride it anymore," Ben says darkly.

Ben walks us upstairs to our bedroom. OUR BEDROOM.

"We share a room?"

"Is that okay? This was actually mine and Dylan's house, and I kind of . . . moved you into my room."

He looks nervous, which makes me brave enough to scoot closer to him. "Very okay," I say, resting my head on his shoulder. "I like being your roommate."

He hooks his arm around my waist and kisses me softly on the forehead.

And something shifts. We don't log out of the game, but Ben slides the laptop back onto his pillow. Then—it's hard to explain, but he pulls me on top of him, and we're not exactly lying down, but we're not exactly upright either. He slides his hands beneath my shirt, and the warmth of his palms on my back makes me giddy. I thread my hands into his hair and kiss him without thinking, and *The Sims*' music and chatter fades into the background, not nearly as loud as the thud of Ben's heartbeat.

He draws back, breathing heavily. "Should we take this off?" He presses his thumb against one of my shirt buttons. He looks slightly terrified.

"Do you want me to?"

He nods quickly.

"Okay." I scoot a few inches sideways, so I'm slightly less on top of him. My heart's beating so fast it's practically buzzing. "FYI, it's hard to unbutton buttons when your hands are shaking," I say, and even though it's not a joke, we both laugh. We're both breathless.

Ben grins up at me, his eyes landing first on my face, then my chest, then the wadded-up button-down in my lap. "Cute undershirt," he says, catching its hem with his fingers. He meets my eyes, and I nod. And the next thing I know, we're in our boxers, horizontal.

"This okay?" he says softly, and I nod into the crook of his neck. He traces his fingertips along my back and my shoulders, and then he kisses me fiercely. I can't get over how warm his skin feels against mine. I run my hands along his stomach, which makes him squirm.

"Should I not—"

"No, you're good." He exhales. We stare at each other, smiling.

"So," I say finally. "Do we want to try . . ."

His eyes widen. "Do you?"

"Maybe. Yeah."

"Okay. Yeah." He hugs me closer. And for a moment, we stay just like that—chest to chest, cheek to cheek. And then, slowly, his fingers trail closer to my boxers, slipping under their waistband. "This still okay?"

Holy shit. I laugh breathlessly. "Yup."

So this is actually happening. It's happening. It's happening, and my whole body knows it. His hand slides down another inch. I don't think I'll ever not be hard again. His eyes never leave mine. He looks nervous. And he holds me like I'm breakable.

Another inch, and my heart leaps into my throat. Because how is this real? How is this possibly real? How is this the same me that woke up this morning in a bunk bed?

"Still good?" Ben asks softly.

I nod, but I'm strangely close to tears. I'm just—I don't know. How is this happening? And how does this work? No, seriously, how does this specifically work? Who puts what parts where and in what order and when does the condom go on, and what about lube? I know fucking *nothing* about lube. And here's Ben, peering at me sweetly, with those eyes and those freckles, and I guess he probably knows the mechanics, and I should probably warn him how much I'm going to suck at this. Unless he's already figured it out. God. He probably already thinks this is a mistake, and I'm a mistake, and sex is a mistake, and also what even is sex? It's so WEIRD. What a weird thing to want to do. Or maybe I'm the one who's—

"You okay?" Ben asks.

"I'm freaking out."

"Oh." His eyes widen. "Okay."

"I'm so sorry."

"No! Arthur." He kisses me gently and opens his arms. "It's fine, okay? Come here."

I tuck my head onto his shoulder, and he wraps his arms around me tightly.

"I'm really sorry," I whisper.

"Don't be sorry." He kisses me again. "If you're not ready, you're not ready. That's fine."

"I am, though! I thought I was." I bury my face. "I just—I don't know."

"So we try again another day. No big deal."

"We don't have a lot of other days."

He rests his head on mine. "I know."

We're quiet for a moment, just breathing.

"Are you disappointed?" I ask.

"No way. I'm just glad you're here."

"Yeah, me too." My throat feels thick. "God. Ben."

"Mmm?"

"I really like you. It's kind of scary."

He shifts back to look at my face. "Scary why?"

"Well, for one thing, you make me not want to leave New York."

"I don't want you to leave either," he says.

"Really?"

He smiles. "You think I'm half-assing this?"

"I don't know." I sigh. "I don't know what it's supposed to look like or feel like. I just know I really like you. This is serious for me."

"I feel serious about you too."

"Really?" I say again.

"God, Arthur." He kisses me. "Te quiero. Estoy enamorado. You don't even know."

And I don't speak a word of Spanish, but when I look at his face, I get it.

CHAPTER TWENTY-SIX

BEN

Monday, July 30

Summer has really stepped its game up.

I may have lost some pretty huge firsts to Hudson, but dating Arthur feels like a do-over. Every kiss with Arthur feels like discovery, like we become more comfortable with each breath. And we haven't had sex yet, which is great. Not great like I didn't want to do it, because wow, I really did and I still do. But great because we're not falling outside of ourselves just to make the other person happier. I'm right for him and he's right for me and that feels beyond right— the universe knew it was love before we did.

I still don't know what comes next for us after Arthur leaves. His seventeenth birthday is on August 4. I don't have the money to buy him something flashy, but my parents don't really drop bank on gifts either. They make them. Instead of buying Pa a coffeemaker that would have to be replaced within a year, Ma made him an *I love you, Diego* mug that he cherishes. Like, if the apartment is on fire, he's grabbing us and that mug. And instead of buying Ma a new prayer book, I helped Pa make an audio file of him reciting her favorite Bible verses to listen to every morning.

For my gift, I'm writing Arthur into *The Wicked Wizard War*. The small, mighty Arturo who is clueless to what chill is. He's traveled from the land of Great Georgia to Ever York to build his reputation in some skills so he can gain access to House Yale. But then he meets Ben-Jamin, and the rest of the story is just going to be Ben-Jamin and Arturo becoming kings who make out a lot.

But before Arthur's big day, we're all celebrating the epic birthdays of Harry Potter and J. K. Rowling at Dylan's tomorrow. We're going to watch *Sorcerer's Stone* and eat Bertie Bott's Every Flavor Beans and send a photo to J. K. Rowling on Twitter and see if she likes our tweet.

I'm so happy everything is coming together.

Though no matter how happy I am, summer school Mondays always especially suck. Thankfully there's only ten minutes left and then later on I get to hang with Arthur. He's going to help me study and then we're having dinner with my parents and Dylan.

A flash of lightning and loud clap of thunder draws

everyone's eyes to the window. Harriett takes a moody photo that will get her more likes in an hour than I would get in a week. And Hudson is the only one staring at his desk, deep in thought, while everyone gets excited over the first rain of this blistering month. Hudson suddenly turns to me like he could feel my gaze on him, and from the corner of my eye I can see he's still staring.

"Let's call it a day," Mr. Hayes says at the front of class. "Quiz tomorrow on identifying subatomic particles. Just hang tight until it's time to go."

Harriett flips around in her chair and talks to Hudson. That used to be me and her in English class. At the beginning, we would talk about what music we liked and then it became all things Hudson. Now we have awkward waves behind Hudson's back.

Hudson gets out of his chair and comes my way, probably to use the back door to get to the bathroom sooner. But then he hovers over my side.

"Can I sit for a sec?"

"Uh. Sure."

Suddenly Hudson and I are face-to-face for the first time since the second day of summer school. "How's it going?" he asks, flicking his fingernails against each other.

"Um. Fine." I really don't know what this is. "Everything okay?"

"Been a while," Hudson says.

"Yup."

"I want to talk."

"About what?"

Hudson takes a deep breath. "I don't want to talk about us. I know that's done because of everything, and I . . . I saw a group picture of you at karaoke with Dylan and some guy—"

"You were looking into me? Aren't you hashtag moving on—"

Damn. I outed myself. Guilty of the same crime.

Hudson grins. "You checked up on me too. Maybe we can just catch up instead of getting all life updates on Instagram. Try and be friends again. Harriett wants to hang too. She also misses you."

Goose bumps run up my arms. I don't like that Hudson has any effect on me. He's the guy who kissed me and had sex with me and told me secrets and let me think something serious was going to happen. Everything would be so much easier if I could just be one of those ex-boyfriends who was happy that Hudson misses me and not care because I have an even more amazing boyfriend. But I really do want to be his friend. Harriett too. And the only reason I really, truly regret dating Hudson is because we couldn't break up and be friends again. Maybe we can bounce back.

"Okay," I say. "I'm having dinner with Arthur and Dylan later, but we can go chill for a bit."

"Cool. No strings attached or weirdness," Hudson says. "Maybe some weirdness."

"Some weirdness is okay," I say. "But I'm running when it gets too weird."

"Like that time we kept calling Harriett 'Mom' like her followers?"

"Exactly. I mean, she's seventeen. How is she a mother to all these fourteen-year-olds?"

Wow, maybe this will be a good thing. I'll get my friends back and tell them all about Arthur, and if it's not too weird for Arthur, maybe there's a chance they can meet him before he leaves. Might be tough talking Arthur into that one, but I think he'll come around. We can make it a group hangout with Dylan and Samantha too.

Mr. Hayes is heading out, and I promised my parents I'd get an update on my progress. "I'll see you guys outside," I say, getting up and chasing after him. He's very fast for someone on crutches, and I'm convinced he's not participating in a Spartan Race because he wouldn't want to hurt the fragile male egos of his opponents.

"Mr. Hayes?"

"Yeah?" Mr. Hayes asks as we slowly go down the stairs.

"Can I help you with your bag? Or crutch?"

"I got it. Thanks. So what's up?"

"Are you liking my chances of passing next week's final? I really don't want to get left back."

"I know school during the summer is no water park, but it's important you study extra hard over the next week. You're not failing the quizzes, but . . ."

"I'm not acing them either," I say. Legit feel like I can throw up. If I suck at homework when I have the internet and textbooks at my disposal, then I'm going to completely fail when it's just me and the blank page.

"You'll get there, Ben. I'm going to be staying late a couple days next week for extra guidance. I do recommend spending extra time studying every night as we lead up to the final. Maybe get a group together and quiz one another," Mr. Hayes says.

We walk outside the building. I'm about to ask which days he'll be doing the extended classes when I see Arthur standing underneath a store's awning, hiding out from the rain. He's waving and smiling. I don't know what he's doing here, but my heart is hammering even harder than before.

I have to get rid of him.

"Okay-Mr.-Hayes-thanks-bye-be-careful-with-your-leg-the-steps-are-wet."

I almost bust my ass running to Arthur, and he rushes toward me.

"Hey." I grab his hand and drag him back under the awning. I hug him and kiss him and spin him so his back is to the school's entrance. "Why aren't you at work?"

"I'm 'out sick,'" he says with air quotes. "Skipping for the rest of the afternoon."

"Why?"

"Because I wanted to be with my boyfriend before his parents get home. I was thinking we could try again. You know."

I keep looking to the entrance. Mr. Hayes passes us on his way to the train.

"Study hard," Mr. Hayes says, leaning in for a fist bump.

"You got it," I say. Is it possible to sweat while your face is already wet?

If I get out of this, I'm going to set everything right. Come on, universe.

"Who's that guy?"

I don't see Hudson, but maybe he came out the side exit. "Who?"

"The one you were talking to. The guy on the crutches."

"Oh! Mr. Hayes. Yeah. That's my teacher."

"Cool." Arthur is smiling. "So should we—"

"BEN!"

I could throw up. Hudson runs down the steps and please, please, please fall and don't get up until Arthur and I are long gone. Arthur turns and he squints and it's too late. It's all too fucking late.

"Harriett can't join us," Hudson says, walking up to me.

He turns to Arthur. "Hey, wait. You're the panini guy, right? Ben, he's the guy I met at Panera a few weeks ago—"

"What's going on here, Ben?" Arthur is red. Pissed? Embarrassed? Both. I don't know.

"It's not what you think," I say. Even though it's true doesn't make me any less of a cliché douchebag.

"What is he doing here?" Arthur asks.

Hudson takes a step back. "I'll give you a sec."

"Ben. Why is he here?"

"He's in summer school too."

Arthur looks like I just punched him in the face. Like I punched him in the heart. He turns his back on me and heads into the rain, dragging his messenger bag on the ground. I stay by his side.

"So, what, you just hang out with your ex-boyfriend after school? Does he even know about me? Are you two-timing both of us?"

"We were literally hanging out so we could talk about you!"

"Since when do you guys hang out at all?!"

"Today was going to be the first time, I swear!"

Arthur throws his messenger bag against the wall. "NO! You just got caught today. That's the only first." He crouches over, holding his stomach. "I'm going to throw up." I put my hand on his lower back and he swipes me off of him. "DON'T TOUCH ME."

"Arthur, please, hear me out. This looks bad. Catastrophic. But I promise you that I love—"

"What ass-backward world are you living in where your ex-boyfriend is more in the loop than your boyfriend?" Arthur stands straight. He grabs his messenger bag and we go on to the next block with a little more distance between us. "How come he gets to know about me but I don't get to know about him?"

"I didn't want to hurt you," I say. "I tried to say something, but it just got harder and harder and looked worse and worse the longer I took and—"

"Then you should've just said something!"

"I should've, but nothing happened between us. I can't control the fact that we're both in summer school. Sorry we don't have it together like you."

"Don't spin this around on me! I'm not pissed you're in summer school, I don't care about that. It would've been nice to know Hudson was there with you."

"Oh yeah, like you would've been really chill about that. You clearly don't even trust me. Why should you, we haven't even known each other for a month." I take a deep breath. "There were so many expectations and I honestly wasn't sure we were going to be able to live up to them and then we did."

"Ben, just stop. I don't need to hear how this wasn't real for you all along."

"It was real, but what's the point? You're leaving the city in a week."

Arthur squeezes his eyes shut and he's shaking. When he reopens his eyes, there's so much hurt and anger. "So you're going to stand there and act like this has all been in my head? All these first dates and meeting your parents and your friends and . . . everything."

"It wasn't—"

"Did you ever send Hudson his box?"

"What?"

"The box that you were going to mail the day we met."

The rain is pounding on us.

I don't say anything.

I can't lie to him, and telling the truth is even worse.

Arthur shakes his head. "And *this* is why I don't trust you. Hope you and Hudson have an awful life together." He looks me in the eyes. "We're over."

I reach for his arm. "Arthur."

"No! I'm done. I can't wait to go home."

I don't think he's talking about Uncle Milton's place.

He walks away, and even though I'm a huge idiot, I'm smart enough to know better than to follow him.

CHAPTER TWENTY-SEVEN

ARTHUR

Of course it's raining. Of fucking course. I'm drenched to my boxers, water dripping from my eyelashes, and everything hurts. Everything's broken.

Ben and Hudson. This whole time. Well done, universe. Way to prove you were never on our side. Way to prove you don't even exist. There's no plan and no fate. It's only us. Only me trying too hard. Only Ben trying not hard enough. But hey—why bother trying for a guy you barely even know. Because I guess that's how he sees me. Just some stupid tourist here to entertain him for the summer.

A sudden buzz in my pocket. I've got my phone rainproofed in a Ziploc, but I duck under an awning anyway. Just to peek. If it's him, I'm not answering.

But it's not. Surprise, surprise. It's just Jessie, swooping in for an impromptu FaceTime. I tug it out of the bag and decline it—but then I feel bad, so I text her. Sorry, am outside and it's raining

She writes back immediately. Can you go somewhere to talk? It's kind of important.

My stomach drops. *Kind of important.* I don't like that phrase at all. It's too serious, too urgent. Maybe this is about the Complicated Thing. Only maybe it's not just a Complicated Thing. Maybe it's Complicated Bad News, really bad news, and she's been trying to tell me for days. Maybe I'm a really bad friend.

Give me one sec

I don't even stop to think. There's a guy in a tank top letting himself into a nearby apartment building. "Hey!" I call. "Sorry, can you hold that. My keys are . . ."

I trail off, at a loss, but I guess I must have sold it, because tank top guy keeps his foot in the door long enough for me to slip in behind him.

The lobby's kind of bare-bones—no couches, not even a bench. Just a small bank of mailboxes, a fake plant, and a single wooden chair. I collapse into it, feeling clammy and strange. Jessie accepts my FaceTime immediately.

She's with Ethan—they're on Ethan's basement couch. I swallow. "Hi. Everything okay?"

"Um, Arthur, are *you* okay?"

"What?" I peek at my face in the little selfie box on my screen, and wow. I look like shit. Like steaming-hot shit. "I'm fine. I'm just wet."

"Okay, good."

She's silent for a moment, and Ethan's not looking at me.

"So . . . ," I say finally. "What's up?"

"Okay, I'm just going to come out with it." She pauses, and my throat feels thicker with every passing second. I've never seen her like this.

"Jess?" I say softly.

She takes a deep breath, and then blurts it out fast. "I have a boyfriend."

My heart skids to a stop. "What?"

"I've been trying to tell you." She smiles nervously.

I force myself to smile back. "A boyfriend. Wow."

I mean, this is good. It's a good thing. Especially considering that thirty seconds ago, I thought she might be dying. And yeah, I'm happy for her. Obviously. Even if it's a little out of nowhere.

"Okay . . . so, what's his name?"

"Well." She glances sideways. "Ethan."

"Really?"

"No, I mean, Ethan and I are a couple."

I freeze. "A couple of what?"

307

"Very funny," says Jessie. She doesn't laugh.

"Wait. So." My chest tightens. "You guys are like . . . a *couple* couple?"

Ethan nods. "Yes."

"With each other?"

"Yes."

"Since when?"

"Well." Jessie smiles faintly. "Prom."

"WHAT?"

"Yeah." She twirls her hair. "Okay, remember that moment—they were playing that Chris Brown song, and we walked off the dance floor to protest, and we found Angie Whaley crying in the hallway, because Michael Rosenfield dumped her, and Ethan was like, that guy's a dick—"

"He is a dick," says Ethan.

"Right, but then she starts crying harder, and Arthur, you were hugging her, and I just kind of dragged Ethan away so he wouldn't make it worse." Jessie bites her lip. "Remember?"

"You hooked up when I was with Angie?"

"Kind of," says Ethan.

I shake my head. "No."

"I mean, that's what happened," Ethan says.

"You're telling me you guys have been a couple for two months, and what? You didn't think to mention it?"

"We tried! We tried so many times. But it was always

weird timing, or you were talking about Ben—"

"Oh, *right*. This is about me and Ben. Of course—"

"No! Art, that's not how I meant it. You're allowed to be excited about Ben. He's your first boyfriend—"

"He's not my boyfriend," I snap.

"WHAT?" Jessie and Ethan say, in creepy, near-perfect unison.

"That seems . . . major," Ethan says. "Want to fill us in?"

"Weird that you don't already know, seeing as I talk about him so much."

"Arthur. Come on. We never said that!"

Wow. So, Ethan and Jessie are *we*. That's beautiful. What a beautiful new era of our friendship. I swallow the lump in my throat. "Whatever. You guys should go make out or have sex or whatever it is—"

"Can we just talk about this?" Jessie says. "I don't want this to be weird—"

"You don't want this to be weird?" I laugh sharply. "You're secretly dating and you didn't tell me for months, but that's not weird?"

Jessie sighs. "We wanted to tell you! Right away. And we were going to—but that was, you know. It was kind of like, *What are we doing, is this going to be a thing*, and we were just figuring everything out. And then, Arthur, you came out to us that night! So obviously, we weren't going to steal your thunder—"

"Oh, I'm so sorry I ruined your moment by coming out. How inconvenient for you."

"Dude, we didn't want to ruin *your* moment."

I stare Ethan down. "And since when do you care about my moment?"

"What's that supposed to mean?"

"Hmm, you've been weird around me since, let's see, *literally* the second I told you I was gay."

His mouth falls open. "You think I'm not cool with you being gay?"

"So, what, it's just a coincidence that you haven't texted me once outside the group chain since prom night? Do you even realize that?" I feel my eyes start to prickle. "We can't even text without Jessie there to chaperone. But sure, you're totally cool with it."

Ethan looks like I've punched him. "I am totally cool with it."

"Yeah, well that's not—"

"Arthur, we knew you were gay."

My heart jumps into my throat. "*What?*"

"I mean, we didn't know, but we figured. You're not really subtle . . . about anything."

"So, wait. You knew I was gay, but you pretended you didn't—"

"Art, it wasn't like that," Jessie says. "We just wanted you to be able to come out when you were ready."

"And you were just going to act surprised when I told you. That was the plan, huh?"

"No. Not at all—"

"I love that y'all had, like, a whole strategy for this. That's just great." I nod. "That must have been very interesting for you guys to talk about behind my back. In between make-outs. Wow. Any more secrets you'd like to fill me in on?"

"Arthur! God. I knew you were going to make this awkward."

"Oh, I'm the one making it awkward? You guys have been dating! All summer!"

"I know. And we tried—"

"Listen, I'm not weird about you being gay," Ethan says suddenly. He presses a hand to his forehead. "I'm weird about Jess. Okay? This is new for me, too. I don't know how to do this. It's like, I wanted to tell you everything, the way you do about Ben—"

"Wow." I laugh harshly. "I guess it's your lucky day, then, because guess who I *never* want to talk about ever—"

"No. Arthur." Ethan looks pained. "That's not what I meant. Okay. This isn't—look, I know our timing sucks, but now you know, and I guess that's . . . that. And I'm sorry. But dude, I just need you to know that I don't have any issues with you. I never have. It's just that we were trying to find the right way to tell you, and we wanted to do it together, and then it dragged on for so long, it started to feel like I was lying to you. And I hate that."

"I mean. You were lying to me. For months."

Ethan frowns. "But it's kind of like how you didn't want to tell us you were gay—"

"Oh, don't you dare." I practically spit. "Don't you fucking dare compare this to coming out. That is not the same thing, and you know it."

"We know!" Jessie's eyes brim with tears. "Arthur, I'm sorry, okay? You're right. You're totally right."

For a moment, we just stare one another down. Ethan, Jessie, and me.

"I don't know," Jessie says finally. "I guess I thought you'd be happy for us."

"I am!"

"And I know this was a shitty time to drop this bomb, because clearly something just happened with—"

"I don't want to talk about Ben."

"That's fine! Art, that's fine."

"And I think you guys should go."

"Are you—"

"Hanging up now." It comes out choked.

Then I hug my messenger bag to my chest and cry until my face hurts.

CHAPTER TWENTY-EIGHT
BEN
Tuesday, July 31

The only person who should be upset on Harry Potter's birthday is Lord Voldemort. But here I am, staring at a wall while *Sorcerer's Stone* is on, pretty pissed off. While I was failing a quiz this morning, Samantha went over to Dylan's early "to help set up." I thought I was going to walk into Dylan's apartment with Hogwarts banners hanging from the walls. Maybe some bowls with color-coded candy for each house. At the very least, streamers from wall to wall. But Dylan's place is just as Dylan's as ever before. The only difference is the freshly made Butterbeer in the fridge, the Bertie Bott's Every Flavor Beans in a cereal bowl, and our T-shirts.

Butterbeer doesn't take six hours to make.

They probably had sex, napped, and had sex again.

"Controversial opinion incoming," Dylan says. He takes a sip from the Butterbeer, getting more foam on his beard. Pretty sure he's doing it on purpose in the hopes Samantha will lick it off, but her self-respect keeps getting in the way. "Michael Gambon is the better Dumbledore."

"Wrong. So wrong," Samantha says. "Richard Harris was perfectly cast. Pure Dumbledore. Demeanor, appearance, delivery, everything."

Dylan raises a skeptical eyebrow. "The court rules that you can only have an opinion on Harry Potter casting if you've been a fan longer than a year."

"I may be late to this world, but I will still out-Harry-Potter you," Samantha says. She grabs the bowl of Bertie Bott's Every Flavor Beans. "I propose a Triwizard Trivia Tournament. If you get a question right, you choose your own bean. If you get it wrong, someone chooses for you."

I play along even though my heart's not really in it. If I could ace chemistry questions the way I'm slaying this Harry Potter trivia, I would've never been in this mess with Arthur because I wouldn't have been stuck in summer school with Hudson in the first place. Where the fuck is a Time-Turner when you need one? I would go back in time and never date Hudson. Maybe not even be his friend at all knowing that's where it started. But then I wouldn't have been at the post office with the breakup box to meet

Arthur. Not like that has a happy ending either.

Dylan gags on a vomit-flavored bean as I watch the movie. Ron's pet rat, Scabbers, comes on the screen, and I think about Arthur singing "Ben" during karaoke. Things weren't easy then, but they were simpler. Sorry was enough to keep it moving. But now Arthur has unfollowed me on Instagram and probably enlisted Namrata and Juliet on putting together restraining orders.

"I'm seriously the worst," I say. I take a swig of the Butterbeer, which we'd planned on spiking with rum thinking Dylan's very Irish parents wouldn't care, but all bets were off on that because they don't want Samantha buzzed on the way home. "I ruined everything. Something good with Arthur. How much he loves New York. He'll probably never want to come back, and . . . I really wanted him to want to come back."

Samantha puts down a bean and sits in front of me. "You've done everything you can right now. He might just need some more time."

"I haven't gone to his house," I say. "Or job."

"Let's not do that."

"Why not? No one invited him to my school."

"No, but you were dating," Samantha says.

I can't believe how quickly everything has gone with Arthur—strangers to boyfriends to exes. We wouldn't be exes if Arthur hadn't tried to surprise me. But that's who he is. Someone who goes the extra step. Someone who puts up a poster to find a boy from a city he doesn't live in even though he's not here to stay.

"I know it couldn't last anyway," I say.

"He was only here for another week, right?" Dylan asks.

"Yeah, but . . . nothing lasts. Me and Hudson didn't last. Me and Arthur didn't last. You and Harriett didn't last. You guys won't last. Nothing lasts."

"Um." Dylan gestures at himself and Samantha. "No need to bring us into this, Bennison."

"D, I'm just saying. We all talk a big game like the universe is actually setting us up for something epic, and then everything ends. If we were all just a little more realistic, we wouldn't keep losing people."

Samantha stands. "I'm going to, uh, get more Butterbeer." She walks out of Dylan's bedroom.

"Dude. Big Ben. The fuck."

"What?"

"You're telling me my relationship with my girlfriend isn't going to last . . . in front of my girlfriend. Like she wasn't standing right there. Which she was."

"Yeah, but for how long is it going to last?"

"Hopefully a long time."

"But probably not. You're hyping up this relationship like last time, and you're just going to disappoint Samantha like you did Harriett."

Dylan pauses *Sorcerer's Stone*, which, wow, dude never pauses a game, but he's pausing a movie we've seen over a dozen times. "It's different with Samantha. She's—"

"What, she's special? Yeah, well, I know some other girls who were special. Gabriella and Heather and Natalia and Zoe and Harriett. That's your pattern. You make your jokes about it being meant to be and you move on. You have no idea what I'm going through right now."

Samantha comes back and grabs her phone off the desk. "I'm going to head out."

"Nope. I'm out," I say, getting up.

"Good. Maybe you can go act like you're the victim with someone who doesn't know better," Dylan says. "You're the one who broke Arthur's heart, Ben. And ended things with Hudson. Never the other way around. You get to be hurt, but don't play dumb like you're any better than me."

"That's me. Stupid Summer School Ben."

"What?"

"Whatever. I don't want to be here." I lock eyes with Dylan. "You don't need your best friend when you've got your future wife around, so I'll just talk to you again in a couple weeks when this is over."

"No idea where my best friend has gone, but I'm definitely glad the dickhead who looks like him is leaving," Dylan says. He takes Samantha's hand and turns his back on me.

I rush out and wow. I have pushed everyone out of my life. Not pushed. Shoved. No Samantha. No Dylan. No Arthur.

But maybe I don't have to be alone.

I know I'm not supposed to go see him. That's common sense. But I'm not ready to go home. I get to his building and I text him that I'm downstairs and I really hope he's here.

Down in a sec, he says immediately.

And yup, Hudson is in the lobby pretty quickly. He tried talking to me at school this morning, but I pushed him away because he's the reason I'm in this mess in the first place. Nope, I am. Dylan is right. We're both heartbreakers, he's just playing dumb. Dylan and I will be friends again in no time and he'll say *I told you so* and I'll say *You did* and he'll say *More sexy time for us now that we're single again* and we'll be all good.

But right now, I look around to make sure Arthur doesn't pop up somewhere, and when I don't see him, I hug Hudson and I cry so damn hard.

CHAPTER TWENTY-NINE
ARTHUR
Wednesday, August 1

How's this for pathetic: me in pajama pants and a questionably clean T-shirt from Mom's law firm picnic, smeared in Cheeto dust, on the couch watching YouTube videos of Pokémon dancing to Kesha songs. I've reached the summit of Suck Mountain. Peak Suck. Suck Everest. Watch me take suck to new and exciting elevations.

The good news is that Charizard can really fucking dance.

But wow. I haven't had an actual conversation in days. Dad's in Atlanta for a job interview, and Mom's been working late every single day. And of course, I'm "out sick" again. Hopefully forever. It doesn't even feel like a lie at this point.

Mom walks in around eight, perching beside me on the

319

arm of the couch. "Honey, how are you feeling?"

I force a cough, but it morphs into a choke halfway through.

"So . . . not good?"

"Not good," I confirm.

She presses a hand to my forehead. "No fever, though. We'll keep an eye on it." She smooths my hair. "You going to be okay this weekend? I hate leaving you alone on your birthday."

"It's fine."

I mean, here's the thing: my birthday's Saturday. Mom's driving upstate tomorrow morning for a bunch of depositions and meetings. She's not coming back until Monday, and Dad's not back until Monday either, so I'll be spending my seventeenth birthday alone in Uncle Milton's apartment. Of course, the worst part is knowing it could have been the most epic birthday ever. This could have been a fucking honeymoon weekend with Ben. No parents. Apartment wide open. Just me and thirty-six condoms and my beautiful sweet boyfriend. Otherwise known as my asshole ex-boyfriend.

"I'm giving Namrata and Juliet your number, okay? I'll have them check in on you."

I shrug.

We're both silent. Mom clears her throat. "So, do you want to talk about—"

"Nope."

I mean, what would I even say? Too bad I won't be losing my virginity while you're gone, Mom, because Ben broke my fucking heart, and now I'm single and alone. Here, have six boxes of condoms. I'll literally never need them.

"Well, if you change your mind . . . ," she says, pursing her lips. Here we go. "I don't know, Arthur. Your dad and I are just so worried about you—"

"Okay, you don't have to do that."

"Do what?"

"The whole parental unity game. *Your dad and I.* Come on."

"Sweetie, I—"

"You know what's awesome? The way everyone—every single one of you—just walks around lying to me. All the time. Because, oh, it's Arthur, and he can't handle our scary big secrets." I thrust my palms up. "You guys want to get a divorce? Fine. Just fucking *tell me.*"

Mom's mouth falls open. "Divorce?"

"Come *on.*"

"Arthur, what? Your dad and I are fine."

"You're not fine."

She peers at me strangely. "How long have you been stressing about this?"

"Since forever! You've been fighting nonstop all summer."

"Sweetie, no. It's just been kind of a tough time, with your dad being out of work and—"

"Oh, believe me, I'm up-to-date. You need to learn how to have quieter fights."

It's like someone sucked all the air from the room. I stare at my hands. I swear I can hear my heartbeat.

"Okay, why don't we call your dad?"

"Right now?" I groan, covering my face.

She presses the phone to her ear and stands, murmuring something under her breath, but I don't even try to eavesdrop. I'm tired of caring about this. I'm tired of *trying*. That's what I need to do: stop giving a shit and stop trying. Just like my parents stopped trying with each other.

Just like Ben stopped trying with me.

Ben, who texted me once. Literally once. And there you have it. That's how hard he was willing to fight for me. But why would he fight? Why would he fight for a boy who's moving back to Georgia when he's had Hudson sitting two feet away from him all summer? And yeah, I know he can't control that. But he lied about it. Every single day. Every word he's ever said. He never even mailed the box.

Mom steps back into the living room and hands me her phone. "Here's Dad. He's on speaker."

"Hi," I say flatly.

"So, who told you we're getting divorced?"

He sounds amused, which is annoying.

"Uh, well, seeing as you can't even go five minutes without being assholes to each other, it doesn't take a rocket scientist—"

"Wow." Mom sits back down on the couch and hooks her arm around me. "Don't hold back."

Dad laughs. "Kiddo, we're not getting divorced."

"You can tell me! Just be honest."

"We are being honest!" Mom shakes her head. "Arthur, we've always argued. That's just us. We're not perfect. Relationships are messy. You and Ben haven't been a hundred percent smooth sailing—"

"This isn't about Ben!"

"Art, I'm just saying, things get stressful. You mess up, you say the wrong thing, you get on each other's nerves—"

"But you guys are married. You should have your shit together."

Mom does this choked little laugh—and when I glance up at her, she's grinning full force at Dad's name on the phone screen. So, that's a little disorienting—it's like catching Valjean and Javert holding hands. But maybe my parents really are a Saturday-night-on-the-sofa kind of couple. And an arguing-over-stupid-shit kind of couple. Maybe they're both.

"So you're just a regular mess," I say finally. "Not a pending-divorce mess?"

"Regular hot mess. Standard-issue," says Dad.

Mom hugs me sideways. "Maybe you should give your hot mess another chance to explain himself?"

"Psh. That's different."

"Oh, Arthur. If you say so."

Maybe the universe doesn't hate all of Team Seuss, but it definitely hates me.

CHAPTER THIRTY
BEN

Hanging out with Hudson and Harriett has felt pretty easy. It's sort of like when I put away my winter boots because it was spring again and I got to slip back into last year's sneakers; I grew a little bit, but they still fit. We've been catching up and filling in the blanks on everything that's been going on since Hudson and I split, though we're not bringing up our breakup at all. Even last night when I went over to Hudson's, he was just listening to me whine about Arthur and Dylan. He's being the friend he used to be.

"I'm living for Mr. Hayes's Instagram," Harriett says as we step out of the frozen yogurt store, a smoothie in one hand and her phone in the other.

"I didn't know he has one."

"When you have a face like Mr. Hayes's, your Instagram magically appears."

On a bench with Harriett in the middle, we lean in as she scrolls through Mr. Hayes's Instagram profile. I expected rows and rows of shirtless selfies, and while some definitely exist, everything else is motivational, like removing the clutter in your home and living minimalistically and balanced breakfasts and this mega cheeseburger he conquered in Germany.

"See, he's living his best life," Harriett says. "Just look at his feed. He's been to so many countries. Prepare for my Instagram to be nothing but ads for organic baby food and sugar-free gum and goat milk shampoo, because I have to save up so I can unleash myself on the world."

"Then you'll return to a life of selfies?" Hudson asks. "The onslaught of selfies is really important; if I go two minutes on Instagram without seeing your face, I'd probably forget what you look like."

"You won't be selfie shaming when you see pictures of me flying solo on boats and on mountains and on hot guys' laps."

"You wouldn't want a travel buddy?" I ask. If I had the money to see the world, I'd want Dylan there. He's in all my other stories, and I'd want him in all the new ones too, when things settle down again. If they do.

"Are you volunteering your company?"

"Yeah, right." I chuckle. Harriett's parents have well-paying jobs and they love spoiling her. I can't side hustle with my Instagram.

"Down the line, I mean," Harriett says. "After you've sold your book and you're raking in that Netflix and amusement park money."

"No pressure." *The Wicked Wizard War* feels like such a waste now. Arthur was my biggest fan, and I doubt anyone would love the story as much as Arthur does. And he was my boyfriend. If I wanted to post somewhere public like Wattpad, I would be opening myself up to feedback from strangers who won't care if this is the story of my heart.

"Just saying. We really missed you, Ben," Harriett says. Hudson shoots her a look. "What. Let's stop acting like there isn't a big gay elephant in the room and try to move on." She holds our hands. "We're all friends, right?"

Not all of us, but I say "Right" anyway.

"Yeah," Hudson says. I hope he means it.

"So let's be friends again," Harriett says. I wonder if she misses Dylan at all. "What are you going to do about Arthur? Reach out? Move on? Let us know where you stand so we can support you."

"I wish Arthur would give me a chance to explain . . . I know it's kind of pointless because he's leaving, but I don't want him leaving like this. And Dylan . . ." I turn to Harriett, who gestures for me to go on. "I stepped out of line.

But I also told the truth. I just think everything would be simpler if I could have my boyfriend and all my friends and not feel like people always have to choose one or the other."

I shut down right there because we've been here before, after Dylan broke up with Harriett. Being Harriett's friend was weird for Dylan, and me trying to be Hudson's friend was weird for Arthur. But maybe this isn't how life works. Maybe it's all about people coming into your life for a little while and you take what they give you and use it on your next friendship or relationship. And if you're lucky, maybe some people pop back in after you thought they were gone for good. Like Hudson and Harriett.

And maybe this is the do-over I needed all along.

CHAPTER THIRTY-ONE
ARTHUR
Friday, August 3

Just me and you tomorrow, Obama.

Alone in Uncle Milton's apartment, surrounded by horses, with only the Grubhub delivery guy for company. I may actually print a picture of Barack's face and tape it to a Popsicle stick, because even if I'm single with no friends or parents in sight, at least I can spend the day partying with my president. And I bet you think I'm kidding, but guess who overcame "sickness" and showed up at work just to use the color printer.

"Arthur, you're depressing me," says Namrata.

"I . . . didn't say anything."

"I know. It's freaking me out."

I shrug and turn back to the Bray-Eliopulos files, which

are as numbingly boring as ever. Maybe I'm feeling mas-ochistic. Or maybe I've unlocked the secret, and this is how people focus. All you have to do is have a cute boy rip your heart out, then let your best friends stomp all over it, and if it's still beating even a little bit, finish the job yourself. Say the worst things and yell your voice raw and destroy every-thing you love until, lo and behold, the monotony of work is a relief. Because if you're balls-deep in Bray-Eliopulos, at least you can't think about your ex-boyfriend. Your un-soul-mate. The guy who bailed in the middle of Act Two.

"What's the plan for tomorrow?" Juliet turns to Nam-rata.

I look up. "What's tomorrow?"

"David's roommates are having a goodbye party," says Namrata.

"The dinosaurotica guys? *Jurassion Passion*?"

"Yeah, and I can't fucking wait. I'm shedding no tears over that departure." Namrata leans back in her chair. "Jules, we're heading up there together, right?"

"Up where?" I ask.

"Upper West Side. David goes to Columbia."

"Oh, that's near me." Neither of them speak. "So. Party, huh?"

Juliet nods. "It's pretty small, though, right?"

"Yeah, just in their apartment," Namrata says.

"Sounds fun," I say slowly, and then I press my lips

together, because it's not like I'm about to sit here begging for an invite to a random party on my own birthday. God. Even I'm not that uncool.

Wait, I AM that uncool.

"Maybe I could stop by?" I ask casually.

Juliet and Namrata glance at each other.

"Or . . . not."

"Arthur, look, it's not personal," Juliet says. "There's going to be booze there."

"I'm comfortable with that."

"Well I'm not."

"You're not comfortable with booze?"

"I'm not comfortable with rolling into a boozy party with my boss's underage son."

"Ha." I grin. "I hear you. I wouldn't actually drink. But my parents have a liquor cabinet, so I could make something! Like a candy corn martini—"

"No, like, Namrata and I could legit get fired for that."

"Yeah, not happening," Namrata says.

"Even on my birthday?"

And there it is. My Hail Mary.

Namrata softens. "It's your birthday?"

"Tomorrow is."

"Oh, Arthur." Juliet bites her lip. "We can't bring you to this, though. You get that, right?"

"Yeah, I . . . never mind."

"But seriously, you don't want to hang out with the dinosaur guys anyway. You should do something fun with Ben."

And wow. Now I'm about to start crying at the conference table. I just stare at my hands, blinking. Fantastic.

"Okay, that's not the reaction I was expecting," Juliet says carefully. "Do you want to talk about it?"

"No."

Juliet and Namrata exchange glances again.

But I don't care. Let them feel bad. I have no shits left to give. Dad's in Atlanta, Mom's halfway to Canandaigua, Ethan and Jessie are probably making out behind Starbucks, and my only two friends in this whole stupid city are spending my birthday at a party in my neighborhood without me.

My seventeenth birthday. Maybe on some planets, that's the kind of thing people look forward to. But all I can think about is Hudson and Ben passing love notes in class. Ben's Instagram, with its fifty-six versions of Hudson's face. Hudson's name on a shipping label for a box that was never sent.

I think about the giant gaping hole in my heart, exactly the size of Ben's fist.

CHAPTER THIRTY-TWO
BEN
Saturday, August 4

I'm at this low-key coffee shop with Hudson since our exam is on Tuesday and I really need a solid study session to handle my weak spots. A couple times I thought I saw Dylan waltzing in, but it wasn't him. That's for the best. I'm not sure Harriett running off an hour ago to celebrate a friend's birthday and leaving me alone with Hudson was for the best, though. I mean. We were fine that night after my showdown with Dylan. But it's just us again for the first time.

We're sitting side by side on stools. We've been quizzing each other, but the only answers I care about are all Arthur-related: How is he celebrating his birthday? Who's making him feel like a king? Namrata and Juliet? Will texting him a happy birthday ruin his day? Does he hate me?

"Earth to Ben," Hudson says, waving.

"Sorry."

"Arthur?"

"Yup. Hard to focus." Hudson and Harriett don't know it's Arthur's birthday. I just jumped into study group so I wouldn't stay home and play *Sims*. Last night my Sim counterpart gave flowers to Sim Arthur and got rejected because fuck my lives, real and digital. It's become really obvious that no one can hurt you if they can't talk to you, so I just locked Sim Ben in a room with no doors or windows. He'll run out of oxygen eventually, but at least no one is breaking his heart. "Today is Arthur's birthday."

"Did you make him something?" Hudson asks. "You're a birthday pro." For Hudson's birthday I teamed up with Dylan to draw Hudson in Wonder Woman's armor since she's his favorite superhero. I wonder if he threw that out or not.

"I wrote Arthur into *The Wicked Wizard War*," I say. I finished the chapter last night after I was done with my homework. I was planning on emailing the chapter to Arthur at midnight, but I couldn't get myself to send another message he would ignore. "I actually shared the book with him."

"Wow. That's huge. You must've really liked him." Hudson asked to read *TWWW* a couple times but never as passionately as Arthur did. Not sharing something so personal to me with the guy I was dating should've been a red flag about how positive I felt about our future. "I'm guessing Hudsonien got the ax?"

"Locked away in a dungeon," I say.

"Cool," Hudson says. "You should just text Arthur. You won't feel better until you do."

"I know I should. But it feels like I'm programmed to do the wrong thing. I walked away from Arthur when we first met. I took too long to open up and earn his trust. I was always late. I never threw away that fucking box, and now he wants nothing to do with me."

"What box?" Hudson asks.

No point hiding anything.

"On the first day of summer school I brought a box of everything you gave me. But you didn't show up, so I was going to mail it to you, and then I met Arthur at the post office. But I didn't mail it because . . ."

"Because what?"

"I was still holding out hope?"

I shouldn't be talking about this, but I can't help myself; these are all the words I've been thinking but couldn't say out loud. Not to Hudson. Not even to myself.

"Where's the box now?"

"In my mom's closet."

"What are you going to do with it?"

My phone rings; it's Dylan. I screen his call. I saw his Instagram post earlier, and I don't need to pick up so he can not-so-casually remind me how well things are going with Samantha.

I don't know how to tell Hudson that I want to throw away a box of things that used to mean everything to me. But that fucking box. I can't keep treating it like something that belongs in a museum's exhibit specializing in one guy's history of breaking hearts.

"I don't know."

"I'm kind of happy to hear you say that, Ben."

"Why?"

My phone rings again. I don't know this number, so I can screen this call too.

"Same reason you never mailed it," he says.

"Hope?"

Hudson leans in, like he thinks we're about to kiss.

My phone buzzes. This time it's a text from that unknown number: Ben, it's Samantha. Call me. Dylan is in the hospital.

"Holy shit." I call Samantha back immediately. While it's ringing, I tell Hudson that Dylan is in the hospital. He's asking me what's going on, but all I can think about are the different things that could've happened. Coffee burn or car accident or jumped by some stranger because he was being too Dylan in a place where that gets you hit or something too scary to even think to myself.

"Ben," Samantha answers.

"What happened? Is he okay?"

"His heart," Samantha says, and she sounds like she's fighting for her air herself. "We had to rush him to the hospital."

"Where are you? What hospital?"

"New York–Presbyterian. His parents are on the way. Are you coming?"

"Of course." The fact that she has to ask makes me feel like the worst best friend ever. "I'll be there as soon as I can," I say, walking toward the train station already. I hang up and Hudson catches up to me. "Dylan's heart is being stupid and I got to get to him."

I'm about to cry, because holy shit, the universe might be setting me up for a painful goodbye.

"Where?"

"Presbyterian."

"That should only take us twenty minutes, maybe ten if we catch an express train."

"No. I have to go . . ." Not alone, because I don't want to be alone, but I don't need Hudson there. "It's okay. You don't have to go."

"He was my friend too," Hudson says.

"But he's my brother." And that's that. Hudson nods. "I'll let you know how he's doing," I say as I take off.

Nothing's going to happen to Dylan. He's going to be

fine. It's Dylan. Nothing ever holds him down. But it still hurts to picture him in a hospital bed. I need him to know that I was there if—no.

Dylan is going to be okay.

He's going to be okay.

One stop away from the hospital and the train is stuck underground because fuck you, universe. It's hard to keep calm. He just had his appointment, where his doctor said he was low-risk for any attack like this. Yeah, he's going to be fine. It's Dylan. Nothing ever holds him down. . . .

I have to talk to someone. My phone has service since we're close enough to the next station, and I type out a text to Arthur:

Dylan is in the hospital. Idk everything yet but his heart is acting up. I haven't been this scared in a long time. It's Dylan, you know. I was a total dick to him a couple days ago because I'm an asshole. And I never really took his heart thing that seriously but maybe I should have and I'm fucking TERRIFIED. And I'm fucking stuck underground because the MTA gods are still The Worst. I know you don't want to hear from me, but you're the only person I want to talk to right now. I'm sorry, Arthur. Happy birthday. I hope hearing from me doesn't ruin your day.

I send the text.

And I wait. I wait to see if he'll respond. I wait for the train to move.

Maybe I should walk it. Just go outside and take my chances on the tracks. I can use my phone light to scare away rats and guide the way.

My phone buzzes.

Arthur.

Oh shit! OK. Who's there with him? He's not alone, right?

That's the scariest thought, Dylan being alone with all this going on. No one at his side who isn't a doctor or nurse. Thankfully someone important is with him.

Samantha is there. His parents are on the way, they're like a quick taxi from Presbyterian Hospital.

Anything I can do? Arthur asks.

Stay with me?

I'm not going anywhere, he says.

And a couple minutes go by without either of us saying anything. But I trust that wherever Arthur is, he's on his phone, keeping me company. He's sticking around.

What happened with Dylan? The argument, I mean.

I told him that relationships never last.

Do you actually believe that?

Of course not. That was the heartbreak talking. Relationships just don't last when there's an idiot in the mix. I really messed up, Arthur. I just wish I could've done everything differently. Told you at the very beginning that I was in summer school with Hudson. But I promise you that everything I said on Monday was true. We were just going to talk.

Arthur isn't typing anything back. I know he's still there, but I want to know what he's thinking.

I have to be honest. I've been hanging with Hudson and Harriett. They used to be my friends and they were the only people I could turn to after ruining things with you and Dylan and Samantha. And I talked about you all the time. And then today it was just me and Hudson and I was beating myself up some more and Hudson tried to kiss me and I pulled away because I'm only into you.

The train starts moving and I send another text.

I'm not sorry for having an ex-boyfriend. But I'm sorry for letting him get in the way of you trusting me. I hope you believe me.

The train stops at the station, and right before the doors open, my phone buzzes again. I have this dread—Arthur telling me to fuck off, Samantha telling me the worst news.

But it's something good in all this chaos.

I believe you, Ben.

I run into the waiting room and Samantha is leaning back in a chair with her head on the wall.

"Samantha!"

"Ben." She hops up, and even though I don't deserve it, she hugs me.

I look around. "How's it going? Where are his parents?"

"Grabbing coffee."

340

"The fuck? Dylan is dy—"

"He's okay! He's okay. It was a false alarm. Panic attack. *Really* bad panic attack. We just found out like five minutes ago. I was going to text you but . . ." Samantha takes a deep breath. "I needed a moment. I will never forget the way he panicked when his heart rate started speeding up . . ."

I hug her when she's tearing up. I know the face she's talking about. When Dylan was admitted overnight three years ago for a heart scare, I was really bummed I couldn't stay there with him, so I skipped school the next day to hang out.

"I'm sorry you had to see that, but I'm happy you were there." I take a step back. "Thanks for telling me."

"I didn't think twice. I know Dylan has a reputation, and I know you were looking out for me."

"He doesn't deserve you," I say with a smile.

"Of course not, but he's stuck with me. At least for another couple weeks," she jokes.

"I'm sorry I said that. I'm really rooting for you both. I just feel threatened."

We take a seat and she shakes her head. "No way. He's obsessed with you. He talks about you as much as I go home and talk about him to my parents. Which he doesn't know I do, by the way. I'm being careful even though it's hard to keep my chill sometimes."

When you spend time with Arthur, you're pretty familiar

with no chill. But Arthur and I didn't have the time Dylan and Samantha do to take it slow. I wonder what our relationship could've looked like if Arthur lived here.

"I'm sure-sure it's going somewhere," I say. "If that counts for anything."

"It does. Big-time."

Dylan's parents come through with coffee, and we catch up for a bit before they go in and see Dylan first. Samantha and I hang out, and I tell her all about the almost kiss with Hudson. It feels odd telling her before Dylan, but I snap out of it. No reason my best friend's girlfriend shouldn't be my best friend too. We're all going to be rotating around each other anyway.

When his parents come back to the waiting room to do some paperwork, Samantha and I get up to see him at the same time.

"You go first," I say.

"Let's go together."

So we do. We enter the emergency room, passing a patient's curtained-off cubicle before reaching Dylan, and wow, what a sight.

"My loves!" Dylan's voice is raspy, and kind of hot. He looks pale and just overall pleased with himself. "Death tried to have its way with me and I flipped the sumbitch off. I have afterlife spoilers."

Samantha shakes her head as she approaches his bedside

and hugs him. "You had a panic attack."

Dylan turns to me. "Don't believe Samantha, she's trying to ruin my good name."

"I'm not even going to shut you up," Samantha says.

"I have just conquered Death, there's no such thing as shutting me up."

I watch his face as he hugs her back, the way his eyes close and lose a lot of his electric Dylan-ness. None of the arrogance, just pure relief he's still alive and able to hold his girlfriend again.

It's really sweet.

I can't wait to make fun of him.

I'm so happy I get to make fun of him.

I hug my best friend. "Thanks for not dying," I say.

And I mean it. Because yeah, it was a false alarm, but I know it felt real to Dylan. It scares him when his heart beats fast. I don't blame him for hauling ass to the ER. I'm glad he did. Better a million false alarms than the alternative.

"I had to come back. Our last words to each other were trash and we would've been some bad cliché, and I'm too iconic for such nonsense."

"Very iconic. The most iconic."

"Speaking of, I almost died living a lie," Dylan says. He takes Samantha's hand. "So hear me out. Dream & Bean coffee is just in my blood. Kool Koffee's coffee doesn't do it for me. You're so passionate about the money being donated to charities, but I have to be honest about buying my coffee elsewhere."

Samantha squints. "What? I don't care. You do you."

"Really?"

"Very really," Samantha says.

"This was never a real problem, D," I say.

"Were you actually stressed about this?" Samantha says.

"Yes. Very much."

She shakes her head and kisses him on the forehead. "You're ridiculous." She takes his hand and squeezes.

My phone buzzes. I grin a little because it's Arthur.

Dylan catches me. "What was that? That little smile? The fuck was that? What's happening?"

"You're being hysterical," I say. "Let's up your drugs."

"Respect your immortal best friend and tell me what's happening. I didn't go to hell and back to not be kept in the loop."

"Arthur is asking how you're doing."

"You guys good again?"

"Well, we're not boyfriends. But we're texting."

"Screw texting. Go see him. I would ask you to swear on my life that you'll be more honest with him, but we've proven today that I'm untouchable. I will walk this world forever."

Samantha takes a step away from him. "A lightning bolt is going to burst in here any second now and shut you up."

"I eat lightning for breakfast."

"Okay," I say. "You're alive and well. So well that maybe I can meet Arthur. I know you just came back from the dead, but it's his birthday."

"No way that's more superior than my resurrection, but sure."

I clap my hands. "Great. Samantha, you can fill him in on all the Hudson stuff, if you want. And make sure he doesn't die again to prove a point."

Samantha returns to his side and takes his hand. "Future husband will live to see another day. Go get your boy."

"What did you just call me?" Dylan asks with the biggest smile, like a kid on Christmas.

"This is my cue to get out of here before you strip out of your gown," I say.

I hug and kiss Dylan and Samantha and bounce.

When I'm out in the hallway, I text Arthur back. **Everything is good. Dylan is very Dylan.** I take a deep breath. **I really want to see you. Can I meet you somewhere?**

My phone buzzes.

Yeah, I'll meet you in the waiting area in ten seconds. Don't be late.

What.

I look up.

There he is.

PART THREE

AND
ONLY US

CHAPTER THIRTY-THREE
ARTHUR

I spent all this time thinking Ben was the king of chill, but I guess no one's chill when their best friend almost dies. You know how you open the door in some houses and a dog rocket-launches toward you with his whole trembling body? That's Ben when he sees me. He flings his arms around me before I can say hello, and now he's just standing here hugging me like a cobra.

"You came." His voice breaks.

"Of course."

He draws back a few inches, still gripping my arms—and suddenly, our eyes lock. For a moment, we just stare.

"So he's okay?" My heart's thudding.

"Who?"

"Dylan!"

"Oh my God." Ben scrunches his nose. "I'm an idiot. Yeah, he's totally fine. It was just a really bad panic attack. He gets those—"

"Right, I remember that." I exhale. "Thank God."

"Yeah. His parents are dealing with paperwork, and Samantha's there. He's getting discharged soon."

I nod. "You should get back in there."

"He kicked me out."

"Really?"

"Well." He smiles faintly. "I kicked myself out. But I had to. Important birthday today."

"Barack Obama?"

"Obviously what I meant." He disentangles our arms. "Should we walk?"

"Okay."

Now we're side by side, all over again. It's sort of nice.

"What do you think Barack's doing today to celebrate?" Ben asks.

"Oh, he's having a party, for sure. Michelle's organizing it, the girls are there, obviously Biden's there, and Trudeau. And maybe Lin-Manuel Miranda? Okay, and Ben Platt, probably Tom Holland, too, and obviously Daveed Diggs and Jonathan Groff. Maybe Mark Cuban?"

"So Obama's basically having your ideal birthday party?"

"I'd call it a universally ideal birthday party."

350

Ben laughs. "I really missed you."

"Me too." I pause. "Where are we going?"

"Oh. I don't know. I should have asked you if it was even okay for me to hang. I totally get if you'd rather—"

"Don't go."

He smiles. "Okay."

"Want to head back to my apartment? No one's home."

"Oh!"

I blush. "I don't mean—I just mean we could talk, if you want."

"I'd like that. I think I owe you a conversation."

I pause. "Right."

"I mean. Ugh. Sorry, we don't have to talk about this on your birthday."

"No, we should. I want to."

We cross an intersection where everyone's honking and yelling and cussing, but somehow Ben's silence is the loudest sound of all.

"Okay," he says finally. "I want to try to explain the Hudson thing. Is that okay?"

I take his hand. "Yeah."

"It's not even about Hudson, really," he says, threading our fingers. "It's just me. I'm really bad at this."

"Bad at what?"

"At relationships? At feeling like I should even be in relationships? I'm so . . ." He stares straight ahead, furrowing his brow. "I have this thing where if someone likes me, I feel like I tricked them into it. Like I can't trust it. I'll fuck it up somehow, like with Hudson."

"But Hudson's the one who fucked up. *He* cheated on *you*."

"Well, maybe I wasn't worth it."

"That's ridiculous." I lift our twined hands. "I'm sorry, but how could anyone think you're not worth it?"

He laughs flatly. "Why wouldn't they?"

"Because you're you! Ben. God. You're funny and smart and—"

"But I'm not! I'm not smart, okay? I mean—I don't know if you'll be able to understand this, but a lot of school things are really hard for me. My mind doesn't want to let that stuff stick."

"Look." I nod emphatically. "I get it. I mean—"

"I know, I know, but Arthur, you're killing it in school. I know you have ADHD, and I'm not saying it's not hard for you, but look—you're applying to Yale. I mean, come on. You're *so* smart, Arthur. It's intimidating."

I can't help but grin. "I'm intimidating?"

"In that way. Only in that specific way." He rolls his eyes, smiling slightly. "But really, Hudson and I had been a done deal for two weeks when you came along, and I'm like *no, no fucking way, too soon*, but the universe was like *I insist*, and I'm sitting there trying to resist it, because you're leaving, and it's pointless, and why would we even—but I don't even know, Arthur. You're just so . . ."

"I'm so . . . what?" I nudge him. "Go on."

"Cute. Charming. Irresistible." He stops suddenly, tugging me toward a Duane Reade. "Wait a second, okay? I need to run in there."

"Should I—"

"Nope. I'll be right back."

And just like that, he disappears. I lean against the storefront to wait for him, pulling my phone out. There's a missed call from Bubbe and another one from Mom, but still no birthday texts from Ethan and Jessie. Which isn't terribly surprising, given what must be an extremely demanding makeout schedule. Not to mention the fact that they probably hate my guts now. And I probably deserve it. Hanging up on them was a dick move, but I guess some part of me was hoping for a birthday do-over. A rewind and redo.

After a minute, Ben emerges from Duane Reade with a bag he won't show me. "Okay, where were we?" he asks. He can't seem to stop smiling.

"You were just about to elaborate on me being irresistible."

He takes my hand again. "You are."

We go on walking without speaking, all the way to the end of the block.

"Hey," he says finally, catching my eye. "Thanks for

being there for me with Dylan."

"Come on. What kind of asshole would ditch you in that moment?"

"An asshole who was justifiably mad at me for not telling him about Hudson?"

"I'm the asshole. I should have believed you when you said it was nothing."

"You're not an asshole," he says.

"I am sometimes—"

"No, you're not. You're so—you're just *good*. Do you even see it? We're not even on speaking terms, and you drop everything to be there at the hospital with me."

"Well, I really like you," I blurt. "And I like us. Even if we are a hot mess as a couple."

He hugs me sideways. "I like us, too. And I feel really lucky to have you, even as a friend."

I stop short. Record scratch. "As a friend?"

"Well, I thought . . . I didn't want to assume anything?"

"Excuse me, we are *not* platonic bros, Ben Alejo."

"Okay then."

"And when we get back to my apartment, we are not going to do platonic-bro things."

"Good to know." He bites his lip. "So we're . . . boyfriends again?"

"Do you want to be?"

"Yeah."

"Okay." I nod, beaming. "This is a really great birthday."

"For you or Obama?"

"Both!"

"Okay, one more thing," Ben says. "I just want you to know I'm going to be open with you about stuff from now on. I'm not going to sugarcoat."

"I like that. Totally open. Me too."

"I don't think you could be closed off if you tried."

"You don't know me." I swat him, but he just laughs and wraps his arms around my waist.

"Here's the thing," he says. "I'm not going to pretend this Hudson stuff isn't confusing, because it is. But I just want you to know that the way I feel about you? Isn't confusing."

"And how do you feel?"

"I mean—"

"Tell me in Spanish again, okay?"

He laughs. "Okay."

"But—"

But then he kisses me right here on Columbus Avenue, and I forget what I'm saying. I forget how to speak.

The next hour is a blur, in the best possible way. Ben insists on a quick detour to Levain Bakery, where he skips all the bullshit and orders the biggest, warmest double-chocolate-chip cookie ever made. "Your favorite."

"How did you know that?"

"I just know." He insists on treating me—and he looks so pleased with himself that I don't even protest. He holds my hand the whole way home, and when the elevator door closes, we're kissing. When it opens again, we're kissing. I kiss him while I root in my pocket for my keys, and I kiss him in the doorway, and I kiss him in our foyer. We shove the bags on the dining room table, and we kiss beneath Uncle Milton's horses. You'd think I'd be tired of kissing right now. You'd think I'd get distracted, but I've never been more focused in my whole entire life.

I just love this. Every part of it. The hitch in his breath and his slightly swollen lips and knowing I'm the one who made both of those things happen. I love the way the spaces between our bodies vanish, like we can't be close enough. I love the feeling of my hands in his hair. I love the softness of the nape of his neck. And most of all, I love it when our lips are touching and our mouths slide open and my heart's a mile a minute, and breath becomes something we share. I've spent my whole life thinking talking was the best thing I could do with my mouth, but maybe talking's overrated. Mouth is still the best organ, though. Hands down.

"What do you think is happening"—I kiss him gently—"at the Obama party right now?"

He kisses me back. "Probably this."

It's strange that you can laugh against another person's

lips. "Barack and Michelle?"

"Barack and Trudeau." He kisses me again.

"With Joe watching wistfully."

"So wistfully."

My phone starts buzzing in my back pocket, which is currently right underneath Ben's palm.

"Someone's calling you," he says.

"Let's ignore it."

"No. No way. Last time I ignored a phone call, Dylan was—"

"Sheesh. Okay." I pull it out and peer at the screen. "It's my dad."

Ben kisses me quickly. "Answer it."

"Hi, Dad." I sound breathless and guilty. I sound exactly like a boy who's been making out with his boyfriend in an empty apartment.

"How's the birthday going?" he says.

"Great."

Ben keeps his eyes fixed on mine.

"I miss you, bud. I'm eating cake tonight in your honor."

"Cool."

"I got them to put your name on it, too, and now I'm like, why don't I always do this? You don't have to wait for a birthday. I'm going to start going once a week and giving the bakery guys some random name, and voilà."

"Great idea, Dad."

"So what have you been up to?"

"Not much." I shake my head slowly. "Actually, Dad, this is kind of a bad—"

"Wait, I'll let you go! But I just wanted to let you know your present from Mom and me just got delivered. It's waiting for you now in the lobby."

Ben just watches me, smiling.

"Okay. I'll go get it in just a—"

"You should go get it now, bud. It's perishable. Let me know what you think, okay?"

We say goodbye and hang up, and Ben wraps his arms around me.

My phone buzzes. Let me know when you get it!! Winky emoji.

"Awesome. Now he's texting me." I roll my eyes. "So apparently I'm supposed to pick up a package from the lobby right this second."

"Okay."

"Come with me."

"You got it."

"There's a ninety percent chance that this is from Harry & David," I tell Ben on the elevator.

"Who are they?"

"You know, the fancy gourmet guys who make Moose Munch and those pears? Fruit of the month?" Ben looks at me blankly. "It's—anyway, let's just grab the box, take a picture, text it to my parents, and then I'm turning my phone off all night."

"That's an extremely good plan."

The first thing I hear when the elevator doors open is a very familiar voice. "Arthur!"

My mouth falls open. "Jess?"

"And Ethan," says Ethan.

"I don't understand." I glance back at Ben, but he's staring at his feet. I turn back to Jessie and Ethan, who look larger than life next to the rows of tiny mailboxes. Ethan's in gym shorts and a Milton High T-shirt, and Jessie's in a sundress, and they're both carrying duffel bags. "What are you doing here?"

Jessie smiles shyly. "Your mom flew us up with her Sky-Miles. Just for the night."

"Wait." I clap my hands over my mouth. "Are you my surprise?"

"Hi, I'm Ben," Ben says suddenly.

Jessie hesitates. "Nice to meet you."

"My boyfriend," I say quickly. "We're dating again now."

"Oh—"

"And they're dating, too," I say to Ben. "Ethan and Jess. They're a couple. Ha. Out of nowhere. But I'm happy for them."

"Arthur, you don't have to—"

"I am! I'm happy for you. Extremely. And totally. Heh. You know what should be a word? Extrotally."

Ben's lips twist up at the corners.

"Anyway, wow. You're here. For my birthday."

"Extrotally," says Ethan.

"And you don't hate me."

"Why would we hate you?" asks Jessie.

"Because I hung up on you? And I was a jerk? But you're here." I look from Jessie to Ethan, grinning. "You're in New York."

Jessie grins back. "Your parents didn't want you to be alone on your birthday. Although . . ." She glances at Ben, who promptly turns bright red.

And in that moment, it hits me. Ben. At my apartment. With no parents. On my birthday. Just us and six unopened boxes of condoms and . . . Ethan and Jessie. I mean, talk about some fucking next-level parental interference.

But as cockblocks go, this is kind of a great one. I keep staring at everyone's faces and smiling. Ethan, Jessie, and Ben, all in a row. My three favorite people in one tiny elevator. And no one hates me. Nothing's broken. Maybe the universe has my back after all.

"Did you guys take the subway from the airport?" asks Ben.

"We Lyfted," says Jessie. "You grew up here, right?"

"Yup. In Alphabet City."

"That sounds like *Sesame Street*."

"That's what he said," Ben says, nudging me, and then he blushes. "Not like that. Not like *that's what he said*. I just mean. Arthur said that. The *Sesame Street* thing. About Alphabet City."

"Got it." Jessie laughs.

The doors slide open, and we step out into the corridor.

"So, how long have you guys been dating?" asks Ben.

Ethan and Jessie glance at each other. "Um. Like two months? A little more?"

It's funny. They're not touching. They're not even standing that close to each other. Which makes me feel weird, like they're walking on eggshells. Like I scared them out of being affectionate. But maybe they're just a really hands-off kind of couple.

"Here's home," I say brightly, opening the door to 3A.

My phone buzzes: Ben, slyly texting from my doorway.

They're a couple????

Yup. Upside-down smiley.

You okay?

"This place is so nice." Jessie peers around the living room.

Extrotally. Five more upside-down smileys.

Laughing-crying emoji. Let me know if you guys need some time to talk. I can head home, no worries.

"No!" I say out loud.

Jessie and Ethan look at me expectantly, while Ben bites back a grin.

I blush down at my phone. Don't go, I need you!!!!!! Do you think your parents would let you stay overnight? Fingers-crossed emoji. Praying-hands emoji.

You got it, I'll just tell them I'm at Dylan's sickbed.

Wow, tell D he's the best wingman ever, A+

Our eyes lock. Ben grins. I grin, too.

"Whoa, is that Catherine the Great?" asks Ethan, blinking up at the walls.

CHAPTER THIRTY-FOUR
BEN
Sunday, August 5

I really wanted some solo time with Arthur, but a double date with his best friends is way better than no date at all. We're all sitting in his uncle's living room, splitting his Levain cookie; I give him my piece, even though I'm hungry. I can only imagine what he's going through right now. It's like, one minute Arthur, Jessie, and Ethan were just the three amigos and now two amigos are dating and the other amigo is spending way more time alone. At least Hudson and I had each other when Dylan and Harriett started dating. Arthur has to go home and roll around like a third wheel.

"So you guys are good," Jessie says.

Arthur nods.

"My best friend was in the hospital and Arthur was there for me," I say. "He's the only person I wanted to talk to when all that was happening."

Arthur and Jessie smile.

"That's sweet. Is your friend okay?"

"He died," I say with a shrug. "It happens." Jessie freezes and Ethan's hand slaps over his mouth. Arthur busts out laughing. "Dylan is alive. A little too alive. Which is a thing."

"I like this guy," Ethan says, pointing at me. "I now feel extra bad that we're cockblocking."

"Whaaaaaaaat," Arthur says. "No. You're not. Okay, maybe a little. But I'm so happy you're here."

"You can be happy that we're here and want to throttle us for cockblocking."

"I am that."

Jessie leans forward. "We can go do something. A whole city of stuff to do."

"Don't be silly," I say.

"Yeah . . ." Arthur side-eyes me. "Don't be silly."

I ask them more about themselves, giving Arthur some extra time to absorb this whole thing unfolding before him. They share stories of all the different ways they used to spend their summers, like roasting marshmallows and camping out in Jessie's backyard and Arthur reading Draco and Hermione fanfiction in dramatic voices and watching

Ethan battle other kids at the mall in Pokémon matches. Everything was simpler when they were just three kids being best friends.

My phone rings. It's Dylan.

"I got to take this," I say. I get up and answer the call in Arthur's bedroom. "Are you dying again?" I ask, a little nervous.

"No. I'm free and living my best rebirth," Dylan says. "I am out of that hellhole. I didn't come back from the dead to pee in a pan."

"No one was making you pee in a pan, the hospital has bathrooms."

"Illusions. Where are you and Arthur?"

"At his place. His best friends just surprised us—flew in from Georgia. They're apparently dating too."

"Wait. Can Samantha and I come over too? It can be an orgy!"

"Or just a birthday party?"

"We'll start there."

I have an idea. "I'll tell Arthur you and Samantha might crash here too, but you have to do me a favor. Pick up a cake that says . . ."

An hour later, Dylan and Samantha have joined the party. Dylan has hijacked the spotlight as he regales his "tale of a young man who flipped off Death" to Ethan and Arthur and gives them tips on how they can also "escape Death's clutches." Ethan wants to know why Dylan's parents are already letting him party, and Arthur is just nodding along while eating pizza. Samantha is already over Dylan's second shot at life, so she's talking with Jessie about her dreams of all the apps she wants to create.

I drag Dylan into the kitchen to make sure the birthday cake is good to go.

"Thanks so much, man." I shut the box and put it back in the fridge. "So. How are you really feeling? Dylan-ness aside."

"I'm good. Panic attacks are a bitch. But I'm glad we went. Better safe than sorry."

"Did something happen? Or was your heart just racing faster like last time and you got nervous?"

"Something happened," Dylan says. "We were in Central Park watching two cyclists making out. I was making jokes about what their dirty talk in bed must be like. Pumping tires. If there are any chains in need of good lubing. Reminders not to forget helmets before they went for another ride. I wanted to keep going because she was laughing so hard, and I said I love you."

"Dylan. Dude. You agreed to take it slow."

"That's what the cyclist said," Dylan says. I glare. "I know. Look, it slipped. And I tried taking it back and I was making an even bigger ass of myself. I was freaking out about losing her for real this time and blood was rushing to my head and my heart was racing. Then Samantha freaked out because I was freaking out and that only made things worse and I was sure I was a goner."

Dylan panicking is my least favorite Dylan.

"Well, you're both obviously okay, Samantha's future husband."

"Surprised me too," Dylan says. "Just like when she dropped that L-bomb after you left. I had to Han Solo her at first, but then I got real, which was very, very hard."

"I bet it was." I hug him. "I'm really happy for you. I can't wait to be the best man at your ridiculous coffee shop wedding."

"I hope there's a ridiculous coffee shop wedding to be had. I know I jump ahead. And I know I'm a superior immortal being, but I'm not psychic, so I just got to keep it moving like it's going to go somewhere good."

"She might be the one," I say.

"And Arthur might be the one," Dylan says.

"What if, right?"

Dylan pats me on the shoulder. "But in case Arthur and Samantha aren't the ones, we should invite Hudson and Harriett over. Make this orgy extra interesting."

The doorbell rings.

What the fuck.

"Impossible," I say.

Dylan snaps his fingers. "I am a man of magic now, Big Ben. I could've summoned them."

I meet Arthur by the door, and even though it's impossible, I'm relieved it's two young women and not Hudson and Harriett.

"YOU CAME!" Arthur shouts as he hugs the two of them, and one playfully rolls her eyes as she hugs him back, like a big-sister type. "Ben, this is Namrata and Juliet."

"The legendary Ben," Juliet says.

"The daily drama behind the fucking Shumaker files never getting done," Namrata says, shaking my hand.

"I brought sparkling cider," Juliet says.

"Yes! Let's get fucked up," Arthur says.

"There's no alcohol. We're not getting drunk with you. Did you not hear us yesterday?" Namrata shakes her head. "We're only here for a few minutes. We just couldn't let you be alone on your birthday." She peeks into the living room. "Which you're clearly not. Your mom knows about this, right?"

"She knows . . . people are here."

"We're so fired," Namrata says. "We were never here."

Arthur holds out his phone at selfie length. "Smile!"

Namrata and Juliet do not smile.

Arthur and I go into the kitchen and grab eight glasses for this one bottle of cider. Not a lot to go around, but there's enough to toast to his birthday and sip away. Dylan

368

takes the empty cider bottle and tries to get a game of spin the bottle going, and literally no one else wants to play.

Juliet taps Arthur's shoulder to give him a hug. "Arthur, we have to go before we're late for the party."

"But we're so happy your birthday made a turn for the better," Namrata says.

"Wait. You can't go. There's a cake," I say.

"There is?!" Arthur asks.

"Stay and sing happy birthday?" I ask them.

Namrata and Juliet nod.

Dylan and Samantha help me out in the kitchen. I'm carrying the cake as we reenter the room and everyone starts singing "Happy Birthday." On top of the chocolate cake, vanilla frosting spells *Do Not Throw Away Your Wish*. Arthur looks around, and we smile for a photo while the cake is still lit. I'm so happy I had a role in flipping this birthday around. I mean, I kind of ruined it in the first place. But I got this ship sailing again, and that's what Arthur will hopefully remember no matter what happens between us.

Arthur finally blows out the candles.

"What'd you wish for?" I ask.

"Can't say. But I did not throw away my wish."

"*Hamilton* tickets before you leave?"

"*Hamilton* tickets before I leave."

★ ★ ★

"I can't believe they showed up," Arthur says as he comes back into the living room after saying goodnight to Namrata and Juliet. He settles back on the floor next to me, plates of half-eaten cake at our feet. "I knew they liked me." He gestures at all of us. "I still can't believe you're all here. Everyone's faces have been the best surprises today."

"You win Best Birthday Plot Twist for sure," I say. No one deserves a birthday party with all his favorite people more than Arthur. He always goes extra for everyone, and it's about time everyone goes extra for him. He has me making things right. Dylan and Samantha coming straight from the hospital. Ethan and Jessie flying from Georgia. Namrata and Juliet popping in to prove he's not just the boss's kid.

"Now it's a triple date," Dylan says. "I have an idea."

"No you don't," I say.

"Why yes I do."

"If it's sexual, just don't."

Dylan grins. "Maybe we should have a six-way—"

"Dylan!"

"—wedding," Dylan finishes. "Six-way wedding since we have three couples. Get your mind out of the gutter, Big Ben." He rolls his eyes at Samantha, who's busy rolling her eyes at him. "Hey, future wife, you're the one who made the future-husband comment. You know what you've gotten yourself into. I will always love you and I will always hate your coffee."

Samantha shakes her head with a smile. "Let's talk about 'always' later. It's Arthur's birthday right now."

"Agreed," I say.

"I'm just saying," Dylan says. "This is huge. Three couples in one room. This feels like the Fellowship of the Wedding Rings."

"His parents met when they were young, and they're still married today," I explain to Ethan and Jessie so they're caught up on why Dylan is the way he is when it comes to love. I turn back to Dylan. "Doesn't mean everyone else is excited to talk about the future." I grab Arthur's hand. "Some of us want to live in our moment." In our do-over.

"You're going to have a lifetime of moments," Dylan says. "It's you guys! Arthur and Ben! You defied the odds. This is that Hollywood love. I have no doubts about you two. Distance be damned." He points at Jessie and Ethan. "You guys seem tight. Just don't pull a Ben and Hudson and ruin the squad."

"Pretty sure you and Harriett ruined the squad first," I say.

Dylan waves me off. "Details."

"It's something we talked about, obviously," Jessie says. "But what were we going to do, not give it a shot? We didn't just wake up one day with feelings."

"Definitely not," Ethan says.

"But we had an opening and we took it. Maybe we'll

regret it down the line, but I doubt it. We've known each other forever. There's no throwing away that friendship."

I hope some of this relieves Arthur. That when he goes home, he won't have to constantly freak out about his squad disbanding.

"Do you guys regret dating your friends?" Ethan asks.

"Yup, sure do," Dylan says without missing a beat.

"You do?" I ask.

"A good thing got ruined for something that went nowhere. Maybe if I'd known Harriett for as long as these two have known each other, it would've been different."

"Yeah, but I knew Hudson for even shorter and . . ." I'm nervous about where this conversation is going.

"Do you regret Hudson?" Arthur asks.

"I miss my friends," I say. "It's not like I need Hudson and Harriett here right now. But I don't want it to be such a ridiculous thought. They were our best friends, and everything feels so split up. Like I can never hang out with Harriett without it feeling weird for Hudson or Dylan. Hudson and Dylan can't clown around. I can't hang alone with Hudson without that awkwardness in the air. No more hanging out just to hang out."

"But do you regret dating Hudson?" Arthur asks. "You can be honest. It's okay."

"I don't regret dating Hudson," I say. I felt differently a

few weeks ago. I would've kept the truth a secret back then too. But Arthur gets all my honesty. "It's like Ethan and Jessie. And Dylan and Harriett. We had to try. What if it had been awesome? It wasn't, but what if it had been? We would've never known. And I'm who I am today because I dated Hudson. I'm the guy you like because I dated Hudson. Who you met because I dated him and broke up with him."

"Cheers to Hudson," Dylan says, raising a glass. No one moves. "Too much?"

I gesture at Dylan's entire being. "Blanket yes. Too much." I turn back to Arthur. "I had to answer that what-if question with Hudson. Just like we answered our own."

"No regrets there either?" Arthur asks.

"There's nothing to regret," I say.

"Not yet," Arthur says.

"Not ever," I say, wrapping my arm around his shoulders.

If I don't regret Hudson, there's no way I could ever regret Arthur. I just have no idea what our next chapters look like. What kind of ending we need to brace ourselves for.

It's getting late, so we're figuring out sleeping arrangements. Arthur's dad was expecting Jessie to take Arthur's bed, for Arthur to stay in his uncle's bed, and Ethan to camp out in the living room. This is clearly not happening anymore. Ethan and Jessie are already in pajamas on the foldout couch. Dylan is dragging Samantha into his shameless world and taking Milton's room. And I'll be with Arthur in his room. Finally alone.

If Dylan ever leaves.

"This room is adorable," Dylan says when it's just the three of us in Arthur's room. "Which bunk do you sleep on?"

"I'm always on the bottom," Arthur says, fitting new sheets onto the mattress.

"Ohhhh," Dylan says.

Arthur freezes. "Wait. That's not what I meant. It's not *not* what I mean. I think. But I wasn't talking about that. Just talking about sleeping. In bunk beds. Nothing else."

"Amazing," Dylan says. "You can't write this shit. On that note, I'm going to go get started on my future child."

"Dylan, do not have sex in that bed," I say.

"We're going to role-play. I'm going to be a vampire and she's going to be the slayer—"

Samantha is standing at the door. "Dylan. We're going to sleep. Let's go." She turns back around and heads into Milton's room.

"'Sleep' is code, FYI," Dylan says, closing the door behind him.

Arthur and I turn off the lights and rest on top of the sheets, face-to-face.

"So. Good birthday?" I ask.

"It started a little on the mopey side."

"I'm sorry."

"Then there was a major improvement."

"You're welcome."

"Then it got a little mopey again."

"I'm sorry for Dylan."

"And now we're here."

"Let's not be mopey," I say. "We're finally alone, and I have something for you."

Arthur lights up. "Really?"

I pull out my phone and open Gmail, where I save all my *Wicked Wizard War* chapters. I learned my lesson after losing *Sorcerer Squad* years ago after the old family laptop crashed. I get the chapter up. "I wrote you into *The Wicked Wizard War*."

Arthur shoots up and bangs his head against the bottom of the top bunk.

I massage his head while laughing. "You okay?"

"Yeah. I mean. I've been written into my favorite story since *Hamilton*. Am I taller?"

"No. But you're a king. King Arturo. You don't have to read it now."

"When did you write this?"

"I started on Monday. And finished yesterday."

"Were you going to send it to me? If we didn't start talking again?"

"I was working up the nerve. I think so, though. Even Hudson told me I should send it to you."

Arthur nods.

"I shouldn't have brought him up again," I say. "Sorry."

"You and Dylan should reach out to Hudson and Harriett. Try to make things right."

"Really? That won't be weird for you?"

"It's only weird if I get in your way. I know you miss your friends. What if all hope isn't lost there? You should find out."

"I'll think about it," I say, lighting up with this possibility of getting Dylan, Harriett, and Hudson in the same room again.

"But only explore the friend stuff," Arthur says. "Do not ask any what-if questions about you and Hudson dating again. That would probably end in literal heartbreak at the hands of someone pretty familiar with the law because of his summer internship but too reckless to care."

"Death threat well received. You got it." I'm lucky that Arthur is keeping his cool about this. "I was going to ask Harriett to swing by this week to pick up the box for Hudson. Get it out of my room. But I can just give it to him myself."

"You don't have to do that," Arthur says.

"I want to."

"No, really. I don't need you getting rid of gifts and deleting fifty-six pictures on Instagram. It's different. I know you love me. I would destroy anyone who tried to get me to erase any trace of you."

"You're really feisty today," I say. "Still. It's something I need to do for me."

I don't need little reminders of the person Hudson stopped being while we were dating. Not when I'm trying to remember who he is as a friend.

I return the focus to Arthur's birthday, which is the most important thing tonight. We get comfortable and he begins reading his chapter. He laughs at all the King Arturo jokes I spent extra time getting right for him. He kisses me whenever King Arturo kisses Ben-Jamin. I can't believe there was ever a chance I wasn't going to see Arthur today. Maybe ever again.

"I love you, Arthur," I say.

Arthur turns to me. "Te amo . . . *too*, Ben."

CHAPTER THIRTY-FIVE
ARTHUR

When my eyes flutter open, Dylan's an inch from my face. "Gentlemen, PLEASE UNHOOK YOUR DICKS IMMEDIATELY. IT'S AN EMERGENCY."

"That's not . . . how dicks work."

Dylan winks. "I know how dicks work."

Ben hugs me closer, mumbling something into my shoulder.

"And cover your naked selves. Think of the children."

"We're like . . . not even close to naked." Ben sits up, tugging his T-shirt down. "We're literally wearing more clothes than you are."

Dylan waggles his eyebrows. "Is that a challenge?"

"For you to put on more clothes? Sure."

"What's the emergency?" I ask.

"We're getting doughnuts," says Dylan. "And we need recommendations."

Ben blinks. "You woke us up to get doughnut recommendations."

"Yes."

"Okay, is Dunkin' Donuts out of business, or—"

"Are you actually suggesting Dunkin' Donuts? Did you just look me in the eye and say that?"

"What's wrong with Dunkin'?"

Dylan shudders. "They're the Starbucks of doughnuts."

"Starbucks has doughnuts," says Ben. "Starbucks is the Starbucks of doughnuts."

"Please stop."

"Doughnuts are doughnuts."

"Bennis the Menace, you're better than this."

Samantha pokes her head in the doorway. "Come on, we're going to Beard Papa's. We'll bring stuff back. Ben, you coming?"

"Put your pants on, Ben 10," says Dylan. "You just got enrolled in Doughnuts 101."

When I wander into the living room, Jessie's legs are in Ethan's lap. It hits me that this is the first time the three of us have been alone together all summer.

I sink into a chair, wrapping my arms around my knees. "This is strange."

Jessie laughs nervously. "What's strange?"

"I don't know. The fact that you're here. In New York. And you're dating!"

"And you have a boyfriend," says Jessie. "A really cute boyfriend."

"Heh. Yeah."

"So everything worked out? You guys are good again?"

"We're good. Totally good. For two more days anyway." I try to smile, but it won't stick.

Jessie looks at me expectantly. "Are you guys gonna—"

"No. I don't know. We haven't talked about it."

"You should," Jessie says.

My chest tightens. "Yeah."

Now Ethan's hands are resting on Jessie's . . . calves? Sort of her knees? I'm trying not to fixate on it, but wow. It's like the time Dad shaved off his beard, and he was Dad, but he wasn't, and my twelve-year-old brain couldn't handle it. And here I am all over again, not handling it. Or maybe this *is* me handling it.

"Art, I'm really, really sorry we didn't tell you about . . . us. I know it's weird for you. Of course it would be."

"No, you weren't weird." I shake my head quickly. "I was weird. It's just—I don't know. I felt like Amneris in

Aida. Like I should have seen it coming."

"Dude." Ethan exhales. "I'm so sorry. We did that. We Amneris'd you."

"Please speak English," says Jessie.

"But I was such a dick. I'm sorry. You guys are happy, and I'm happy for you!"

"No—"

"And I hate how I reacted. I hate that I made you feel weird."

"Well," says Ethan, "I hate that I made you think I had issues with you being gay."

"Yeah, but that was in my mind"

"I should have made it really clear." Ethan shakes his head. "I should have been in your texts every day. I'm really sorry, Art."

"It's fine."

"I know. I just wish I'd handled it differently."

For a moment, no one speaks.

"Well, maybe we should have a do-over," I say.

"A do-over?"

"Jessie . . . Ethan. I have something to tell you." I pause. "I'm gay."

They both look at me expectantly.

"We know?" says Jessie.

"No, this is a do-over. Now you guys say something."

"Okay." Jessie nods. "What do you want us to say?"

"Whatever you want to say. Like, 'sweet' or 'two thumbs up' or 'oh, cool, that's badass' or—"

"Oh, cool, that's badass," says Jessie.

"Two thumbs up," says Ethan.

"Okay, good. And now it's your turn."

Jessie furrows her brow. "You mean—"

"Hey, guys, what's up? What's your big news?" I ask loudly.

"Well," Jessie says.

Ethan grins down at his phone screen.

"Ethan and I are dating."

"What? That's great!" I clasp my hands together. "I'm so happy for you, THIS IS ROMANTIC AS FUCK."

Jessie laughs. "I think dial it back two notches."

"Okay, but I am happy for you. You know that, right?"

"I know. But it's a little weird, too. It's different." Jessie shrugs. "I get that."

"Well, you guys are my best friends. That's not different."

"True." Jessie smiles wetly, sliding her legs off of Ethan's. "Come on."

And the next thing I know, she's squeezing into my chair beside me. "Excuse me. Personal space." I push her away, biting back a grin.

"Not a chance." She flings her arms around my shoulders and nuzzles closer.

My phone buzzes with a text. Jessie shamelessly reads over my shoulder.

I love you, dude.

From Ethan. And not the group chat. It's in our solo thread.

And when I look up to catch his eye, he's already halfway to the armchair. "I want in," he says, planting himself firmly in both of our laps.

I collapse beside Ben on the couch. "They're all gone. All those terrible people are gone."

"Finally." He tugs me closer. Ben's funny. He's weird about touching in front of our friends, but now that they're gone, there can't be an inch of space between us. "I like Jessie and Ethan, though."

"JessieandEthan. One word. I'm still . . . wow."

"Must be hard to get used to."

"It's weird. I think I really am happy for them." I smile up at him. "Maybe I'm just happy."

He buries his face in my shoulder. "I know what you mean."

"This is the best. It's like we're dads."

He laughs. "Dads?"

"Like we're an old New York couple just sitting around doing nothing."

"I like doing nothing with you."

"Me too."

And I do. I like it so fucking much. I always thought love was about the showstopper moments. No dialogue, no filler. But if the quiet parts are filler, maybe filler's underrated.

"We should do this every day," I say.

"All two of them?" asks Ben with this sad half smile.

My heart sinks. "Oh."

"Sorry to be a downer."

"No." I kiss his head. "You're being real with me, just like you said."

He nods.

"But I hate this."

"Me too," he says softly.

"Hey. Come here." I shift over to lie down, and then I pull him down with me—chest to chest, limbs in a tangle. He tucks his head in the crook of my neck and sniffs, and my heart beats in triple time. He's so palpably sad. It almost catches me off guard.

I pull back, and for a moment, I just study his face—the thick eyelashes fanning across his flushed cheeks, the constellation of freckles on his nose. It's one of those silences that's so thick, it feels solid. I press my lips to his forehead.

Deep breath.

"So," I ask finally, "what happens in two days?"

Ben pauses. "I don't know."

"I move back to Georgia."

He catches my gaze. "I've never had a long-distance boyfriend."

"I've never had any kind of boyfriend until you," I say. "I don't even know how it works."

"How what works?"

"Time apart." My hands linger on his jawline. "Like in movies, it's just a montage. You know, they're pining, maybe they talk on the phone a few times, someone gets a haircut or grows a beard or whatever, so you can see the passage of time. But I don't know if that's realistic. I kind of think we'd just FaceTime and text and miss each other a lot. And maybe masturbate on the phone with each other sometimes. Is that a thing?"

Ben looks taken aback. "Um. I have no idea."

"But then what if it goes south? Like, I'll be the guy who's sad, drunk, and alone, and you'll be going to raves and kissing boys, and I'll try to call, but you'll be in a sex den with a bunch of hot guys with celebrity parents, but they're all dead around the eyes, and there's probably cocaine—"

"Jesus, Arthur. You realize I spend ninety-nine percent of my time writing about wizards and playing *The Sims*, right?"

"I know."

"You just have no filter, do you?"

"None."

He kisses my cheek. "Okay, I have to go do something now."

"Ooh, what? Is it a secret? Should I close my eyes?"

"You don't have to close your eyes. Just hang tight. Listen to three *Dear Evan Hansen* songs, and I'll be ready."

I sit up straight, beaming. "You got it!"

But I'm barely past Zoe's part in "Only Us" when my FaceTime app pops up with a call.

I press accept. "Hi, Mom."

"Hi, sweetie!" She's in the most generic-looking hotel room I've ever seen in my life. Stark white bedding, plush headboard, framed picture of the beach. "How did the surprise go?"

"It was great."

"What are Ethan and Jessie like as a couple? I can't picture it."

"Oh, they're the worst," I start to say, but then my bedroom door creaks open.

And I lose the ability to speak.

Because—wow. *Wow.* There's my boyfriend. Wearing only boxers. Looking straight at me like—

"You okay, sweetie?" Mom asks.

Ben's hand flies over his mouth. He scurries back into my room, yanking the door shut behind him.

"I've got to go, Mom. Sorry." I end the call before she can ask why.

When I walk into my room, my bed's covered in heart stickers, with a line of tea lights trailing from my door. And then there's Ben, perched in the middle of the bottom bunk, next to his laptop. "I didn't light the candles. I'm sorry. I didn't want to set your apartment on fire. And Duane Reade didn't have rose petals, so I went with stickers."

"Ben."

"I know it looks ridiculous—"

"It's perfect."

"You like it?" The corners of his mouth quirk up.

"I love everything in this room," I tell him. "Every single thing."

CHAPTER THIRTY-SIX
BEN

This morning I got to wake up next to Arthur, and I can't believe there was almost a world where that never happened. I felt the same way last night when we were passing out with my face pressed against his shoulder, breathing in his T-shirt. And this afternoon we're lying on our sides, shirtless, with our locked hands resting between our faces.

"We seriously don't have to do this," I say. "We don't know what's next for us and . . . It's a big moment. You can't take it back. It's okay if you want to wait for someone else and—"

"You're the only one I want to do this with, Ben. Do you want to?"

"So much."

"Me too. I just . . . I don't know how to . . ."

"I know."

"I know *you* know. Just be patient with me."

"Of course." If Arthur psyches himself out like last time, I'll be cool with it. I just never want him to feel uncomfortable. I kiss his knuckles. "I love you."

"I love you too."

We get going and we go slow. I want this to be the unforgettable experience Arthur has been dreaming of for who knows how long. And it's a different kind of first time for me. Arthur is a completely different boy, and we're in a completely different bed. This apartment isn't home for either of us, but we're home to each other, and that's what makes every wall fall away so I only focus on him. I really want this to last as long as possible for him. No one starts a movie and immediately wants to see the credits rolling, so when this is over, I hope he looks back on this and considers it a win.

The pressure is getting to me. I can't ruin this for him.

I snap out of it. It's nonsense. Arthur and I have never done anything that's perfect. Perfect for us, yeah. But not on paper. And I know his thoughts are extra busy with his own concerns, especially after some technical difficulties slow us down, and we get through everything together with patience and reassuring smiles.

I kiss him and I call him beautiful and I tell him I love

him and we go on past that finish line.

We laugh and we catch our breaths and we peel stickers off each other.

No do-over needed.

Monday, August 6

My birthday—April 7—was the last time my group chat with Dylan, Harriett, and Hudson was active. I had sent out a text seeing if everyone wanted to meet up for lunch before Hudson took me to the concert. Harriett texted me and Hudson separately because she literally couldn't stand the idea of her text bubble even being near Dylan's, so the three of us grabbed breakfast. Dylan didn't want any drama anyway, so I just met up with him at his place and he cooked me cauliflower tacos and we played video games, just the two of us. And then Hudson and I went off to do our own thing, and I couldn't even vent about how disappointing a day it had been because his own spirits were really low from his parents' divorce earlier that week. I really wish I would've been enough to unite everyone the way Arthur was able to do on his birthday, but that's in the past now. Different times.

After I got home from hanging with Arthur last night, I resurrected the group chat. Just told everyone I wanted to meet up after class today to see if we could talk things out.

I put it out into the universe—with a GIF of Puss in Boots begging with his huge glassy eyes. Dylan responded with a GIF of SpongeBob giving two thumbs up and said he'll be there. An hour later Harriett responded with an "As you wish" GIF from *The Princess Bride*. And a few minutes after that, Hudson sent a GIF of Stewie Griffin bouncing around in anticipation.

The air was different in class this morning. No more weirdness. Like Hudson and Harriett are going to be my friends again and not just because they were the only people I could turn to after messing things up with Arthur, Dylan, and Samantha.

Everyone's willingness was enough to make me feel super hopeful about everything in life until Mr. Hayes handed me back a quiz where I got a C-plus. I was so sure I was going to score an A-minus or a B-plus. The exam that determines everything is tomorrow—same day Arthur leaves. I just . . . I don't have the hang of this, and I was ready to break down and cry, so I texted Arthur. We're canceling our plans to run around the city so Arthur can be a Super Tourist, and he's just going to help me study instead. I'd be surprised if we get any studying done—too many reasons to not keep our hands off each other and one big talk we need to have. One we've been avoiding.

But one big talk at a time.

When we get out of class, I keep the conversation about

391

grades as we walk over to Dream & Bean. Harriett and Hudson fared better than me, as I knew they would. It's weird how everything could fall back into place with our squad and Harriett, Hudson, and Dylan might be moving on to senior year without me. Graduating without me. Going to college without me. I'll always be one year behind them in life.

I have to kick this test's ass tomorrow.

We get to Dream & Bean, and Dylan is seated in a corner with four drinks and a box at his feet.

"These aren't all for you, right?" I ask as I sit next to him.

Harriett sits across from me and Hudson across from Dylan.

"Peace offerings," Dylan says. He gives me a pink lemonade, Hudson an iced mocha, and Harriett a cappuccino with caramel drizzle. "The barista drew a cat that you could've Instagrammed, but it got messed up."

"Thought that counts. Thanks." Harriett takes a sip. "So how are you feeling?"

"Been okay. Summer has been pretty slow. I did start seeing someone—"

"That's wonderful, but I'm talking about you being admitted to the hospital," Harriett interrupts. "Not your summer. You seem physically okay. What happened? Panic attack?"

"Yup. I'm okay."

"Good," Hudson says. "I wanted to text yesterday, but it didn't feel like my place."

"What do you mean?" Dylan asks.

"Ask him," Hudson says, pointing at me.

"Because I didn't let you go with me to the hospital? It didn't make sense."

"I have love for him too," Hudson says. "He's not just your friend."

Dylan props his face into his hands. "Are you guys about to fight over me?"

I glare at Dylan. "I know you love him too. But you never even tried to be his friend after we broke up."

"Your friend game went down before you guys broke up too," Dylan says.

Hudson is blushing.

"So you're ganging up on him," Harriett says.

I call time-out with my hands. "No ganging up. I know you guys have your loyalty to each other and we have our own. But this is keeping us apart." I take a deep breath. "Look, this has to be weird before it gets better. I know it's awkward, but I'm glad we're doing this."

"What exactly are we doing?" Hudson asks. "What's the point of all of this? A group hug? Instagram refollows?"

"For starters, yeah," I say. "I want us to try and hit the reset button. Get a do-over. You're both really important to us, and you're obviously not here just for fun. You want to make this right too."

Harriett stares at her cappuccino. "You've never been to the hospital for a panic attack, Dylan. I was freaking out, but I felt like I wasn't allowed to be there. All because my ego refused to let me trust you with any relationship, not even friendship, after the way you dropped me out of nowhere."

"I'm really sorry," Dylan says. "I just didn't want to waste your time."

"I get that. I guess I'm grateful for it in retrospect. It still messed with my head. But no matter how angry I was, when I thought the worst was happening to you, I really wanted to be by your side like old times." Harriett stares into his eyes and then mine. "I don't think I would've been open to this conversation if I didn't lose sleep over all of this on Saturday."

"Wow, you lost sleep over me?" Dylan asks. "You love sleep."

"Precious beauty sleep over you," Harriett says.

"It means the world to me." Dylan places a hand on his heart. "I'm no longer the odd man out. Between you three reconnecting when Ben and I weren't talking and all the hanging out in summer school, you guys had me wishing I failed chemistry too."

"D, enough with the summer school jabs, okay?"

"Whoa." He leans in and lowers his voice. "We're on the same team here."

"No teams. The only team is the one we're all trying to be on again." I rap my knuckles against the table. "It's just been a day. Almost failed a quiz, and I'm pretty sure I'm going to fail tomorrow. I just need support from you."

"Sorry, Big B. You know I'm just joking."

"Time and a place. I could probably stand a summer school joke once I come out on the other side of this. If I pass. Not looking likely. Pretty sure I'm going to be repeating junior year in a different school. No you and no you and no you." I almost add Arthur won't be there either, but Arthur not being around for school or anything is a bigger problem eating away at me. "I'm going to be the actual odd man out who gets left out and forgotten."

Dylan grabs my hand. "Big Ben, if you get left back and kicked out, I would transfer to your new school. You know I'm not messing around."

I squeeze his hand back. No matter the outcome with Hudson and Harriett, I know Dylan will be in my life forever. It's the kind of comforting thought I need on the eve of Arthur leaving. "No coming to my new school if you're going to make fun of me for getting left back."

"Deal." He turns to Hudson. "Okay. So I went to war against Harriett and Ben. You got any complaints or can we get our group hug on?"

"We're good," Hudson says. "I want to talk to Ben though."

"Same," I say.

"Have at it," Dylan says. Waiting.

"We should give them some space," Harriett says.

"Why? We aired out our business in front of them."

Harriett gets up. "Come buy me a hot cappuccino and tell me about this new girlfriend."

Dylan follows, always ready to talk about Samantha. I can't believe I'm watching Dylan and Harriett walk off together like they don't have this history of not speaking for the past four months.

I slide across the bench so I'm face-to-face with Hudson. "So. Good start, right?"

"For the group, yeah," Hudson says. "I'm sorry I tried kissing you. I shouldn't have jumped on you like that. Some wires got crossed."

"Yeah, you thought I wanted to get back together."

"Not just that. Talking about my own wires. I don't think I wanted us to bounce back as boyfriends, I was just confused because . . . my parents weren't the only ones who made me believe in love. You're my first, and I wanted to feel that specialness again. But I think we're better friends than we were boyfriends and that's how we should keep it. You're so hard on yourself, so I almost didn't even want to tell you this because I never want to make you feel worthless again. But I have to air this out so you can trust I'm ready to be friends again. You're important to me, and we shouldn't have messed with our friendship in the first place."

"I'm really glad we did, Hudson. D and I were talking about this last night. I don't regret us dating, and I wouldn't throw any of it away. Literally." I bring out the box from underneath the table. "Everything in here reminds me of when you didn't think love was total bullshit. Do whatever you want with it, obviously. But if you want to toss it, maybe it'll help if you look through it again? You're one of the kindest people out there. I wouldn't have been so heartbroken about us not working out if falling for you wasn't so awesome in the first place."

Hudson slides the box closer to him. "That means a lot, Ben. Thanks." He taps the box. Deep breath. "So what are you going to do about Arthur?"

"I'm not sure. I get that it doesn't make sense because he leaves tomorrow, but . . . I think there's something more to us. I should head out and go see him."

"You should definitely do that."

I look into Hudson's eyes, and I know he's not only rooting for my love, but he's aching for the heartbreak that may be coming my way.

I hail Dylan and Harriett back over. We tell them we're all good. No jokes are cracked. They don't ask questions about us just like we don't ask if they really just talked about

Samantha or if the conversation revolved around them. Just because we're friends doesn't mean we're entitled to one another's private moments.

I open up my arms and we come together. If I'm being honest, the group hug feels a little forced. But maybe that's not a bad thing. We're fighting to be close again, and that's beautiful. Maybe one day it'll feel easy again. We can start slow by following each other on Instagram again and keeping the group chat thread alive. We can plan hangouts instead of the good old days where we would just show up at each other's apartments. We can fall back in place, or somewhere close enough to where we were before. This summer with more do-overs than I can count gives me hope that the four of us will figure it out.

CHAPTER THIRTY-SEVEN
ARTHUR

I don't want to go home.

I'm on my stomach on this too-small bed in Ben's too-small room with its warm, gooey air and index cards everywhere, and I'm literally reading a chemistry textbook. Chemistry, the most molecularly shitty of all subjects, and I don't mean that ionically.

I really wish I could stop time.

Ben flops onto his stomach beside me, pressing his hands to his face. "I can't believe we're spending your last night studying for my fucking exam."

"I love studying with you for your fucking exam."

"I'd rather forget the exam part and go straight to—"

I clap my hand over his mouth. "Don't say 'fucking.' Don't you dare."

His laugh is muffled. "Why not?"

"Because." I let my hand drift to his cheek. "It's the least romantic sex word ever."

"But what about 'coitus'?"

"Okay, that's another strong contender."

"'Fornicate.' 'Copulate.' 'Sexual congress.'"

"That one sounds like a political-themed porn."

Ben bursts out laughing.

"Starring Mitch McConnell and Paul Ryan."

"Thank you so much for that mental image, Arthur."

"And the sequel: *Congressional Cock-us*."

"I hate you." He kisses me, and I just gaze at his face. I'm pretty sure I'd be happy devoting the rest of my life to kissing each and every Ben freckle. I'm pretty sure he can tell.

I cup his cheeks in my hands. "Hey."

"Hey."

"Question. In sodium chloride, which element has the negative charge?"

"Chloride."

"Yup!"

He smiles self-consciously.

"Next question. How does adding salt change the freezing and boiling points of water?"

"The freezing point decreases and the boiling point increases."

"How are you so good at these?"

"I mean, I have to impress my Yale-major boyfriend."

I laugh and kiss his cheek. "You can't major in Yale."

"You'll be the first."

"Yeah, about that." My heartbeat quickens. "I had an interesting conversation today with Namrata and Juliet."

"Oh yeah?"

"About NYU. Excellent school. Excellent theater program."

"You're majoring in theater?"

"No, but I want to know famous actors before they're famous. Oh, and Namrata's boyfriend is going to talk to me about Columbia."

"I . . . okay."

"I just mean"—I shoot him a tentative smile—"maybe this doesn't have to be my last night in New York."

Ben doesn't smile back. He doesn't say a word.

"Okay, wow, your expression right now. I'm freaking you out. I'm so sorry. I'm just going to—"

"Arthur, no. You're not freaking me out, but listen." He rubs his forehead. "You can't plan your future around me."

And just like that, my words evaporate. My heart's thudding so quickly, it's almost painful.

Ben's eyebrows furrow. "Arthur?"

"What?" I clear my throat. "Right. Sorry. Next question."

"You okay?"

I ignore him. "Is silver chloride soluble in water?"

"Um. No."

"How about silver nitrate?"

"Yes."

"Not bad, Alejo," I say, and Ben buries his face in his pillow—but I catch a flicker of a tiny, proud smile first. This boy.

My heart twists every time I look at him. The way his hair curls around his ears. The way it brushes the nape of his neck.

"I have a question," I say softly.

"You have a whole stack of questions."

"This one's not about chemistry."

"Oh." He rolls onto his back and looks up at me. "Okay."

So I just let it spill out. "I know you don't like making plans for the future, but we're almost seniors—"

"Unless I'm still a junior. Again."

"You're going to pass." I tug his hand up to my chest, lacing our fingers together.

"But what if I don't?"

"You will. You're going to ace the crap out of this test."

He laughs shortly. "I'm not in summer school because I ace tests."

"Ben. Come on. We've got this." I shift closer. "I'm going to teach you all my mnemonic devices—"

"Those don't actually work."

"Try me. First nine elements of the periodic table. Go."

"Um. Hydrogen . . ."

"Hydrogen, helium, lithium, beryllium, boron, carbon, nitrogen, oxygen, fluorine," I say. "Happy Hudson loves boners but can never overcome flaccidity. I made that one just for you."

He laughs. "Wow."

"And if it's not true, I don't want to know."

"Arthur, you are so fucking cute." He kisses me lightly on the mouth. "Don't go."

"I don't want to." Then I disentangle our hands and reach for an index card and a pen, because fuck it. I have to ask him.

I write. Deep breath. And then I hold up the card.

"'What about the United States?'" Ben reads.

"No, us. You and me. What about US? The caps are for emphasis." He's grinning. I grin back and swat him in the arm. "Shut up. You know what I'm asking."

"I mean . . . I don't know." His eyes find mine. "Can I be real with you?"

"You should always be real with me."

"Okay." He pauses. For a minute, his eyes catch mine, but then he squeezes them shut. "I think we have to let go."

"Let go?"

And there's this silence—the kind that rearranges your organs.

I press both palms to my chest. "Like . . . we break up?"

"I don't know." He sighs. "I guess I'm scared."

He takes my hand and tugs me closer, until we're both horizontal. And for a moment we just lie there, our faces a breath apart on the pillow.

"Scared of what?" I ask finally.

"I don't know." He squeezes my hand. "That I'll hold you back from meeting other guys. That I'll lose you, even as a friend. I'm so scared of that."

"But you won't."

"You never know." He starts to smile, but it falters—and when he speaks again, his voice is so soft. "I'm scared I'll break your heart."

I don't speak. If I do, I think I'll cry.

"I don't want to." His voice cracks. "But I might. Relationships are so hard. Maybe it's just me. I don't know. But I couldn't make it work with Hudson, even when he was right in front of my face."

I feel my eyes start to brim. "I wish I could stay."

"Yeah, me too." He wipes his cheek with the heel of his hand and smiles wetly. "I'm going to miss you so fucking much."

"I miss you already."

The next tear slides all the way down his cheek. "Well, we have one more day."

"The grand finale. Or intermission. Because we're going to keep in touch, right?"

"Are you kidding?" he says. "I plan to know you forever."

I drink him in: rumpled hair, brown eyes, shiny, tear-streaked cheeks. "I love you," I say. "I'm really glad the universe made us happen."

"Arthur, the universe just got the ball rolling," he says. "We made us happen."

Tuesday, August 7

Ben wakes me with a FaceTime on my last morning in New York.

"Hey, I'm kidnapping you."

"Wait—what?" I yawn. "Where are you?" He's clearly outside, but his face is so close to the camera, I can't make out what's behind him.

"You'll find out. Your first instruction: let me know when you're at the subway. And then I'll text your next instruction. Okay?"

As soon as we hang up, I scramble out of bed. I don't bother with contacts or actual clothes. Glasses, T-shirt, and gym shorts for the win. I find Mom pacing around the living room, on the phone with the movers—the ones

Ben couldn't believe we hired when we aren't even moving furniture. But I'm glad we did, because guess who's not lugging boxes onto the elevator right now. Guess who's not loading up a U-Haul. Guess who's already at the subway by six forty-five in the morning.

I'm here!!

Good. Now take the 2, transfer at 42nd St, and take the 7 to Grand Central

Are you taking me to the office? Side-eye emoji.

He sends me an Aladdin GIF. Do you trust me?

Eye-roll emoji. Heart-eyes emoji.

Of course, the 2 train's packed with commuters, and the 7's even worse. I'm on my way to say goodbye to a boy I'm head over heels for. I'll wake up tomorrow in a city where I didn't have my first kiss, in a bed where I didn't lose my virginity.

I'll wake up single.

But to everyone around me, it's just a regular workday. Headphones and pantsuits and scrolling through phones. It boggles the mind.

I text Ben from Grand Central. Okay, now what?

He texts me a picture of a street map, where he's clumsily traced my route in red. I don't even have to read the street names. WHY ARE YOU SENDING ME TO WORK BEN ALEJO??? I ask.

He texts me a thinker emoji.

This better not be about the Shumaker files. Side-eye, side-eye, side-eye.

But somehow, I can't stop grinning. I'm the worst New Yorker ever. I'm floating through the intersections, smiling at strangers, totally captive to my own triple-knotted stomach. Maybe when I get there, Ben will be waiting naked in the conference room. Or maybe a literary agent works in this building, and I'll find Ben signing a contract for a book deal with movie rights, and the movie's filming in Atlanta, because things always film in Atlanta, and they'll need Ben there for filming, so—

"Doctor!" says Morrie. He sips a cup of coffee with one hand and extends the other one toward me—but he's not going for a fist bump. "I'm supposed to give you this," he says.

He hands me an envelope with my name on it, but when I start tearing into it, he snatches it back. "You have to find all four. See?" Morrie flips the envelope over, and sure enough, in Ben's messy handwriting, there's a message.

#1 out of 4. Find them all and read in order.
NO PEEKING, ARTHUR.

"Okay . . ." I glance at the letter again and back up at Morrie. "Where are the others?"

"You have to find them," says Morrie, shrugging. And

then he turns his cup around.

It's from Dream & Bean.

My mouth falls open. "Is that a clue?"

"I don't know. Is it?"

Two blocks to Dream & Bean. I don't think my feet touch the ground the whole way there. I don't even know what I expect to find. An envelope, I guess? A whole bunch of envelopes, swarming around Harry Potter–style?

But when I push through the door, there's no flying stationery. No magic. Just a whole bunch of anonymous New Yorkers lining up for their jolt of caffeine.

A bunch of anonymous New Yorkers . . . and Juliet and Namrata.

"What are you guys doing here?"

"Keeping you on task, as usual." Namrata points her chin toward the bulletin board. "Go get him, kid."

"My next clue!"

Right away I see the envelope. It's in the exact spot once occupied by my poster. *#2/4*, it says. *Arturo, you got this!!!!*

I stack it under the first envelope, hugging them both to my chest. Then I text Ben. **Treasure hunt, huh??**

He writes back immediately with a shrugging-guy emoji. **Where do I go next?**

Hmm, if only there were someone you could ask . . . Thinker emoji.

Ohhhhhh, I write—and sure enough, when I look up from

my phone, the girls are watching me with matching amused smiles. My heart flips in my chest. I drift back to their table.

"Here's your clue," Juliet says, holding up her phone. "I don't really get it."

It's a picture. Of a rat.

"Got it!" I make a break for the door—but then I skid to a stop. "Wait."

"Wait what?" asks Juliet.

"Wow. Oh my God. I'm leaving. This is . . . goodbye."

"No it's not," says Namrata. "Your Shumaker docs are a hot mess. I'll be calling you with questions every day for a month."

I hug her. "Good."

"But we'll miss your face," says Juliet.

"A little," Namrata says.

"A lot," says Juliet.

I hug them both again and take off running—until I reach the corner and hail the first taxi I see. I don't care if it's just a few blocks: I'm not fucking around with time today. I stare out the back-seat window, practically jumping out of my skin. When the driver pulls up to the karaoke place at last, I fling money at him and burst out the door.

And there's Dylan on the sidewalk, holding his phone, a pair of headphones, and a giant thermos of coffee. He visibly starts when he sees me. "Shit. Seussical, you're early. Okay, take these." He shoves the headphones over my ears and does this giant, gaping yawn. "Fucking Benosaur. It's too early—okay, wait, we're on mute. Hold up." He taps his phone screen. "And . . . you good?"

"So . . . reggae?" I start to ask—but then a moment later, I place it. Not just any reggae. It's Ziggy Marley. "Is this—"

"A song about an aardvark?" says Dylan. "Absolutely."

Arthur Read, my bespectacled alter ego. King of the yellow V-neck. The fist that launched a thousand memes.

Dylan looks pensive. "I'm not the only one wondering what it would look like if a rat and an aardvark mated, right?"

"Mmm. You might be."

"Arthur!" I look up to find Samantha turning the corner. She jogs toward us, immediately crushing me in a hug. "You're early! Your next clues aren't here yet, but they're coming in, like, one second."

"Clues, plural?"

"Definitely plural."

"You done with my headphones, Seussical?" Dylan plucks them off my head before I can answer. "Hey, don't look now . . ."

And right away, I see them. They're crossing the street, walking toward us, their steps perfectly synchronized. But they're not wearing rompers this time. They're wearing lederhosen.

"Holy. Shit," I murmur.

"I . . ."

"So this is Wilhelm, and this is Alistair," Samantha says. "And they're here to escort you to your last stop."

I can't stop staring. The handlebar mustaches. The man buns. The way they're even more identical up close. They're each holding an envelope with Ben's handwriting.

"How did he . . . find you?" I ask.

Wilhelm smiles, mustache twitching. "Craigslist."

"I'm just."

Holy shit. Ben put up a missed connection. For me. Well, for the twins. But I'm the reason he did it. Me.

"We check Craigslist every day," says Alistair. "We've had thirty-six missed connections since we moved here."

"Is that . . . a good thing?" asks Dylan.

"It's a very good thing," says Wilhelm. "Open the envelopes."

"In order," Samantha reminds me.

Ben's handwriting. Four sentences.

Arthur, I know you're the one with the grand gestures and no chill.
But the truth is, no one deserves a grand gesture more than you.
I'm not as creative as you, but this is me going the extra mile.
And making you walk an extra mile. I love you.

My eyes prickle with tears—I feel so achy and happy and strange. The next thing I know, the twins are herding me back uptown. It doesn't even feel real. If it weren't for my rioting heart, I'd swear I'd left my body. The twins keep asking me chatty questions about music and movies and Ben, but I can barely form words. It's hard to be a fully functioning Arthur when your heart lives in four envelopes.

I try to catch my breath. Be normal. Make conversation. "So do you guys live in, uh, Brooklyn?"

"Nah, Upper West Side. Well, we *used* to live on the Upper West Side, but we just moved back in with our parents on Long Island."

"We're writing a webcomic," says Wilhelm.

"About dinosaurs," adds Alistair.

I stop short. "Of course you are."

Wilhelm points up the street. "Look, we're almost there."

I follow his gaze. And without a doubt, I know.

I break off from them at full speed, weaving around strollers, shoving between couples, clutching the envelopes to my chest. I'm sure I look ridiculous, or at least ridiculously determined. I didn't even know I could run this fast. I'm a five-foot-six southerner in glasses, and I'm the fastest fucking dude in New York.

I see its awning from a full block away—its white stone exterior gleams in the sun.

United States Post Office.

And there's Ben, leaning next to the doorway, balancing a cardboard box on his knee.

CHAPTER THIRTY-EIGHT
BEN

We're back at the start.

Arthur walks into the post office, and wow. His face is winning the game. Like always. It doesn't matter if he's just reading chemistry trivia off index cards or eating a hot dog or embarrassed because his parents are talking about his childhood or even now, looking tired and wearing glasses. My heart is running wild, which wasn't the case when we first met. It should've been love at first sight like all the great stories, but I wasn't ready yet. And that's okay. We still got somewhere great. The worst story would've been never finding each other again, or never meeting in the first place.

I put down the box as he hugs me.

"How'd I do?" I ask. Mapping out memory lane seemed like an epic way to close out this summer.

"Best curtain call ever," Arthur says. "I really don't want this to be over."

"Me either. Super me either."

"I want a time machine. Go back and do everything right. Literally everything would've been different if I had just gotten your name. I would've just followed you on Instagram and taken it from there."

"The universe knew that was too easy and outsmarted us." I kiss his forehead. "Everything means so much more because of all the hoops we jumped through, right?"

I don't know if we're a love story or a story about love. But I know whatever we are that it's great because we kept jumping through the hoops in the first place.

"I still want the time machine," Arthur says. "So we can jump ahead. I want to leave right now and see where we end up."

"Won't fight you there," I say.

He looks down at the box. "That better not be what I think it is. Don't bring this full circle with my very own breakup box."

"It's not." I pick up the box. "It's a best friend box."

"Really?" His smile will still be wonderful on FaceTime, but it won't be the same.

"Really. But don't tell Dylan. He doesn't believe in multiple best friends, and he might hire someone to make you go missing."

"Noted. What's inside?"

"Just some things so you always remember our summer."

Arthur shakes his head. "I don't need this box to remember."

"Fine. I guess I'll keep this very sexy scene between Ben-Jamin and King Arturo on the back of a Central Park postcard—"

"—I want the box."

"—And the packaged cookie from Levain Bakery that was supposed to be one hundred percent for you."

"I said I want the box!"

I'm going to miss him and his no-chill energy so much. "There's also a touristy magnet with my name. I'm keeping the one with yours." I take a deep breath in his silence. "And I framed the photo Dylan took of us with your birthday cake. I have one in my room too."

Arthur is tearing up. "Thanks for this. For everything. This morning. This summer. I know I'm a lot, and you've been so cool about it."

I laugh a little. "We're the worst. I mean, we're the best. But we're the worst. You always think you're too much, and I feel like I'm not enough."

"I will say it a hundred more times, but you are more than enough."

"I'm starting to believe you."

We get to the clerk's window and I kiss Arthur's name on the box before handing it over. The clerk gives me a what-the-hell look because he doesn't know what Arthur and I have gone through in the past few weeks to be back here right now.

Once the box is off on its way, so are we.

This time when I leave the post office, I'm holding Arthur's hand. We stop underneath the metallic lettering of the post office.

"One last pic to hold us over," Arthur says, pulling out his phone.

I close my eyes and kiss his cheek while he takes the picture. When I look at the picture, Arthur has this *Hamilton*-ticket-lottery-winning smile.

That smile is gone when I look up at him. "I can't believe I'm actually leaving."

"Me either."

There couldn't be a worse morning to have to say goodbye to Arthur. We're walking to school, where I have to pass an exam that will determine my future. Like things aren't complicated enough. But I'm feeling okay. Sad and nervous, but hopeful. I bet I'll be the only person laughing in the classroom since Arthur's ridiculous but super-helpful mnemonic devices will lead me to victory.

"I'm not ready," I say outside my school.

He's crying. "Me either."

"Arthur, you know I would try if I thought we could beat the world, right?"

"I know. We never let anything stand in our way before, but this is . . ."

"Next-level. I can't lose you forever. You can't be someone I just knew for one summer. I have to know you every summer."

"You will," Arthur promises.

We press our foreheads together and he wipes away my tears.

"I should get in there," I say, holding on to him like I'm hanging over the side of a building and he's the ledge.

"I should catch my flight," Arthur says through tears.

"Okay, King Arturo."

"Okay, Ben-Jamin."

He leans in. Our last kiss. I stay pressed against him because this is it, this is all we have to get us through the coming days when we can't hold hands or kiss or wake up next to each other. I try pulling away, but I'm sucked back into him. It's not enough and it's never going to be enough, so I slowly count down from ten in my head and at zero we're done.

"I'm about to walk away," Arthur says. "I can't turn

around once I get moving. But you shouldn't be standing here and watching me in case I cheat. Just run into the school. Okay?" He takes a step back.

I nod.

"I love you, Ben."

"Te amo too, Arthur."

Our fingers unlock and that's it. Arthur somehow finds the strength to turn away, and I feel emptier with each rapid footstep he takes. He gets to the end of the block and he stops. Long enough that I'm expecting him to spin a one-eighty and run back for one more kiss. But he keeps on moving. It's for the best. I run up the steps into school and my phone buzzes. It's Arthur texting me the picture of me kissing him in front of the post office. One picture sparks summer memories and I don't feel empty. I feel like I'm breathing in hope.

The universe wouldn't get us together for just one summer, right?

WHAT IF IT'S YOU AND WHAT IF IT'S ME?

ARTHUR

Fifteen Months Later
Middletown, Connecticut

Ethan's not picking up.

I feel ridiculous, scrunched up against the wall, two halls down from Mikey's dorm room. I'm supposed to be at a party, living that College Arthur life. But College Arthur and college parties don't mix well. It's more than two months into freshman year, so I can officially say that. I mean, I keep trying anyway, mostly for the Life Experience, but also because I highly doubt Lin-Manuel Miranda stayed in his dorm all night watching YouTube and throwing away his shot. But parties make me nervous, which makes me talk too much, and then everyone thinks I'm drunk, which I'm not, because let's be real: no one's ready to meet Drunk Arthur, not even me.

Anyway, I told Mikey I'd be there, so I'm here. Or at least I *was* here, until I saw Ethan's Instagram Story. Now I'm the best friend, reporting for duty.

I try texting. **You okay my dude?**

Nothing. Five minutes later, still nothing, not even an ellipsis, and I feel a little sick about it. When Jessie broke the news to me yesterday, she made it sound like it was mutual. I've talked to her twice since then, and she seems okay—sad, but okay. But Ethan won't answer my calls. He's barely responding to my texts.

I rest my head on the cinder-block wall, shutting my eyes. I mean, I'm sure Ethan's fine. Maybe he's ignoring my texts because he already met an awesome new girl who can sing and play piano and looks like Anna Kendrick. Maybe she *is* Anna Kendrick. Though you just know Ethan would blurt out that he likes the original cast soundtrack of *The Last Five Years* better than the film, which, duh, but how rude is it to say that to Anna Kendrick? So obviously she'll dump him, which means he's double-dumped, which means we're back where we started, but worse.

Guess I better call again.

I'm sent straight to voice mail. For a minute, I just stare at my phone, only half listening to the Radiohead song drifting out of someone's dorm room. I hate how helpless I feel. And not the romantic kind of helpless. Not the Eliza Schuyler kind. It's more like the feeling you get watching the end of *Titanic*. You want to reach into your screen and tip the boat back upright. You want to fix the unfixable.

A text from Mikey: Hey, where'd you go?

I should text him back. Actually, I should just suck it up and go back to the party. It's not even the intimidating kind of party. It's mostly just a cappella people sitting on Mikey's bed and drinking. College is like that—at least Wesleyan's like that. It's like the nerds rose to power, kicked out all the popular kids, and stole their weed and alcohol. Which isn't to say everything's about smoking and drinking here. A lot of people just sit around talking or gaming or making art, and they're sometimes naked, and I kind of love that. Not the nudity in particular. But I love that give-no-shits mentality. Also Wesleyan has the cutest boys, far cuter than a certain other Connecticut school that shall remain nameless until I name them. I'm not even bitter that Yale waitlisted me. That's how cute the boys are here. Case in point: Mikey, with his bleached hair and wire-framed glasses and above-average kissing ability. I'd say he's the third-best kisser out of the six boys I've kissed. Second best was this guy I met when I visited Jessie at Brown. First best was Ben.

Ben. That's who I should FaceTime. He knows breakups, and more importantly, he knows Ethan. And *most* importantly, I'm wearing a button-down shirt and a cardigan and glasses, and I'm kind of feeling myself tonight. Also, a few weeks ago, Ben drunk-texted me to say I look hot in my glasses. So there's that.

Ben answers right away. "I was just thinking about you!"

"You were?"

He nods.

"But you're going to leave me hanging on the details, aren't you?"

"Yup." His face breaks into a grin, and wow. We need to FaceTime more often, because his smile is my favorite smile ever. He's gotten a haircut since the last selfie he posted—sort of longer on top, but it's subtle. He looks perfect. Which is a thing I notice in a strictly platonic way. I'll just be here thinking all the platonic Ben thoughts. Even though he's on his bed. It's not like I'm thinking about all the things *we* did on that bed. I can appreciate the bed as a well-crafted, functional item of furniture. Ben leans back on his pillows and yawns. "So, what's up?"

Might as well spit it out. "Jessie dumped Ethan."

Ben sits up. "Whoa."

"Right? It's weird."

"I bet. Wow. How are they holding up?"

I stretch my legs out in front of me, settling in for the long haul. "Jessie's good, I think. Ethan, though. Have you looked at his Instagram?"

"Not recently."

"Ben, it's bad. He posted this story where he's singing

'I'll Cover You' from *Rent* and crying, and like . . . I don't know. Can you pull a muscle from cringing?"

Ben winces. "Uh-oh."

"Whatever you're picturing, it's worse. Just watch it."

"Poor Ethan."

"I know." I press a hand to my face. "Tell me this gets less awkward."

"You mean breakups?"

"Yeah, I mean. I've only ever had ours, and ours was awesome."

Ben laughs. "Best breakup ever."

"I know. We rocked it." I sigh. "Maybe Ethan and Jess will bounce back, too."

"They might. I bet they will."

"Should I go visit him at UVA? I don't want it to be like I'm picking sides. Jessie's my friend, too."

"That's tricky." Ben wrinkles his nose, and it's so cute, it makes my heart flip. I'll never get over those freckles. Not ever. "But it gets easier. You'll see. Look at me and Hudson."

I narrow my eyes. "I try not to."

"I love that you're still jealous of Hudson. Still."

"Always."

He shakes his head, smiling. "I'm just saying, it's not exactly like it used to be, but we're cool. We can text. We don't really talk much, but—"

A door bursts open, and I'm suddenly surrounded by girls in scarves and gloves and pom-pom hats. They're loud and happy and flushed, probably tipsy, and one of them fist-bumps me when she walks by.

"Where are you?" Ben asks.

"In the Butts. The Butterfield dorms."

"You call it the Butts? People live in the Butts?"

"Yup. People are literally partying in the Butts right now. That's why I'm here. I escaped a Butt party."

"Wow." Ben laughs. "Whose Butt?"

I feel myself blushing. "Just this guy."

"Oh, right. That guy from your a cappella group?"

"Mikey."

"Cool." He pauses. "So . . . are you guys, like—"

"No," I say quickly. "I don't think so. I mean, he's sweet. But he has the same name as my dad."

"He can't help that."

"Okay, and get this. He thought *Hamilton* was fine, but not great. And he doesn't like arcades! That's weird, right?"

"Arthur, you don't like arcades."

"I know, but he seems like he would, and he doesn't, and I don't like that." I shrug. "Anyway, what about you? Are you . . ."

"Single as fuck," Ben says happily. "But Dylan and Samantha are back in town this weekend and are coming over later."

"Oh my God, I miss them! Remember that night at Milton's apartment?"

"Of course."

"Kind of weird, huh, that out of all three couples that night, Dylan and Samantha are officially the last couple standing."

"That is weird. Wow."

And for a minute, we just look at each other, and I swear the air gets thicker. I haven't even been in the same state as Ben since we said goodbye that summer. But my heart and brain and lungs never remember that.

The truth is, I don't know how to do this. I've spent so much time googling. *How to turn off a feeling. How to make myself like him platonically.*

When Ben finally speaks, his voice is low and soft. "We're still standing."

"What?" I look at him strangely. I'm sitting in a dorm hallway against a wall. He's sitting on a bed.

"I mean, we're still here. We're still us. You're still in my life."

"Very good point."

And it's true. I love his smile. I love his voice. I love his face. I love that he lives in my phone, even now. I love being his friend. His *best* friend.

My best friend, Ben.

Maybe that's what the universe wanted. Maybe that's us.

BEN

One Month Later
New York, New York

This is it. This is actually it. The end.

I can't believe I did it.

The final chapter of *The Wicked Wizard War* is up on Wattpad.

I'm sitting cross-legged on my bed, the same spot against my wall where I finished the first draft last December. A couple days before New Year's. Met my goal. I was listening to Lana Del Rey then, and tonight I'm mellowing out to the Chromatics cover of "I'm on Fire." What's missing now is this sense of privacy. No one waiting on new chapters. Except Arthur. It's so different now. I've been posting my edited chapters serially since January. Started off with a few hundred reads and it moved into the thousands in February.

I'm pretty sure this final chapter is going to push me over fifty thousand reads, which is mind-blowing. I owe a lot of that to the awesome book cover Dylan commissioned Samantha to design last Christmas. The community loves it; readers have even found me and Samantha on Instagram to tell us.

The chapter has only been up for a couple minutes and I'm already wanting to keep refreshing the page for new reads and reviews. Just to see that the previous thirty-nine chapters weren't some fluke. I want to go on Tumblr and check my tags, as if fans have already had the time to whip up some epic fan-art for the scene where Ben-Jamin single-handedly annihilates the Life Swallowers and rescues King Arturo, Duke Dill, and Sovereign Harrietta. Or where Ben-Jamin teams up the Crowned Sorceress, Sam O'Mal, to exorcise the vicious spirits that were possessing Hudsonien so he can find happiness again.

But instead of trying to scratch those itches, I pick up my phone and FaceTime the person who encouraged me to post the story in the first place. Feels extra full circle since I also called Arthur when I finished the very first draft.

Arthur answers immediately. Beaming smile and glasses. "I got the Wattpad notification that BennisTheMenace uploaded a new chapter! I was *just* about to call you."

"You say that all the time," I say, shaking my head.

"You do too!"

"Truth." We always seem to call each other when we need to talk the most. Like last week when I FaceTimed him from Dave & Buster's to show him the claw machine from our first date and discovered Arthur panicking in his dorm room and ready to quit a cappella because he cut things off with Mikey. He really needed to hear from someone who survived summer school with his ex-boyfriend, and he promised me he would sing even louder.

Arthur is in his bedroom, back in Georgia for the holidays. Sometimes I forget that I've never been there because I feel like I know his house, especially his bedroom, so well from all the hours we've clocked in on FaceTime. "I'm so proud of you," Arthur says. "You did it."

Arthur telling me I did it makes this whole book thing extra real. It sinks in deeper than seeing the final chapter live online or when I switched the story's status from In-Progress to Complete.

"I couldn't have done it without you," I say.

"You're the one who wrote the book," Arthur says.

"I'm not sure I would've finished without you cheering me on."

Arthur lounges on the bed where he read the first few chapters before anyone else. "I, King Arturo, am your first fan, Ben-Jamin."

In more ways than one—I really do believe in myself because of him.

I've thanked him a thousand times for helping me study on his last night in New York because those pneumonic devices helped me pass summer school so I could move into senior year with Dylan, Hudson, and Harriett. I got serious about school after that scare of failing. I set a challenge to not only be early—or at least on time—but also having a perfect attendance so I wouldn't ever feel left behind on material like before. I was late a few times and absent twice because I'm still me, but not bad overall. Dylan, Harriett, Hudson, and I made it to graduation without killing one another, and our picture in our caps and gowns hangs right beside the one of me and Arthur on his birthday.

College in the city has been tougher, but I'm getting through it. Whenever I pictured college life, I thought I would be sharing a dorm room with Dylan and hanging a Hufflepuff tie out on the doorknob whenever I had a guy over and Dylan would barge in anyway. But I'm home with my parents while Dylan and Samantha are getting their college on in Illinois. Thankfully, Hudson and Harriett are still in the city, even if our friendship is probably never going to be what it used to be. Maybe we peaked as a group before we started dating one another. But better where we are now than when things were messy.

"I don't know what's next for me," I say. My fingers are restless.

"I'm always going to beg you for a sequel," Arthur says.

"Keep the story going."

"But what if the story should quit while it's ahead?"

"How do you know unless you give the story another chance?"

I smile. "Like a do-over."

I'm pretty sure we're not talking about my book anymore. At least Arthur is a lot subtler than he used to be. Unlike last year when he was heavily hinting that he should come to New York so we could spend New Year's Eve together and watch the ball drop at midnight and if we happened to kiss that would be cool with him. That didn't happen, but Arthur is still the last person I've kissed. One time I thought I was developing a crush on this guy in my creative writing class, but that didn't last long. I just need more time with me, I think. To really believe in my worth without anyone's help. Doesn't mean I don't find myself tracing the letters of Arthur's name on the magnet I bought myself to match the one he has with my name. Or staring at the photo of when I kissed him in front of the post office where we met. Or constantly thinking about the future and asking myself: *What if?*

"Never say never," Arthur says. "Right?" So much hope hangs on one word.

"Right," I say. "Never know what the universe has planned for us."

I don't know what *we* have planned for us.

What if there's a do-over down the line for us? What if we end up in the same city again and pick up where we left off? What if we go as far as we once hoped we would, and boom, happy ending for us? But what if this is it for us? What if we never get to kiss again? What if we're there for each other's big moments, but *we* aren't at the heart of those big moments anymore? What if the universe always wanted us to meet and stay in each other's lives forever as best friends? What if we rewrite everything we expect from happy endings?

Or . . .

What if we haven't seen the best us yet?

ACKNOWLEDGMENTS

This book is a collaboration in every way, and we're so grateful the universe brought us:

- Our editors, Donna Bray and Andrew Eliopulos, who helped us through infinite do-overs until we found our dream love story. ("Need?")

- Our wonderful team at HarperCollins, including but not limited to Caroline Sun, Megan Beatie, Alessandra Balzer, Rosemary Brosnan, Kate Morgan Jackson, Suzanne Murphy, Michael D'Angelo, Jane Lee, Tyler Breitfeller, Bethany Reis, Veronica Ambrose, Patty Rosati, Cindy Hamilton, Ebony LaDelle, Audrey Diestelkamp, Bess Braswell, Tiara Kittrell, and Bria Ragin. You're all wizards who made this magic happen.

- Erin Fitzsimmons, Alison Donalty, and Jeff Östberg, who gave us the dreamiest cover we've ever seen and have loved since day one.

435

- Wendi Gu, Stephanie Koven, and the rest of our hard-working team at Janklow & Nesbit.
- Mary Pender, Jason Richman, and our badass team at UTA.
- All our international publishers who are bringing Arthur and Ben's love story across the globe.
- Our friends who kept us sane, including Aisha Saeed, Angie Thomas, Arvin Ahmadi, Corey Whaley, Dahlia Adler, Jasmine Warga, Kevin Savoie, Nic Stone, Nicola Yoon, and Sabaa Tahir. Veteran collaborators Dhonielle Clayton + Sona Charaipotra and Amie Kaufman + Jay Kristoff, who cheered us on and offered wisdom. Matthew Eppard, who kept the ship running smoothly. David Arnold, who made writing Ben and Dylan's bromance the easiest thing possible.
- Our early readers who made this book better: Jacob Batchelor, Shauna Sinyard, Sandhya Menon, Celeste Pewter, and Dakota Shain Byrd.
- Our loyal readers who have followed us into this collaboration without knowing what they were getting themselves into. Librarians and booksellers for connecting books like this with the readers who need them.
- Our families, including but not limited to: James Arthur Goldstein, who made it through two books with no dads. Persi Rosa for always helping with summer school

homework. Great-Uncle Milton, who is great. The Thomas–Berman family, who let Arthur stay in their apartment. Anna Overholts for knowing chemistry.

- And our agent, Brooks Sherman, without whom none of this would've been possible.